世界名作家小小说选译

张经浩 选译

商务印书馆
2018年·北京

图书在版编目（CIP）数据

世界名作家小小说选译 / 张经浩选译 . —北京：商务印书馆，2018
ISBN 978-7-100-16062-9

Ⅰ. ①世⋯　Ⅱ. ①张⋯　Ⅲ. ①小小说—小说集—世界　Ⅳ. ①I14

中国版本图书馆 CIP 数据核字（2017）第 095018 号

权利保留，侵权必究。

世界名作家小小说选译
张经浩　选译

商 务 印 书 馆 出 版
（北京王府井大街36号　邮政编码100710）
商 务 印 书 馆 发 行
北京市艺辉印刷有限公司印刷
ISBN 978 - 7 - 100 -16062 - 9

2018年7月第1版　　　开本880×1230　1/32
2018年7月北京第1次印刷　　印张13 ³/₄

定价：58.00 元

前 言

本书含欧、亚、美三大洲12个国家38位名作家的38篇小说，作品题材广泛，风格各异，有喜剧，也有悲剧，还有滑稽剧。有能博人一笑的，也有叫人想而生畏的，有包含深刻哲理的，也有如中国《聊斋志异》般奇异的，每篇都足见匠心。那丰富的想象，巧妙而严密的构思，意料之外情理之中的结局，都不能不叫人赞叹。

本书为英汉对照读本。就方法而论，翻译界无论中外，无论古今，都存在"直译"与"意译"之分，而且译者各执己见。英国的著名语言学家纽马克认为，翻译就是译"字"，因为纸上有的只是字。美国的翻译理论家奈达则认为"翻译即译意"。中国的鲁迅主张"保留原作的丰姿"，有的地方"宁可译得不顺口"。傅雷则大不同，认为"不妨假定理想的译文是原作者的中文写作"。两种观点可谓泾渭分明。

然而，纵观历史，读者对于译文的选择却相当一致：喜爱意译而不喜爱直译。佛经最早的翻译家安世高主张直译，其译本不被人看好，使用时间很短。鸠摩罗什采用意译，虽然这位译家离世已1604年，他译的经今天仍在念。朱生豪的莎士比亚意译本远比梁实秋的直译本被读者看好，虽然梁实秋在整个社会的知名度远超朱生豪。杨宪益的夫人戴乃迭坦率地说，霍克思译的《红楼梦》比他们夫妇译的《红楼梦》"更有创造性"，他们夫妇的"读者不爱看"，因为"偏于直译"，这并非过谦之词。

本人一贯采用意译。认为原文作者用原语写作时，自然而然会遵循原语的表达习惯和原语使用民族的文化传统，原文读来流畅，文学作品更是色彩缤纷。译者想要使译文流畅，甚至色彩缤纷，就必须遵循译语的表达习惯和使用译语民族的文化传统。译者对原文的"忠实"绝非使译文尽量保留原文形式，而是使译文读者读译文的感受能与原文读者读原文的感受尽量接近，译文尽量反映出原文的意思和风格。

中国文坛有句名言：文不厌改。这话千真万确，对翻译尤甚。本书的大部分译文是第四次出版，又做了修改，包括文字和意义上的修改。本人要借写前言的机会，对本书的责任编辑表示感谢。能遇上一位这样认真细致、善于发现问题的编辑非常幸运。希望本书能得到读者喜爱，欢迎读者批评指正。

张经浩
2017年12月22日

目 录

How Light Belief Bringeth Damage ················Bidpai   1
　轻信的后果 ······················〔印〕比德派   4

Neifile's Story ·····························Boccaccio   6
　急中生智 ·························〔意〕薄伽丘   10

Tom Varnish ···························Richard Steele   13
　花花公子 ···················〔英〕理查德·斯梯尔   16

The Disabled Soldier ················Oliver Goldsmith   18
　残疾军人 ···············〔英〕奥利弗·哥尔斯密   25

The Beggar-Woman of Locarno ········Heinrich von Kleist   30
　洛迦诺的叫花婆 ·······〔德〕海因里希·冯·克莱斯特   34

The Wife ·························Washington Irving   37
　妻子 ·························〔美〕华盛顿·欧文   47

The Hollow of the Three Hills ········Nathaniel Hawthorne   54
　阴阳之间 ···················〔美〕纳撒尼尔·霍桑   61

The Oval Portrait ····················Edgar Allen Poe   66
　椭圆形画像 ···················〔美〕埃德加·爱伦·坡   71

1

The Fiddler	Herman Melville	75
小提琴家	〔美〕赫尔曼·梅尔维尔	84
The Heavenly Christmas Tree	Fyodor Dostoevsky	91
天国的圣诞树	〔俄〕陀思妥耶夫斯基	98
The Three Hermits	Leo Tolstoy	102
三隐士	〔俄〕列夫·托尔斯泰	112
The Father	Björnstjerne Björnson	120
父亲	〔挪〕比昂斯滕·比昂松	125
How the Devil Lost His Poncho	Ricardo Palma	129
魔王怎样丢了大氅	〔秘〕里卡多·帕尔马	133
Luck	Mark Twain	136
运气	〔美〕马克·吐温	143
The Doctor's Heroism	Villiers de L'Isle-Adam	148
医生的勇敢精神	〔法〕维利埃·德·利尔-亚当	154
A Game of Billiards	Alphonse Daudet	159
打台球	〔法〕阿方斯·都德	165
Absent-Mindedness in a Parish Choir	Thomas Hardy	169
乱弹琴	〔英〕托马斯·哈代	174
A Psychological Shipwreck	Ambrose Bierce	177
魂游	〔美〕安布罗斯·比尔斯	184
An Attempt at Reform	August Strindberg	189
尝试改革	〔瑞典〕奥古斯特·斯特林堡	194

The Jewels of M. Lantin	Guy de Maupassant	198
兰廷先生的珠宝	〔法〕莫泊桑	208
The Boy Who Drew Cats	Koisumi Yakumo	215
爱画猫的孩子	〔日〕小泉八云	220
The Crime on Calle de la Persequida	Palacio Valdes	223
佩塞基达街凶杀案	〔西〕帕拉西奥·瓦尔德斯	232
A Wicked Boy	Anton Chekhov	238
小缺德鬼	〔俄〕安东·契诃夫	242
Witches' Loaves	O. Henry	245
多情女的面包	〔美〕欧·亨利	251
Her Lover	Maxim Gorky	256
她的情人	〔苏〕马克西姆·高尔基	265
Mrs. Packletide's Tiger	Saki	272
帕克尔泰夫人打老虎	〔英〕萨基	278
The Ant and the Grasshopper	William Somerset Maugham	282
蚂蚁和蟋蟀	〔英〕威廉·萨默塞特·毛姆	288
Three Letters … and a Footnote	Horacio Quiroga	293
三封信与一条脚注	〔乌拉圭〕奥拉西奥·基罗加	299
The Ghosts	Lord Dunsany	303
鬼	〔爱尔兰〕邓萨尼勋爵	309
A Dangerous Guy Indeed	Damon Runyon	314
十足的祸害	〔美〕达蒙·鲁尼恩	319

The Guardian Angel	André Maurois	323
保护神	〔法〕安德烈·莫洛亚	331
Kong at the Seaside	Arnold Zweig	337
康康在海边	〔德〕阿诺尔德·茨维格	345
Germans at Meat	Katherine Mansfield	351
餐桌上的德国人	〔英〕凯瑟琳·曼斯菲尔德	357
Mr. Preble Gets Rid of His Wife	James Thurber	362
普雷布尔先生杀妻	〔美〕詹姆斯·瑟伯	368
Fard	Aldous Huxley	373
胭脂	〔英〕奥尔德斯·赫胥黎	381
The Bedchamber Mystery	C. S. Forester	387
闺房秘事	〔英〕C. S. 福雷斯特	393
Over the Hill	John Steinbeck	397
开小差	〔美〕约翰·斯坦贝克	401
Charles	Shirley Jackson	404
查尔斯	〔美〕雪莉·杰克逊	412

附录：作家简介 ······ 418

How Light Belief Bringeth Damage

Bidpai

Two skillful thieves one night entered the house of a wealthy knight, no less wise than worshipped in the community. The gentleman, hearing the noise of their feet in the house, awakened and suspected that they were thieves. They were upon the point of opening the door of the chamber wherein he lay, when he jogged his wife, awakened her, and whispered, "I hear the noise of thieves who have come to rob us. I would have you, therefore, ask me straight, and with great insistence, whence and by what means I came by all I own. Ask me loudly and earnestly, and, as I shall appear reluctant, you must plead and wheedle until, at length, I shall succumb and tell you." The Lady, his wife, being wise and subtle, began in this manner to question her husband—"O, dear sir. Grant me one thing this night that I have for so long desired to know. Tell me how you have come by all these goods you now possess." He, speaking at random and carelessly, scarce answered. Finally, after she kept pleading, he said, "I can but wonder, Madam, at what moves you to know my secrets. Be contented, then, to live well, to dress richly, and to be waited upon and served. I have heard that all things have ears, and that many things are spoken which are later repented. Therefore, I pray you, hold your peace."

But even this did not deter the Lady. Sweetly and lovingly enticing, she besought him to tell her. Finally, wearying of her speech, the knight said, "All we have—and I charge you to say nothing of this to anyone—is stolen. Indeed, of all I own I got nothing truly.①" The Lady, unbelieving, so berated her husband that he answered farther, "You think what I have already told you is a wonder. Listen then. Even in my cradle I delighted in stealing and filching. And I lived among thieves so that my fingers might never be idle. One friend among them loved me so well that he taught me a rare and singular trick. He taught me a conjuration which I made to the moonbeams—enabling me to embrace them suddenly. Thus I sometimes came down upon them from a high window—or served myself with them to go up again to the top of the house. So I used them as I would. The Moon, hearing my conjuration seven times, showed me all the money and treasure of the house and with her beams I flew up and down. And thus, good wife, I made me rich. Now, no more."

One of the thieves, listening at the door, heard all that was said and bore it away. Because the knight was known to be a man of credit and integrity, the thieves believed his story. The chief thief, desirous to

---

① of all I own I got nothing truly：此句的 of 义为"在……中"，作状语修饰 got；all 后省略了关系代词 that；truly 在本句义为"诚实""正当"。

prove in deeds what he had heard in words, repeated the conjuration seven times, and then, embracing the moonbeams, he cast himself upon them thinking to go from window to window, and he fell headlong to the ground. The moon, however, favored him so that he was not killed, but broke his legs and one arm. He cried aloud in his pain and at his stupidity in trusting too much to another's words.

So, lying on the ground expecting death, he was found by the knight who beat him sorely. The thief begged for mercy, saying that what hurt him most was that he was such a fool to believe such words. And he besought him, since he had hurt him so with words, he would not also hurt him in deeds.

轻信的后果

〔印〕比德派

从前有位家道充裕的爵爷,不但受四邻敬重,而且头脑灵活。一天夜晚,两个惯偷溜进了他家。他听到屋子里有脚步声,警惕起来,猜准是来了贼。没等贼进房门,他忙推醒妻子,轻声说:"我听到有贼进来,要偷东西。你照我的办,追问我从哪儿挣来这么大一份家当,有什么生财之道。你要大声问,求我说。我假装不肯,你就又求又哄,让我到头来没办法,只好说。"爵爷夫人也聪明过人,按爵爷吩咐的话问了起来:"好老爷,有件事我一直想知道,今天晚上你非告诉我不可。你现在金银财宝不少,说说吧,是怎么弄到手的。"他支支吾吾,答非所问。后来禁不住一再恳求,说道:"我的太太,奇怪得很,你为什么要刨我的根底呢?你住得好,穿得好,有人侍候,该心满意足了。我听人说隔墙有耳,好些话说过了会后悔。算我求你,还是别多操心。"

爵爷夫人不依。她用尽甜言蜜语,叫他别瞒她。爵爷终于招架不住,说:"我的金银财宝——你千万不能走漏风声——全是偷来的。老实告诉你吧,没有一件来路正当。"爵爷夫人不相信,逼着爵爷交代明白。"你只当我刚才对你说的话是胡诌。那就听着吧！我从小爱干偷偷摸摸的事，又住在贼窝里，两只手从来没有闲过。有位贼朋友与我很有交情，教了我一个绝招。他传给我一套咒语，让我对着月光念，一念就能驾着月光走。所以有时候我驾着月光从楼上的窗口下来，有时候又驾着月光回到楼上，随心所愿。我念过七遍咒语月亮会告诉我这家人家的金银财宝藏在哪里，我驾着月光上下自如。好太太，我就这样发了财，秘诀算是全告诉你了。"

有一个贼躲在门边偷听，把话牢牢记着。这位爵爷的诚实可靠出了名，贼深信不疑。为首的想试试偷听到的诀窍，念了七遍咒语，然后把月光当梯子，想从窗口出窗口进，可是刚跨一步就一头栽到了地上。还好，总算月神慈悲，他没伤及性命，只摔断两条腿，一只胳膊。他痛得哇哇叫，悔不该轻信别人的话，上了大当。

这家伙躺在地上等死，等到爵爷来了，又挨一顿痛打。他苦苦求饶，说他主要不是痛在身上，而是痛在心上，后悔上当，既然伤了他的心，就别再伤他的身了。

Neifile's Story

Boccaccio

Chichibio, cook to Currado Gianfigliazzi, by a sudden reply which he made to his master, turns his wrath into laughter, and so escapes the punishment with which he had threatened him.

Though ready wit and invention furnish people with words proper to their different occasions, yet sometimes does Fortune, an assistant to the timorous, tip the tongue with a sudden and yet more pertinent reply than the most mature deliberation could ever have suggested, as I shall now briefly relate to you.[①]

Currado Gianfigliazzi, as most of you have both known and seen, was always esteemed a gallant and worthy citizen, delighting much in hounds and hawks, to omit his other excellencies, as no way relating to our present purpose.[②] Now he having taken a crane one day with his

---

① as I shall now briefly relate to you：此处作定语从句，先行词为主句。
② as no way relating to our present purpose：此处 as 仍是个介词，relating 是修饰 way 的定语，整个介词短语修饰紧靠前的名词。

hawk, near the village of Peretola, and finding it to be young and fat, sent it home to his cook, who was a Venetian, and called Chichibio, with orders to prepare it delicately for supper. The cook, a poor simple fellow, trussed and spitted it, and when it was nearly roasted, and began to smell pretty well, it chanced that① a woman in the neighbourhood called Brunetta, of whom he was much enamoured, came into the kitchen, and, being taken with the high savour, earnestly begged of him to give her a leg. He replied very merrily, singing all the time, "Donna Brunetta, you shall have no leg from me." Upon this she was a good deal nettled, and said, "As I hope to live,② if you do not give it to me, you need never expect any favour more from me." The dispute, at length, was carried to a great height between them; when, to make her easy, he was forced to give her one of the legs. Accordingly the crane was served up at supper, with only one leg, whereat a friend whom Currado had invited to sup with him expressed surprise. He therefore sent for the fellow, and demanded what was become③ of the other leg. The Venetian (a liar by nature) answered directly, "Sir, cranes have only one leg." Currado, in great wrath, said, "What the devil does the man talk of? Only one leg! Thou rascal, dost thou think I never saw a crane before?" Chichibio still persisted in his denial, saying, "Believe me, sir, it is as I say, and I will convince you of it whenever you please, by such fowls as are living," Currado was willing to have no more words, out of

---

① it chanced that: it happened that

② As I hope to live: 直译为"正如同我希望活着一样", 意即"实话告诉你吧"。

③ was become: had become; to become of; to happen to

regard to his friend; only he added. "As thou undertakest to show me a thing which I never saw or heard of before, I am content to make proof thereof tomorrow morning; but I vow and protest, if I find it otherwise, I will make thee remember it the longest day thou hast to live." [①]

Thus there was an end for that night, and the next morning Currado, whose passion would scarcely suffer[②] him to get any rest, arose betimes, and ordered his horses to be brought out, taking Chichibio along with him towards a river where he used early in the morning to see plenty of cranes; and he said, "We shall soon see which of us spoke truth last night." Chichibio, finding his master's wrath not at all abated, and that he was now to make good what he had asserted, not yet knowing how to do it, rode on first with all the fear imaginable; gladly would he have made his escape but he saw no possible means, whilst he was continually looking about him, expecting everything that appeared to be a crane with two feet. But being come near to the river he chanced to see, before anybody else, a dozen or so of cranes, each standing upon one leg, as they use to do when they are sleeping; whereupon, showing them quickly to his master, he said, "Now, sir, you yourself may see that I spoke nothing but truth, when I said that cranes have only one leg: look at those there, if you please." Currado, beholding the cranes, replied. "Yes, sirrah! but stay a while, and I will show thee that they have two." Then riding something nearer to them,

---

① remember it the longest day thou hast to live: remember it forever
② suffer: allow

he cried out, "Shough! Shough!" which made them set down the other foot, and after taking a step or two they all flew away. Then Currado, turning to him, said, "Well, thou lying knave, art thou now convinced that they have two legs?" Chichibio, quite at his wits' end, and knowing scarcely what he said himself, suddenly made answer, "Yes, sir, but you did not shout out to the crane last night, as you have done to these; had you called to it in the same manner, it would have put down the other leg, as these have now done." This pleased Currado so much that, turning all wrath into mirth and laughter, he said, "Chichibio thou sayest right; I should have done so indeed."

By this sudden and comical answer, Chichibio escaped a sound drubbing, and made peace with his master.

急中生智

〔意〕薄伽丘

库拉多·詹恩菲利亚齐的厨师基基比奥急中生智,妙语惊人,使主人转怒为喜,本要受的一顿处罚就此免了。

我来给诸位讲个小故事,说明虽然机灵、善辩的人巧舌如簧,在各种场合应付自如,有时却不如胆怯的人碰得巧,突然说出句巧妙的话,那是你无论怎样深思熟虑也想不到的。

在座诸公大都见过和了解库拉多·詹恩菲利亚齐,知道他是位潇洒过日子的老爷,爱养鹰犬。至于其他与我们现在要说的事无关的佳话,我们就不提了。有一天,他的鹰在佩雷托拉村附近捕到一只鹤,又肥又嫩,他便叫人送到家,交给厨师,准备晚上美餐一顿。厨师是威尼斯人,叫基基比奥,是个头脑简单的可怜虫。他把鹤捆好,放到炉上烤。就在烤到七八成、开始闻到香味时,邻近一个叫布鲁内塔的女人闯进了厨房,厨师正迷着这女人。她闻到香味嘴馋,向他要一条烤鹤腿吃。厨师唱个没停,得意洋洋地答道:"唐娜·布鲁内塔,这腿我不能给。"她一听很不高兴,说:"实话告诉你吧,如果你不给,以后别对我抱什么指望。"两人你一言我一语，斗得热闹。他最后不得不让步，给了她一条腿。所以，晚上端上桌的鹤只有一条腿，库拉多邀来吃饭的一位朋友一见，连说奇怪。库拉多把厨师叫了来，问另一条腿怎么不见了。这威尼斯人生性爱说谎，答道："老爷，鹤只有一条腿。"库拉多发了火，说："这是什么鬼话！只有一条腿！你这混蛋，难道以为我没见过鹤吗？"基基比奥仍然毫不让步，答道："老爷，您得相信我，的确是这么回事。等您哪天愿意的时候，我让您看看活的鹤，您就相信了。"库拉多碍着朋友在场，不想再争，只说道："这样的怪物我没听过，没见过，既然你说让我看看，好吧，明天早上见个分晓。如果我见到的鹤有两条腿，看我不剥了你的皮才怪！"

这一夜事情到此结束。第二天，库拉多急不可耐，一早起身，吩咐备马，带着基基比奥往河边去，他每天早上在那儿都看到成群的鹤。"昨天晚上我们谁是谁非马上可以见分晓。"他说。基基比奥见主人依然怒气冲冲，说过的话眼见要当真，一路上胆战心惊，其不安可想而知。他本打算溜之大吉，只可惜没法溜，只好走在前面；主人正不停地东张西望，盼着看见长着两条腿的鹤。快到河边时，还是数他运气好，第一个看见了十几只鹤，全是一条腿站着，鹤睡觉时就是这姿势。他赶快叫主人看，说："老爷，我说了鹤只有一条腿，您看吧，一点没错。您看那群鹤。老爷看啦！"库拉多看着鹤道："去你妈的！你等着瞧，我叫它们一条腿变两条腿。"他催马过去，吆喝两声："哟！哟！"鹤马上放下另一条腿，跑两步，飞了。库拉多转身对厨师说："你这混蛋，瞧吧！现在看看，是不是两条腿！"基基比奥狡辩不了，正愁无言以对时却脱口说道："没错，老爷。可是您昨天晚上没有像现在这样大叫一声。要是您也这样叫,那只鹤准会把另一条腿伸出来。"库拉多的怒火被这句话浇灭了,忍不住大笑起来,说:"基基比奥,你说的是,我要是也这么大叫一声就好了。"

基基比奥偶然说句俏皮话,免了一顿痛打,与主人又相安无事了。

Tom Varnish[①]

Richard Steele

  Because I have a professed aversion to long beginnings of stories, I will go into this at once, by telling you, that there dwells near the Royal Exchange as happy a couple as ever entered into wedlock. These live in that mutual confidence of each other, which renders the satisfaction of marriage even greater than those of friendship, and makes wife and husband the dearest appellations of human life. Mr. Balance is a merchant of good consideration, and understands the world, not from speculation, but practice. His wife is the daughter of an honest house, ever bred in a family-way[②]; and has, from a natural good understanding and great innocence, a freedom which men of sense know to be the certain sign of virtue, and fools take to be an encouragement to vice.

  Tom Varnish, a young gentleman of the Middle Temple, by the bounty of a good father, who was so obliging as to die, and leave him,

---

① Tom Varnish: 译文标题是根据小说情节重拟的，文学翻译中这样译并非罕见。
② in a family-way: 习惯用语，义为"不拘礼节地"。

in his twenty-fourth year, besides a good estate, a large sum which lay in the hands of Mr. Balance, had by this means an intimacy at his house; and being one of those hard students who read plays for the improvement of the law, took his rules of life from thence. Upon mature deliberation, he conceived it very proper, that he, as a man of wit and pleasure of the town, should have an intrigue with his merchant's wife. He no sooner thought of this adventure, but he began it by an amorous epistle to the lady and a faithful promise to wait upon her at a certain hour the next evening, when he knew her husband was to be absent.

The letter was no sooner received, but it was communicated to the husband, and produced no other effect in him, than that he joined with his wife to raise all the mirth they could out of this fantastical piece of gallantry. They were so little concerned at this dangerous man of mode, that they plotted ways to perplex him without hurting him. Varnish comes exactly at his hour; and the lady's well-acted confusion at his entrance gave him opportunity to repeat some couplets very fit for the occasion with very much grace and spirit. His theatrical manner of making love was interrupted by an alarm of the husband's coming; and the wife, in a personated terror, beseeched him, "if he had any value for the honour of a woman that loved him, he would jump out of the window." He did so, and fell upon featherbeds placed there on purpose to receive him.

It is not to be conceived how great the joy of an amorous man is, when he has suffered for his mistress, and is never the worse for it. Varnish the next day writ a most elegant billet, wherein he said all that imagination could form upon the occasion. He violently protested, "going out of the window was no way terrible, but as it was going from her"; with several other kind expressions, which procured him a second assignation. Upon his second visit, he was conveyed by a faithful maid into her bed chamber, and left there to expect the arrival of her mistress. But the wench, according to her instructions, ran in again to him, and locked the door after her to keep out her master. She had just time enough to convey the lover into a chest before she admitted the husband and his wife into the room.

You may be sure that trunk was absolutely necessary to be opened; but upon her husband's ordering it, she assured him, "she had taken all the care imaginable in packing up the things with her own hands, and he might send the trunk abroad as soon as he thought fit."

The easy husband believed his wife, and the good couple went to bed; Varnish having the happiness to pass the night in the mistress's bedchamber without molestation. The morning arose, but our lover was not well situated to observe her blushes; so all we know of his sentiments on this occasion is, that he heard Balance ask for the key, and say, "he would himself go with this chest, and have it opened before the captain of the ship, for the greater safety of so valuable a lading."

The goods were hoisted away; and Mr. Balance, marching by his chest with great care and diligency, omitting nothing that might give his passenger perplexity. But, to consummate all, he delivered the chest, with strict charge, "in case they were in danger of being taken, to throw it overboard, for there were letters in it, the matter of which might be of great service to the enemy."

花花公子

〔英〕理查德·斯梯尔

我最讨厌在故事的开头说上一大堆话，就开门见山告诉你吧。在皇家交易所附近住着一对夫妇，要多美满有多美满。他们互相信任，把夫妻情分看得比朋友情分还重，认为世上最亲切的称谓只有两个：丈夫、妻子。丈夫巴兰斯先生是一位大商人，熟稔世情（不是投机有术，而是见多识广）。他太太是位良家女，从小自由自在。由于她生性大方，天真无邪，在人前无拘无束，有头脑的人知道这是纯洁的表现，傻瓜蛋才只当是轻佻。

中坦普尔有位少爷，名叫汤姆·瓦尼什，得了父亲的福。老人心肠好，撒手归天前，在汤姆24岁那年，把一大笔产业，外加一大笔存在巴兰斯先生手中的钱，全留给了他。这一来，他与巴兰斯家来往密切。这人是以剧本为师学生活之道的人，以为剧本中有的事生活中必定有。他自以为是伦敦有数的几个聪明、逗人爱的人物之一，准能勾搭上这位巨商的太太。主意打定后，他马上给她写了封情书，说一定在第二天晚上趁她丈夫不在家的时候侍奉她。

妻子收到信后马上交给丈夫，丈夫不但没有醋意，而且与妻子合谋，要好好捉弄一下这个乱献殷勤、异想天开的家伙。他们不怕这位风流哥儿不好惹,想了个能捉弄他又不致伤他的妙计。瓦尼什准点到来,巨商的妻子装作慌慌张张。他趁机潇潇洒洒、情深意长地念了一些非常得体的对句。正装腔作势求爱时,丈夫回来了。妻子假装害怕,求他道:"哪个女人如果爱你,你就得珍惜人家的名誉。现在你就从窗口跳出去吧。"他果真跳了窗,却落在鸭绒被上,没伤着,原来鸭绒被是特地为他准备的。

花花公子猎艳只虚惊一场,安然无恙,不用说喜不自胜。第二天,瓦尼什写了封深情的信,在信上说在当时那种情况下,什么想象都会产生。他口口声声表明"跳窗不可怕,只是舍不得你"。另外还有好些温存话,总算没白说,换来了第二次幽会。第二次去时,一位可靠的女仆把他领进太太的卧室,叫他在里面等。过了一会儿,女仆按太太安排的巧计又跑进来,锁上门,说老爷来了。她刚把这位有情郎藏进大箱子,一打开门,老爷和太太便进来了。

这口箱子本来非打开不可,但老爷刚一吩咐,太太就抢着说:"所有东西都是我一件件亲手收拾的,错不了,你什么时候叫人把箱子搬走都行。"

丈夫是随和人,相信妻子的话,夫妻俩便去睡觉了。瓦尼什好福气,在情妇的卧室里过了一夜,只是什么也没捞着。第二天早上,多情郎仍闷在箱子里,当然没看到她红扑扑的脸,却听见了巴兰斯要钥匙,说:"我亲自押送箱子。里面装的东西很值钱,我要当面打开让船长过目,这样做才万无一失。"这时有情郎心里是何感想,我们不难得知。

大箱子被人抬走了,巴兰斯先生不辞劳苦,寸步不离地跟着,一路上尽说些叫箱子里的人犯愁的话,但最叫他胆战心惊的是巴兰斯先生托运箱子时说的一句:"如果你们遇到危险,就把箱子扔到海里去。箱子里装着重要文件,落到对方手里不是闹着玩的。"

The Disabled Soldier

Oliver Goldsmith

No observation is more common, and at the same time more true, than that one half of the world are ignorant how the other half lives. The misfortunes of the great are held up to engage our attention; are enlarged upon in tones of declamation; and the world is called upon to gaze at the noble sufferers: the great, under the pressure of calamity, are conscious of several others sympathising with their distress; and have, at once, the comfort of admiration and pity.

There is nothing magnanimous in bearing misfortunes with fortitude, when the whole world is looking on: men in such circumstances will act bravely even from motives of vanity; but he who, in the vale of obscurity, can brave adversity; who without friends to encourage, acquaintances to pity, or even without hope to alleviate his misfortunes, can behave with tranquility and indifference, is truly great: whether peasant or courtier, he deserves admiration, and should be held up for our imitation and respect.

While the slightest inconveniences of the great are magnified into calamities; while tragedy mouths out their sufferings in all the strains of eloquence, the miseries of the poor are entirely disregarded; and yet some of the lower ranks of people undergo more real hardships in one day, than those of a more exalted station suffer in their whole lives. It is inconceivable what difficulties the meanest of our common sailors and soldiers endure without murmuring or regret; without passionately declaiming against providence, or calling their fellows to be gazers of their intrepidity. Every day is to them a day of misery, and yet they entertain their hard fate without repining.

With what indignation do I hear an Ovid, a Cicero, or a Rabutin complain of their misfortunes and hardships, whose greatest calamity was that of being unable to visit a certain spot of earth, to which they had foolishly attached an idea of happiness. Their distresses were pleasures, compared to what many of the adventuring poor every day endure without murmuring. They ate, drank, and slept; they had slaves to attend them and were sure of subsistence for life; while many of their reflow creatures are obliged to wander without a friend to comfort or assist them, and even without shelter from the severity of the season.

I have been led into these reflections from accidentally meeting, some days ago, a poor fellow, whom I knew when a boy, dressed in a sailor's jacket, and begging at one of the outlets of the town, with a wooden leg. I knew him to have been honest and industrious when in the country, and was curious to learn what bad reduced him to his present situation. Wherefore, after giving him what I thought proper, I desired to know the history of his life and misfortunes, and the manner in which he was reduced to his present distress. The disabled soldier, for such he was, though dressed in a sailor's habit, scratching his head, and leaning on his crutch, put himself into an attitude to comply with my request, and gave me his history as follows.

"As for my misfortunes, master, I can't pretend to have gone through any more than other folks; for except for the loss of my limb and my being obliged to beg, I don't know any reason, thank Heaven, that I have to complain. There is Bill Tibbs, of our regiment, he has lost both his legs, and an eye to boot; but, thank Heaven, it is not so bad with me yet.

"I was born in Shropshire; my father was a labourer, and died when I was five years old, so I was put upon the parish. As he had been a wandering sort of man, the parishioners were not able to tell to what parish I belonged, or where I was born, so they sent me to another parish, and that parish sent me to a third. I thought in my heart, they kept sending me about so long, that they would not let me be born in any parish at all; but at last, however, they fixed me. I had some disposition to be a scholar, and was resolved at least to know my letters: but the master of the workhouse put me to business as soon as I was able to handle a mallet; and here I lived an easy kind of life for five years. I only wrought ten hours in the day and had my meat and drink provided for my labour. It was true, I was not suffered to stir out of the house, for fear, as they said, I should run away; but what of that? I had the liberty of the whole house, and the yard before the door, and that was enough for me. I was then bound out to a farmer, where I was up both early and late; but I ate and drank well; and liked my business well enough, till he died, when I was obliged to provide for myself; so I was resolved to go seek my fortune.

"In this manner I went from town to town, worked when I could get employment, and starved when I could get none; when, happening one day to go through a field belonging to a justice of the peace, I spied a hare crossing the path just before me; and I believe the devil put it into my head to fling my stick at it. Well, what will you have on't? I killed the hare, and was bringing it away, when the justice himself met me; he called me a poacher and a villain, and collaring me, desired I would give an account of myself. I fell upon my knees, begged his worship's pardon, and began to give a full account of all that I knew of my breed, seed, and generation; but though I gave a very true account, the justice said I could give no account; so I was indicted at the sessions, found guilty of being poor, and sent up to London to Newgate, in order to be transported as a vagabond.

"People may say this and that of being in jail, but for my part, I found Newgate as agreeable a place as ever I was in all my life. I had my belly full to eat and drink, and did no work at all. This kind of life was too good to last forever; so I was taken out of prison, after five months, put on board of ship, and sent off, with two hundred more, to the plantations. We had but an indifferent passage, for being all confined to the hold, more than a hundred of our people died for want of sweet air, and those that remained were sickly enough, God knows. When we came ashore we were sold to the planters, and I was bound for seven years more. As I was no scholar, for I did not know my letters, I was obliged to work among the negroes, and I served out my time, as in duty bound to do.

"When my time was expired, I worked my passage home, and glad I was to see old England again, because I loved my country. I was afraid, however, that I should be indicted for a vagabond once more, so did not much dare to go down into the country, but kept about the town, and did little jobs when I could get them.

"I was very happy in this manner for some time till one evening, coming home from work, two men knocked me down, and then desired me to stand. They belonged to a press-gang. I was carried before the justice, and as I could give no account of myself, I had my choice left, whether to go on board a man-of-war, or list for a soldier. I chose the latter, and in this post of a gentleman, I served two campaigns in Flanders, was at the battles of Val and Fontenoy, and received but one wound through the breast here; but the doctor of our regiment soon made me well again.

"When the peace came on I was discharged; and as I could not work, because my wound was sometimes troublesome, I listed for a landman in the East India Company's service. I have fought the French in six pitched battles; and I verily believe that if I could read or write, our captain would have made me a corporal. But it was not my good fortune to have any promotion, for I soon fell sick, and so got leave to return home again with forty pounds in my pocket. This was at the beginning of the present war, and I hoped to be set on shore, and to

The Disabled Soldier

have the pleasure of spending my money; but the Government wanted men, and so I was pressed for a sailor, before ever I could set foot on shore.

"The boatswain found me, as he said, an obstinate fellow: he swore he knew that I understood my business well, but that I shammed Abraham to be idle; but God knows, I knew nothing of sea-business, and he beat me without considering what he was about. I had still, however, my forty pounds, and that was some comfort to me under every beating; and the money I might have had to this day, but that our ship was taken by the French, and so I lost all.

"Our crew was carried into Brest, and many of them died, because they were not used to life in a jail; but, for my part, it was nothing to me, for I was seasoned. One night, as I was asleep on the bed of boards, with a warm blanket about me, for I always loved to lie well, I was awakened by the boatswain, who had a dark lantern in his hand. 'Jack,' says he to me, 'will you knock out the French sentry's brains?' 'I don't care,' says I, striving to keep myself awake, 'if I lend a hand.' 'Then follow me,' says he, 'and I hope we shall do business.' So up I got, and tied my blanket, which was all the clothes I had, about my middle, and went with him to fight the Frenchman. I hate the French, because they are all slaves, and wear wooden shoes.

"Though we had no arms, one Englishman is able to beat five French at any time; so we went down to the door where both sentries were posted, and rushing upon them, seized their arms in a moment, and knocked them down. From thence nine of us ran together to the quay, and seizing the first boat we met, got out of the harbor and put to sea. We had not been here three days before we were taken up by the *Dorset* privateer, who were glad of so many good hands; and we consented to run our chance. However, we had not as much luck as we expected. In three days we fell in with the *pompadour* privateer of forty guns, while we had but twenty-three, so to it we went, yard-arm and yard-arm. The fight lasted three hours, and I verily believe we should have taken the Frenchman, had we but some more men left behind; but unfortunately we lost all our men just as we were going to get the victory.

"I was once more in the power of the French, and I believe it would have gone hard with me had I been brought back to Brest; but by good fortune we were retaken by the *Viper*. I had almost forgotten to tell you, that in that engagement, I was wounded in two places: I lost four fingers off the left hand, and my leg was shot off. If I had had the good fortune to have lost my leg and the use of my hand on board a king's ship, and not aboard a privateer, I should have been entitled to clothing and maintenance during the rest of my life; but that was not my chance: one man is born with a silver spoon in his mouth, and another with a wooden ladle. However, Blessed be God, I enjoy good health, and will for ever love liberty and old England. Liberty, property, and Old England, for ever, huzza!"

Thus saying, he limped off, leaving me in admiration at his intrepidity and content; nor could I avoid acknowledging that an habitual acquaintance with misery serves better than philosophy to teach us to despise it.

残疾军人

〔英〕奥利弗·哥尔斯密

世界上有一半人不知另一半人是怎样生活的，这是句最有普遍意义、最真实的话。大人物的不幸我们能见到，会添油加醋地说，巴不得普天下的人都关心贵人的疾苦。所以，大人物要是遭了难，总有几个人同情他们的苦处，这一来，他们便崇敬与惋惜双丰收。

万众瞩目时，你能毅然决然忍受不幸，这不算什么了不起的行为。在这种情况下，即使为了爱面子，你也会拿出勇敢的行动来。真正伟大的是默默无闻地勇对逆境的人。他们既无朋友鼓励，也无熟人怜悯，甚至连减轻不幸的希望也见不到，却处之泰然。无论是种地的也好，当差的也好，他们都应引为我们的楷模，受到我们的尊敬。

大人物芝麻大的不顺心事会夸成西瓜大，一传十，十传百，他们的烦恼变成了大悲剧，而穷人的痛苦却完全无人提起。其实，下层社会的某些人一天经受的苦难比地位显赫的人一辈子经受的还多。我们的普通水手、普通士兵究竟无声无息地吃着怎样的苦头，人们是想象不出的。他们既不责怪命运，也不向人夸耀自己的英雄气质。每一天对他们来说都很不幸，然而他们身逢厄运却从不怨尤。

如果是哪位诗人、哪位政治家或诸如此类的非等闲之辈对我说起他们的忧愁苦恼，我听了反而会生气，他们的倒霉事充其量不过是没有去成世界上他们莫名其妙设想的一片什么乐土。与每天默默受煎熬、苦苦挣扎的可怜人比起来，他们的苦实际上是福。他们好吃好喝，睡得香，有奴婢侍候，生活舒舒服服，而他们的同胞却有许多人被迫流浪，得不到朋友的安慰、帮助，甚至无栖身之地。

我产生这些看法的原因是，好些天前我偶然遇见了一个儿时就认识的可怜人，他穿着件水手的衣服，拖着条假腿，在城边的路口讨钱。我知道他在乡下时一贯守本分又勤快，看到他落到这步田地，觉得很奇怪。我给了他一些钱，问起他的经历和不幸的由来，想把他落魄的原因打听清楚。他穿着水手衣服，其实是个残废军人。他搔搔头皮，靠在拐杖上，没有拒绝我的要求，说了自己的经历。

"老爷，我虽很可怜，但总算比上不足比下有余。谢天谢地，我只缺了条腿，当了乞丐，别的倒没什么。我们团的比尔·蒂伯斯断了两条腿，还瞎了一只眼。谢天谢地，我没有他弄得惨。

"我生在什罗普郡，父亲给人帮工，在我五岁时他死了，教区收养了我。我父亲是走南闯北的人，教区的人弄不清我该归哪个区管，也不知道我在哪个地方生，把我送到了别的教区，别的教区又把我往外送。他们把我送来送去，好像我是从天上掉下来的。还算好，最后他们查清楚了。我想上学，至少也要能识字。可是贫民院的老爷没让，等我长到能拿木槌时便叫我干活。在那地方过得倒不错，有五年好日子。一天只干十小时，干了活有肉吃，有酒喝。他们不让我出贫民院，担心我逃跑，我倒不想跑。在屋子里我自由自在，出了门在院子里也自由自在，这就满足了。后来我跟着一个庄稼汉过活，早出晚归，也有吃有喝，干得痛快。等到他死了，我只好一个人过日子，就打算碰碰运气。

"从那以后，我在城里流浪，四处跑，找得到活时干干活，找不到就饿肚皮。有一天，我从一块地里走过，看到一只野兔从面前蹿过去。这块地是治安官的。不知有什么鬼使神差，我把手里的棍子扔了过去。偏有那么巧的事，把兔子打死了。我提着兔子正要走，没想到治安官看到了，骂我是小偷、流氓，揪住我的衣领，问我的来历。我跪下求饶，把祖宗八代的事都告诉了他。我的话句句是实话，但治安官硬说我来路不正，把我送上法庭，说我是穷鬼，把我当无业游民①押进伦敦新门监狱②。

"大家都说蹲监狱受这个罪那个罪，我倒觉得大牢里最舒服。我有吃有喝，又不用干活。可惜好景不长，蹲了五个月我出来了，让人押上一条船，往庄园里送，同船的有两百多人。一路上我们吃够了苦，全闷在船舱里，一百多人活活闷死了，剩下的也只有半条命。上岸以后，我们被卖给庄园主，我的期限是七年。我不识字，没知识，只能跟着黑人干活。最后我的期限总算熬到了头。

"期满以后我回国了，又看到了英国，心里高兴得很。我喜爱的还是自己的国家。可是我也担心再被当成无业游民，不敢下乡去，只在城市转，找一点零活干。

---

① 1536年英国法律规定，身强力壮的无业游民要割耳朵，第三次被抓获要处死刑。
② Newgate Prison，又译"纽盖特监狱"，King John 在位时的第一座监狱，于1880年关闭，1902年拆除，以环境恶劣著名，很多小说中都提到过它。

"这样快快活活过了些日子以后,一天晚上我下工回来,被两个人打倒在地,接着又拉了起来。这两人是拉夫队的人,把我带去见法官。我说不出身份,只有两条路可走,要么上军舰,要么进陆军。我宁愿进陆军。当兵以后,我在弗兰德打过两次大仗,瓦尔和丰特努瓦的仗也有我一份,只在胸口负了一处伤,我们团的医生很快给我治好了。

"停战以后,军队用不着我了。我的伤口有时会发痛,干不了活,进了东印度公司当差。我与法国人面对面干过六仗,如果能读会写,照理说上司少不了叫我当个上等兵。可惜我没福气,提升不了,没多久反倒生了场病,又回国了,口袋里放着四十镑钱。这是现在这场战争开始时的事。我原指望能住下来,用这笔钱享受享受,可是政府缺人,没等我跨上岸又叫我当了水手。

"水手长责怪我性子倔,硬说我其实懂行,是在偷懒。老天知道,船上的事我的确不懂,他便没头没脑地打我。这时候我还有四十镑钱,每次挨打我就想着这笔钱,安慰自己。本来我把钱会留到今天,可谁知我们的船被法国人掳去,全完了。

"船上的人被送进布雷斯特大牢,好些人没蹲过监狱,死了。我坐牢是吃家常便饭,满不在乎。一天晚上,我照老样包着毯子在硬板床上睡得正香,水手长叫醒了我。他手里提着盏灯笼,没点着。'老兄,我们把法国哨兵的脑袋砸了,怎么样?'他问。我睡得蒙蒙眬眬,说:'要我去就去呗!'他说:'好,那你跟我来。我们要干得干净利索。'于是我起身了,跟着他去干掉法国人。毯子捆在腰上,也是我的衣服。我恨死了法国人,他们全是乌龟王八蛋。

"我们没有武器,可是一个英国人什么时候都打得过五个法国人。我们摸到门边，向两个哨兵猛扑过去，夺下武器，干掉了他们。我们九个人跑到码头边，赶紧抢了条船，划出港，逃了。在海上还没出三天，被多塞号武装民船俘虏了。这些人见我们全是好手，叫我们入伙，我们说入就入吧。谁知道运气不好。三天以后我们又遇上了一艘法国武装民船，有40条枪，我们才23条，双方摆开阵势交起火来。前后打了三个小时，如果人手够，我们准会打败法国人，可是眼看就要胜利时我们的人全完了。

"我又一次落到了法国人手里。要是再送到布雷斯特，那我一定完了。还算幸运，我们没有。我忘了告诉你，这次交火我有两处受伤：左手断了四个手指，少了一条腿。如果是在国王陛下的船上断了一条腿，废了一只手，那倒走运，一辈子吃穿不愁。可我是在武装民船上，没有这福分。本来，有的人生来命好，用银勺子吃饭，有的人生来命苦，用木勺子吃饭。现在谢天谢地，我总算身体好。我爱自由，爱英国。英国永远自由繁荣。英国万岁！"

他说完一瘸一拐地走了，我不由得对他的无所畏惧和无怨无求的精神肃然起敬。然而我也不能不承认，一位天天苦苦挣扎的人比哲学家更能使我们懂得，为什么我们要藐视不幸。

The Beggar-Woman of Locarno

Heinrich von Kleist

At the foot of the Alps, near Locarno in Upper Italy, stood once a castle, the property of a marquis; of this castle, as one goes southward from the St. Gotthard, one sees now only the ashes and ruins. In one of its high and spacious rooms there once lay, on a bundle of straw which had been thrown down for her, an old, sick woman who had come begging to the door, and had been taken in and given shelter out of pity by the mistress of the castle. The Marquis, returning from the hunt, happened to enter this room, where he usually kept his guns, while the old woman lay there, and angrily ordered her to come out of the corner where the bundle of straw had been placed and to get behind the stove. In rising the old woman slipped on the polished floor and injured her spine severely; so much did she hurt herself that only with unspeakable agony could she manage to cross the room, as she was ordered, to sink moaning behind the stove and there to die.

Some years later the Marquis, owing to war and bad harvests, having lost most of his fortune, decided to sell his estates. One day

The Beggar-Woman of Locarno

a nobleman from Florence arrived at the castle which, on account of its beautiful situation, he wished to buy. The Marquis, who was very anxious to bring the business to a successful conclusion, gave instructions to his wife to prepare for their guest the above-mentioned room, which was now very beautifully furnished. But imagine their horror when, in the middle of the night, the nobleman, pale and distracted, entered their room solemnly assuring them that his room was haunted by something which was not visible, but which sounded as if somebody lying on straw in one corner of the room got up slowly and feebly but with distinct steps crossed the room to lie down moaning and groaning behind the stove.

The Marquis, horrified, he did not know himself why, laughed with forced merriment at the nobleman and said he would get up at once and keep him company for the rest of the night in the haunted room, and when the morning came the nobleman ordered his horses to be brought round, bade farewell, and departed.

This incident, which created a great sensation, unhappily for the Marquis frightened away several would-be buyers; and when amongst his own servants strangely and mysteriously the rumor arose that queer things happened in the room at midnight, he determined to make a definite stand in the matter and to investigate it himself the same night. For that reason he had his bed moved into the room at twilight, and watched there without sleeping until midnight. To his horror, as the clock began to strike midnight, he became aware of the mysterious noise; it sounded as though somebody rose from straw which rustled beneath him, crossed the room, and sank down sighing and groaning behind the stove. The next morning when he came downstairs his wife inquired what he had discovered; he looked around with nervous and troubled glances, and after fastening the door assured her that the rumor was true. The Marquise was more terrified than ever in her life, and begged him, before the rumor grew, to make a cold-blooded trial in her company. Accompanied by a loyal servant, they spent the following night in the room and heard the same ghostly noises; and only the pressing need to get rid of the castle at any cost enabled the Marquise in the presence of the servant to smother the terror which she felt it would be easy to discover. On the evening of the third day, as both of them, with beating hearts, went up the stairs to the guestroom, anxious to get at the cause of the disturbance, they found that the watch-dog, who happened to have been let off his chain, was standing at the door of the room; so that, without giving a definite reason, both perhaps unconsciously wishing to have another living thing in the room besides themselves, they took him into the room with them. About eleven o'clock the two of them, two candles on the table, the Marquise fully dressed, the Marquis with dagger and pistol which he had taken from the cupboard beside him, sat down one on each bed; and while they entertained one another as well as they could by talking, the dog lay down, his head on his paws, in the middle of the room and slept. As the clock began to strike midnight the horrible sound began; somebody whom human eyes could not see raised himself on crutches in the corner of the room; the straw could be heard rustling beneath him; and at the first step the dog woke, pricked up his ears, rose from the ground growling and barking, and just as though somebody were making straight for him, moved backwards towards the stove. At the sight the Marquise, her hair rising, rushed from the room, and while the Marquis, who had snatched up his dagger, called "Who is there?" and received no answer, she like a madwoman had ordered the coach to be got out, determined to drive away to the town immediately. But before she had packed a few things together and got them out of the door she noticed that all around her the castle was in flames. The Marquis, overcome with horror, and tired of life, had taken a candle and set fire to the wooden panelling on all sides. In vain she sent people in to rescue the wretched man; he had already found his end in the most horrible manner possible; and his white bones, gathered together by his people, still lie in that corner of the room from which he had once ordered the beggar-woman of Locarno to rise.

洛迦诺的叫花婆

〔德〕海因里希·冯·克莱斯特

在阿尔卑斯山下，意大利北边的洛迦诺①附近，原来有一座古堡，为一位侯爵所有；现在如果你从圣哥达往南走，看到的却只是古堡的废墟和焦土。古堡里的房间又高又大，其中有一间房里放过一捆干草，是给讨饭讨到古堡来的一个病老婆子的；古堡的女主人出于怜悯之心让她住了进来。这间房是侯爵放猎枪的地方，侯爵打猎回来，进房后看见一个老太婆在里面躺着，发了火，叫她从角落里的干草上滚到火炉后去。地板很光，老婆子起身时脚一滑，肋骨受了重伤。她这跤摔得很重。但让人逼着，只得忍着剧痛，一步步从房间这头的角落，挪到那头的火炉后，哼着躺下等死。

几年以后，侯爵因为战祸和歉收，家产去之大半，决定卖掉古堡。有一天，佛罗伦萨的一位贵族到了古堡，看中古堡的环境幽邃，想买。侯爵急于脱手，吩咐妻子收拾上面说的房间给客人住，那间房现在摆设得十分漂亮。但到了半夜，那位贵族闯进侯

---

① 洛迦诺，属瑞士，离意大利很近。

爵的房间，脸色发白，慌慌张张，一口咬定他住的房间闹鬼，见不着，听声音像是什么人，先躺在角落的草堆上，以后慢慢站起来，走到房间的另一头，脚步软绵绵，但听得清清楚楚，走到火炉后哼着躺了下来。这一说引起的恐慌可想而知。

侯爵不明原因，心里害怕，但表面装镇静，听了贵族的话笑起来，马上答应起身陪他到闹鬼的房间过夜。到第二天早上，贵族还是吩咐备马，告辞了。

这件事传得很广，侯爵算是倒霉，好几个愿买的人都吓退了。奇怪得很，不知为什么，他自己的仆人后来也开始传说那间房半夜里有怪事，这使他下了决心采取果断办法应付，当晚亲自去看看是否果有其事。所以，他叫人在黄昏把他的床搬进那间房，没有睡，守到半夜。时钟刚敲12点，他害怕起来，听到了一个奇怪的声音，好像是有人窸窸窣窣地从他床边的干草堆上站起来，走到房间的另一头，又在炉子后哼着躺下来。第二天早上他到楼下，妻子问他见到听到了什么，他慌慌张张四下先看了看，闩上门，告诉妻子流传的事果然是真。侯爵夫人一辈子从未遇过这种可怕的事，担心闹得满城风雨，要丈夫陪她去冒险看个究竟。第二天夫妻俩叫了个可靠的仆人，夜晚住进那间房，结果又听到有鬼声。侯爵夫人的恐惧本来连她自己也知道难以掩饰，只是她急于卖掉古堡，价钱贵贱不论，又当着仆人的面，才装出了镇静。到第三天晚上，夫妻俩又战战兢兢去客房，想看看究竟是什么在作怪。凑巧守夜狗的链条放开了，狗跑到了客房门口。可能不是由于别的原因，而是因为想找个有生命的东西做伴，他们把狗带进了客房。大约11点钟时，两人各坐在一张床上，桌上点着两支蜡烛，侯爵夫人穿戴整齐，侯爵带着匕首和身旁小柜上拿来的手枪。他们闲谈着消磨时间，狗躺在客房当中睡着了，头枕在爪子上。当时钟开始敲12点时，那可怕的声音又响起来，看不见却听得到有人在屋角撑着拐杖站起来，踩得干草沙沙响的声音清清楚楚。刚走出一步，狗醒了过来，竖起耳朵，直起身，狂叫乱吠，往炉子后退，好像有人向它逼过来。侯爵夫人见了毛发倒竖，忙跑出去。侯爵亮出匕首，喝道："是谁！"可是没有人回答。侯爵夫人像是发了疯，吩咐套马来，决定连夜离开去城里。但她才收拾了不多几件东西拿出门，便发现古堡四处已经着火。原来侯爵吓昏了头，觉得活着没意思，拿着蜡烛，把古堡各处的木饰板点着了。她叫人来救可怜的侯爵，可是为时太晚，侯爵已经惨死。他家的人找到了他的白骨，就在他原来叫洛迦诺的叫花婆站起来的那个房间的一个角落里。

The Wife

Washington Irving

The treasures of the deep are not so precious
As are the conceal'd comforts of a man
Locked up in woman's love. I scent the air
Of blessings, when I come but near the house.
What a delicious breath marriage sends forth ...
The violet bed's not sweeter.

MIDDLETON

I have often had the occasion to remark the fortitude with which women sustain the most overwhelming reverses of fortune. Those disasters which break down the spirit of a man, and prostrate him in the dust, seem to call forth all energies of the softer sex, and give such intrepidity and elevation to their character, that at times it approaches to sublimity. Nothing can be more touching than to behold a soft and tender female, who had been all weakness and dependence, and alive to every trivial roughness, while treading the prosperous paths of life, suddenly rising in mental force to be the comforter and support of her husband under misfortune, and abiding, with unshrinking firmness, the bitterest blasts of adversity.

As the vine, which has long twined its graceful foliage about the oak, and been lifted by it into sunshine, will, when the hardy plant is rifted by the thunderbolt, cling round it with its caressing tendrils and bind up its shattered boughs, so is it beautifully ordered by Providence, that woman, who is the mere dependent and ornament of man in his happier hours, should be his stay and solace when smitten with sudden calamity; winding herself into the rugged recesses of his nature, tenderly supporting the drooping head, and binding up the broken heart.

I was once congratulating a friend, who had around him a blooming family, knit together in the strongest affection. "I can wish you no better lot," said he with enthusiasm, "than to have a wife and children. If you are prosperous, there they are to share your prosperity; if otherwise, there they are to comfort you." And indeed, I have observed that a married man falling into misfortune is more apt to retrieve his situation in the world than a single one; partly because he is more stimulated to exertion by the necessities of the helpless and beloved beings who depend upon him for subsistence; but chiefly because his spirits are soothed and relieved by domestic endearments, and his self-respect kept alive by finding that, though all abroad is darkness and humiliation, yet there is still a little world of love at home, of which he is the monarch. Whereas a single man is apt to run to waste and self-neglect; to fancy himself lonely and abandoned, and his heart to fall to ruin like some deserted mansion, for want of an inhabitant.

These observations call to mind a little domestic story, of which I was once a witness. My intimate friend, Leslie, had married a beautiful and accomplished girl, who had been brought up in the midst of fashionable life. She had, it is true, no fortune, but that of my friend was ample; and he delighted in the anticipation of indulging her in every elegant pursuit, and administering to those delicate tastes and fancies that spread a kind of witchery about the sex.—"Her life," said he, "shall be like a fairy tale."

The very difference in their characters produced a harmonious combination: he was of a romantic and somewhat serious cast; she was all life and gladness. I have often noticed the mute rapture with which he would gaze upon her in company, of which her sprightly powers made her the delight; and how, in the midst of applause, her eyes would still turn to him, as if there alone she sought favor and acceptance. When leaning on his arm, her slender form contrasted finely with his tall manly person. The fond confiding air with which she looked up at him seemed to call forth a flush of triumphant pride and cherishing tenderness, as if he doted on his lovely burden for its very helplessness. Never did a couple set forward on the flowery path of early and well-suited marriage with a fairer prospect of felicity.

It was the misfortune of my friend, however, to have embarked his property in large speculations; and he had not been married many months when, by a succession of sudden disasters, it was swept from him, and he found himself reduced almost to penury. For a time he kept his situation to himself, and went about with a haggard countenance and a breaking heart. His life was but a protracted agony; and what rendered it more insupportable was the necessity of keeping up a smile in the presence of his wife; for he could not bring himself to overwhelm her with the news. She saw, however, with the quick eye of affection, that all was not well with him. She marked his altered looks and stifled sighs, and was not to be deceived by his sickly and vapid attempts at cheerfulness. She tasked all her sprightly powers and tender blandishments to win him back to happiness; but she only drove the arrow deeper into his soul. The more he saw cause to love her, the more torturing was the thought that he was soon to make her wretched. A little while, thought he, and the smile will vanish from that cheek—the song will die away from those lips—the lustre of those eyes will be quenched with sorrow; and the happy heart, which now beats lightly in that bosom, will be weighed down like mine by the cares and miseries of the world.

At length he came to me one day, and related his whole situation in a tone of the deepest despair. When I heard him through I inquired, "Does your wife know all this?" —At the question he burst into an agony of tears. "For God's sake!" cried he, "if you have any pity on me, don't mention my wife; it is the thought of her that drives me almost to madness!"

"And why not?" said I. "She must know it sooner or later: you cannot keep it long from her, and the intelligence may break upon her in a more startling manner, than if imparted by yourself; for the accents of those we love soften the harshest tidings. Besides, you are depriving yourself of the comforts of her sympathy; and not merely that, but also endangering the only bond that can keep hearts together—an unreserved community of thought and feeling. She will soon perceive that something is secretly preying upon your mind; and true love will not brook reserve; it feels under-valued and outraged, when even the sorrows of those it loves are concealed from it."

"Oh, but my friend! to think what a blow I am to give to all her future prospects—how I am to strike her very soul to the earth by telling her that her husband is a beggar; that she is to forego all the elegancies of life—all the pleasures of society—to shrink with me into indigence and obscurity! To tell her that I have dragged her down from the sphere in which she might have continued to move in constant brightness—the light of every eye—the admiration of every heart!—How can she bear poverty? she has been brought up in all the refinements of opulence. How can she bear neglect? she has been the idol of society. Oh! it will break her heart—it will break her heart!—"

I saw his grief was eloquent, and I let it have its flow; for sorrow relieves itself by words. When his paroxysm had subsided, and he had relapsed into moody silence, I resumed the subject gently, and urged him to break his situation at once to his wife. He shook his head mournfully, but positively.

"But how are you going to keep it from her? It is necessary she should know it, that you may take the steps proper to the alteration of your circumstances. You must change your style of living—nay," observing a pang to pass across his countenance, "don't let that afflict you. I am sure you have never placed your happiness in outward show—you have yet friends, warm friends, who will not think the worse of you for being less splendidly lodged; and surely it does not require a palace to be happy with Mary—"

"I could be happy with her," cried he, convulsively, "in a hovel!—I could go down with her into poverty and the dust! —I could—I could—God bless her!—God bless her!" cried he, bursting into a transport of grief and tenderness.

"And believe me, my friend," I said, stepping up and grasping him warmly by the hand, "believe me she can be the same with you. Ay, more: it will be a source of pride and triumph to her—it will call forth all the latent energies and fervent sympathies of her nature; for she will rejoice to prove that she loves you for yourself. There is in every true woman's heart a spark of heavenly fire, which lies dormant in the broad daylight of prosperity; but which kindles up and beams and blazes in the dark hour of adversity. No man knows what the wife of his bosom is—no man knows what a ministering angel she is—unless he has gone with her through the fiery trials of this world."

There was something in the earnestness of my manner, and the figurative style of my language, that caught the excited imagination of Leslie. I knew the auditor I had to deal with; and following up the impression I had made, I finished by persuading him to go home and unburden his sad heart to his wife.

I must confess, notwithstanding all I had said, I felt some little solicitude for the result. Who can calculate on the fortitude of one whose life has been a round of pleasures? Her gay spirits might revolt at the dark downward path of low humility suddenly pointed out before her, and might cling to the sunny regions in which they had hitherto reveled. Besides, ruin in fashionable life is accompanied by so many galling mortifications, to which in other ranks it is a stranger.—In short, I could not meet Leslie the next morning without trepidation. He had made the disclosure.

"And how did she bear it?"

"Like an angel! It seemed rather to be a relief to her mind, for she threw her arms round my neck, and asked if this was all that had lately made me unhappy.—But, poor girl, " added he, "she cannot realize the change we must undergo. She has no idea of poverty but in the abstract; she has only read of it in poetry, where it is allied to love. She feels as yet no privation; she suffers no loss of accustomed conveniences nor elegancies. When we come practically to experience its sordid cares, its paltry wants, its petty humiliations—then will be the real trial."

"But," said I, "now that you have got over the severest task, that of breaking it to her, the sooner you let the world into the secret the better. The disclosure may be mortifying; but then it is a single misery and soon over: whereas you otherwise suffer it in anticipation, every hour of the day. It is not poverty so much as pretence, that harasses a ruined man—the struggle between a proud mind and an empty purse— the keeping up a hollow show that must soon come to an end. Have the courage to appear poor and you disarm poverty of its sharpest sting." On this point I found Leslie perfectly prepared. He had no false pride himself, and as to his wife, she was only anxious to conform to their altered fortunes.

Some days afterwards he called upon me in the evening. He had disposed of his dwelling house and taken a small cottage in the country, a few miles from town. He had been busied all day in sending out furniture. The new establishment required few articles, and those of the simplest kind. All the splendid furniture of his late residence had been sold, excepting his wife's harp. That, he said, was too closely associated with the idea of herself; it belonged to the little story of their loves; for some of the sweetest moments of their courtship were those when he had leaned over that instrument and listened to the melting tones of her voice. I could not but smile at this instance of romantic gallantry in a doting husband.

He was now going out to the cottage, where his wife had been all day superintending its arrangements. My feelings had become strongly interested in the progress of this family story, and, as it was a fine evening, I offered to accompany him.

He was wearied with the fatigues of the day, and as he walked out, fell into a fit of gloomy musing.

"Poor Mary!" at length broke, with a heavy sigh, from his lips.

"And what of her?" asked I: "has anything happened to her?"

"What," said he, darting an impatient glance, "is it nothing to be reduced to this paltry situation—to be caged in a miserable cottage—to be obliged to toil almost in the menial concerns of her wretched habitation?"

"Has she then repined at the change?"

"Repined! she has been nothing but sweetness and good humor. Indeed, she seems in better spirits than I have ever known her; she has been to me all love, and tenderness, and comfort!"

"Admirable girl!" exclaimed I. "You call yourself poor, my friend; you never were so rich—you never knew the boundless treasures of excellence you possess in that woman."

"Oh! but, my friend, if this first meeting at the cottage were over, I think I could then be comfortable. But this is her first day of real experience; she has been introduced into a humble dwelling—she has been employed all day in arranging its miserable equipments—she has, for the first time, known the fatigues of domestic employment—she has, for the first time, looked round her on a home destitute of everything elegant, —almost of everything convenient; and may now be sitting down, exhausted and spiritless, brooding over a prospect of future poverty."

There was a degree of probability in this picture that I could not gainsay, so we walked on in silence.

After turning from the main road up a narrow lane, so thickly shaded with forest trees as to give it a complete air of seclusion, we came in sight of the cottage. It was humble enough in its appearance, for the most pastoral poet; and yet it had a pleasing rural look. A wild wine had overrun one end in a profusion of foliage; a few trees threw their branches gracefully over it; and I observed several pots of flowers tastefully disposed about the door and on the grassplot in front. A small wicket gate opened upon a footpath that wound through some shrubbery to the door. Just as we approached, we heard the sound of music—Leslie grasped my arm; we paused and listened. It was Mary's voice singing, in a style of the most touching simplicity, a little air of which her husband was peculiarly fond.

I felt Leslie's hand tremble on my arm. He stepped forward to hear more distinctly. His step made a noise on the gravel walk. A bright beautiful face glanced out at the window and vanished—a light footstep was heard—and Mary came tripping forth to meet us: she was in a pretty rural dress of white; a few wild flowers were twisted in her fine hair; a fresh bloom was on her cheek; her whole countenance beamed with smiles—I had never seen her look so lovely.

"My dear George," cried she, "I am so glad you are come! I have been watching and watching for you; and running down the lane, and looking out for you. I've set out a table under a beautiful tree behind the cottage; and I've been gathering some of the most delicious strawberries for I know you are fond of them—and we have such excellent cream—and everything is so sweet and still here—Oh!" said she, putting her arm within his, and looking up brightly in his face, "Oh, we shall be so happy!"

Poor Leslie was overcome. He caught her to his bosom—he folded his arms round her—he kissed her again and again—he could not speak, but the tears gushed into his eyes; and he has often assured me, that though the world has since gone prosperously with him, and his life has, indeed, been a happy one, yet never has he experienced a moment of more exquisite felicity.

妻 子

〔美〕华盛顿·欧文

别希罕海底的宝藏，
最可贵的
是爱妻的贤良；
每当我走进家门，
就感到一阵清香，
美满姻缘，
比紫罗兰更加芬芳。
——米德尔顿[①]

我常发现，女人在受到命运最无情的打击时，具有坚强的忍受能力。那些打击落到男人头上，会使男人精神崩溃，一蹶不振；落到女性头上反而会激起无穷的力量，表现出她们的无畏和崇高品质，而且往往是最充分地表现。如果你看到一个温和驯良的女性本来过惯舒适生活，依附他人，懦弱无能，不堪一击，在不幸降临时，却突然成了勇士，安慰和支撑丈夫，用不屈不挠的毅力，与逆运的最残酷打击抗争，那你真会感动至极。

---

① 托马斯·米德尔顿（1570？—1627），英国戏剧家。

藤一圈圈盘在橡树的干上,靠着橡树见到了阳光,当坚实的大树被雷劈开时,藤便用它的细蔓给它包扎,缝合裂开的枝条:这是上帝的巧妙安排。女人像是一根藤,当男人走运时,她依附于男人,是男人的装饰;一朝灾祸临头,女人便成了他的依靠和安慰,解除他的痛苦,鼓起他的勇气,治愈他心灵的创伤。

我有一位朋友,一家和睦,相亲相爱,我曾为他感到高兴。他深情地说:"你最大的幸福是有妻子和孩子。在你幸运的时候,他们会分享你的幸运;如果遇上不幸,他们会成为你的安慰。"的确,我发现有家有室的人比单身汉更易于摆脱逆境,其原因之一是想到心爱的妻儿要靠他生活,他不能倒下,但主要的原因是亲人能给以精神上的安慰。他看到尽管出家门凄凄惨惨,进家门却有一个小小的爱的天地,而他就是这个天地的主宰,便不会失去自尊。单身汉不同,他孤灯独影,感到冷冷清清,心就像一座空屋,因为无人居住势必倒塌。

说到这些话我想起一家人家的经历,是我亲眼目睹的。我有位朋友,叫莱斯利,娶了位受过时髦生活熏陶,才貌双全的姑娘。说实话,她没有大家产,但是我的朋友家当大,就希望让她尽情享受,凡女人会有的爱好追求都尽量满足她。他说过:"我要让她过天堂般的生活。"

两人性格不同,但相处和谐。他浪漫而不失认真,她则活泼开朗。我常注意到他默默地看着她,内心甜滋滋;她活泼的性格的确逗人喜爱。在获得一片掌声时,她的眼只朝向他,似乎只看重他的赞赏。她依偎在他的怀里时,她的苗条与他的魁梧正好相映成趣。她抬头看着他时,眼神中充满信赖,使他好不得意,更加温情脉脉,似乎她越依赖他,他会越喜爱她。婚后不久,他们使人觉得真是天生一对，地造一双，最有希望过得幸福的要算这夫妻俩。

然而，不幸的是，我的朋友把家产拿去进行了大投机，结婚没几个月，由于接二连三失利，钱财耗尽，几乎落得两手空空。他的脸憔悴了，心破碎了，但没有声张。他感到的只有痛苦，特别令他难受的是得在妻子面前装出一副笑脸，不敢把实情告诉她，让她心焦。然而感性给了她慧眼，她看得出来他心事重重。尽管强作欢颜，他骗不了她。她发现了他脸上气色的变化，发现了他有苦难言。她想靠着自己的活泼温柔使他高兴起来，结果这样做只是雪上加霜。他越看到她值得爱，越因不久后要使她过穷日子而痛苦。他明白，不要等多少日子，她脸上的笑容就会消失，再听不到歌声，眼神因忧愁而变得呆滞，现在轻轻快快地跳动的幸福的心会像他的一样，被人世的忧愁苦恼压得无法动弹。

终于有一天他找上我的门，用一筹莫展的声气向我说出了全部情况。我听完以后问他："你太太知道这一切吗？"一听这话，他立刻流出了辛酸的泪，大声道："看在上帝的分上，如果你还可怜我，请别提起她。正因为想到她，我才几乎发疯。"

我问道："为什么别提？她迟早得知道，你不能长时间瞒着她，与其使她受到突然打击，还不如由你亲口对她说明，最坏的消息从亲人的嘴里说出来就没那么可怕了。而且，你现在没有让她替你分忧，不但没有，而且还要断送把你们两颗心联在一起的纽带，即思想和感情的无保留的交流。她很快会发现你有心事，而真正的爱情是无所隐瞒的，即使所爱的人隐瞒的是苦恼，爱情也会感到委屈，受到损害。"

"可是朋友，你不想想，她受到这种打击时对未来的希望就统统完啦！如果告诉她，丈夫已经一贫如洗，她得放弃一切享受，不能出入交际场所，只好与我默默无闻过穷苦日子，她不会伤心透顶吗？她是人人眼中的明星，个个敬重，本可以走到哪儿都荣耀，我怎么开得了口对她说我已经让她完蛋了呢？她从小生活优裕，过得了穷日子吗？她在交际场中风光无限，以后默默无闻受得了吗？她一定会伤心透顶，伤心透顶！"

我知道他一口气说出这番话是因为内心苦恼，就没有打断他。只有吐出苦水，人才会好受。等他冷静下来不再说话了，我开始劝他，叫他马上对妻子说明实情。他难过地，然而毫不含糊地摇摇头。

"你怎么能长期瞒住她呢？家境变了，你得让她知道才能想办法让她慢慢适应。现在的派头你非改不可，别忍下下心。"我发现他脸上掠过一丝痛苦的表情。"我相信你的幸福并不在于表面的排场。你还有朋友，热心的朋友，他们不会因为你搬出了富丽堂皇的住地就看不起你。再说，并不一定要在宫殿里才能与玛丽一道快快乐乐过日子。"

"有了她我就幸福！"他嚷道，声音颤抖着，"哪怕是住在茅屋里，哪怕再穷，再苦，我都——我都——上帝保佑她！上帝保佑她！"他大声说着，又伤心，又充满温情。

"相信我的话，朋友！"我走过去热情地握住他的手。"相信吧，她能与你过一样的日子。而且她会因此而自豪、得意，发挥出所有潜在的天生本领，可以体贴你，能证明她爱的是你本人她会打心底里高兴。每个忠诚的女人的心里都有天国之火的火星，在走运的时候，火星不会烧起来，到倒霉的时候火星会变亮，发光。只有生活上经过磨难，你才能真正了解自己心爱的妻子，知道原来她是保佑你的天使。"

我的态度诚恳,话说得委婉,打动了莱斯利。我了解听我说话的人,见他已经被我说动心,最后进一步劝他回家去把内心的苦恼告诉妻子。

话虽如此说,我却必须承认,对最终结果我并无多大把握。对于一个享乐惯了的人,谁能指望她有多坚强呢?突然间眼见要走下坡路,低人一等,她这个生性快活的人也许会不快活,会留恋过去了的荣华。况且,好生活一旦化为乌有,接着来的是无穷苦恼,还不如原来没过过的生活。总之,第二天见到莱斯利我难免提心吊胆。他把结果告诉了我。

"她受得了吗?"

"她太好了,她像是卸下了心头重负,伸出手搂住我的脖子,问我最近不高兴是不是就因为这件事。可是——"他接着说,"可怜她哪儿知道以后会变得怎样。她见过'贫穷'这个字眼,却没有尝过贫穷的滋味,仅在诗歌里读过对贫穷的歌颂,只当贫穷与爱情分不开。她还没有感到缺吃少穿的危险,没有失去享受惯了的舒适和体面。要等我们尝到了贫穷的酸咸苦辣,才能算真正受到了考验。"

我说:"你对她说了实话,既然最大的难关已经过了,真相越快对外面公开越好。公开也许是件丢脸的事,但只是一时的痛苦,如果瞒着,你会每天每日每时每刻因害怕公开而苦恼。对破产了的人来说最可怕的不是贫困,而是装门面。死要面子,钱袋却空空。明明西洋镜就要被人戳穿,却死抱着西洋镜。别怕,穷了拿出穷样,这样你就避开了贫穷最大的忌讳。"我发现莱斯利在这方面是有充分准备的。他没有虚荣心,而他的妻子正一心想着怎样穷日子穷过。

几天以后他到了我这儿,是在晚上。他卖掉了住房,在离城好些里的乡下买了一栋小屋。白天处理家具,忙了一整天。新住所里摆不了几件家具,而且是最简陋的。老住所的豪华家具全卖了,只剩下妻子的一张竖琴。他说,看到竖琴就会想到妻子。它是两人爱情的见证,在相恋的最甜蜜时刻,他边弹着这把琴边听她美妙的歌喉唱歌。见痴情的丈夫这样有心计,我忍不住笑了。他打算回家了,妻子一天都在家料理。我很想看看这对夫妻的亲近,正巧天气好,陪他走了一趟。

他劳累一天,已精疲力竭。走出我家以后,默默无言,心事又重起来。

"玛丽可怜!"最后他长叹一声,说。

"怎么啦?"我问,"她出了什么事?"

"什么事!"他说,现出了不耐烦的神情,"现在已经一无所有,蹲在小茅屋里,看着她受尽委屈,这不叫人难过吗?"

"难道搬家以后她有了怨言?"

"怨言?她仍那样惹人喜爱,那样开朗。一点不夸张,她的情绪比以往任何时候都好。她一心爱我,体贴我,安慰我。"

"多好的姑娘!"我说,"朋友,你以为穷了,其实是更富了,你没想到有这样的人做妻子等于有了无价之宝?"

"说的也是!不过朋友,要等在小屋里第一次见了她的面,我才能放下心。今天是她真正吃苦的第一天。她住进了不像样的屋子,为整理一个烂摊子忙了一整天,头一遭尝到了家务活的辛苦,也头一遭发现家里好东西一件没有,事事不便。也许现在累倒了,无精打采地坐着,想以后的穷日子怎样熬。"

对于他的这种估计,我无法否认有一定的可能性,于是两人默默地走着。

从大路走到小路后,我们看见了那所小房子。路旁的树长得郁郁葱葱,给人一种与世隔绝之感。在最田园的诗人看来,这所房子已显得简陋,不过,它也有乡间房屋叫人喜爱的特点。房子的一角长着根野藤,枝繁叶茂;房子边长着几棵大树,树枝遮盖住了房顶;门前有草地,门口摆着好几盆花。过了扇小柳条园门有条弯弯曲曲的小路通到小屋,路旁长着些灌木。快进房子时,我们听到了歌声,莱斯利一把抓住我的手臂。是玛丽的歌声,唱得纯朴动人,是丈夫最喜爱的风格。

我只觉得莱斯利抓着我的那只手颤抖着。他向前走了几步,想听个清楚,脚踩在卵石路上发出了咯咯的声音。一张美丽、年轻的脸在窗口晃了一下,接着听到阵轻盈的脚步声:玛丽出来迎接我们了。她穿着件漂亮的乡下式的白衣裳,一头金发上插着几朵野花,脸红扑扑,笑容可掬;我发现她比以往任何时候都惹人喜爱。

"乔治,你总算来了!"她大声道,"我一直在等你来,还跑到路上看。我把桌子摆在屋后的一棵大树下面,拣了些最好吃的草莓,我知道你爱吃。我们的奶油真好。这儿什么都好,又安静。"说着,她挽起他的手臂,热情地直看着他的脸,"看,我们会过得幸福的!"

莱斯利感动极了。他一把把她抱到怀里,紧紧地搂着,吻了又吻,说不出话,流出了眼泪。他常对我说,虽然以后他变得顺利了,日子美满,但感到最幸福还是这一刻。

The Hollow of the Three Hills[①]

Nathaniel Hawthorne

In those strange old times, when fantastic dreams and madmen's reveries were realised among the actual circumstances of life, two persons met together at an appointed hour and place. One was a lady, graceful in form and fair of feature, though pale and troubled, and smitten with an untimely blight in what should have been the fullest bloom of her years; the other was an ancient and meanly-dressed woman, of ill-favoured aspect, and so withered, shrunken and decrepit, that even the space since she began to decay must have exceeded the ordinary term of human existence. In the spot where they encountered, no mortal could observe them. Three little hills stood by each other, and down in the midst of them sunk a hollow basin, almost mathematically circular, two or three hundred feet in breadth, and of such depth that a stately cedar might but just be visible above the sides. Dwarf pines

---

① The Hollow of the Three Hills：直译为"三座山之间的盆地"，根据小说内容，可译为"阴阳之间"。

were numerous upon the hills, and partly fringed the outer verge of the intermediate hollow; within which there was nothing but the brown grass of October, and here and there a tree-trunk, that had fallen long ago, and lay mouldering with no green successor from its roots. One of these masses of decaying wood, formerly a majestic oak, rested close beside a pool of green and sluggish water at the bottom of the basin. Such scenes as this (so grey tradition tells) were once the resort of a power of evil and his plighted subjects; and here, at midnight or on the dim verge of evening, they were said to stand round the mantling pool, disturbing its putrid waters in the performance of an impious baptismal rite. The chill beauty of an autumnal sunset was now gilding the three hill-tops, whence a paler tint stole down their sides into the hollow.

"Here is our pleasant meeting come to pass," said the aged crone, "according as thou hast desired. Say quickly what thou wouldest have of me, for there is but a short hour that we may tarry here."

As the old, withered woman spoke, a smile glimmered on her countenance, like lamplight on the wall of a sepulchre. The lady trembled, and cast her eyes upward to the verge of the basin, as if meditating to return with her purpose unaccomplished. But it was not so ordained.

"I am a stranger in this land, as you know," said she, at length. "Whence I come it matters not; but I have left those behind me with whom my fate was intimately bound, and from whom I am cut off for ever. There is a weight in my bosom that I cannot away with, and I have come hither to inquire of their welfare."

"And who is there by this green pool that can bring thee news from the ends of the earth?" cried the old woman, peering into the lady's face. "Not from my lips mayest thou hear these tidings; yet, be thou bold, and the daylight shall not pass away from yonder hill-top before thy wish be granted."

"I will do your bidding though I die," replied the lady, desperately.

The old woman seated herself on the trunk of the fallen tree, threw aside the hood that shrouded her grey locks, and beckoned her companion to draw near.

"Kneel down," she said, "and lay your forehead on my knees."

She hesitated a moment, but the anxiety that had long been kindling burned fiercely up within her. As she knelt down, the border of her garment was dipped into the pool; she laid her forehead on the old woman's knees, and the latter drew a cloak about the lady's face, so that she was in darkness. Then she heard the muttered words of prayer, in the midst of which she started, and would have arisen.

"Let me flee—let me flee and hide myself, that they may not look upon me!" she cried. But, with returning recollection, she hushed herself, and was still as death.

For it seemed as if other voices—familiar in infancy, and unforgotten through many wanderings, and in all the vicissitudes of her heart and fortune—were mingling with the accents of the prayer. At first the words were faint and indistinct, not rendered so by distance, but rather resembling the dim pages of a book which we strive to read by an imperfect and gradually brightening light. In such a manner, as the prayer proceeded, did those voices strengthen upon the ear; till at length the petition ended, and the conversation of an aged man, and of a woman broken and decayed like himself, became distinctly audible to the lady as she knelt. But those strangers appeared not to stand in the hollow depth between the three hills. Their voices were encompassed and re-echoed by the walls of a chamber, the windows of which were rattling in the breeze; the regular vibration of a clock, the crackling of a fire, and the tinkling of the embers as they fell among the ashes, rendered the scene almost as vivid as if painted to the eye. By a melancholy hearth sat these two old people, the man calmly despondent, the woman querulous and tearful, and their words were all of sorrow. They spoke of a daughter, a wanderer they knew not where, bearing dishonour along with her, and leaving shame and affliction to bring their grey heads to the grave. They alluded also to other and more recent woe, but in the midst of their talk their voices seemed to melt into the sound of the wind sweeping mournful among the autumn leaves; and when the lady lifted her eyes, there was she kneeling in the hollow between three hills.

"A weary and lonesome time yonder old couple have of it," remarked the old woman, smiling in the lady's face.

"And did you also hear them?" exclaimed she, a sense of intolerable humiliation triumphing over her agony and fear.

"Yea; and we have yet more to hear," replied the old woman. "Wherefore cover thy face quickly."

Again the withered hag poured forth the monotonous words of a prayer that was not meant to be acceptable in heaven; and soon in the pauses of her breath strange murmurings began to thicken, gradually increasing, so as to drown and overpower the charm by which they grew. Shrieks pierced through the obscurity of sound, and were succeeded by the singing of sweet female voices, which in their turn gave way to a wild roar of laughter, broken suddenly by groanings and sobs, forming altogether a ghastly confusion of terror and mourning and mirth. Chains were rattling, fierce and stern voices uttered threats, and the scourge resounded at their command. All these noises deepened and became substantial to the listener's ear, till she could distinguish every soft and dreamy① accent of the love songs, that died causelessly into funeral hymns. She shuddered at the unprovoked wrath which blazed up like the spontaneous kindling of flame, and she grew faint at the fearful merriment raging miserably around her. In the midst of this wild scene, where unbound passions jostled each other in a drunken career, there was one solemn voice of a man, and a manly and melodious voice it might once have been. He went to and fro continually, and his feet sounded upon the floor. In each member of that frenzied company, whose own burning thoughts had become their exclusive world, he sought an auditor for the story of his individual wrong, and interrupted their laughter and tears as his reward of scorn or pity. He spoke of women's perfidy, of a wife who had broken her holiest vows, of a home

---

① dreamy：此处的 dreamy 与梦幻无关，指音乐时，义为 soft（轻柔的）、soothing（给人以安慰的）。

The Hollow of the Three Hills

and heart made desolate. Even as he went on, the shout, the laugh, the shriek, the sob, rose up in unison, till they changed into the hollow, fitful, and uneven sound of the wind, as it fought among the pine-trees of those three lonely hills. The lady looked up, and there was the withered woman smiling in her face.

"Couldest thou have thought there were such merry times in a madhouse?" inquired the latter.

"True, true," said the lady to herself, "there is mirth within its walls, but misery, misery without."

"Wouldest thou hear more?" demanded the old woman.

"There is one other voice I would fain listen to again," replied the lady faintly.

"Then lay down thy head speedily upon my knees, that thou mayest get thee hence before the hour be past."

The golden skirts of day were yet lingering upon the hills, but deep shades obscured the hollow and the pool, as if sombre night were rising thence to overspread the world. Again that evil woman began to weave her spell. Long did it proceed unanswered, till the knolling of a bell stole in among the intervals of her words, like a clang that had travelled far over valley and rising ground, and was just ready to die in the air. The lady shook upon her companion's knees as she heard that boding sound. Stronger it grew and sadder, and deepened into the tone of a deathbell knolling dolefully from some ivy-mantled tower, and bearing tidings of mortality and woe to the cottage, to the hall and to the solitary wayfarer, that all might weep for the doom appointed in turn to them. Then came a measured tread, passing slowly, slowly on, as of mourners with a coffin, their garments trailing on the ground, so that the ear could measure the length of their melancholy array. Before them went the priest reading the burial service, while the leaves of his book were rustling in the breeze. And though no voice but his was heard to speak aloud, still there were revilings and anathemas whispered, but distinct, from women and from men, breathed against the daughter who had wrung the aged hearts of her parents, the wife who had betrayed the trusting fondness of her husband, the mother who had sinned against natural affection and left her child to die. The sweeping sound of the funeral train faded away like a thin vapour, and the wind, that just before had seemed to shake the coffin-pall, moaned sadly round the verge of the hollow between three hills. But when the old woman stirred the kneeling lady she lifted not her head.

"Here has been a sweet hour's sport," said the withered crone, chuckling to herself.

阴阳之间

〔美〕纳撒尼尔·霍桑

　　以往有段时间说来奇怪，荒唐的梦和疯子的狂想在实际生活中竟会成真。就是在这段时间，有两人在约定的地点与时刻碰面了。一个是妙龄女郎，身段苗条，相貌清秀，然而面色苍白，显出病态，有些未老先衰；另一位是老婆子，穿着朴素，相貌丑陋，憔悴枯槁无以复加。在她们会面的地点，再没有旁人。这儿被三座小山环抱，中间是一块凹下去的盆地，几乎像圆规画出来的，两三百米方圆，很深，一棵杉树摆下去大概只能见到个树梢。山上长了无数小松树，有些地方一直延伸到盆地边。盆地里除了10月发黄的草什么也没有长，树多年前就倒下了，只剩下零零落落的树墩，在慢慢腐烂，根上没有发出新枝。有一个腐烂的树墩，原来是株参天大橡树，生在盆底一潭绿色的死水边。这种地方在古老的传说中是鬼怪出没的地方，到半夜或黄昏，他们围在水潭边，搅动一潭死水，算是洗礼，实际上是亵渎神明。秋日的余晖冷清清照着三座山的山巅，顺山坡落到盆地里的就只有惨淡的光了。

　　"我按照你的希望到这么个好地方与你见面，"干瘪的老婆子说,"你对我有什么要求赶紧说吧,我们在这儿只能停留短短一个小时。"

瘦老婆子边说边露出笑容,活像坟墓上出现了一道灯光。女郎颤抖着,两眼望着盆地的边,似乎想不达到目的就回去。然而,这样做是不行的。

她终于说话了:"我是这地方的新客。无论我从何处来,反正是离开了亲人,与他们永远不能见面。我的心头压着一个摆不脱的重负,来这儿想问问亲人的消息。"

"这潭绿水边有谁能带给你世上亲人的消息呢?"老婆子紧盯着女郎的脸说道,"你从我嘴里听不到,但是如果你有胆量,在太阳下山前你的愿望可以得到满足。"

"一切听从你的吩咐。"女郎无可奈何地答道。

老婆子在树墩上坐下,掀去头巾,露出一头白发,招手叫女郎过来。

"跪下来,把额头靠在我的膝上。"

她有些犹豫,但毕竟想见亲人心切,就跪了下来,裙边拖到了水里,额头靠在老婆子的膝上。老婆子把外衣蒙住女郎的脸,蒙得不透一丝光。接着女郎听到了低声祈祷,吃了一惊,想站起身。

"放开我,放开我,让我躲起来别让他们看到!"她大叫起来。可是她一转念又静下来,一声不响了。

她仿佛听到祈祷声中混有别的声音,是从小熟悉的,虽然以后到处漂流,心绪和命运都变化无常,还是没有忘记。开始,这些声音很微弱,听不清楚,倒不是因为距离隔得太远,而是像在光线暗淡时我们无法看清书上的字,后来光线渐渐强了才看清。

祈祷使这些声音渐渐变得大了。最后祈祷停止,听清了有两人在说话,一个是老头,另一个是女人,也老态龙钟了。女郎仍旧跪着。这两个人似乎不站在三座山之间的盆地里,听声音是在房间里说话,房间的窗户被风吹得咯咯响,一架时钟在很有规律地嘀嘀嗒嗒,火炉在噼噼啪啪,炭屑掉进灰里又咚咚作响,女郎虽是耳闻,却也无异于目见。这两位老人在一个孤零零的火炉边坐着,老头垂头丧气,老太婆声泪俱下,两人说的都是伤心话。他们谈的是自己的女儿,下落不明,声名狼藉,也使老两口丢脸、痛苦,会至死难以瞑目。他们还谈到近来遇到的其他伤心事,女郎听着听着,只觉得他们的声音变成了萧萧瑟瑟的秋风,抬眼一看,原来还是跪在三座山之间的盆地里。

"这对老夫老妻遇上了这种事真落得凄凄惨惨!"老婆子看着女郎边笑边说。

"他们的话你也听见了?"女郎大声问道,又痛苦又害怕,更羞愧难当。

"听到了!还有呢,快把脸蒙上。"老婆子回答。

瘦老婆子又用单调的声音祈祷起来,但这种祈祷不是为说给上天听的。她停下换气时,另外的声音越来越响了,终于盖过了召来它们的咒语。起先听得清清楚楚的是尖叫声,接着是女人悦耳的歌声,往后是一阵狂笑。突然,笑声中夹进了呻吟、哭泣,有怕的,有愁的,也有乐的,乱七八糟。链条叮叮当当在响,有人厉声吆喝,随着吆喝声响起的是鞭笞声。所有这些声音女郎听起来都清晰可辨,甚至连柔和的情歌的每个音符都能识别,只可惜情歌无缘无故变成了挽歌。她又听到有人突然生起气来,像是哪里突然烧出一片火来,打了个哆嗦;还有人在她四周狞笑,她怕得差点昏了过去。在这一片混乱中，各种感情尽情发泄，像醉汉，独有一个男人的声音是庄重的，也许他原来说话是很有男子气、很动听的。他不停地走来走去，脚踩得地板咯咯响。这群发了狂的人心中各打各的算盘，然而他还是在对人讲自己的不幸，不时打断他们的笑声、哭声，就这样来表示他的鄙视或同情。他讲到女人的不贞，讲到妻子违背海誓山盟，弃家而走，伤透了他的心。他不停地说，还有人在不停地嚷、笑、叫、哭，最后所有的声音都化成时有时无、时急时慢的呜呜风声，在三座孤寂的山中的松树间吹。女郎抬起头，仍只看到瘦老婆子在对着她笑。

"疯人院里还有这么些快活人，没想到吧？"老婆子问。

"的确没有。疯人院里的人快活，外边的人痛苦。"女郎自言自语道。

"还想听吗？"老婆子问。

"有一个人的话我还想听。"女郎轻声答道。

金色的夕阳还在山顶流连，但山谷和水潭变暗了，似乎夜是从这儿开始，很快主宰了整个世界。巫婆又施展了魔法。很久没见反应，后来才听到间断的钟声，是在她的嘴暂歇时，很弱，像已经越过山谷，飞向远方，即将消逝的声音。女郎听到不祥之声，靠在老婆子膝上直发抖。钟声越来越响，越凄惨，变成了某个爬满常春藤的塔上传来的丧钟声，把死讯和悲哀送到贫苦人家、富贵人家和路上的独身行人，使谁都要伤心落泪，哀叹自己终有这么一天。接着听到的是一队送葬的人在慢慢地、慢慢地走，长衫拖在地上，女郎凭着声音能判断出队伍的长短。走在最前的是牧师，念着送葬文，风把他手中的书吹得沙沙响。大声讲话的只有他，但低声说的还有别人，清清楚楚听得出来是在咒骂，有男有女，骂做女儿的把老父老母折磨得肝断肠裂，骂做妻子的不贞，辜负了丈夫的恩爱，骂做母亲的伤天害理，害死了孩子。送葬队伍渐渐远去，声音像薄雾一样消失了，原来好像在掀动柩衣的风变成了在三座山之间的盆地上哀号的风。但是当老婆子推推伏在膝上的女郎时，她却再没能抬起头来。

"这一个钟点倒玩得够意思！"瘦老婆子咯咯笑着说。

The Oval Portrait

Edgar Allen Poe

The chateau in which my valet had ventured to make forcible entrance, rather than permit me, in my desperately wounded condition, to pass a night in the open air, was one of those piles of commingled gloom and grandeur which have so long frowned[①] among the Apennines, not less in fact than in the fancy of Mrs. Radcliffe. To all appearance it had been temporarily and very lately abandoned. We established ourselves in one of the smallest and least sumptuously furnished apartments. It lay in a remote turret of the building. Its decoration were rich, yet tattered and antique. Its walls were hung with tapestry and bedecked with manifold and multiform armorial trophies, together with an unusually great number of very spirited modern paintings in frames of rich golden arabesque. In these paintings, which depended from the walls not only in their main surfaces, but in very

---

① 此处 frown 相当于 exist 或 stand。frown 一词用得非常形象，因为这种别墅看起来阴森森的。

The Oval Portrait

many nooks which the bizarre architecture of the chateau rendered necessary—in these paintings my incipient delirium, perhaps, had caused me to take deep interest; so that I bade Pedro to close the heavy shutters of the room, since it was already night, to light the tongues of a tall candelabrum which stood by the head of the bed, and to throw open far and wide the fringed curtains of black velvet which enveloped the bed itself. I wished all this done that I might resign myself, if not to sleep, at least alternately to the contemplation of these pictures, and the perusal of a small volume which had been found upon the pillow, and which purported to criticize and explain them.

Long, long I read—and devoutly, devotedly I gazed. Rapidly and gloriously the hours flew by and the deep midnight came. The position of the candelabrum displeased me, and outreaching my hand with difficulty, rather than disturb my slumbering valet, I placed it so as to throw its rays more fully upon the book.

But the action produced an effect altogether unanticipated. The rays of the numerous candles (for there were many) now fell within a niche of the room which had hitherto been thrown into deep shade by one of the bed-posts. I thus saw in vivid light a picture all unnoticed before. It was the portrait of a young girl just ripening into womanhood. I glanced at the painting hurriedly, and then closed my eyes. Why I did this was not at first apparent even to my own perception. But while my lids remained thus shut, I ran over in my mind my reason for so shutting them. It was an impulsive movement to gain time for thought, to make sure that my vision had not deceived me, to clam and subdue my fancy for a more sober and more certain gaze. In a very few moments I again looked fixedly at the painting.

That I now saw aright I could not and would not doubt; for the first flashing of the candles upon that canvas had seemed to dissipate the dreamy stupor which was stealing over my senses, and to startle me at once into waking life.

The portrait, as I have already said, was that of a young girl. It was a mere head and shoulders, done in what is technically termed a vignette manner, much in the style of the favorite heads of Sully. The arms, the bosom, and even the ends of the radiant hair melted imperceptibly into the vague yet deep shadow which formed the background of the whole. The frame was oval, richly gilded and filagreed in Moresque. As a thing of art nothing could be more admirable than the painting itself. But it could have been neither the execution of the work, nor the immortal beauty of the countenance, which had so suddenly and so vehemently moved me. Least of all, could it have been that my fancy, shaken from its half slumber, had mistaken the head for that of a living person. I saw at once that the peculiarities of the design, of the vignetting, and of the frame, must have instantly dispelled such idea—must have prevented even its momentary entertainment. Thinking earnestly upon these points, I remained, for an hour perhaps, half sitting, half reclining, with my vision riveted upon the portrait. At length, satisfied with the true secret of its effect, I fell back within the bed. I had found the spell of the picture in an absolute *life-likeness* of expression, which, at first startling, finally confounded, subdued, and appalled me. With deep and

The Oval Portrait

reverent awe I replaced the candelabrum in its former position. The cause of my deep agitation being thus shut from view, I sought eagerly the volume which discussed the paintings and their histories. Turning to the number which designated the oval portrait, I there read the vague and quaint words which follow:

> She was a maiden of rarest beauty, and not more lovely than full of glee. And evil was the hour when she saw, and loved, and wedded the painter. He, passionate, studious, austere, and having already a bride in his Art: she a maiden of rarest beauty, and not more lovely than full of glee; all light and smiles, and frolicsome as the young fawn; loving and cherishing all things; hating only the Art which was her rival; dreading only the palette and brushes and other untoward instruments which deprived her of the countenance of her lover. It was thus a terrible thing for this lady to hear the painter speak of his desire to portray even his young bride. But she was humble and obedient, and sat meekly for many weeks in the dark high turret-chamber where the light dripped upon the pale canvas only from overhead. But he, the painter, took glory in his work, which went on from hour to hour, and from day to day. And he was a passionate and wild, and moody man, who became lost in reveries; so that he *would* not see the light which fell so ghastly in that lone turret withered the health and the spirits of his bride, who pined visibly to all but him. Yet she smiled on and still on, uncomplainingly, because

she saw that the painter (who had high renown) took a fervid and burning pleasure in his task, and wrought day and night to depict her who so loved him, yet who grew daily more dispirited and weak. And in sooth some who beheld the portrait spoke of its resemblance in low words, as of a mighty marvel, and a proof not less of the power of the painter than of his deep love for her whom he depicted so surpassingly well. But at length, as the labor drew nearer to its conclusion, there were admitted none into the turret; for the painter had grown wild with the ardor of his work, and turned his eyes from the canvas rarely, even to regard the countenance of his wife. And he *would* not see that the tints which he spread upon the canvas were drawn from the cheeks of her who sat beside him. And when many weeks had passed, and but little remained to do, save one brush upon the mouth and one tint upon the eye, the spirit of the lady again flickered up as the flame within the socket of the lamp. And then the brush was given, and then the tint was placed; and for one moment, the painter stood entranced before the work which he had wrought; but in the next, while he yet gazed, he grew tremulous and very pallid, and aghast, and crying with a loud voice, "This is indeed *Life* itself!" turned suddenly to regard his beloved—*She* was dead.

椭圆形画像

〔美〕埃德加·爱伦·坡

我的仆人见我伤得很重,不让我在露天过夜,冒昧住进了一栋大别墅。亚平宁山脉中的古老大别墅的确气派十足,却又阴森森,与拉德克利夫夫人①想象中的别墅的确相差无几,我们闯进去的就属这一种。从各种迹象看,这儿不久前还有人住。我们挑了一套最小、陈设最简单的房间,在整栋别墅一个偏僻的角楼里。房内的装饰价值昂贵,然而破旧了。墙上挂着绣帷,各种各样带纹章的纪念品,还有许许多多很见功夫的现代画,框在有讲究的金色图案的画框里。这些画不但挂在墙上最显眼的地方,而且各个角落里都有。别墅的设计奇特,势必角落多。我有些好奇,想细看这些画。所以,我吩咐佩德罗把笨重的百叶窗关上(天已经黑了),床头的高烛台上的蜡烛点着,床四周有须边的黑天鹅绒床帘全部拉开。这样,如果睡不着,我可以欣赏欣赏画,也可以看看在枕边找到的一本小册子,那上面介绍了画的来历,还有评价。

---

① 拉德克利夫夫人(1764—1823),英国女小说家。

小册子我看了很久很久,欣赏画时目不转睛,全神贯注。时间一小时接一小时不知不觉迅速过去,到了午夜,我嫌烛台摆的位置不合适,又不愿叫醒睡熟的仆人,便伸出一只手,费了很大劲把烛台移了个地方,让烛光正照到书上。

这一移带来了意外的收获。房间里有个壁龛,原来被一根床柱挡住,在暗处,现在被很多支蜡烛(烛台上有很多支蜡烛)一齐照着了。这样,我在明亮的烛光下看到了一幅还没发现的画。是一位豆蔻年华少女的肖像。我匆匆扫了一眼便合上了眼睛。开始连我自己也不明白为什么这样做,但后来眼皮合久了,我悟出了这样做的缘由。原来,这个迅速的反应是为了进行思考,想想视觉有没有出差错,静下心来,好再看个仔细。过了好一会,我又张开眼,盯着画看。

现在我对所看到的不可能、也不会产生怀疑了,眼光一落到蜡烛照着的画像上,偷偷袭来的云雾顿时消散,感官从梦境般迷离恍惚的状态中蓦地清醒过来。

这幅画如我前面所说,是位妙龄女郎的肖像,仅画出了头和肩,行家们称之为晕映画像,很像萨利[①]画的头像,手臂、胸,甚至一头金发的尾段全隐没在黑影里,看不出来,成了整个背景的一部分。画框是椭圆形的,有摩尔式的金边。这幅画算得上是登峰造极的艺术品。然而,使我突然入迷的既非画师的技艺,也非画中人倾国倾城的容貌,更不是因为在神情恍惚中错把画像当活人。我一眼便看出了画的布局、手法和画框的特点,不会产生错觉,甚至暂时的错觉也不可能。我半坐半躺,眼不离画,对这

---

① 萨利(1783—1872),美国肖像画家。

些特点认真思考了足足一个钟头。最后，我自以为研究出了它成功的奥妙所在，在床上躺了下来。我发现这幅画的魅力在于绝对逼真，使我看了先是吃惊，然后迷惑，佩服，叹为观止。我把烛台放回原处，看不到使我深深激动的杰作了，心里却仍赞叹不已。接着我连忙拿起评价这许多画和有关它们来历的小册子，翻到介绍这幅椭圆形画像的一页，看到下面一段没有说出有关人姓名的不寻常的话：

  她是一位绝代佳人，而且她的活泼并不亚于她的可爱。不幸，她遇上了、爱上了、嫁给了这位画家。他是一位勤奋好学、不苟言笑的人，早已把艺术当作了新娘；她是一位绝代佳人，可爱又活泼，无忧无虑，笑容可掬，像小鹿一样好动，什么都喜爱，唯独憎恨艺术这个情敌，就怕调色板、画笔等讨厌的工具剥夺她与爱人相见的时间。所以，当画家说想给新娘画一幅肖像时，年轻的新娘听了也大不乐意。但是她温和、顺从，接连好些星期乖乖地坐在高高的、幽暗的角楼里，角楼只有顶上进光，照着白画布。画家埋头作画，一小时接一小时，一天接一天。他如醉如痴，不言不语，沉浸在梦幻般的想象里，没有发现静悄悄的角楼里暗淡的光损害了新娘的健康，败坏了她的精神。除了他，人人都能看出来，她明显消瘦了。但是她嘴上总挂着笑，毫无怨言，因为她看到画家（他很有名气）干得那样热心、高兴，不分昼夜画她的肖像。她非常爱他，只是一天天变得没精神、虚弱。有人看到过这幅画，说画得像极了，简直是大奇迹，不但表现了画家的才能，而且证明画家对她爱得深，所以才有这样的杰作。最后，当工作接近尾声时，谁也不让进角楼了，画家的热情变成了疯狂，眼睛难得离开画布，甚至也不看看妻子。他并没发现自己牺牲了坐在身边的妻子脸上的红润，画布上才有了各种颜色。许多个星期过去了，大功即将告成，就差嘴上还要加一笔，眼睛里还要涂一点色彩。正在这时候，女郎的精神突然好起来，就像即将燃尽的灯会突然亮起来一样。最后一笔加上了，最后一点色彩也涂上了，画家站在他的杰作前愣了愣。接着，尽管眼前仍注视着画，身子却发起抖来，脸色发白，惊呆了，大声嚷道："这真是活人呀！"突然，他一看亲爱的妻子，发现她却已经成了死人！

The Fiddler

Herman Melville

So my poem is damned, and immortal fame is not for me! I am nobody forever and ever. Intolerable fate!

Snatching my hat, I dashed down the criticism, and rushed out into Broadway, where enthusiastic throngs were crowding to a circus in a side-street near by, very recently started, and famous for a capital clown.

Presently my old friend Standard rather boisterously accosted me.

"Well met, Helmstone, my boy! Ah! What's the matter? Haven't been committing murder? Ain't flying justice? You look wild!"

"You have seen it, then?" said I, of course referring to the criticism.

"Oh yes; I was there at the morning performance. Great clown, I assure you. But here comes Hautboy. Hautboy—Helmstone."

Without having time or inclination to resent so mortifying a mistake, I was instantly soothed as I gazed on the face of the new acquaintance so unceremoniously introduced. His person was short and full, with a juvenile, animated cast to it. His complexion rurally ruddy; his eye sincere, cheery, and gray. His hair alone betrayed that he was not an overgrown boy. From his hair I set him down as forty or more.

"Come, Standard," he gleefully cried to my friend, "are you not going to the circus? The clown is inimitable, they say. Come; Mr. Helmstone, too—come both; and circus over, we'll take a nice stew and punch at Taylor's."

The sterling content, good humor, and extraordinary ruddy, sincere expression of this most singular new acquaintance acted upon me like magic. It seemed mere loyalty to human nature to accept an invitation from so unmistakably kind and honest a heart.

During the circus performance I kept my eye more on Hautboy than on the celebrated clown. Hautboy was the sight for me. Such genuine enjoyment as his struck me to the soul with a sense of the reality of the thing called happiness. The jokes of the clown he seemed to roll under his tongue as ripe magnum bonums. Now the foot, now the hand, was employed to attest his grateful applause. At any hit more than ordinary, he turned upon Standard and me to see if his rare pleasure was shared. In a man of forty I saw a boy of twelve; and this too without the slightest abatement of my respect. Because all was so honest and natural, every expression and attitude so graceful with genuine good-nature, that the marvelous juvenility of Hautboy assumed a sort of divine and immortal air, like that of some forever youthful god of Greece.

But much as I gazed upon Hautboy, and much as I admired his air, yet that desperate mood in which I had first rushed from the house had not so entirely departed as not to molest me with momentary returns. But from these relapses I would rouse myself, and swiftly glance round the broad amphitheatre of eagerly interested and all-applauding human faces. Hark! claps, thumps, deafening huzzas; the vast assembly seemed frantic with acclamation; and what, mused I, has caused all this? Why, the clown only comically grinned with one of his extra grins.

Then I repeated in my mind that sublime passage in my poem, in which Cleothemes the Argive vindicates the justice of the war. Aye, aye, thought I to myself, did I now leap into the ring there, and repeat that identical passage, nay, enact the whole tragic poem before them, would they applaud the poet as they applaud the clown? No! They would hoot me, and call me doting or mad. Then what does this prove? Your infatuation or their insensibility? Perhaps both; but indubitably the first. But why wail? Do you seek admiration from the admirers of a buffoon? Call to mind the saying of the Athenian, who, when the people vociferously applauded in the forum, asked his friend in a whisper, what foolish thing had he said?

Again my eye swept the circus, and fell on the ruddy radiance of the countenance of Hautboy. But its clear honest cheeriness disdained my disdain. My intolerant pride was rebuked. And yet Hautboy dreamed not what magic reproof to a soul like mine sat on his laughing brow. At the very instant I felt the dart of the censure, his eye twinkled, his hand waved, his voice was lifted in jubilant delight at another joke of the inexhaustible clown.

Circus over, we went to Taylor's. Among crowds of others, we sat down to our stews and punches at one of the small marble tables. Hautboy sat opposite to me. Though greatly subdued from its former hilarity, his face still shone with gladness. But added to this was a quality not so prominent before: a certain serene expression of leisurely, deep good sense. Good sense and good humor in him joined hands. As the conversation proceeded between the brisk Standard and him—for I said little or nothing—I was more and more struck with the excellent judgment he evinced. In most of his remarks upon a variety of topics Hautboy seemed intuitively to hit the exact line between enthusiasm and apathy. It was plain that while Hautboy saw the world pretty much as it was, yet he did not theoretically espouse its bright side nor its dark side. Rejecting all solutions, he but acknowledged facts. What was sad in the world he did not superficially gainsay; what was glad in it he did not cynically slur; and all which was to him personally enjoyable, he gratefully took to his heart. It was plain, then—so it seemed at that moment, at least—that his extraordinary cheerfulness did not arise either from deficiency of feeling or thought.

Suddenly remembering an engagement, he took up his hat, bowed pleasantly, and left us.

"Well, Helmstone," said Standard, inaudibly drumming on the slab, "what do you think of your new acquaintance?"

The two last words tingled with a peculiar and novel significance.

"New acquaintance indeed," echoed I. "Standard, I owe you a thousand thanks for introducing me to one of the most singular men I have ever seen. It needed the optical sight of such a man to believe in the possibility of his existence."

"You rather like him, then," said Standard, with ironical dryness.

"I hugely love and admire him, Standard. I wish I were Hautboy."

"Ah? That's a pity, now. There's only one Hautboy in the world."

This last remark set me to pondering again, and somehow it revived my dark mood.

"His wonderful cheerfulness, I suppose," said I, sneering with spleen, "originates not less in a felicitous fortune than in a felicitous temper. His great good sense is apparent; but great good sense may exist without sublime endowments. Nay, I take it, in certain cases, that good sense is simply owing to the absence of those. Much more, cheerfulness. Unpossessed of genius, Hautboy is eternally blessed."

"Ah? You would not think him an extraordinary genius, then?"

"Genius? What! such a short, fat fellow a genius! Genius, like Cassius, is lank."

"Ah? But could you not fancy that Hautboy might formerly have had genius, but luckily getting rid of it, at last fatted up?"

"For a genius to get rid of his genius is as impossible as for a man in the galloping consumption to get rid of that."

"Ah? You speak very decidedly."

"Yes, Standard," cried I, increasing in spleen, "your cheery Hautboy, after all, is no pattern, no lesson for you and me. With average abilities; opinions clear, because circumscribed; passions docile, because they are feeble; a temper hilarious, because he was born to it—

how can your Hautboy be made a reasonable example to a heady fellow like you, or an ambitious dreamer like me? Nothing tempts him beyond common limit; in himself he has nothing to restrain. By constitution he is exempted from all moral harm. Could ambition but prick him; had he but once heard applause, or endured contempt, a very different man would your Hautboy be. Acquiescent and calm from the cradle to the grave, he obviously slides through the crowd."

"Ah?"

"Why do you say *Ah* to me so strangely whenever I speak?"

"Did you ever hear of Master Betty?"

"The great English prodigy, who long ago ousted the Siddons and the Kembles from Drury Lane, and made the whole town run mad with acclamation?"

"The same," said Standard, once more inaudibly drumming on the slab.

I looked at him perplexed. He seemed to be holding the master-key of our theme in mysterious reserve; seemed to be throwing out his Master Betty, too, to puzzle me only the more.

"What under heaven can Master Betty, the great genius and prodigy, an English boy twelve years old, have to do with the poor commonplace plodder, Hautboy, an American of forty?"

"Oh, nothing in the least. I don't imagine that they ever saw each other. Besides, Master Betty must be dead and buried long ere this."

"Then why cross the ocean, and rifle the grave to drag his remains into this living discussion?"

"Absent-mindedness, I suppose. I humbly beg pardon. Proceed with your observations on Hautboy. You think he never had genius, quite too contented, and happy and fat for that—ah? You think him no pattern for men in general? affording no lesson of value to neglected merit, genius ignored, or impotent presumption rebuked?—all of which three amount to much the same thing. You admire his cheerfulness, while scorning his commonplace soul. Poor Hautboy, how sad that your very cheerfulness should, by a by-blow, bring you despite!"

"I don't say I scorn him; you are unjust. I simply declare that he is no pattern for me."

A sudden noise at my side attracted my ear. Turning, I saw Hautboy again, who very blithely reseated himself on the chair he had left.

"I was behind time with my engagement," said Hautboy, "so thought I would run back and rejoin you. But come, you have sat long enough here. Let us go to my rooms. It is only a five minutes' walk."

"If you will promise to fiddle for us, we will," said Standard.

Fiddle! thought I—he's a jiggumbob *fiddler*, then? No wonder genius declines to measure its pace to a fiddler's bow. My spleen was very strong on me now.

"I will gladly fiddle you your fill," replied Hautboy to Standard. "Come on."

In a few minutes we found ourselves in the fifth story of a sort of storehouse, in a lateral street to Broadway. It was curiously furnished with all sorts of odd furniture which seemed to have been obtained, piece by piece, at auctions of old-fashioned household stuff. But all was charmingly clean and cozy.

Pressed by Standard, Hautboy forthwith got out his dented old fiddle and, sitting down on a tall rickety stool, played away right merrily at "Yankee Doodle" and other off-handed, dashing, and disdainfully care-free airs. But common as were the tunes, I was transfixed by something miraculously superior in the style. Sitting there on the old stool, his rusty hat sideways cocked on his head, one foot dangling adrift, he plied the bow of an enchanter. All my moody discontent, every vestige of peevishness, fled. My whole splenetic soul capitulated to the magical fiddle.

"Something of an Orpheus, ah?" said Standard, archly nudging me beneath the left rib.

"And I, the charmed Bruin," murmured I.

The fiddle ceased. Once more, with redoubled curiosity, I gazed upon the easy, indifferent Hautboy. But he entirely baffled inquisition.

When, leaving him, Standard and I were in the street once more, I earnestly conjured him to tell me who, in sober truth, this marvelous Hautboy was.

"Why, haven't you seen him? And didn't you yourself lay his whole anatomy open on the marble slab at Taylor's? What more can you possibly learn? Doubtless, your own masterly insight has already put you in possession of all."

"You mock me, Standard. There is some mystery here. Tell me, I entreat you, who is Hautboy?"

"An extraordinary genius, Helmstone," said Standard, with sudden ardor, "who in boyhood drained the whole flagon of glory; whose going from city to city was a going from triumph to triumph. One who has been an object of wonder to the wisest, been caressed by the loveliest, received the open homage of thousands on thousands of the rabble. But to-day he walks Broadway and no man knows him. With you and me, the elbow of the hurrying clerk, and the pole of the remorseless omnibus, shove him. He who has a hundred times been crowned with laurels, now wears, as you see, a bunged beaver. Once fortune poured showers of gold into his lap, as showers of laurel leaves upon his brow. To-day, from house to house he hies, teaching fiddling for a living. Crammed once with fame, he is now hilarious without it. *With* genius and *without* fame, he is happier than a king. More a prodigy now than ever."

"His true name?"

"Let me whisper it in your ear."

"What! Oh, Standard, myself, as a child, have shouted myself hoarse applauding that very name in the theatre."

"I have heard your poem was not very handsomely received," said Standard, now suddenly shifting the subject.

"Not a word of that, for Heaven's sake!" cried I. "If Cicero, traveling in the East, found sympathetic solace for his grief in beholding the arid overthrow of a once gorgeous city, shall not my petty affair be as nothing, when I behold in Hautboy the vine and the rose climbing the shattered shafts of his tumbled temple of Fame?"

Next day I tore all my manuscripts, bought me a fiddle, and went to take regular lessons of Hautboy.

小提琴家

〔美〕赫尔曼·梅尔维尔

就这样我的诗歌完蛋了,我没有资格流芳百世!我永远永远是无名之辈。倒霉!

我抓起帽子,把批评文章一扔,跑到了百老汇。街上成群成群兴致勃勃的人往附近一条路上新开张的马戏团走,那个马戏团靠一个演技高超的小丑出了名。

没走多久,遇上了老朋友斯坦达德,他一见我便大声打招呼:

"老兄,是你呀,赫尔姆斯通!哟,怎么回事?杀了人想逃法网啦?看你这发了疯的模样!"

"这么说你也看过了?"当然我指的是批评文章。

"那当然!看的早场。小丑当真演得好。看,豪特博侬来了。豪特博侬,这位是赫尔姆斯通。"

闹出这个误会本叫人气恼,但我顾不得也不愿气恼,因为新结识的人虽是这样随随便便介绍的,可他的一张脸却立刻引起了我的注意。他矮胖个子,但显得年轻,有活力。皮肤透出乡下人的红润,灰色的眼睛表现出诚恳、快乐。唯有头发说明他不是一个发育过头的孩子,从他的头发看,估计年已四十或四十开外。

"怎么啦，斯坦达德，你不是去看马戏吗？"他高兴地大声问我的朋友，"据说小丑的表演很出色。赫尔姆斯通先生也来吧——两位都来。等马戏完了，我们到泰勒餐馆吃吃炖肉，喝喝混合饮料。"

这位与众不同的新相识心地纯洁，性格开朗，面色红润，表情诚恳，像有魔力一样吸引了我。似乎，只有接受这样一位无疑善良、诚实的人的邀请，才顺乎人的天性。

在马戏场，我注意看的不是名小丑，而是豪特博依。豪特博依才值得我看。他真心的高兴使我领会到了什么叫快乐。他听到小丑的俏皮话像是吃到美味的水果。一会儿手舞，一会儿足蹈，表示他由衷的欣赏。看到特别精彩处，会望望斯坦达德和我一眼，看看我们是不是与他一样高兴至极。我发现一个四十岁的人竟成了一个十二岁的孩子，却同样令我起敬。由于一切都那么纯朴、自然，每一个表情、动作都出自真正的好天性，豪特博依的孩子气就显得圣洁，仿佛会永不泯灭，像那些永远年轻的希腊之神一样。

然而，尽管我这样注意观察豪特博依，尽管我喜爱他的模样，我刚出门时的懊丧却没有完全消失，时不时地弄得我不痛快。到了这种时候我便克制自己，扫一眼圆型大剧场里观众入迷的笑脸。你听，满场人又是拍巴掌，又是跺脚，又是大喊大叫，高兴得快要发狂了。这是什么原因呢？我在想。其实，小丑不过又做了个怪笑而已。

后来我回想起我的写希腊人克里奥西姆证明战争有理的最精彩的那段诗。我暗暗问自己，如果我跳上台，朗诵这一段，甚至朗诵整首悲剧诗，他们会像为小丑拍手叫好那样为诗人拍手叫好吗？不会！他们一定要起哄，骂我神经病，发疯。这说明什么呢？是自己走火入魔还是他们愚昧无知？也许兼而有之，但前者是肯定无疑的。那为什么伤心？难道你能得到一群喜爱小丑的人的欢心吗？请想想有一位雅典人：每当满场人拍手叫好时，他便小声问朋友，他说了什么傻话。

我的眼光又掠过台上，然后落到豪特博依红扑扑、容光焕发的脸上。他由衷地高兴，根本无视我的轻蔑，我极度的自傲受到了责备。但豪特博依做梦也想不到，他笑的时候会使一个像我这样的人奇怪地感到内疚。就在我感到被这种责备刺痛了时，他听到了不停搞笑的小丑又说了一句俏皮话，眼一眨，手一挥，乐得提高嗓门叫。

马戏演完了，我们去了泰勒餐馆。客人还有很多，我们在一张小大理石桌边坐下吃炖肉，喝混合饮料，豪特博依与我面对面。他不像刚才那样欢喜若狂，脸上却仍露出高兴的神情。但除此之外，我有一个新发现：他谈吐冷静，深刻，高明。冷静与开朗他兼而有之。他与思路敏捷的斯坦达德不停地谈，我很少说话或根本不说话，越听越感到他见解过人。话题很多，他谈起来恰到好处，不偏不倚。显然，世界怎样美，豪特博依就看得怎样美，既没有夸大光明面的话，也没有夸大黑暗面的话。他不看重哪家之说，只承认事实。对世界上叫人伤心的事他不随口否认，对世界上叫人高兴的事，他不视而不见；该他自己喜爱的，他真心喜爱。所以，显然——至少当时我觉得——他快快活活既不是因为感觉迟钝，也不是因为头脑简单。

忽然他想起了一件事要办，拿起礼帽，有礼貌地一鞠躬，告退了。

"你说说，赫尔姆斯通，你对第一次见到的这人印象如何？"斯坦达德轻轻敲着大理石桌面问。

他说"第一次见到"是意味深长的。

"的确是第一次见到。"我赞同说，"斯坦达德，非常感谢你介绍我认识这样一位不寻常的人。如果不是亲眼看见，还不会相信真有其人。"

"看来你相当喜欢他,是吗?"斯坦达德明知故问。

"我喜爱得不得了,斯坦达德,恨不得自己就是豪特博依。"

"当真?那可不行,世界上只有一个豪特博依。"

他的后一句话又触动了我的心事,使我犯起心病来。

我没好气地说起挖苦话来:"他快快活活,一因脾气好,二也靠运气好。一看就知道他见解过人,但见解过人不一定绝顶聪明。刚好相反,有时候我认为见解过人是因为缺乏天资。豪特博依多的是快活,少的是天才,倒有享不尽的好处。"

"当真?你不把他看成难得的天才人物?"

"天才?哪儿的话!矮胖子还有天才?天才人物像卡修斯①,是瘦高个子。"

"当真?你就没想过豪特博依也许以前有天才,后来不幸天才泯灭,发了胖?"

"蠢材变不了天才,天才同样变不了蠢材。"

"当真?你说得很肯定啊。"

"没错,斯坦达德。"我更没好气,大声答道,"你那个乐呵呵的豪特博依不值得你我学,不值得你我想。他能力平庸,说话道理清楚是因为所论有限,待人随和是因为麻木不仁,快快活活是因为生来就这个性格。你是头脑灵活的人,我是雄心勃勃的人,你那个豪特博依怎么能成为我们的榜样呢?他绝不会越出常规一步,完全是个平平庸庸的人。由于身体条件的关系,他不会干有违道德的事。如果他还懂得雄心二字,如果他被鼓过一次

---

① 卡修斯系古罗马大将,死于公元前42年。

掌，或者忍受过一次轻蔑，你那位豪特博依都值得刮目相看。他从生到死无声无息，是在人世上混。"

"当真？"

"对我的话你为什么要怪声怪气地问那么多'当真'？"

"你有没有听说过神童贝蒂？"

"是不是那位英国的奇才，很久前出尽风头，使人人喝彩的那位神童贝蒂。"

"正是！"斯坦达德说，又轻轻敲着大理石桌面。

我看着他，愣了。万能钥匙似乎掌握在他手中，他秘而不宣，抛出一个神童贝蒂看来也只是为了使我更觉得玄。

"神童贝蒂是大天才，人中之杰，十二岁的英国孩子，而豪特博依可怜巴巴、平平庸庸，是美国人，有四十岁了，他们怎能相提并论？"

"的确没有共同之处，两人也一定从未见过面。再说，神童贝蒂一定早死了，埋进了地里。"

"那你为什么要跨洋越海，把死人与活人拉扯到一起。"

"是失言了，请原谅。你再谈谈对豪特博依的看法吧。你是不是认为他根本没有天才，容易满足，所以就过得快快活活，长得肥肥胖胖？你觉得他不值得人们仿效吗？对那些长处被忽视，天才被埋没，或者无端被人猜测为无能的人，他不能提供一点有益的启示吗？当然这三种情况实际上是一回事。你喜欢他开朗的性格，却看不起他的平庸。豪特博依真冤，要是知道就因为快快活活而被人瞧不起，会多难受。"

"我没有说看不起他，你曲解了我的意思，我只是说他没有什么值得我仿效。"

我突然觉得身旁来了人，一看，是豪特博依，乐呵呵在原来的位子上坐下了。

"我有件事耽误了，所以快步赶回来再与两位聚会。"豪特博依说，"两位在这儿坐得太久，还是去我家吧。不远，走五分钟就到。"

"你答应拉小提琴我们就去。"斯坦达德说。

小提琴！他还是个能拉弓的提琴师？我暗想。难怪大家说，有天才的人不会在乎什么拉琴不拉琴。现在我更加不服气了。

"拉就拉，让你听个够。"豪特博依对斯坦达德答道，"走吧！"

没走几分钟，我们到了百老汇旁的一条大街，进了幢仓库似的房子，上了五层楼。房间里摆设独特，家具式样奇怪，像是在老古董拍卖时东一件西一件买来的。然而整个房间干净、舒适。

豪特博依被斯坦达德催促不过，取出把老掉牙的小提琴，坐到张摇摇晃晃的高凳上，拉起了《美国人之歌》和别的熟悉、轻快、没有伤感情绪踪影的曲子。曲子虽然平常，没想到演奏技巧却超群。他坐在一条旧凳上，褪了色的帽子歪罩在头上，一只脚悬着，拉动着弓，叫人听得入迷。我的满心委屈消失了，百结愁肠解开了，我忘记了苦恼，被这把有魔力的小提琴整个征服了。

"得了真传的吧，嗯？"斯坦达德用手肘碰碰我的左肋。

"我佩服得五体投地。"我轻声说。

琴声停了。我又一次注视着这位随和、平凡的豪特博依，好奇心更重，但打量是打量不出个名堂的。

我和斯坦达德出了他的家，走到街上后，我恳求他告诉我这位少见的豪特博依是何许人。

"怎么，你不是亲眼见了吗？坐在泰勒餐馆的饭桌旁不是把他分析透了吗？还能听得进去什么？你明察秋毫，当然该什么都知道！"

"别挖苦我，斯坦达德。我算是遇上了个奇怪人。求求你了，告诉我豪特博依是什么人吧！"

"一位超群绝伦的天才！赫尔姆斯通！"斯坦达德的话里一下充满了热情，"小时候他红极一时，走到哪座城市红到哪座城市，最聪明的人把他当成奇才，最引人喜爱的人也来爱抚他，为他捧场的更是成千累万。可今天，他走在百老汇也无人认识，跟你我这样的人混在一起，连阿猫阿狗碰他一下也没什么。以前他戴过一百次桂冠，现在你看，戴的是顶旧海狸皮帽。过去走红运，金钱像流水一样来，荣誉要多少有多少。现在他为了生活，上门教小提琴。过去他名声卓著，现在没有了名声反而快快活活。他有天才没名声，比国王还快乐。以前了不起，现在更是。"

"他的真名实姓呢？"

"我得悄悄说。"

"什么！哎呀，斯坦达德，我小时候上剧院听到这个名字就喝彩，把嗓门都喊哑了。"

"我听说人家对你的诗评价不大好。"斯坦达德突然换了话题，说道。

"天哪，别提了吧！"我说，"西塞罗[①]看到一座繁华一时的城市后来成了不毛之地，不胜哀伤，后来走到东方，精神得到了安慰。我在豪特博依身上看到他倒塌了的名誉殿堂的残垣断壁上爬满了青藤，长着玫瑰，我的小事比较起来又算得了什么呢？"

第二天我把诗稿全撕了，买了把小提琴，按期请豪特博依来教。

---

① 西塞罗（公元前106—前43），罗马政治家、雄辩家、哲学家。

The Heavenly Christmas Tree

Fyodor Dostoevsky

I am a novelist, and I suppose I have made up this story. I write "I suppose," though I know for a fact that I have made it up, but yet I keep fancying that it must have happened on Christmas Eve in some great town in a time of terrible frost.

I have a vision of a boy, a little boy, six years old or even younger. This boy woke up that morning in a cold damp cellar. He was dressed in a sort of [1] little dressing-gown and was shivering with cold. There was a cloud of white steam from his breath, and sitting on a box in the corner, he blew the steam out of his mouth and amused himself in his dullness watching it float away. But he was terribly hungry. Several times that morning he went up to the plank bed where his sick mother was lying on a mattress as thin as a pancake, with some sort of bundle under her head for a pillow. How had she come here? She must have

---

[1] a sort of: 有时 a sort of 并非表示"一种"的意思,有贬义,意为"勉强凑合的""蹩脚(货)"。"This is a desk." 意为"这是一张桌子",但"This is a sort of desk." 意为"这东西凑合着当桌子用"。

come with her boy from some other town and suddenly fallen ill. The landlady who let the "corners" had been taken two days before to the police station, the lodgers were out and about as the holiday was so near, and the only one left had been lying for the last twenty-four hours dead drunk, not having waited for Christmas. In another corner of the room a wretched old woman of eighty, who had once been a children's nurse but was now left to die friendless, was moaning and groaning, with rheumatism, scolding and grumbling at the boy so that he was afraid to go near her corner. He had got a drink of water in the outer room, but could not find a crust anywhere, and had been on the point of waking his mother a dozen times. He felt frightened at last in the darkness: it had long been dusk, but no light was kindled. Touching his mother's face, he was suprised that she did not move at all, and that she was as cold as the wall. "It is very cold here," he thought. He stood a little, unconsciously letting his hands rest on the dead woman's shoulders, then he breathed on his fingers to warm them, and then quietly fumbling for his cap on the bed, he went out of the cellar. He would have gone earlier, but was afraid of the big dog which had been howling all day at the neighbour's door at the top of the stairs. But the dog was not there now, and he went out into the street.

Mercy on us, what a town! He had never seen anything like it before. In the town from which he had come, it was always such black darkness at night. There was one lamp for the whole street, the little, low-pitched, wooden houses were closed up with shutters, there was no one to be seen in the street after dusk, all the people shut themselves up

The Heavenly Christmas Tree

in their houses, and there was nothing but the howling of packs of dogs, hundreds and thousands of them barking and howling all night. But there it was so warm and he was given food, while here—oh, dear, if he only had something to eat! And what a noise and rattle here, what light and what people, horses and carriages, and what a frost! The frozen steam hung in clouds over the horses, over their warmly breathing mouths; their hoofs clanged against the stones through the powdery snow, and everyone pushed so, and—oh, dear, how he longed for some morsel to eat, and how wretched he suddenly felt. A policeman walked by and turned away to avoid seeing the boy.

There was another street—oh, what a wide one, here he would be run over for certain; how everyone was shouting, racing and driving along, and the light, the light! And what was this? A huge glass window, and through the window a tree reaching up to the ceiling; it was a fir tree, and on it were ever so many lights, gold papers and apples and little dolls and horses; and there were children clean and dressed in their best running about the room, laughing and playing and eating and drinking something. And then a little girl began dancing with one of the boys, what a pretty little girl! And he could hear the music through the window. The boy looked and wondered and laughed, though his toes were aching with the cold and his fingers were red and stiff so that it hurt him to move them. And all at once the boy remembered how his toes and fingers hurt him, and began crying, and ran on; and again through another window-pane he saw another Christmas tree, and on a table cakes of all sorts—almond cakes, red cakes and yellow cakes, and three grand young ladies were sitting there, and they gave the cakes to any one who went up to them, and the door kept opening, lots of gentlemen and ladies went in from the street. The boy crept up, suddenly opened the door and went in. Oh, how they shouted at him and waved him back! One lady went up to him hurriedly and slipped a kopeck into his hand, and with her own hands opened the door into the street for him! How frightened he was. And the kopeck rolled away and clinked upon the steps; he could not bend his red fingers to hold it right. The boy ran away and went on, where he did not know. He was ready to cry again but he was afraid, and ran on and on and blew his fingers. And he was miserable bacause he felt suddenly so lonely and terrified, and all at once, mercy on us! What was this again? People were standing in a crowd admiring. Behind a glass window there were three little dolls, dressed in red and green dresses, and exactly, exactly as though they were alive. One was a little old man sitting and playing a big violin, the two others were standing close by and playing little violins, and nodding in time, and looking at one another, and their lips moved, they were speaking, actually speaking, only one couldn't hear through the glass. And at first the boy thought they were alive, and when he grasped that they were dolls he laughed. He had never seen such dolls before, and had no idea there were such dolls! And he wanted to cry, but he felt amused, amused by the dolls. All at once he fancied that some one caught at his smock behind: a wicked big boy was standing beside him and suddenly hit him on the head, snatched off his cap and tripped him up. The boy fell down on the ground, at once there was a shout, he was numb with fright, he jumped up and ran away. He ran, and not knowing where he was going, ran in at the gate of some one's courtyard, and sat down behind a stack of wood: "They won't find me here, besides it's dark!"

He sat huddled up and was breathless from fright, and all at once, quite suddenly, he felt so happy: his hands and feet suddenly left off aching and grew so warm, as warm as though he were on a stove; then he shivered all over, then he gave a start, why, he must have been asleep. How nice to have a sleep here! "I'll sit here a little and go and look at the dolls again," said the boy, and smiled thinking of them. "Just as though they were alive! ..." And suddenly he heard his mother singing over him. "Mammy, I am asleep; how nice it is to sleep here!"

"Come to my Christmas tree, little one," a soft voice suddenly whispered over his head.

He thought that this was still his mother, but no, it was not she. Who it was calling him, he could not see, but someone bent over and embraced him in the darkness; and he stretched out his hands to him, and ... and all at once—oh, what a bright light! Oh, what a Christmas tree! And yet it was not a fir tree, he had never seen a tree like that! Where was he now? Everything was bright and shining, and all round him were dolls; but no, they were not dolls, they were little boys and girls, only so bright and shining. They all came flying round him, they all kissed him, took, him and carried him along with them, and he was flying himself, and he saw that his mother was looking at him and laughing joyfully. "Mammy, Mammy; oh how nice it is here, Mammy!"

And again he kissed the children and wanted to tell them at once of those dolls in the shop window.

"Who are you, boys? Who are you, girls?" he asked, laughing and admiring them.

"This is Christ's Christmas tree," they answered. "Christ always has a Christmas tree on this day, for the little children who have no tree of their own ..." And he found out that all these little boys and girls were children just like himself; that some had been frozen in the baskets in which they had as babies been laid on the doorsteps of well-to-do Petersburg people, others had been boarded out with Finnish women by the Foundling[①] and had been suffocated, others had died at their starved mother's breasts (in the Samara famine), others had died in third-class railway carriages from the foul air; and yet they were all here, they were all like angles about Christ, and He was in the midst of them and held out his hands to them and blessed them and their sinful mothers ... And the mothers of these children stood on one side weeping; each one knew her boy or girl, and the children flew up to them and kissed them and wiped away their tears with their little hands, and begged them not to weep because they were so happy.

And down below in the morning the porter found the little dead body of the frozen child on the woodstack; they sought out his mother too ... She had died before him. They met before the Lord God in heaven.

---

① the Foundling：指 the foundling hospital（育婴堂）。

The Heavenly Christmas Tree

Why have I made up such a story, so out of keeping with an ordinary diary, and a writer's above all? And I promised two stories dealing with real events! But that is just it, I keep fancying that all this may have happened really—that is, what took place in the cellar and on the woodstack; but as for Christ's Christmas tree, I cannot tell you whether that could have happened or not.

天国的圣诞树

〔俄〕陀思妥耶夫斯基

我是小说家,假定这篇小说是我创作的。我说"假定"是因为尽管我知道我的确创作了这篇小说,却一直猜想,在圣诞节前夕,在某个冰封雪盖的大城市,的确发生过这种事。

我仿佛看到一个孩子,一个6岁,甚至不足6岁的孩子。他睡在又冷又潮湿的地窖里,圣诞节前夕一早醒了过来,身上只穿了件不成样子的小睡衣,冻得打哆嗦,呼出的气成了一团白雾。他坐在角落里的一只小箱上,好玩似地老吐着气,又看着白雾消散。可是他的肚子饿得咕咕叫。他妈妈正生病,躺在一张燕麦饼一样薄的席子上,头下塞了个包袱,算是枕头,这天早上他几次走到木板搭的床边。她怎么会在这地方呢?她一定是外地人,带着孩子来的,却不料突然害病。出租"屋角"的房东太太两天前被带到了警察局。因为节日临近,房客们也走了,散了,唯独剩下一个烂醉如泥的人,一躺就是24小时,没打算过圣诞节。房间的另一角还有一个80岁的老太婆,当过保姆,现在无亲无故,在等死,正害风湿痛,痛得厉害,对着孩子骂骂咧咧,所以他不敢靠近她。他在外面房间喝了几口水,但哪儿也找不到面包皮,有十几次想叫醒妈妈。终于,他在黑漆漆的地方受不了了:天早已暗下来,灯却没有点着。他摸摸妈妈的脸,吃了一惊,妈妈已不动了,全身冰凉。"这儿真冷!"他想。他站了一会儿,两只手不知不觉放到了死人肩上,然后又把手指放到嘴边哈气,哈热后在床上悄悄摸到自己的帽子,走出了地窖。隔壁门口台阶上守着一只大狗,叫了一天。要不是怕狗,他早出去了。现在狗没守在那儿,他才上了街。

哎哟,多漂亮的地方!以前他从没饱过这样的眼福。他原来住的那小镇夜晚黑漆漆,整条街就那么一盏灯,又矮又小的木头房子的百叶窗关着,天黑以后人人守在自己家里,只有成群的狗叫得热闹,几百上千条嚎一个通宵。但是那地方使人感到暖融融,他还能得到吃的——天哪,他现在急需的就是吃!这地方真闹翻了天,灯太亮,人多,马车多,天也太冷!马喷着鼻息,呼出的热气结成一团团云雾。马蹄踏碎积雪,踩在石头路上发出嗒嗒的声音。所有人都急匆匆地走着。可是,哎,他多想吃到一块面包!突然间他感到自己真可怜。一名警察走了过去,把头偏到一边,装作没见到孩子。

又是一条马路。哟,多宽!他准会被轧死。所有的人拉开嗓门叫着,跑着,飞快赶着车。多亮堂哦,多亮堂哦!这又是什么?一扇大玻璃窗。玻璃窗里有一棵树,齐天花板高。这是棵枞树,扎满灯,还有金纸、苹果、小玩偶和马。穿戴得整整齐齐、漂漂亮亮的孩子在房间里跑着,笑着,玩着,又吃又喝。后来,一个小女孩与一个男孩跳起舞来,她真漂亮!隔着窗他还听到了音乐。孩子看得入神,笑着,脚趾却冷得痛,手指发红、发僵,一动就痛。孩子这才清醒过来,感觉到了痛,大哭起来,往前跑。他又看到了一扇窗后有棵圣诞树,一张桌上摆着各式糕点,有杏仁的,有红的,有黄的。三位阔气的小姐坐在桌边,谁来了给谁一块,而门不断开着,街上有许多先生和太太走进屋子。孩子爬上台阶,打开门,走了进去。哟,那些人朝他嚷开了,挥手叫他出去。一位小姐赶忙过来,塞给他一分小硬币,打开门,请他出去。他吓坏了。硬币当啷一声滚到了台阶上;他冻红的手捏不拢,抓不住。孩子跑开了,漫无目标地走着。他想哭又不敢哭,一个劲儿跑,哈着手指。这小可怜突然感到无依无靠,害怕起来。天哪,就一下子感觉到了!这又是什么呢?一堆人站着看得津津有味。原来,一扇玻璃窗里放着三个穿红着绿的小玩偶,活像真人一般。一个是老头,在拉大四弦琴,另外两个紧靠他站着,在拉小四弦琴,不时点点头,你看看我,我看看你,嘴唇还能动,是在说话,当真在说话,不过隔着玻璃窗听不见罢了。孩子起初以为他们是活的,后来看出是玩偶,笑了。他从来没有见过这样的玩具,也不知道有这样的玩具。他想哭,但看玩具又看得高兴。突然,他发现有人从后面拽住了他的衣服。原来,他身后站了个捣蛋的大孩子,猛地打他的头,抢走他的帽子,还用脚绊他。他栽倒在地上,接着只听到一阵起哄,他吓坏了,跳起来就跑。他漫无目标地往前跑,跑到了一户人家院子的门口,在一堆木柴后面坐了下来。"这儿可找不着我,天又黑了!"

他缩成一团坐着,吓得不敢出气,可是一刹那间他高兴起来,这真是意外的事。他的手和脚突然不痛了,变暖和了,暖得像在火炉上烤。他浑身一颤,吃了一惊,心想刚才一定是睡着了。能在这地方睡一觉多美!"我再坐一会儿去看玩具!"孩子心里在打算,想到那三个玩偶他笑了,"真跟活的一模一样……"突然,他听到妈妈在唱歌,"妈,我睡着了,睡在这里真舒服!"

"孩子,来看我的圣诞树吧!"忽然一个温和的声音在他头上说。

他以为是妈妈的声音,可是错了,这不是妈妈的声音。他认不出是谁在叫他，只知道黑暗中有人伸出手来抱他，他也向那人伸出手，而且……而且转眼之间——哟，多亮堂！多漂亮的圣诞树！这不是一棵枞树，他从没见过这样的树。他现在在哪儿呢？这地方光彩夺目，四周摆满玩偶。不，不是玩偶，是小朋友们，太漂亮了！他们都是飞到他身边的，他们吻他，把他带走，他跟着也飞起来了，发现妈妈在看着他，开心地笑着。"妈，妈！呀，这里真好，妈！"他也吻了那些小朋友，巴不得把在商店橱窗看到玩偶的事一股脑全告诉他们。

"你们是谁呀？你们是谁呀？"他笑着，很喜欢他们，问道。

小朋友们回答："这是基督的圣诞树。每年今天基督有一棵圣诞树，给没有圣诞树的小朋友……"他这才发现这些孩子原来与他一样，有的生下来就被放进篮子里，送到有钱的彼得堡人家的台阶上，冻死了；有的让育婴堂送给芬兰女人养，结果咽了气；有的妈妈在大饥荒中饿死，他们跟着死在妈妈怀里；还有的是在三等车厢里闷死的。现在他们聚到了一起，都像是基督身边的天使。基督站在孩子们当中，向他们伸出手，祝福他们和他们有罪的妈妈……孩子们的母亲站在一旁哭，各人认识各人的子女。孩子们飞到她们的身边，吻她们，用小手揩干她们的眼泪，叫妈妈别哭，因为他们很快乐。

第二天早上看门人发现了冻死在柴堆上的孩子，他妈妈也被发现了。妈妈比他死得早，两人一道进了天堂，在上帝面前相会。

为什么我要创作这样一篇小说，一个一般人日记里不记，特别是作家们不写的故事呢？我曾说过要写两篇写实小说。但的确如此，我一直认为这种事——就是发生在地窖里和柴堆上的事——的确是有的。至于基督的圣诞树，我不敢说是否确有其事。

The Three Hermits

An Old Legend Current in the Volga District

Leo Tolstoy

"And in praying use not vain repetitions, as the Gentiles do: for they think that they shall be heard for their much speaking. Be not therefore like them: for your Father knoweth what things ye have need of, before ye ask Him."

Matthew vi: 7, 8.

A Bishop was sailing from Archangel to the Solovetsk Monastery, and on the same vessel were a number of pilgrims on their way to visit the shrines at that place. The voyage was a smooth one. The wind favorable and the weather fair. The pilgrims lay on deck, eating, or sat in groups talking to one another. The Bishop, too, came on deck, and as he was pacing up and down he noticed a group of men standing near the prow and listening to a fisherman, who was pointing to the sea and telling them something. The Bishop stopped, and looked in the direction in which the man was pointing. He could see nothing, however, but the sea glistening in the sunshine. He drew nearer to listen, but when the man saw him, he took off his cap and was silent. The rest of the people also took off their caps and bowed.

"Do not let me disturb you, friends," said the Bishop. "I came to hear what this good man was saying."

"The fisherman was telling us about the hermits," replied one, a tradesman, rather bolder than the rest.

"What hermits?" asked the Bishop, going to the side of the vessel and seating himself on a box. "Tell me about them. I should like to hear. What were you pointing at?"

"Why, that little island you can just see over there," answered the man, pointing to a spot ahead and a little to the right. "That is the island where the hermits live for the salvation of their souls."

"Where is the island?" asked the Bishop. "I see nothing."

"There, in the distance, if you will please look along my hand. Do you see that little cloud? Below it, and a bit to the left, there is just a faint streak. That is the island."

The Bishop looked carefully, but his unaccustomed eyes could make out nothing but the water shimmering in the sun.

"I cannot see it," he said. "But who are the hermits that live there?"

"They are holy men," answered the fisherman. "I had long heard tell of them, but never chanced to see them myself till the year before last."

And the fisherman related how once, when he was out fishing, he had been stranded at night upon that island, not knowing where he was. In the morning, as he wandered about the island, he came across an earth hut, and met an old man standing near it. Presently two others came out, and after having fed him and dried his things, they helped him mend his boat.

"And what are they like?" asked the Bishop.

"One is a small man and his back is bent. He wears a priest's cassock and is very old; he must be more than a hundred, I should say. He is so old that the white of his beard is taking a greenish tinge, but he is always smiling, and his face is as bright as an angel's from heaven. The second is taller, but he also is very old. He wears a tattered peasant coat. His beard is broad, and of a yellowish grey color. He is a strong man. Before I had time to help him, he turned my boat over as if it were only a pail. He too is kindly and cheerful. The third is tall, and has a beard as white as snow and reaching to his kness. He is stern, with overhanging eyebrows; and he wears nothing but a piece of matting tied round his waist."

"And did they speak to you?" asked the Bishop.

"For the most part they did everything in silence, and spoke but little even to one another. One of them would just give a glance, and the others would understand him. I asked the tallest whether they had lived there long. He frowned, and muttered something as if he were angry; but the oldest one took his hand and smiled, and then the tall one was quiet. The oldest one only said: 'Have mercy upon us,' and smiled."

The Three Hermits

While the fisherman was talking, the ship had drawn nearer to the island.

"There, now you can see it plainly, if your Lordship will please to look," said the tradesman, pointing with his hand.

The Bishop looked, and now he really saw a dark streak—which was the island. Having looked at it a while, he left the prow of the vessel, and going to the stern, asked the helmsman:

"What island is that?"

"That one," replied the man, "has no name. There are many such in this sea."

"Is it ture that there are hermits who live there for the salvation of their souls?"

"So it is said, your Lordship, but I don't know if it's true. Fishermen say they have seen them; but of course they may only be spinning yarns."

"I should like to land on the island and see these men," said the Bishop. "How could I manage it?"

"The ship cannot get close to the island," replied the helmsman, "but you might be rowed there in a boat. You had better speak to the captain."

The captain was sent for and came.

"I should like to see these hermits," said the Bishop. "Could I not be rowed ashore?"

The captain tried to dissuade him.

"Of course it could be done," said he, "but we should lose much time. And if I might venture to say so to your Lordship, the old men are not worth your pains. I have heard say that they are foolish old fellows, who understand nothing, and never speak a word, any more than the fish in the sea."

"I wish to see them," said the Bishop, "and I will pay you for your trouble and loss of time. Please let me have a boat."

There was no help for it; so the order was given. The sailors trimmed the sails, the steersman put up the helm, and the ship's course was set for the island. A chair was placed at the prow for the Bishop, and he sat there, looking ahead. The passengers all collected at the prow, and gazed at the island. Those who had the sharpest eyes could presently make out the rocks on it, and then a mud hut was seen. At last one man saw the hermits themselves. The captain brought a telescope and, after looked through it, handed it to the Bishop.

"It's right enough. There are three men standing on the shore. There, a little to the right of that big rock."

The Bishop took the telescope, got it into position, and he saw the three men: a tall one, a shorter one, and one very samll and bent, standing one the shore and holding each other by the hand.

The captain turned to the Bishop.

"The vessel can get no nearer in than this, your Lordship. If you wish to go ashore, we must ask you to go in the boat, while we anchor here."

The cable was quickly let out; the anchor cast, and the sails furled. There was a jerk, and the vessel shook. Then, a boat having been lowered, the oarsmen jumped in, and the Bishop descended the ladder and took his seat. The men pulled at their oars and the boat moved rapidly towards the island. When they came within a stone's throw, they saw three old men: a tall one with only a piece of matting tied round his waist, a shorter one in a tattered peasant coat, and a very old one bent with age and wearing an old cassock—all three standing hand in hand.

The oarsmen pulled in to the shore, and held on with the boathook while the Bishop got out.

The old men bowed to him, and he gave them his blessing, at which they bowed still lower. Then the Bishop began to speak to them.

"I have heard," he said, "that you, godly men, live here saving your own souls and praying to our Lord Christ for your fellow men. I, an unworthy servant of Christ, am called, by God's mercy, to keep and teach His flock. I wished to see you, servants of God, and to do what I can to teach you, also."

The old men looked at each other smiling, but remained silent.

"Tell me," said the Bishop, "what you are doing to save your souls, and how you serve God on this island."

The second hermit sighed, and looked at the oldest, the very ancient one. The latter smiled, and said:

"We do not know how to serve God. We only serve and support ourselves, servant of God."

"But how do you pray to God?" asked the Bishop.

"We pray in this way," replied the hermit. "Three are ye, three are we, have mercy upon us."

And when the old man said this, all three raised their eyes to heaven, and repeated:

"Three are ye, three are we, have mercy upon us!"

The Bishop smiled.

"You have evidently heard something about the Holy Trinity," said he. "But you do not pray aright. You have won my affection, godly men. I see you wish to please the Lord, but you do not know how to serve Him. That is not the way to pray; but listen to me, and I will teach you. I will teach you, not a way of my own, but the way in which God in the Holy Scriptures has commanded all men to pray to Him."

And the Bishop began explaining to the hermits how God had revealed Himself to men; telling them of God the Father, and God the Son, and God the Holy Ghost.

"God the Son came down on earth," said he, "to save men, and this is how He taught us all to pray. Listen, and repeat after me: 'Our Father.'"

And the first old man repeated after him, "Our Father," and the second said, "Our Father," and the third said, "Our Father."

"Which art in heaven," continued the Bishop.

The first hermit repeated, "Which art in heaven," but the second blundered over the words, and the tall hermit could not say them properly. His hair had grown over his mouth so that he could not speak plainly. The very old hermit, having no teeth, also mumbled indistinctly.

The Bishop repeated the words again, and the old men repeated them after him. The Bishop sat down on a stone, and the old men stood before him, watching his mouth, and repeating the words as he uttered them. And all day long the Bishop labored, saying a word twenty, thirty, a hundred times over, and the old men repeated it after him. They blundered, and he corrected them, and made them begin again.

The Bishop did no leave off till he had taught them the whole of the Lord's Prayer so that they could not only repeat it after him, but could say it by themselves. The middle one was the first to know it, and to repeat the whole of it alone. The Bishop made him say it again and again, and at last the others could say it too.

It was getting dark and the moon was appearing over the water, before the Bishop rose to return to the vessel. When he took leave of the old men they all bowed down to the ground before him. He raised them, and kissed each of them, telling them to pray as he had taught them. Then he got into the boat and returned to the ship.

And as he sat in the boat and was rowed to the ship he could hear the three voices of the hermits loudly repeating the Lord's Prayer. As the boat drew near the vessel their voices could no longer be heard, but they could still be seen in the moonlight, standing as he had left them on the shore, the shortest in the middle, the tallest on the right, the middle one on the left. As soon as the Bishop had reached the vessel and got on board, the anchor was weighed and the sails unfurled. The wind filled them and the ship sailed away, and the Bishop took a seat in the stern and watched the island they had left. For a time he could still see the hermits, but presently they disappeared from sight, though the island was still visible. At last it too vanished, and only the sea was to be seen, rippling in the moonlight.

The pilgrims lay down to sleep, and all was quiet on deck. The Bishop did not wish to sleep, but sat alone at the stern, gazing at the sea where the island was no longer visible, and thinking of the good old men. He thought how pleased they had been to learn the Lord's Prayer; and he thanked God for having sent him to teach and help such godly men.

So the Bishop sat, thinking, and gazing at the sea where the island had disappeared. And the moonlight flickered before his eyes, sparkling, now here, now there, upon the waves. Suddenly he saw something white and shining, on the bright path which the moon cast across the sea. Was it a seagull, or the little gleaming sail of some small boat? The Bishop fixed his eyes on it, wondering.

"It must be a boat sailing after us," thought he, "but it is overtaking us very rapidly. It was far, far away a minute ago, but now it is much nearer. It cannot be a boat, for I can see no sail; but whatever it may be, it is following us and catching us up."

And he could not make out what it was. Not a boat, nor a bird, nor a fish! It was too large for a man, and besides a man could not be out there in the midst of the sea. The Bishop rose, and said to the helmsman:

"Look there, what is that, my friend? What is it?" the Bishop repeated, though he could now see plainly what it was—the three hermits running upon the water, all gleaming white, their grey beards shining, and approaching the ship as quickly as though it were not moving."

The steersman looked, and let go the helm in terror.

"Oh, Lord! The hermits are running after us on the water as though it were dry land!"

The passengers, hearing him, jumped up and crowded to the stern. They saw the hermits coming along hand in hand, and the two outer ones beckoning the ship to stop. All three were gliding along upon the water without moving their feet. Before the ship could be stopped, the hermits had reached it, and raising their heads, all three as with one voice, began to say:

"We have forgotten your teaching, servant of God. As long as we kept repeating it we remembered, but when we stopped saying it for a time, a word dropped out, and now it has all gone to pieces. We can remember nothing of it. Teach us again."

The Bishop crossed himself, and leaning over the ship's side, said:

"Your own prayer will reach the Lord, men of God. It is not for me to teach you. Pray for us sinners."

And the Bishop bowed low before the old men; and they turned and went back across the sea. And a light shone until daybreak on the spot where they were lost to sight.

三隐士

——伏尔加地区广为流传的一个古老传说

〔俄〕列夫·托尔斯泰

你们祷告,不可像外邦人,用许多重复话。他们以为话多了必蒙垂听。

你们不可效法他们。因为你们没有祈求以先,你们所需要的,你们的父亲早已知道了。

《马太福音》第六章7、8节

一位主教乘船从阿尔汉格尔去索洛维茨克修道院,同船的还有一大帮朝圣者,是去那地方朝圣的。一路上他们顺利得很,风是顺风,天气相当好。朝圣者有的躺在甲板上,有的在吃,有的在一起聊天。主教也上了甲板,踱来踱去,后来发现一群人站在靠近船头的地方,围着一个打鱼人。打鱼人指着海上,对他们在说些什么。主教停住脚,往打鱼人指的方向看去,然而除了在阳光下一闪一闪的大海,什么也没见着。他也凑过去听,打鱼人发现了他,摘下帽,不言语了。其他人跟着脱帽,躬身行礼。

"朋友们，我不想打搅各位，只是来听听这位热心人在说些什么。"主教说。

"这位师傅在对我们说隐士的事。"一个生意人胆大些，答道。

"什么隐士？"主教问道，走到船边，在一口木箱上坐下，"请说说吧，我想听听。你刚才手指的方向有什么？"

"是一个小岛，你在这儿看得见。"打鱼人说，指着右前方的一个黑点，"几个隐士就住在那岛上，盼望灵魂得救。"

"岛在哪儿？"主教问，"我什么也没看见。"

"还远着，你顺我手指的方向看吧。你看见了那一小团云吗？在云下面靠左边的地方有一线黑乎乎的东西，就是那个岛。"

主教仔细看着，但他的眼对着太阳不中用，除了在太阳下闪光的水，什么也见不到。

"我看不见。"他说，"住在岛上的隐士是什么人？"

"都是圣洁的人。"打鱼人说，"我早听说过他们，但是在前年才有机会亲眼见到。"

打鱼人说有一次他出海打鱼，夜晚漂到了岛上，可并不知道到了什么地方。早上他在岛上走，看到一所小土屋，屋边站着一位老人。没多久又出来两位，给了他吃的，烘干了他的衣服，又帮他修船。

"这些人什么模样？"主教问。

"有一个是小个子，驼背，穿着牧师的法衣，年龄很大，看来准有一百多岁了，胡须白里带青，满脸是笑，神采比得过天上来的天使。第二个的个子高些，年纪也很大，穿着破旧的庄稼人衣裳，胡须宽，带灰黄色，身体结实。他还没等我过去帮一把，就把船翻了个身，像是倒过来一只桶。他也是又和气，又开朗。

第三个的个子很高,胡须像雪一样白,拖过了膝盖。他没有笑容,眉毛长得垂了下来,没穿衣,只在腰上捆了一片破麻袋。"

"他们对你说过话吗?"主教问。

"无论做什么他们大都一声不响,相互间也难得说一句话,只要使个眼色,另外两个就能明白。我问个子最高的人,他们来岛上的时间长不长。他一听皱起眉头,咕噜几句,像是生气了。但年纪最大的拉起他的手,笑了笑,个子高的便不生气了。年纪最大的人说了声'可怜我们吧',然后笑笑。"

打鱼人说着说着,船离岛近了。

"主教大人,你如果现在看看,就看得清楚了。"生意人指着海岛说。

主教一看,果然发现了一线黑乎乎的东西,就是那岛。他细看了一会儿,离开船头,走到船尾,问舵手道:

"那岛是什么地方?"

"那岛没有名字,这一带海上这种岛很多。"舵手说。

"岛上真住着隐士,盼望灵魂得救吗?"

"话虽这么说,但我也不知道是真是假,主教大人。打鱼的人都这样说,但谁知道他们是不是信口开河。"

"我想到岛上看看这些人,怎么上岸呢?"主教问。

"大船靠不了岸,"舵手说,"但可以划一条小船去。你最好与船长谈谈。"

船长被请了来。

"我想见见这几位隐士,能划小船上岸吗?"主教问。

船长劝主教道:

"划小船当然能上岸,但是耽误的时间多。依我看,这几个老头用不着主教大人劳神费力。我听说他们是几个老糊涂,什么也不懂,一句话也不说,跟海里的鱼差不多。"

"我想见见他们,有劳之处和损失的时间由我补偿,只是还请借给我一条小船。"主教说。

事情只好这样办,船长发出了命令。水手调整船帆,舵手扳过舵,大船往海岛驶去。船头摆了一张椅子,是给主教的,他坐在椅上眺望前方。旅客一齐聚集到船头,看着海岛。没多久,眼尖的人看见了岛上的大岩石,后来又发现了小屋。终于有人看见隐士了。船长拿来望远镜,望了望以后递给主教,说:

"果然有!岸上站着三个人,在那块大岩石的右边,离岩石不远。"

大主教接过望远镜望去,果然见到三个人:一个高个子,一个矮些,还有一个个子很小,驼背。三人手牵手站在岸上。

船长对主教道:

"大人,船不能再往前了。如果你想登岸,请坐上小船,我们在这儿抛锚恭候。"

铁缆马上放开了,锚抛了下去,帆收了起来。船受到震动,晃了一下。一条小船放下了海,划桨的人跳进船里,主教从梯子上爬下,坐到船里。几个人划着桨,船很快往海岛靠近。约离一箭之地时,他们看见了三位老人:一个高个子,只在腰间捆了一块麻袋片;个子矮些的穿着一件破庄稼人衣裳;年岁很大的老人背也驼了,穿着一件旧法衣。三人手牵手站着。

船靠了岸,划桨的人用钩撑稳船,让主教下船。

三个老人向主教深深鞠躬,主教向三个老人表示祝福,他们把腰弯得更低了。祝福完,主教对他们说道:

"我听说,你们是虔诚信仰上帝的人,住在这儿是为拯救自己的灵魂，同时也为同类向我主基督祈祷。我是基督不称职的仆人，奉我主之命，保护和教诲众生。我想见见你们，上帝的仆人，并且尽我之所能教诲你们。"

老人互相看看，笑了，但仍然不吭声。

主教说："请告诉我，你们是怎样拯救自己的灵魂，在这座岛上为上帝效劳的。"

第二个隐士叹口气，看看年岁最长的那位。那位笑了，说："我们不知道怎样为上帝效劳，只是为自己——上帝的仆人——效劳，出力。"

"那你们是怎样向上帝祈祷的呢？"主教问。

那位答道："是这样的：你们是三位，我们是三位，请怜悯我们。"

年岁最长的说完，三人都抬头看着天，重复道：

"你们是三位[①]，我们是三位，请怜悯我们！"

主教笑了。

"你们对三位一体[②]之说显然已略知一二，"他道，"但你们祈祷的方式不对。你们几位可谓虔诚，深得我的好感。我知道，你们希望让主高兴，但不知道怎样为主效劳。祷告不是这样做的，听好了，我来教你们。我教给你们的不是我自己的一套，而是主在《圣经》中教所有人向主祈祷时说的话。"

主教向三隐士说起了上帝怎样向人类显灵和圣父、圣子、圣灵是怎么回事。

[①] 指圣父、圣子、圣灵。
[②] 指基督教中圣父、圣子、圣灵合成一位神。

他说:"圣子来到人间拯救人们,他教我们这样祈祷,你们听着,跟我说:'我父'。"

第一位老人跟着道"我父",第二个也道"我父",第三个也道"我父"。

"你在天国,"主教又道。

第一个隐士跟着说了"你在天国",但第二个就走了样,高个子也说不好。高个子嘴上长满了胡须,口齿不清;年岁特别大的那位没有了牙齿,也念得含混不清。

主教又说了一遍,三个老人跟着学。主教坐到一块石头上,老人站到他面前,看着他的嘴,一个字一个字模仿。主教累了一天,每个字得说上二十、三十、上百遍,老人跟着学。他们念错了他就纠正,叫他们重新来过。

主教直到把主的祈祷文全教给他们,使他们不但能跟着念,而且能独立念以后,才离开岛上。当中一个首先学会,单独从头至尾念了一遍。主教叫他反复说,终于另外两个也会了。

天快黑了,月亮从海面升起,主教才起身回船。临走时,老人一齐鞠躬,头弯到地上。他扶起他们,一个个亲吻,叫他们按他教的祈祷,然后坐上小船,回到大船。

他坐在小船上,小船往大船划,他还听见三隐士高声念主的祈祷。小船靠近大船后,他们的声音听不到了,但借着月光他还看见他们仍旧站在岸边没动,最矮的居中,高个子在右,中等个在左。主教一上大船,船起锚了,帆张了开来。风鼓满帆,船起航了,主教坐在船尾,看着岛渐渐远去。开始他还能见到三隐士,但不久人消逝了,只有海岛依稀可辨。最后岛也消逝了,见到的就是海,在月光下泛着银波。

朝圣者躺下睡了，甲板上静悄悄的。主教没有睡意，独自坐在船尾，凝视着海岛消逝的方向，想着几位好老人。他猜他们学会了主的祈祷词一定高兴，他感谢上帝派他来指教和帮助了这几个至诚至信的人。

主教就这样坐着，想着，凝视着海岛消逝的方向。月光在他眼前随着海波的起伏而跳动、闪烁。突然，顺着海面反射的一道月光看去，他发现了一个白东西在闪光。是只海鸥呢？还是一艘小船的帆？主教定睛瞧着，在猜。

"一定是艘小船在追我们，"他想，"但奇怪，这船行驶得非常快，刚才离得很远，现在近多了。不可能是船，是船怎么没有帆呢？是什么不知道，反正跟在我们后面，想赶上我们。"

他看不清那东西是什么：既不是船，也不是鸟，也不是鱼！说是人又太大，而且人不可能在海面跑。主教起身对舵手说：

"你看，朋友，那是什么？那是什么？"主教连问了两声，他还没有看清，原来是三位隐士在水上跑，周身洁白，胡须亮闪闪，飞快向大船靠近，似乎船根本就没有动。

舵手一看，吓得丢开了舵。

"哟，天哪！隐士追上来啦，踩在水里就像走在平地一样快！"

旅客听他一叫，连忙起身，涌到船尾，见三隐士手牵手追了上来，旁边的两个打着手势要船停下来。三人的脚没有动，是在水上滑行。船还没有来得及停，三隐士就到了船边，昂着头同声说：

上帝的仆人，我们把你教的忘了。我们反复念的时候还记得，刚一停马上忘了一个字，现在全忘了，什么都不记得了，请你再教教吧。"

主教划了个十字，躬身站在船边，说：

"上帝的使臣,各位自己的祈祷能上达天听,我教不了各位。请为我们这些罪人祈祷吧!"

主教向老人们深深鞠着躬,老人们回转身,往来的方向去了。在他们消失的地方,出现了一道亮光,直到天明后才消失。

The Father

Björnstjerne Björnson

The man whose story is here to be told was the wealthiest and most influential person in his parish; his name was Thord Overaas. He appeared in the priest's study one day, tall and earnest.

"I have gotten a son," said he, "and I wish to present him for baptism."

"What shall his name be?"

"Finn—after my father."

"And the sponsors?"

They were mentioned, and proved to be the best men and women of Thord's relations in the parish.

"Is there anything else?" inquired the priest, and looked up.

The peasant hesitated a little.

"I should like very much to have him baptized by himself," said he, finally.

"That is to say on a week-day?"

"Next Saturday, at twelve o'clock noon."

"Is there anything else?" inquired the priest.

"There is nothing else"; and the peasant twirled his cap, as though he were about to go.

Then the priest rose. "There is yet this, however," said he, and walking toward Thord, he took him by the hand and looked gravely into his eyes: "God grant that the child may become a blessing to you!"

One day sixteen years later, Thord stood once more in the priest's study.

"Really, you carry your age astonishingly well, Thord," said the priest; for he saw no change whatever in the man.

"That is because I have no troubles," replied Thord.

To this the priest said nothing, but after a while he asked: "What is your pleasure this evening?"

"I have come this evening about that son of mine who is going to be confirmed tomorrow."

"He is a bright boy."

"I did not wish to pay the priest until I heard what number the boy would have when he takes his place in church tomorrow."

"He will stand number one."

"So I have heard; and here are ten dollars for the priest."

"Is there anything else I can do for you?" inquired the priest, fixing his eyes on Thord.

"There is nothing else."

Thord went out.

Eight years more rolled by, and then one day a noise was heard outside of the priest's study, for many men were approaching, and at their head was Thord, who entered first.

The priest looked up and recognized him.

"You come well attended this evening, Thord," said he.

"I am here to request that the banns may be published for my son; he is about to marry Karen Storliden, daughter of Gudmund, who stands here beside me."

"Why, that is the richest girl in the parish."

"So they say," replied the peasant, stroking back his hair with one hand.

The priest sat a while as if in deep thought, then entered the names in his book, without making any comments, and the men wrote their signatures underneath. Thord laid three dollars on the table.

"One is all I am to have," said the priest.

"I know that very well; but he is my only child, I want to do it handsomely."

The priest took the money.

"This is now the third time, Thord, that you have come here on your son's account."

"But now I am through with him," said Thord, and folding up his pocket-book he said farewell and walked away.

The men slowly followed him.

A fortnight later, the father and son were rowing across the lake, one calm, still day, to Storliden to make arrangements for the wedding.

"This thwart is not secure," said the son, and stood up to straighten the seat on which he was sitting.

At the same moment the board he was standing on slipped from under him; he threw out his arms, uttered a shriek, and fell overboard.

"Take hold of the oar!" shouted the father, springing to his feet and holding out the oar.

But when the son had made a couple of efforts he grew stiff.

"Wait a moment!" cried the father, and began to row toward his son. Then the son rolled over on his back, gave his father one long look, and sank.

Thord could scarcely believe it; he held the boat still, and stared at the spot where his son had gone down, as though he must surely come to the surface once again. There rose some bubbles, then some more, and finally one large one that burst; and the lake lay there as smooth and bright as a mirror again.

For three days and three nights people saw the father rowing round and round the spot, without taking either food or sleep; he was dragging the lake for the body of his son. And toward morning of the third day he found it, and carried it in his arms up over the hills to his gard.

It might have been about a year from that day, when the priest, late one autumn evening, heard someone in the passage outside of the door, carefully trying to find the latch. The priest opened the door, and in walked a tall, thin man, with bowed form and white hair. The priest looked long at him before he recognized him. It was Thord.

"Are you out walking so late?" said the priest, and stood still in front of him.

"Ah, yes! it is late," said Thord, and took a seat.

The priest sat down also, as though waiting. A long, long silence followed. At last Thord said:

"I have something with me that I should like to give to the poor; I want it to be invested as a legacy in my son's name."

He rose, laid some money on the table, and sat down again. The priest counted it.

"It is a great deal of money," said he.

"It is half the price of my gard. I sold it today." The priest sat long in silence. At last he asked, but gently:

"What do you propose to do now, Thord?"

"Something better."

They sat there for a while, Thord with downcast eyes, the priest with his eyes fixed on Thord. Presently the priest said, slowly and softly:

"I think your son has at last brought you a true blessing."

"Yes, I think so myself," said Thord, looking up, while two big tears coursed slowly down his cheeks.

父 亲

〔挪〕比昂斯滕·比昂松

我要讲的这个故事中的人是他所在教区最富裕、最有影响的人,名叫索德·奥弗拉斯。有一天,这位高个子虔诚地来到牧师的书斋。

"我生了个儿子,"他说,"想请您给他行洗礼。"

"取什么名字?"

"与我父亲的一样,叫芬恩。"

"教父母呢?"

他说了姓名,原来是本教区索德的亲戚中品德最好的人。

"还有什么事吗?"牧师说完抬头看看他。

庄稼人犹豫起来。

"能不能——能不能单独给他行洗礼?"他终于说出了口。

"那得不在星期天。"

"就星期六中午12点吧。"

"还有事吗?"牧师问。

"没有了。"庄稼人转着手中的帽子,准备告退。

"别走,还有呢,"这时牧师却站了起来,走到索德跟前,握住他的手,看着他,衷心祝愿道:"上帝保佑,这孩子是你的福分!"

16年后的一天,索德又一次来到牧师的书斋。

"索德,你保养得真好,一点没见老。"牧师看到他一点没变样,说道。

"那是因为我没有心事。"索德答道。

牧师没有接下去说,过了一会儿才问:"你今晚来有何贵干?"

"明天我儿子要行坚信礼,我这才晚上来了。"

"这孩子挺好。"

"钱我一定付,只是想先问问,明天上教堂您让他站在什么地方。"

"让他站首位。"

"那就好,这是10元谢金。"

"你还有什么事吗?"牧师问,眼盯着索德。

"没有了。"

索德告辞了。

一晃又是8年。有一天牧师的书斋外闹哄哄,来了许多人,走在最前面的是索德,第一个进了书斋。

牧师一眼认出了他。

"你今天怎么带着这么一大帮人,索德?"他问。

"我来请您给我儿子发个结婚预告,他准备与古德芒德的女儿卡伦·斯托丽登结婚。我身边这位就是亲家。"

"好极了,本教区这姑娘家最有钱。"

"大家都这么说。"庄稼人答道,用一只手往脑后理理头发。

牧师端坐了一会儿,像在仔细考虑什么,然后在册子里将两人的名字登记下来,没说话,两亲家在册子下方签了名。索德把3元钱摆到桌上。

父　亲

"只要1元。"牧师说。

"这我知道。我只有一个儿子,多花些钱心甘情愿。"

牧师把钱收下了。

"索德,你为儿子的事这是第三趟来。"

"以后不需要为他再跑了。"索德说,合上钱包,告退了。

其他人在他后面慢慢跟着。

两星期后,父子俩划着船过湖往斯托丽登家,为办喜事做准备,湖上风平浪静。

"这横板不牢靠。"儿子说,站起身把他坐的一块板放平。

就在这时,脚下的板一滑,他手一伸,尖叫一声,掉下了水。

"抓住桨!"父亲高喊着,一纵身起来,伸出桨。

然而,儿子挣扎几下,不行了。

"坚持一下!"父亲喊着往儿子身边划,可是儿子翻个身,看父亲一眼,沉下去了。

索德简直不敢相信,停住船,直望着儿子沉下去的地方,仿佛儿子一定会浮上来。然而浮上来的只有一串小气泡,没一会儿又是一串,最后是一个大气泡,浮上来便爆了。湖水恢复了平静,像是一面明镜。

人们只见父亲划着船在出事地点打转,接连三天三夜没吃没睡,他在湖上打捞儿子的尸体。大约到第三天上午,他终于看到了尸体,把他抱到自家山上埋了。

这以后一年左右,在一个秋天的深夜,牧师听到门外的过道里有人在轻轻摸着找门闩。他打开门,一个又高又瘦、驼着背、满头白发的人走了进来。牧师看了很久才认出是索德。

"你这么晚了还出门?"牧师问道,一动没动站在他面前。

"是呀，是晚了。"索德说，坐了下来。

牧师也坐下了，像在等对方说话。一阵长时间的沉默。最后，索德开口了。

"我有笔钱送给穷苦人，想以我儿子的名义捐赠。"

他起身把钱放在桌上，然后又坐下。牧师点了数。

"这是相当大一笔钱！"他说。

"这是我产业的半数，今天卖掉的。"

牧师坐着很久没说话。最后他发问了，但声音很轻。

"索德，那你今后怎么办呢？"

"您尽管放心。"

两人坐了好长时间，索德的眼垂着，牧师的眼光始终落在索德身上。牧师后来说话了，又慢又轻：

"我认为，你的儿子最后使你受到了真正的祝福。"

"您的话对，我也这样想。"索德说，抬起头，两滴大大的泪珠慢慢流下了他的双颊。

How the Devil Lost His Poncho

Ricardo Palma

Once, when Our Lord was traveling about the world upon His gentle little donkey, restoring sight to the blind and recovering the use of their limbs to the lame. He came into a region where there was nothing at all but sand. Here and there was a rustling, slender palm under whose shade Gentle Jesus would stop with His disciples, who would fill their sacks with dates.

As eternal as the Lord Himself seemed that desert, with neither beginning nor end. The travelers, heavy-hearted, prepared to spend the night with only a starry sky for shelter, when, picked out by the last ray of the setting sun, the silhouette of a belfry showed upon the horizon.

Lord Jesus, shading His eyes to see better, said: "I see a town over there. Peter, you know all about geography. Could you tell me what city that is?"

St. Peter grinned at the compliment.

"Master, that is the city of Ica."

"Well, then. Let us move along."

The donkeys jogged along briskly, and they all soon reached town. Jesus, just before they entered, gently reminded Peter that he must not lose his temper. "You're always getting us into trouble with your temper," said Our Lord. "Please try to keep it under control."

The people of the city rolled out the welcome mat for these illustrious visitors. Even though the little party was anxious to be on its way, the townsfolk made everything so pleasant that a week had passed before you could whistle. During that week the city of Ica seemed like the alcove of Paradise. Doctors and dentists sat idly in their offices, and the druggists made up no prescriptions. Not a complaint was registered before the advocates. There was not even a cross word between husband or wife, nor any—miracle of miracles!—nor any malice expressed by mothers and sisters-in-law.

How long this idyllic existence might have gone on nobody knows, for on the eighth day Our Lord received a message calling Him to return to Jerusalem to stand between Mary Magdalene and the unfriendly Samaritan women. Rather than bother the hospitable folk of Ica with long-winded excuses and explanations, the Gentle Traveler decided to leave suddenly, during the night, with His companions.

Early the next morning, then, when the city council called to give a special morning concert, they found their guests gone.

But after He and His party had gone several miles from the city, the Lord turned and blessed the little town of Ice in the name of the Father, the Son, and the Holy Ghost.

Naturally such a succession of events could not remain out of the newspapers. The Devil, therefore, received the news by the earliest mail. He gnashed his teeth with chagrin and swore that no one could steal a march on him. Calling together the chief of his demons he had them disguise themselves as disciples. The art of make-up and disguise is certainly close to the heart of the Horned One. So, putting on high boots and ponchos, he and his party started on their journey.

The citizens of Ica, seeing the travelers in the distance, rushed out to greet them, hoping this time that The Lord and His companions would remain with them forever.

Up to this time, of course, there had been happiness and content in Ica such as existed nowhere else. The citizens paid their taxes without complaint, let the politicians run politics, and regarded helping their neighbors as the most important thing in life.

Needless to say this bliss made the Devil quiver with rage, and he determined to upset the apple cart at the first opportunity.

Just at the time the Devil arrived, a marriage was about to take place between a young man and a young girl made for each other as ewe for ram; here was a perfect match.

Satan waited his time, as he always does, and when the toasts began to go down the thirsty gullets, the liquor produced not the friendly elevation of spirits that banquets should foster, but a coarse, indecent frenzy. Insulting remarks were hurled at the bride, and several women made advances towards the handsome groom.

And things went further than this. For all the doctors and dentists and druggists and advocates began to do a rushing business. Family squabbles flourished, mothers-in-law seemed to make up for time lost; wives remembered it was their duty and prerogative to whine and cry for new dresses and expensive jewelry. To top it all, the city council decided it was time to levy new taxes. It was obvious, wasn't it, that only the Devil could be at the bottom of this?

In the meantime the poor bride, trying desperately to stop the fighting and brawling, kept muttering, "It must be the Devil gotten into them. That's what it must be."

She rushed to the Evil One in disguise and tugged at his poncho.

"Oh, Lord," she cried. "They are all going to kill one another."

"What do I care?" sneered old Cloven Hoof. "It's no concern of mine. The worse it gets, the better I like it."

The poor girl, amazed, berated him.

"What a heart Your Excellency has. It's like a stone. You must be the Devil himself." And she made the sign of the cross with her fingers.

No sooner had the Evil One seen her gesture than he tried to race from the scene. But she had a strong hold on his poncho, and he had to duck his head through the opening, leaving the cape in the girl's hand.

The Devil's party disappeared in a puff, but, since then, every once in a while, old Satan comes back to Ica, searching for his poncho. Whenever this happens the liquor starts flowing, of course; and things get really lively all over again.

魔王怎样丢了大氅

〔秘〕里卡多·帕尔马

有一次我主骑着他那匹温和的小毛驴巡视世界，使双目失明的人重见光明，使瘸子的腿恢复正常。他来到一个地方，那儿是片茫茫沙漠，走不多远就有一棵舞姿婆娑、体态苗条的棕榈树，仁慈的耶稣和他的门徒到了树荫下便停下来，把棕榈果装进袋子里。

我主是永生的，而这片沙漠似乎无边无际。这一行人见没有了走出沙漠的希望，打算在星空下过夜。正在这时，在地平线上，在落日的最后一道光辉中，隐隐约约出现了一座钟楼。

耶稣手搭凉棚，看了个清楚，说："那是一座城。彼得，你熟悉地理，知道那座城是什么地方吗？"

圣彼得受到称赞，笑了。

"我主，那是伊卡城。"

"好吧，我们上那儿去。"

驴子加快脚步，不久到了伊卡城。快进城时耶稣轻声提醒彼得，火性子千万不能发作。我主说："你脾气不好，总是给我们招来麻烦。无论如何你得耐住性子。"

伊卡城的人铺了地毯欢迎贵宾。虽然耶稣与门徒急于赶路，但伊卡人的盛情难却，过了一星期，还是叫人开口告辞不得。这一星期里，伊卡城成了乐园：大夫坐着无事可干，药剂师没处方可配，律师那儿无人上门，夫妻不见拌嘴，而奇迹中的奇迹是，婆媳不见失和。

这种升平景象可能维持多久不得而知，只知到第八天，我主得到消息，要回耶路撒冷调解玛利亚①与不大友好的撒马利亚女人之间的纠纷。仁慈的耶稣不愿费尽口舌向好客的伊卡人解释，决定连夜带着门徒不辞而别。

第二天一大早，市议会准备特地举行一次音乐晨会，才发现客人已不见踪影。

其实这一行人出城数里后，耶稣回转身以圣父、圣子、圣灵的名义向小小的伊卡城表示了祝福。

自然这一连串的事不可能不见报。所以第一班邮差一到，魔王就知道了消息，气得咬牙切齿。他不甘心让人占了上风，把手下魔头找来，叫他们化装成耶稣的门徒。这头上长角的家伙最爱乔装打扮。于是，他和手下一伙人穿上高统靴，披上大氅，上路了。

伊卡城的人远远看见客人便跑来迎接，希望这一次耶稣和门徒能永远留下来。

当然，这以前伊卡城的人快快乐乐，心满意足，哪个地方的人也比不上他们。他们纳税没有怨言，让政治家经营政治，把帮助邻居看成生活中的头等大事。

不用说，这样的好光景叫魔王气得发抖，他决定一有机会便下手。

---

① 玛利亚原为一邪恶淫荡的女人，后悔罪向善而得救，载于圣经路加福音。

魔王到时，一位青年与一位姑娘正要举行婚礼，他们是天生的一对。

撒旦等待着，他从不缺乏耐心。客人大口喝下酒以后，不像在一般宴会上那样，喜气洋洋，说说笑笑，却粗暴无礼，发起狂来，大骂新娘，好些女人往漂亮的新郎身上靠。

事情并没有这样收场。医生、药剂师、律师的生意兴隆起来，家庭纠纷层出不穷，做婆婆的无事生非，做妻子的大吵大闹要买新衣，要戴昂贵的宝石，认为这是理所应当的事。最糟的是，市议会决定开征新税。这一切都是因为魔王在捣乱，难道还用说吗？

可怜巴巴的新娘费尽苦心也没能阻止客人胡闹，嘴里不停地嘀咕："这些人一定是着了魔，一定是这么回事。"

她跑到乔装打扮的魔王身边，扯着他的大氅，叫道：

"主哦，他们要厮杀起来啦！"

"那怕什么？"撒旦冷笑道，"不关我的事。闹吧，闹得越凶越好。"

可怜的姑娘吃了一惊，骂起来。

"你这家伙心肠多硬！像是石头！你一定是魔王。"她用手指画了个十字。

魔王一看到她的手势，拔腿想溜。但是姑娘紧紧拽住了他的大氅，他只好一缩头钻出大氅跑了。大氅脱在了姑娘手里。

魔王的喽啰们转眼间也无影无踪。但后来撒旦常回伊卡城找他的大氅。每当他来时，酒不免又把人醉得昏昏沉沉，什么都弄得乱七八糟。

Luck

Mark Twain

It was at a banquet in London in honor of one of the two or three conspicuously illustrious English military names of this generation. For reasons which will presently appear, I will withhold his real name and titles and call him Lieutenant-General Lord Arthur Scoresby, Y. C., K. C. B., etc, etc, etc. What a fascination there is in a renowned name! There sat the man, in actual flesh, whom I had heard of so many thousands of times since that day, thirty years before, when his name shot suddenly to the zenith from a Crimean battle field, to remain forever celebrated. It was food and drink to me to look, and look, and look at that demigod; scanning, searching, noting: the quietness, the reserve, the noble gravity of his countenance; the simple honesty that expressed itself all over him; the sweet unconsciousness of his greatness—unconsciousness of the hundreds of admiring eyes fastened upon him, unconsciousness of the deep, loving, sincere worship welling out of the breasts of those people and flowing toward him.

The clergyman at my left was an old acquaintance of mine—

clergyman now, but had spent the first half of his life in the camp and field and as an instructor in the military school at Woolwich. Just at the moment I have been talking about a veiled and singular light glimmered in his eyes and he leaned down and muttered confidentially to me—indicating the hero of the banquet with a gesture:

"Privately—he's an absolute fool."

This verdict was a great surprise to me. If its subject had been Napoleon, or Socrates, or Solomon, my astonishment could not have been greater. Two things I was well aware of: that the Reverend[①] was a man of strict veracity and that his judgment of men was good. Therefore I knew, beyond doubt or question, that the world was mistaken about this hero: he *was* a fool. So I meant to find out, at a convenient moment, how the Reverend, all solitary and alone, had discovered the secret.

Some days later the opportunity came, and this is what the Reverend told me:

About forty years ago I was an instructor in the military academy at Woolwich. I was present in one of the sections when young Scoresby underwent his preliminary examination. I was touched to the quick with pity, for the rest of the class answered up brightly and handsomely, while he—why, dear me, he didn't know anything, so to speak. He was evidently good, and sweet, and lovable, and guileless; and so it was exceedingly painful to see him stand there, as serene as a graven image, and deliver himself of answers which were verily miraculous for stupidity

---

① the Reverend：指"牧师"，注意首字母大写。

and ignorance. All the compassion in me was aroused in his behalf. I said to myself, when he comes to be examined again he will be flung over, of course; so it will be simply a harmless act of charity to ease his fall as much as I can. I took him aside and found that he knew a little of Caesar's history; and as he didn't know anything else, I went to work and drilled him like a galley-slave on a certain line of stock① questions concerning Caesar which I knew would be used. If you'll believe me, he went through with flying colors on examination day! He went through on that purely superficial "cram,"② and got compliments too, while others, who knew a thousand times more than he, got plucked③. By some strangely lucky accident—an accident not likely to happen twice in a century—he was asked no question outside of the narrow limits of his drill.

It was stupefying. Well, all through his course I stood by him, with something of the sentiment which a mother feels for a crippled child; and he always saved himself, just by miracle apparently.

Now, of course, the thing that would expose him and kill him at last was mathematics. I resolved to make his death as easy as I could; so I drilled him and crammed him, and crammed him and drilled him, just on the line of questions which the examiners would be most likely to use, and then launched him on his fate. Well, sir, try to conceive of the

---

① stock：此处义为 common（常见的）。
② on that purely superficial "cram"：此处 on 义为 "依照" "根据"，cram 指为应付考试而临时强记的东西。
③ pluck：此词有一义为 "拔毛"，本处可说是个幽默用法，义为这些学生没有得到多少分，考糟了。

Luck

result: to my consternation, he took the first prize! And with it he got a perfect ovation in the way of compliments.

Sleep? There was no more sleep for me for a week. My conscience tortured me day and night. What I had done I had done purely through charity, and only to ease the poor youth's fall. I never had dreamed of any such preposterous results as the thing that had happened. I felt as guilty and miserable as Frankenstein. Here was a wooden-head whom I had put in the way of glittering promotions and prodigious responsibilities, and but one thing could happen: he and his responsibilities would all go to ruin together at the first opportunity.

The Crimean War had just broken out. Of course there had to be a war, I say to myself. We could have peace and give this donkey a chance to die before he is found out. I waited for the earthquake. It came. And it made me reel when it did come. He was actually gazetted to a captaincy in a marching regiment! Better men grow old and gray in the service before they climb to a sublimity like that. And who could ever have foreseen that they would go and put such a load of responsibility on such green and inadequate shoulders? I could just barely have stood it if they had made him a cornet; but a captain—think of it! I thought my hair would turn white.

Consider what I did—I who so loved repose and inaction. I said to myself, I am responsible to the country for this, and I must go along with him and protect the country against him as far as I can. So I took my poor little capital and went with a sigh and bought a cornetcy in his regiment, and away we went to the field.

And there—oh, dear, it was awful. Blunders?—why, he never did anything *but* blunder. But, you see, nobody was in the fellow's secret. Everybody had him focused wrong, and necessarily misinterpreted his performance every time. Consequently they took his idiotic blunders for inspirations of genius. They did, honestly! His mildest blunders were enough to make a man in his right mind cry; and they did make me cry—and rage and rave, too, privately. And the thing that kept me always in a sweat of apprehension was the fact that every fresh blunder he made always increased the luster of his reputation! I kept saying to myself, he'll get so high that when discovery does finally come it will be like the sun falling out of the sky①.

He went right along up, from grade to grade, over the dead bodies of his superiors, until at last, in the hottest moment of the battle of— down went our colonel, and my heart jumped into my mouth, for Scoresby was next in rank! Now for it, said I; we'll all land in Sheol② in ten minutes, sure.

The battle was awfully hot; the allies were steadily giving way all over the field. Our regiment occupied a position that was vital; a blunder now must be destruction. At this crucial moment, what does this immortal fool do but detach the regiment from its place③ and order

---

① it will be like the sun falling out of the sky：此处 it 指 discovery。
② Sheol：指"阴间"，典出圣经。
③ what does this immortal fool do but detach the regiment from its place：此处按语法规范的说法是 what this immortal fool does is but detach ... 本句的 but 是副词，义即 only; detach 前省略了不定式符号 to。

a charge over a neighboring hill where there wasn't a suggestion of an enemy! "There you go!" I said to myself; "this *is* the end at last."

And away we did go, and were over the shoulder of the hill before the insane movement could be discovered and stopped. And what did we find? An entire and unsuspected Russian army in reserve! And what happened? We were eaten up? That is necessarily what would have happened in ninety-nine cases out of a hundred. But no; those Russians argued that no single regiment would come browsing around there at such a time. It must be the entire English army, and that the sly Russian game was detected and blocked; so they turned tail, and away they went, pell-mell, over the hill and down into the field, in wild confusion, and we after them①; they themselves broke the solid Russian center in the field, and tore through, and in no time there was the most tremendous rout you ever saw, and the defeat of the allies was turned into a sweeping and splendid victory! Marshal Canrobert looked on, dizzy with astonishment, admiration, and delight; and sent right off for Scoresby, and hugged him, and decorated him on the field in presence of all the armies!

And what was Scoresby's blunder that time? Merely the mistaking his right hand for his left②—that was all. An order had come to him to fall back and support our right; and instead, he fell *forward* and went over the hill to the left. But the name he won that day as a marvelous

---

① we after them: 此处 we 与 after 间按语法规范应有动词 ran。
② the mistaking his right hand for his left: 此处按语法规范不应用定冠词 the。

military genius filled the world with his glory, and the glory will never fade while history books last.

He is just as good and sweet and lovable and unpretending as a man can be, but he doesn't know enough to come in when it rains. Now that is absolutely true. He is the supremest ass in the universe; and until half an hour ago nobody knew it but himself and me. He has been pursued, day by day and year by year, by a most phenomenal and astonishing luckiness. He has been a shining soldier in all our wars for a generation; he has littered his whole military life with blunders, and yet has never committed one that didn't make him a knight or a baronet or a lord or something. Look at his breast; why, he is just clothed in domestic and foreign decorations. Well, sir, every one of them is the record of some shouting stupidity or other; and, taken together, they are proof than the very best thing in all this world that can befall a man[①] is to be born lucky. I say again, as I said at the banquet, Scoresby's an absolute fool.

---

① that can befall a man: 作定语从句，其先行词为 thing。

运 气

〔美〕马克·吐温

事情得从伦敦的一次宴会说起,宴会是为一位赫赫有名的英国军事家举行的,他这样的军事家在当代是数一数二的。由于诸位马上会知道的原因,我不说他的真名实姓和头衔了,就称他为阿瑟·斯科斯比中将爵爷吧。当然,称他为别的什么也完全可以。显赫的声名多叫人倾倒呀!30年前,克里米亚战争①让他威震环宇,功勋永垂青史,其大名我已听过成千上万次了,而这个人现在就坐在我眼前。我朝着这位神明似的人物看呀,看呀,看呀,像吃着佳肴,饮着美酒。我观察着,思索着,领悟着,发现他脸上有一种平静、矜持和贵人的庄重,而周身又露出一种朴质的诚实,而且他对自己的伟大无知无觉,对注视着他的几百双眼无知无觉,对满座出自肺腑的深厚、热烈、诚挚的崇拜无知无觉。

坐在我左边的牧师是我的老相识。他现在是牧师,但曾在伍

---

① 1853—1856年的克里米亚战争中,一方为英国、法国、土耳其和萨丁尼亚(当时为一王国,现属意大利),另一方为俄国。

利奇①军校当过教员,前半辈子都在军营和战场度过。在我上面说的那一刻,他的眼亮了一下,就那么偷偷一下。他凑过身子,指指宴会的主角,轻声对我说:

"私底下说,他是个地道的傻瓜。"

听到这话我大吃一惊。如果听到拿破仑、苏格拉底、所罗门是地道的傻瓜,我吃惊的程度也不过如此。有两点我是十分清楚的:一是这位牧师严格尊重事实,二是他看人很有眼光。所以,我知道,毫无疑问大家都搞错了,这位英雄不是英雄,一定是个傻瓜。于是我决心等到一个方便的时候打听打听,牧师先生怎样独具慧眼,发现了这个秘密。

过几天机会来了。牧师先生对我是这样说的:

大约40年前,我在伍利奇军校当教员。斯科斯比参加初试时,我也在考场上。全班别的学生对答如流,可他——哟,我的天,他什么也不知道,叫我觉得怪可怜的。看外表他挺好,逗人喜欢,可爱、诚实,所以眼见他站在那儿像尊雕像一动不动,答话牛头不对马嘴,觉得特别难受。我打心底里怜悯他。我想,等到下次考试,不用问,他非被刷下来不可,所以尽我最大的力量帮他一把,不让他败得太惨,就纯粹成了一件问心无愧的善事。我把他找去,发现他还知道凯撒②的一些事情。由于他别的什么都不懂,我就越俎代庖、煞费苦心地教他准备回答我估计会问到的有关凯撒的常识问题。不容你信不信,反正考试那天他大获全胜!就凭那点完全现买现卖的货色,他过关了,还受到称赞,而别的人虽然知识比他多

---

① 这个故事虽纯属虚构,但伍利奇一地却并非虚构,它是伦敦东部一自治区,且确为一兵工厂与陆军军官学校所在地。
② 凯撒(公元前102—前44),罗马将领,曾远征大不列颠。

一千倍，倒考糟了。说来也巧，巧得遇上了千载难逢的机会，问他的问题没有一个超出他准备的那点儿范围。

事情真是那么令人难以思议。你看，在整个学习期间，我都关心他，就出自一种类似母亲可怜瘸腿孩子的同情，而他总是遇到奇迹，化险为夷。

当然，他终究要露馅，要完蛋的功课是数学。我决心不让他完蛋得太难堪，于是教他，给他划范围；给他划范围，教他，准备那些主考人很可能会问到的问题，然后让他听天由命。唉，先生，你想想结果如何？谁知他得了一等奖！由于是一等奖，他受到热烈称赞，大出了风头。

还想睡觉吗？我有一星期时间睡不着。良心日日夜夜严厉责备着我。我做的事单纯出于怜悯，仅仅为了不让这可怜的年轻人败得太惨。我做梦也没有料到会有现在这样的荒唐结果。我尝到了弗兰肯斯坦①经历过的内疚和痛苦。他长了个木瓜脑袋，而我却使他能飞黄腾达，肩负重任。但是，有一种情况也许会发生：时机一到，他和他肩负的责任要一股脑儿地完蛋。

刚好克里米亚战争爆发了。我想，就是得打仗。我们不能安享太平，让这笨猪似的家伙至死都不被人识破。我等待着发生地震。地震的确发生了，可是震得我昏头转向。打开公报一看，他竟被任命为一个即将开拔的团的上尉。比他强的人在军队中熬到头发全白还爬不上那样的位子。谁会料到他们竟把这样的重担放在这样一个乳臭未干、一无所能的人肩上？如果叫他当个旗官，

---

① 弗兰肯斯坦系英国作家玛丽·雪莱1818年出版的《弗兰肯斯坦》一书的男主角。他是一位年轻的医学研究生，创造了一个怪物，但自己为怪物所毁。

那还差不多，可现在是上尉，你想想！我真要愁白了头。

猜猜吧，我怎么办？我本是个多一事不如少一事的好静的人，然而我想，这件事我对不起国家，我得跟着他去，尽自己的力量别让国家在他手里遭殃。于是，我拿出自己的一份小小家当，长叹一声，买了他那个团的旗官头衔。就这样我们上战场了。

可真是——哎哟哟，太糟糕了。是干荒唐事了吗？哼！他一辈子除了荒唐事，别的事一件也干不来。但是，你知道，没有人清楚这家伙的底细。谁都错看了他，每次都对他的行为做了错误的理解。因此，他们把傻瓜的荒唐看成了天才的机灵。他们诚心佩服！如果头脑清醒，谁见到他干的荒唐事，哪怕最小的一件，都准会大吃一惊。这些事的的确确叫我吃惊，还暗地里生气、发急。我百思不得其解的是，为什么他每多干一件荒唐事，名声就多一份光彩。我总认为，他要是爬得太高了，一朝失足，非摔个粉身碎骨不可。

他一帆风顺，步步高升，上司的尸体成了他的垫脚石。到最后，当仗打到某个地方时，我们的上校完了。我的心一下提到了嗓子眼儿，因为斯科斯比只比他官低一级！这下可好，我想，不出十分钟我们就得一命呜呼。

仗打得十分激烈，盟军在整个战场节节败退。我们团占据着一个决定胜负的阵地，哪怕出一个差错就会全盘完蛋。在这个关键时刻，这位百世流芳的傻瓜干了什么！他把全团撤离阵地，下令往邻近一个连敌人的影子也见不到的山头上冲。"等着瞧吧，"我暗暗地想，"这一次总算是完了！"

我们果然转移了，还没等人发现和阻止这种疯狂的举动，就上了半山腰。我们看到了什么？整整一个没有预料到的俄国军团！接着怎么样呢？我们被吃掉了吗？本来，百分之九十九的可能是这样。可是没有。俄国人断定在这种时刻，单单一个团的兵力不会往那儿闯，一定是英军全体出动了，俄军的暗中行动被侦察到了，被破坏掉了。于是他们转身就走，乱套了，山上山下全是人，仓皇逃命。我们追了过去。俄国人在战场上的中坚力量被自己搞垮了，摧毁了，马上出现了你难得见到的全线崩溃，原先败退的盟军反而大获全胜，战果辉煌。康罗贝尔元帅①看得眼花缭乱，又吃惊，又佩服，又高兴，马上催人把斯科斯比叫来，拥抱他，在战场上当着所有军队的将士给他授勋。

那次斯科斯比荒唐在哪里呢？没别的，仅因为把右手当成了左手。他奉命后撤，支援右翼，结果弄反了，向前进，往左边的山头冲。但是那天他打了胜仗，赢得军事天才的美名，让全世界都知道了他的荣誉，只要有历史书存在，他的荣誉就不会消失。

他这个人要说多好、多可亲可爱、多朴实，就有多好、多可亲可爱、多朴实，可是他屁也不懂，连下雨都不知道进屋。这一点不假。他是天下第一号大笨猪，半小时前了解这个底细的只有他自己和我。没有哪一天、哪一年，他不是福星高照。在一代人的时间里，无论哪次打仗，他都是位出色的战将；他的整个军事生涯充满了荒唐事，然而他干的荒唐事没有一件不使他升官晋级，晋级升官。你看他胸前，挂满了本国的、外国的勋章。嘿，先生，他的每枚勋章都记载着一件荒谬绝伦的事，但所有的勋章加起来却成了一条真理的最好证明：世界上最好的事是生来走运。我再说一遍，这话我在参加宴会时就说过：斯科斯比是个地道的傻瓜。

---

① 历史上确有其人，为法国元帅（1809—1895）。

The Doctor's Heroism

Villiers de L'Isle-Adam

To kill in order to cure!
—*Official Motto of the Broussais Hospital*

The extraordinary case of Doctor Hallidonhill is soon to be tried in London. The facts in the matter are these:

On the 20th of last May, the two great waiting rooms of the illustrious specialist were thronged with patients, holding their tickets in their hands.

At the entrance stood the cashier, wearing a long black frock coat; he took the indispensible fee of two guineas from each patient, tested the gold with a sharp tap of the hammer, and cried automactically, "All right."

In his glassed-in office, around which were ranged great tropical shrubs, each growing in a huge Japanese pot, sat the stiff little Doctor Hallidonhill. Beside him, at a little round table, his secretary kept writing out brief prescriptions. At the swinging doors, covered with red velvet studded with gold-headed nails, stood a giant valet whose duty it was to carry the feeble consumptives to the lobby whence they were lowered in a luxurious elevator as soon as the offcial signal, "Next!" had been given.

The patients entered with dim and glassy eyes, stripped to the waist, with their clothes thrown over their arms. As soon as they entered they received the application of the plessimeter and the tube on back and chest.

"Tick! tick! plaff! Breathe now! ... Plaf ... Good ..."

Then followed a prescription dictated in a second or two; then the well-known "Next!"

Every morning for three years, between nine o'clock and noon, this procession of sufferers filed past.

On this particular day, May 20th, just at the stroke of nine, a sort of long skeleton, with wild, wandering eyes, cavernous cheeks, and nude torso that looked like a parchment-covered cage lifted occasionally by a racking cough—in short a being so wasted that it seemed impossible for him to live—came in with a blue-fox skin mantle thrown over his arm, and tried to keep himself from falling by catching at the long leaves of the shrubs.

"Tick, tick, plaff! Oh, the devil! Can't do anything for you!" grumbled Doctor Hallidonhill. "What do you think I am—a coroner? In less than a week you will spit up the last cell of this left lung—the right is already riddled like a sieve! Next!"

The valet was just about to carry out the client, when the eminent therapeutist suddenly slapped himself on the forehead, and brusquely asked, with a dubious smile:

"Are you rich?"

"I'm a millionaire—much more than a millionaire," sobbed the unhappy being whom Hallidonhill thus peremptorily had dismissed from the world of the living.

"Very well, then. Go at once to Victoria Station. Take the eleven-o'clock express for Dover! Then the steamer for Calais. Then take the train from Calais to Marseilles—secure a sleeping car with steam in it! And then to Nice. There try to live on watercress for six months—nothing but watercress—no bread, no fruit, no wine, nor meats of any kind. One teaspoonful of iodized rainwater every two days. And watercress, watercress, watercress—pounded and brayed in its own juice ... that is your only chance—and still, let me tell you this: this supposed cure I know of only through hearsay; it is being dinned into my ears all the time; I don't believe in it the least bit. I suggest it only because yours seems to be a hopeless case, yet I think it is worse than absurd. Still, anything is possible ... Next!"

The consumptive Croesus[①] was carefully deposited in the cushioned car of the elevator; and the regular procession commenced through the office.

Six months later, the 3rd of November, just at the stroke of nine o'clock, a sort of giant, with a terrifying yet jovial voice whose tones

---

① 克罗伊斯, 吕底亚最后一代国王, 以财富甚多闻名。

shook every pane of glass in the doctor's office and set all the leaves of all the tropical plants atremble, a great chubby-cheeked colossus, clothed in rich furs—burst like a human bombshell through the sorrowful ranks of Doctor Hallidonhill's clients, and rushed, without ticket, into the sanctum of the Prince of Science, who had just come to sit down before his desk. He seized him round the body, and, bathing the wan and worn cheeks of the doctor in tears, kissed him noisily again and again. Then he set him down in his green armchair in an almost suffocated state.

"Two million francs—if you want," shouted the giant. "Or three million. I owe my breath to you—the sun, resistless passions, life—everything. Ask me for anything—anything at all."

"Who is this madman? Put him out of here," feebly protested the doctor, after a moment's prostration.

"Oh, no you don't," growled the giant, with a glance at the valet that made him recoil as from a blow. "The fact is," he continued, "I understand now, that even you, you my savior, cannot recognize me. I am the watercress man, the hopeless skeleton, the helpless patient. Nice. Watercress, watercress, watercress! Well, I've done my six months of watercress diet—look at your work now! See here—listen to that!"

And he began to drum upon his chest with two huge fists solid enough to shatter the skull of an ox.

"What!" cried the doctor, leaping to his feet, "you are—my gracious, are you the dying man whom I ..."

"Yes, yes, a thousand times yes!" yelled the giant. "I am the very man. The moment I landed yesterday evening I ordered a bronze statue of you; and I will secure you a monument in Westminster when you die."

Then dropping himself upon an immense sofa, whose springs creaked and groaned beneath his weight, he continued with a sigh of delight, and a beatific smile: "Ah, what a good thing life is!"

The doctor said something in a whisper, and the secretary and the valet left the room. Once alone with his resuscitated patient, Hallidonhill, stiff, wan and glacial as ever, stared at the giant's face in silence for a minute or two. Then, suddenly:

"Allow me, if you please, to take that fly off your forehead!"

And rushing forward as he spoke, the doctor pulled a short "Bulldog revolver" from his pocket, and quick as a flash fired into the left temple of the visitor.

The giant fell with his skull shattered, scattering his greatful brains over the carpet of the room. His hands thrashed automatically for a few moments.

In ten cuts of the doctor's scissors, through cloak, garments and underwear, the dead man's breast was laid bare. The grave surgeon cut open the chest lengthwise, with a single stroke of his broad scalpel.

When, about a quarter of an hour later, a policeman entered the office to request Doctor Hallidonhill to go with him, he found him sitting calmly at his bloody desk, examining with a strong magnifying glass, an enormous pair of lungs that lay spread out before him. The Genius of Science was trying to find, from the case of the deceased, some satisfactory explanation of the more than miraculous action of watercress.

"Constable," he said as he rose to his feet, "I felt it necessary to kill that man, as an immediate autopsy of his case might, I thought, reveal to me a secret of the gravest importance, regarding the now degenerating vitality of the human species. That is why I did not hesitate, let me confess, *to sacrifice my conscience to my duty.*"

Needless to add that the illustrious doctor was almost immediately released upon a nominal bond, his liberty being of far more importance than his detention. This strange case, as I have said, is shortly to come up before the British Assizes.

We believe that this sublime crime will not bring its hero to the gallows; for the English, as well as ourselves, are fully able to comprehend *that the exclusive love of the Humanity of the Future without any regard for the individual of the Present is, in our own time, the one sole motive that ought to justify the acquittal under any circumstances, of the magnanimous Extremists of Science.*

医生的勇敢精神

〔法〕维利埃·德·利尔-亚当

> 杀人是为了治病。
> ——布劳赛斯医院院训

哈利登希尔医生的奇怪案件即将在伦敦审理,有关事实是这样的:

今年5月20日,这位著名专家的两间大候诊室里挤满了病人,个个手里拿着号码单。

出纳员站在大门口,穿件黑长衫,向每个病人收取两个金币,无一例外,用锤当啷一敲,检验是否真金,然后机械地叫一声:"没错!"

哈利登希尔医生的诊室四壁装着玻璃,靠墙摆着日本大花盆,盆里种的是热带灌木。小个子医生坐得笔挺,他旁边摆了一张小圆桌,坐着他的助手,代他写没几个字的处方。旋转门上罩着红天鹅绒,钉天鹅绒的钉是金头的,门边站了个大个子当差,他的工作是把虚弱无力的痨病鬼扶到走廊,只等听到一声"下一个!"病人便被一架豪华的电梯从走廊送了下去。

进诊室的病人一个个眼睛呆滞无神,上身脱光,衣服挽在手臂上。进去以后医生用叩诊板和管子在病人背上敲敲。

"嗒！嗒！吸气……嘟……好……"

接着口授处方，只一两秒钟功夫，完了是一声熟悉的"下一个！"

三年来，每天从上午9点到正午，患这种病的人就这样一个个按次序来了又走。

就在5月20日这天，时钟刚敲过9点，进来个高个子，与骷髅没两样，身上的肋骨一根根往外突，就包着一层皮，痛苦地咳一声鼓一下，面颊深陷，眼珠乱转。总而言之是病得可怕，定死无疑。他手臂上挽着一件蓝狐皮斗篷，要抓着热带灌木的长叶子才能勉强站住。

"嗒，嗒，嘟！哎哟！简直没办法了！"哈利登希尔医生咕噜道，"你来找我干什么？验尸呀？不出一星期，左肺会咳得一个细胞不剩，右肺也已经成筛子了。下一个！"

当差的正准备把病人扶出门，却不料这位名医突然拍拍前额，现出一丝没把握的微笑，问了个唐突的问题：

"你是富翁吗？"

"我是百万富翁——家财远不止百万。"哈利登希尔断定活不成的可怜虫上气不接下气地说道。

"那很好。你赶快到维多利亚车站，乘11点钟的快车去多佛，再坐船到卡利斯，然后从加来乘火车到马赛，注意一定要坐有暖气的卧铺。再到尼斯，在尼斯吃上六个月的水田芥。就吃水田芥，其他什么都别沾，比方说面包、水果、酒、肉类。每两天服一调羹加碘的雨水。水田芥加水田芥加水田芥——捣碎了连汁一道吃……就看这办法行不行了。不过我得声明，这是我道听途说得来的偏方，说的人多得不得了，但我根本不相信。我叫你试试是把死马当活马医，其实认为这办法荒唐透顶。不过，任何事都有可能……下一个！"

这位骨瘦如柴的富豪病人于是被轻轻扶进了铺着软垫的电梯，其他病人一个个依次进诊室就诊。

过了半年，到11月3日，也是在时钟刚敲过9点时，医生刚坐到办公桌前，一位巨人从愁眉苦脸的病人中冲了过去，闯进科学大王哈利登希尔医生的圣殿，没有号码单，脸圆鼓鼓的，身穿阔气的毛皮衣，说话的声音很不悦耳，但非常兴奋，震动了医生诊室的每块玻璃，叫所有热带植物的所有叶子都直颤抖。他一把抱住医生的腰，吻了又吻，亲得叭叭响，眼泪直往医生苍白、瘦削的脸上流。然后将他一把按进绿色的大扶手椅里，差点让他窒息。

巨人说道："200万、300万法郎随你要吧！多亏你我才能够呼吸，产生无可抗拒的热情，才能见到太阳，有了生命，一切都多亏了你。要我怎样酬谢都可以，非酬谢不可。"

"哪儿来的疯子？把他赶出去！"医生缓过气来后有气无力地抗议。

"哟，那可不行！"巨人嚷道，瞪了当差的一眼，吓得他往后退，像是挨了一棍子。"我明白了，"他又道，"原来连你，我的救命恩人，也没认出我来。我就是吃水田芥的那人，那活骷髅，没法救的病人。药到病除。水田芥，水田芥！水田芥！我吃了半年的水田芥，现在你看看你的功劳吧！你看看我，听听这儿！"

他挥起一对结实得能砸碎公牛头的拳头，把胸口敲得咚咚响。

"什么？"医生跳起来，大声道，"你就是——天哪——就是那个快死的人？我还以为你……"

"没错，没错，一点没错，我就是那个人。"巨人嚷着，"昨天晚上我一到，就为你定了一座铜像，还打算你死后在威斯敏斯特区为你树一座纪念碑。"说完，他往大沙发上一坐，把弹簧压得嘎嘎直响，高兴地舒了口气，一笑："哎，能活着有多好！"

医生轻声说了句什么，助手和当差便出了诊室，房间里只剩下他从死亡线上救回来的病人了。哈利登希尔站得笔直，显得体弱，又恢复了冷冰冰的表情，一声不吭地瞪大眼看着病人的脸，足足看了一两分钟，然后突然说：

"你额头上有只苍蝇，我把它赶开，行吗？"

医生说着一个箭步向前，从口袋里掏出支左轮手枪，来个迅雷不及掩耳，给了客人的左太阳穴一枪。

巨人倒下了，脑袋开了花，他本是为道谢来的，却把脑浆撒了一地。两只手还机械地挥动了好一会儿。

医生用剪刀剪了十下，把斗篷、外衣、内衣统统剪开，让尸体的胸口露了出来。这位外科大夫表情严肃，用宽手术刀仅划一刀，就把整个胸口纵向划开了。

一刻钟以后，一名警察进了哈利登希尔医生的诊室，要把他带走，只见他镇静地坐在血糊糊的桌边，拿着高倍放大镜，在仔仔细细看放在桌上的一副特大的肺。原来，这位天才的科学家要从死者身上找出一个满意的答案，解开水田芥的神奇作用之谜。

他站起身说："警察，我觉得非把这人杀了不可，因为只有将他即刻解剖，我才能揭开一个最重要的奥秘，了解到为什么人类现在生命力会退化。所以，老实说吧，我这才毫不犹豫地为职责而牺牲了良心。"

不用说，这位名医只是象征性地关押后便被保释了，放掉他比关押他的好处不知要大多少。前面说过，这件奇怪的案子不日便要开庭审理。

  我们认为这桩大案并不会使作案人上绞架,我们与全英国人一样能充分理解,在我们这个时代,那些酷爱科学、心地高尚的极端人物无论干了什么都可宣告无罪,只要是出于一种动机——全心爱未来的整个人类,尽可不在乎现在的某个人如何如何。

A Game of Billiards

Alphonse Daudet

Even veterans are exhausted after two day's fighting, especially if they have passed the night, knapsacks on their backs, standing in torrents of rain. Yet for three mortal houres they had been left to wait in puddles along the highway; in the mire of rain-soaked fields.

Heavy with fatigue, weakened by the effects of previous nights, their uniforms drenched, they press together for warmth and support. Here and there, leaning upon a comrade's knapsack, a man falls asleep—standing; and upon the relaxed faces of these men, overcome by sleep, may be read more plainly than before the traces which weariness and privation have made. In the mud and rain, without fire, without food; overhead the sky heavy and lowering—around them, on every side, the enemy.

Their cannon, mouths turned towards the woods, seem to be lying in wait. The machine guns, from their hiding places, stare fixedly at the horizon. All is ready for an attack. Why is none made? What are they waiting for?

They await orders from headquarters, but none come.

And yet it is only a short distance to headquarters, to that beautiful Louis XIII chateau whose red brick walls, washed by the rain, are seen half way up the hill, glistening through the thickets. Truly a princely dwelling, well worthy of bearing the banner of a Marshal of France. Upon an artificial pond which sparkles like a mirror, swans are swimming, and under the pagoda-shaped roof of a large aviary, peacocks and golden pheasants strut about, spreading their wings and sending their shrill cries through the foliage. Though the owners of the house have departed, nowhere is there a perceptible sign of that ruin and desolation which war brings in its train; not the smallest flower dotting the lawn has been destroyed and it is indescribably charming to observe. Such evenly trimmed shrubbery, such silent avenues of shade; yet so near the battlefield! The scene is peaceful. Were it not for the flag floating from the top of the roof, and the sight of two sentinels before the gate, one would never believe headquarters were here.

In the dining room, whose windows front the entrance of the chateau, is seen a partly cleared table—bottles uncorked, tarnished empty glasses resting upon the wrinkled cloth—in short, every indication that a repast is ended. The guests have departed; but in a side room loud voices are heard, peals of laughter, the rolling of billiard balls, and the clinking of glasses. The Marshal has just started upon his game, and that is why the army is waiting for orders. Once the Marshal has begun, the heavens might fall, but nothing on earth will hinder him from finishing his game.

A Game of Billiards

For if the mighty soldier has a single weakness, it is his fondness for billiards. There he stands, as grave as though a battle had begun, in full uniform, his breast covered with decorations; his repast, the grog he has drunk, and the excitement of the game animate him. His eyes sparkle, and his cheek-bones are flushed. About him gather his aides-de-camp, most assiduous in their attentions, deferential and overcome with admiration at each of his shots. When the Marshal makes a point, they lunge towards the mark. When the Marshal desires a drink, each one rushes to prepare his grog. Such a rustling of epaulettes and panaches; such a rattling of crosses and aiguillettes. How these flunkies bow and smile. What elegance and charm of manner. And such embroideries; so many new uniforms in this lofty chamber carved in oak, opening upon parks and courts of honor[①]. It reminds one of these autumns of Compiègne, and makes him forget, for a moment, those figures in muddied cloaks, gathered yonder in the roads, making such somber groups[②] as they wait in the rain.

The Marshal's adversary is a staff officer, a little captain with curls, laces and light gloves; he is an excellent shot at billiards, and could beat all the marshals on earth, but he understands his chief, and exercises all his skill in playing so that he shall neither win nor seem to lose, too readily. Evidently an officer with a future.

---

① parks and courts of honor: honor 义为"荣誉"。如将此短语直译为"享有盛誉的园林和庭院"会很费解。

② 文章一开头就说到那些待命的士兵因过于疲倦与寒冷互靠在一起，所以此处出现的 groups 一词即指此现象。

Beware, Captain. The Marshal is five points ahead. If you can complete the game as you have begun it, your promotion is surer than it would be, were you standing outside with the others, beneath those torrents of water. It would be a pity, too, to soil that fine uniform.

The game is fascinating. The balls roll, graze, pass; they rebound. Every moment the play grows more interesting. A flash of light is seen in the sky, and the report of a cannon is heard. A heavy rumbling sound shakes the windows. Everyone starts and casts an uneasy glance about. The Marshal alone remains unmoved. He sees nothing, hears nothing, for, leaning over the table, he is about to make a magnificent draw shot. Draw shots are his forte!

Again that flash! Again! From the cannon, fresh reports, and closer together. The aides-de-camp run to the window. Are the Prussians attacking?

"Let them!" says the Marshal, chalking his cue. "Your turn, Captain."

The staff glows with admiration. Turenne, asleep on the gun-carriage, was nothing compared to this marshal, calmly absorbed in his game at the moment of action. But the tumult increases. The rattling of the machine guns mingles with the blast of the cannon and the rumbling of steady volleys. A reddish cloud, dark at the edges, rises from the further end of the lawn. All the rear of the park is ablaze. Frightened peacocks and pheasants shriek in the aviary. Arabian horses, in their stalls, scent the powder and rear in terror. At headquarters a general commotion begins. Despatch follows despatch. Messengers arrive at a gallop. Everywhere they are asking for the Marshal.

But the Marshal remains unapproachable. Nothing—nothing in the world could hinder him from finishing a game once begun.

"Your play, Captain ..."

But the captain is distracted. He loses his head; forgets where he is, and he makes two successive runs which almost win the game for him. The Marshal is furious. Surprise and indignation mark his features. At this very moment a horse gallops into the courtyard at full speed. An aide-de-camp, covered with mud, forces the sentry, makes one bound over the stone steps crying, "Marshal, Marshal!" The Marshal, red and swelling with anger, appears at the window, cue in hand.

"Who is there? What is it? Is there no sentry there?"

"But Marshal ..."

"Oh, yes, yes—later—let them wait for my orders—in God's name!"

And the window closes with a bang.

Let them wait for his orders. That is exactly what they are doing, those poor fellows. The wind drives rain and grapeshot in their faces. Battalions are slaughtered, while others stand useless, bearing arms, unable to understand why they remain inactive. They wait for orders. But men may die without orders, and these men die in hundreds, falling behind bushes, dropping in trenches in front of that great silent chateau. Even after their death, the grapeshot continues to lacerate their bodies; from those gaping wounds flows a silent stream—the generous blood of France. Above, in the billiard room, all is excited as upon the battlefield. The Marshal has regained his advantage, and the little captain is playing like a lion.

Seventeen! eighteen! nineteen! Scarcely time to mark the points. The sound of battle grows nearer and nearer. The Marshal has but one more point to play. Already shells are falling in the park. One has burst in the pond. The glassy sheen reddens, and a terrified swan is seen swimming amid a whirl of bloody plumage. And now the last shot.

And then—deep silence. Only the sound of rain falling; only an indistinct rumbling noise at the foot of the hill, and along the muddy roads a sound like the tramping of hurrying herds. The army is utterly routed. The Marshal has won his game.

打台球

〔法〕阿方斯·都德

打了两天仗,特别是之后又背着背包在瓢泼大雨中站了一夜,连老兵也难以支撑。然而,他们还是在公路边的烂泥坑里,在被水淹没的野外等了足足三小时。

衣服水淋淋,接连两个夜晚的煎熬耗费了大量体力,这些人倦得不行,挤在一起,好保保暖,也得个依靠。到处都有人靠在同伴的背包上睡着了,可依旧站着;这些人战胜不了瞌睡虫,脸上的肌肉松弛了,但这一来更可看出他们又倦又饿。没有火,没有吃的,脚下是泥,是水,头上乌云压顶,四面八方受到敌人的包围。

他们的大炮似乎也在等待,炮口对着树林。隐蔽的机枪瞪大眼注视着远方。进攻的准备已经就绪。为什么不进攻呢?他们在等待什么?

他们在等待指挥部的命令,可是命令没有下达。

指挥部离得不远,在半山腰灌木丛中路易十三的漂亮别墅里。别墅的红砖墙被雨水冲刷得发亮,清晰可见。这地方不愧是国王的行宫,也配得上法兰西元帅的帅旗。人工挖的池塘闪亮如镜,浮着几只天鹅。大鸟舍宝塔形的顶上孔雀和金雉鸡踱着慢步,伸开翅膀,发出的尖利叫声能传到林子外。虽然别墅的主人已离世,这里却看起来仍美得叫人难以置信,丝毫见不到连绵战祸带来的凄凉破败景象。草地上没有一朵小花被践踏,灌木丛修剪得那么齐整,林荫道那么幽静,战场却偏偏近在咫尺!气氛是平静的。如果不是房顶上有军旗在飘,大门口站着两名卫兵,没人会相信司令部竟设在这里。

别墅前门正对着餐厅的窗户,透过窗户可看到餐厅的一张桌上的东西已吃了大半,酒瓶空空,杯盘狼藉,分明宴会已经结束。客人已经告退,但旁边一个小间里还人声喧哗,有人大笑,有人打台球,有人碰杯。元帅刚开始玩,大军只好待命。元帅要么不玩,一旦玩起来,哪怕天塌地陷也要玩到底。

如果说这位大帅有什么弱点,那就是爱打台球。他穿着制服,胸佩勋章,表情严肃,似乎大战已经开始。他吃饱了,喝足了,又打起了台球,所以精神抖擞,眼发亮,脸透红。身边站着的是副官,大都看得出神,对元帅的每一杆都佩服得五体投地。元帅每得一分,他们便抢着记。等到他酒瘾上来,人们又争先恐后端酒。叮叮当当,当当叮叮,肩章、盔饰、十字勋章、绶带扣,响得好不热闹!这帮马屁精又鞠躬,又微笑,真够殷勤!多高雅的情趣,多动人的风度!你看看这儿的刺绣吧,看看这所橡木雕出的宽敞房间,房里这一套套簇新的军装,窗外这美妙的风光!你会想起贡比涅的金秋而暂时忘却披着带泥的斗篷、冒着大雨站在路上安安静静待命的士兵。

元帅的对手是位参谋,上尉军衔,小个子,蓄着卷发,挂着缎带,戴着浅色手套。他打台球是神手,天底下无论哪路元帅都不在他的话下。但他了解自己的统领，玩起来很有分寸，既不取胜，又不显得故意输掉。显然他会官运亨通。

小心啦，上尉！元帅领先5分。如果这一盘你开始得巧妙结束得也巧妙，那就提升有望，比与那些人一道站在野外淋瓢泼大雨前程远大。再说，弄坏了漂亮的军装也太可惜。

打台球真够味。那圆溜溜的东西滚着，有时擦到边，有时连边也擦不着，弹回来，越玩越带劲。突然天上一道闪光，接着听到一声炮响，窗子震动了。人人大吃一惊，不安地四处张望，只有元帅稳如磐石。他既没听见也没看见什么，正把身子俯在台子上，准备来一手漂亮的回旋球。那可是他的拿手戏。

又一闪！又一闪！炮声又起，越响越近。副官们涌到窗口。难道普鲁士人发起进攻了吗？

"别理他！"元帅说，给球杆擦了点白粉，"上尉，该你啦！"

参谋佩服得不得了。大战近在眉睫，这位元帅仍镇定自若，专心打台球。倒在炮架上便睡着了的蒂雷纳元帅[①]与他相比简直是望尘莫及。然而，炮火越来越密集。机枪嗒嗒嗒，大炮咚咚咚，排炮隆隆隆，响成一片。草地对过升起一团中间红四周黑的云，后院整个便烧着了。孔雀和雉鸡吓得在笼里尖叫，马厩里的阿拉伯战马闻到火药味，惊跳着。指挥部里开始人心惶惶。紧急报告一个接一个，快马一匹接一匹。各路兵马在请元帅发令。

然而，元帅闭门不见。台球一旦打起来，天塌地陷他都不收场。

"该你打，上尉……"

上尉分了心。他昏了头，忘了在与谁对垒，连中两下，快赢

---

① 法国元帅（1611—1675）。

了。元帅动了肝火，只见他又吃惊，又生气。恰在这时，一匹快马冲进了院子。一名副官满身泥浆，闯过岗哨，纵身跳上石阶，高喊："大帅！大帅！"元帅气得满面通红，腮帮鼓起来，站到窗边，手里拿着球杆。

"是谁呀？有什么事？哨兵哪儿去啦？"

"可是大帅……"

"嗯，知道啦，知道啦——别急——叫他们等待命令——看在上帝的分上！"

窗砰地一声关上了。

等待命令，可怜这帮人不是一直在等待命令吗？风把雨点和霰弹倾泻到他们脸上。大批人完蛋了，活着的手拿武器，却无能为力，猜不透为什么会按兵不动。他们在待命。没有命令就会出现牺牲，而且已经有成百成百的人死去，倒在灌木丛后，倒在静悄悄的别墅前的战壕里。甚至在倒下以后，还有霰弹飞来落在他们身上。伤口的血静静地流着——是法兰西男儿慷慨的血！山上的台球室与山下的战场一样热闹。元帅重新取得优势，小个子上尉也打得顽强。

17！18！19！连记分也来不及。炮火声越响越近。元帅还差1分就可取胜。炮弹落到了围墙里，有一颗在池塘中爆炸，水面变红了。一只天鹅惊慌失措，搅着带血的羽毛在水中团团转。可现在还差1分。

接着，一阵死寂，然后只听到雨声，山脚下一声模糊的轰响，泥水路上脚步乱响，听上去像四散的畜群发出的声音。全军乱了套，元帅打台球却得了胜。

Absent-Mindedness in a Parish Choir

Thomas Hardy

"It happened on Sunday after Christmas—the last Sunday they ever played in Longpuddle church gallery, as it turned out[①], though they didn't know it then. As you may know, sir, the players formed a very good band—almost as good as the Mellstock parish players that were led by the Dewys[②]; and that's saying a great deal. There was Nicholas Puddingcome, the leader, with the first fiddle; there was Timothy Thomas, the bass-viol man; John Biles, the tenor fiddler; Dan'l Hornhead, with the serpent; Robert Dowdle, with the clarionet; and Mr. Nicks, with the oboe—all sound and powerful musicians, and strongwinded men—they that blowed. For that reason they were very much in demand Christmas week for little reels[③] and dancing-parties; for they could turn a jig or a hornpipe out of hand as well as ever they

---

① as it turned out: 表示结果
② the Mellstock parish players that were led by the Dewys: 此处教区名与人名无从查考,很可能是虚构的。
③ 里尔舞,轻快活泼的苏格兰民间舞蹈。

could turn out a psalm, and perhaps better, not to speak irreverent. In short, one half-hour they could be playing a Christmas carol in the squire's hall to the ladies and gentlemen, and drinking tay and coffee with 'em as modest as saints; and the next, at the Tinker's Arms[①], blazing away[②] like wild horses with the 'Dashing White Sergeant'[③] to nine couple of dancers and more, and swallowing rum-and-cider hot as flame.

"Well, this Christmas they'd been out to one rattling randy after another every night, and had got next to no sleep[④] at all. Then came Sunday after Christmas, their fatal day. 'Twas so mortal cold that year that they could hardly sit in the gallery; for though the congregation down in the body of the church had a stove to keep off the frost, the players in the gallery had nothing at all. So Nicholas said at morning service, when 'twas freezing an inch an hour, 'Please the Lord I won't stand this numbing weather no longer; this afternoon we'll have something in our insides to make us warm if it cost a king's ramsom.'

"So he brought a gallon of hot brandy and beer, ready mixed, to church with him in the afternoon, and by keeping the jar well wrapped up in Timothy Thomas' bass-viol bag it kept drinkably warm till they wanted it, which was just a thimbleful in the Absolution, and another after the Creed, and the remainder at the beginning o' the sermon. When

---

① the Tinker's Arms：一个虚构的地点。
② blazing away：指使劲地吹奏。
③ Dashing White Sergeant：舞曲名。
④ had got next to no sleep：had almost got no sleep

Absent-Mindedness in a Parish Choir

they'd had the last pull they felt quite comfortable and warm, and as the sermon went on—most unfortunately for 'em it was a long one that afternoon—they fell asleep, every man jack of 'em; and there they slept on as sound as rocks.

"'Twas a very dark afternoon, and by the end of the sermon all you could see of the inside of the church were the pa'son's two candles alongside of him in the pulpit, and his soaking face behind 'em. The sermon being ended at last, the pa'son gied① out the Evening Hymn. But no choir set about sounding up the tune, and the people began to turn their heads to learn the reason why, and then Levi Limpet, a boy who sat in the gallery nudged Timothy and Nicholas, and said, 'Begin! begin!'

"'Hey, what?' says Nicholas, starting up; and the church being so dark and his head so muddled he thought he was at the party they had played at all the night before, and away he went, bow and fiddle, at 'The Devil among the Tailors', the favorite jig of our neighborhood at that time. The rest of the band, being in the same state of mind and nothing doubting, followed their leader with all their strength, according to custom. They poured out that there② tune till the lower bass notes of 'The Devil among the Tailors' made the cobwebs in the roof shiver like ghosts; then Nicholas, seeing nobody moved, shouted out as he scraped (in his usual commanding way at dances when folks didn't know the

---

① gied 是动词 gie 的过去式，gie 即 give，是苏格兰语。
② 此处 there 显多余。

figures), 'Top couples cross hands! And when I make the fiddle squeak at the end, every man kiss his pardner under the mistletoe!'

"The boy Levi was so frightened that he bolted down the gallery stairs and out homeward like lightning. The pa'son's hair fairly stood on end when he heard the evil tune raging through the church; and thinking the choir had gone crazy, he held up his hand and said; 'Stop, stop, stop! Stop, stop! What's this?' But they didn't hear 'n for the noise of their own playing, and the more he called the louder they played.

"Then the folks came out of their pews, wondering down to the ground, and saying: 'What do they mean by such wickedness? We shall be consumed like Sodom and Gomorrah[①]!'

"Then the squire came out of his pew lined wi' green baize, where lots of lords and ladies visiting at the house were worshipping along with him, and went and stood in front of the gallery, and shook his fist in the musicians' faces, saying, 'What! In this reverent edifice! What!'

"And at last they heard 'n through their playing, and stopped.

"'Never such an insulting, disgraceful thing—never!' says the squire, who couldn't rule his passion.

"'Never!' says the pa'son, who had come down and stood beside him.

"'Not if the angels of Heaven,' says the squire, (he was a wickedish man, the squire was, though now for once he happened to be on the Lord's side) —'not if the angels of Heaven come down,' he says,

---

① Sodom and Gomorrah：典出圣经，为两城市名，均因居民罪恶重大，人与城同毁。

Absent-Mindedness in a Parish Choir

'shall one of you villainous players ever sound a note in this church again, for the insult to me, and my family, and my visitors, and God Almighty, that you've perpetrated this afternoon!'

"Then the unfortunate church band came to their senses, and remembered where they were; and 'twas a sight to see Nicholas Puddingcome and Timothy Thomas and John Biles creep down the gallery stairs with their fiddles under their arms, and poor Dan'l Hornhead with his serpent, and Robert Dowdle with his clarionet, all looking as little as ninepins; and out they went. The pa'son might have forgi'ed 'em when he learned the truth o't[1], but the squire would not. That very week he sent for a barrel-organ that would play two-and-twenty new psalm tunes, so exact and particular that, however sinful inclined you was[2], you could paly nothing but psalm tunes whatsomever. He had a really respectable man to turn the winch, as I said, and the old players played no more."

---

[1] forgi'ed 'em ... o't: forgive them ... of it
[2] sinful inclined you was: sinfully inclined you were

乱弹琴

〔英〕托马斯·哈代

事情发生在圣诞节后的星期天,这帮人没想到,他们在长池教堂吹吹打打了这一次,以后就永远滚蛋了。各位也许都已听说,他们是一支顶呱呱的乐队,能与在教堂奏乐的天下第一流乐队相提并论,好到什么程度可想而知。领班尼古拉斯·布丁科姆是第一小提琴手,拉低音古提琴的是蒂莫西·托马斯,拉中音提琴的是约翰·拜尔斯,吹蛇形管的是丹尔·霍恩赫德,吹单簧管的是罗伯特·多德尔,吹双簧管的是尼古斯先生。皆系名家高手,肺活量又大——我是说吹号吹管的。所以圣诞节这一周他们忙得不亦乐乎,无论小型舞会、大型舞会,无有不请。他们固然合唱赞美诗,但对快步子的吉格舞曲和角笛舞曲同样内行,甚至更为拿手,别看这两者并不相关。一言以蔽之,前半小时他们能在东家为老爷太太们演奏圣诞颂歌,文质彬彬地饮茶喝咖啡,后半小时又能在西家给阿狗阿猫演奏野马般疯狂的舞曲,喝火一样厉害的烈酒。

且说这一年圣诞节,他们天天晚上出去一次又一次狂吹乱打,几乎没合过眼。到了圣诞节后的星期天,闹出了大乱子。这年天气冷得要命，台上简直没法坐。教堂的大厅生了火驱寒，台上的乐队可什么也没有。做早礼拜时天冷得一小时结一寸冰，所以尼古拉斯说："天哪，这种冻死人的天怎么受得了？今天下午肚皮里非灌点东西不可，犯王法也得灌。"

果然，下午他带了一加仑白兰地和啤酒到教堂，把两种酒混合在一起，瓶子包在蒂莫西·托马斯的琴袋里，到喝时酒不会冷，准备在读赦罪文时喝一点，念过十二门徒信条后喝一点，剩下的在布道开始时喝。喝完最后一口他们觉得身上暖烘烘，舒舒服服。不巧得很，这天下午牧师布道时间特别长，才讲到一半他们便睡着了，全睡着了，一个个跟死猪差不多。

这天天色也暗，等讲道完了教堂里能看清的只有讲坛上的两支蜡烛和站在蜡烛后的牧师的满面泪痕。讲道终于完结，牧师宣布唱晚祷歌。但唱诗班里没有声音，大家莫名其妙，伸头探脑地瞧。后来还是台子上一个叫利瓦伊·林彼特的孩子推了蒂莫西和尼古拉斯一把，催道："吹呀！吹呀！"

"嗯，怎么啦？"尼古拉斯醒了过来，问道。教堂里黑乎乎，他的脑子昏沉沉，只当是前一晚开的舞会，拿起弓和琴，奏起当时我们那儿跳吉格舞常奏的曲子《裁缝店的魔鬼》。乐队其他人也糊里糊涂，不问青红皂白，照习惯跟着领班使劲吹奏起来。他们吹个不停，连屋梁上的蜘蛛网也让《裁缝店的魔鬼》的低音搅得摆呀摆，活像是闹鬼。尼古拉斯呢，看到没有人起身，一边拉琴一边叫："领头的一对手牵手！听到我的琴末尾一声响，男的都吻自己的女伴！"每次舞会遇到人们不懂行时，他都要这样指挥。

叫利瓦伊的孩子吓得魂出了窍，冲下台，兔子似地跑回了家。牧师听到教堂里奏起这种乌七八糟的曲子，怒发冲冠，认为唱诗班中了邪,举起手来叫道:"快停,停,停!快停,停!究竟怎么啦?"乐队正吹奏得起劲,没有听见,而且他越叫,他们越卖力。

坐在长椅上的人全站了出来,吓蒙了,直叫:"这是造什么孽呀!我们统统要给毁啦!"

一区之长从铺着绿坐垫的长椅上也站了出来;到他家做客的老爷太太全跟着他来做礼拜了。他走到台前,冲着乐队的人挥拳头。"搞什么名堂!这儿是圣殿!搞什么名堂!"

这帮人总算听见了,收了场!

一区之长怎么也压不住心中的火气,骂起来:"天下哪有这种丢人现眼的事!天下哪有!"

"是没有!"牧师走下讲坛,站到他身边,附和道。

"如果不是天使下凡——如果不是天使下凡,你们这班混蛋再别想到这儿来吹!今天下午真给我丢脸,给我一家人,给我的客人丢脸!也太得罪上帝啦!"他叫道。其实他这人心术并不太正,可这次碰巧站到了上帝一边。

教堂的倒霉乐队这才清醒过来,知道他们搞错了地方。尼古拉斯·布丁科姆、蒂莫西·托马斯、约翰·拜尔斯夹着琴,丹尔·霍恩赫德提着蛇形管,罗伯特·多德尔抱着单簧管灰溜溜地下了台,出了教堂。这情景你要是看到真会觉得有意思。牧师如果知道事情真相也许会原谅他们,但一区之长可不会。就在那个星期,他叫人弄来一台手摇风琴,可以奏出22首新圣歌的曲子,准确动听,无论你怎么中邪,奏出的总是圣歌的曲子。他请了一位百分之百的君子做琴师,之前那个班子的人再没来过。

A Psychological Shipwreck

Ambrose Bierce

In the summer of 1874 I was in Liverpool, whither I had gone on business for the mercantile house of Bronson & Jarrett, New York. I am William Jarrett; my partner was Zenas Bronson. The firm failed last year, and unable to endure the fall from affluence to poverty he died.

Having finished my business, and feeling the lassitude and exhaustion incident to its dispatch, I felt that a protracted sea voyage would be both agreeable and beneficial, so instead of embarking for my return on one of the many fine passenger steamers I booked for New York on the sailing vessel *Morrow*, upon which I had shipped a large and valuable invoice of the goods I had bought. The *Morrow* was an English ship with, of course, but little accommodation for passengers, of whom there were only myself, a young woman and her servant, who was a middle-aged Negress. I thought it singular that a traveling English girl should be so attended, but she afterward explained to me that the woman had been left with her family by a man and his wife from South Carolina, both of whom had died on the same day at the house of the young lady's father in Devonshire—a circumstance in itself sufficiently uncommon to remain rather distinctly in my memory, even had it not afterward transpired in conversation with the young lady that[①] the name of the man was William Jarrett, the same as my own. I knew that a branch of my family had settled in South Carolina, but of them and their history I was ignorant.

The *Morrow* sailed from the mouth of the Mersey on the 15th of June and for several weeks we had fair breezes and unclouded skies. The skipper, an admirable seaman but nothing more, favored us with very little of his society, except at his table; and the young woman, Miss Janette Harford, and I became very well acquainted. We were, in truth, nearly always together, and being of an introspective turn of mind I often endeavored to analyze and define the novel feeling with which she inspired me—a secret, subtle, but powerful attraction which constantly impelled me to seek her; but the attempt was hopeless. I could only be sure that at least it was not love. Having assured myself of this and being certain that she was quite as whole-hearted, I ventured one evening (I remember it was on the 3rd of July) as we sat on deck to ask her, laughingly, if she could assist me to resolve my psychological doubt.

For a moment she was silent, with averted face, and I began to fear I had been extremely rude and indelicate; then she fixed her

---

① even had it not afterward transpired in conversation with the young lady that：这是个省略了连词 if 的虚拟语气句，助动词 had 置于形式主语 it 前。真实主语为 that 引导的从句。

A Psychological Shipwreck

eyes gravely on my own. In an instant my mind was dominated by as strange a fancy as ever entered human consciousness. It seemed as if she were looking at me. Not *with*, but *through*, those eyes—from an immeasurable distance behind them—and that a number of other persons, men, women and children, upon whose faces I caught strangely familiar evanescent expressions, clustered about her, struggling with gentle eagerness to look at me through the same orbs. Ship, ocean, sky—all had vanished. I was conscious of nothing but the figures in this extraordinary and fantastic scene. Then all at once darkness fell upon me, and anon from out of it, as to one who grows accustomed by degrees to a dimmer light, my former surroundings of deck and mast and cordage slowly resolved themselves. Miss Harford had closed her eyes and was leaning back in her chair, apparently asleep, the book she had been reading open in her lap. Impelled by surely I cannot say what motive, I glanced at the top of the page; it was a copy of that rare and curious work, "Denneker's Meditations," and the lady's index finger rested on this passage:

"To sundry it is given to be drawn away, and to be apart from the body for a season; for, as concerning rills which would flow across each other the weaker is borne along by the stronger, so there be certain of kin whose paths intersecting, their souls do bear company, the while their bodies go fore-appointed ways, unknowing."

Miss Harford arose, shuddering; the sun had sunk below the horizon, but it was not cold. There was not a breath of wind; there were no clouds in the sky, yet not a star was visible. A hurried tramping sounded on the deck; the captain, summoned from below, joined the first officer, who stood looking at the barometer. "Good God!" I heard him exclaim.

An hour later the form of Janette Harford, invisible in the darkness and spray, was torn from my grasp by the cruel vortex of the sinking ship, and I fainted in the cordage of the floating mast to which I had lashed myself.

It was by lamplight that I awoke. I lay in a berth amid the familiar surroundings of the stateroom of a steamer. On a couch opposite sat a man, half undressed for bed, reading a book. I recognized the face of my friend Gordon Doyle, whom I had met in Liverpool on the day of my embarkation, when he was himself about to sail on the steamer *City of Prague*, on which he had urged me to accompany him.

After some moments I now spoke his name. He simply said, "Well," and turned a leaf in his book without removing his eyes from the page.

"Doyle," I repeated, "did they save *her*?"

He now deigned to look at me and smiled as if amused. He evidently thought me but half awake.

"Her? Whom do you mean?"

"Janette Harford."

His amusement turned to amazement; he stared at me fixedly, saying nothing.

"You will tell me after a while," I continued; "I suppose you will tell me after a while."

A moment later I asked: "What ship is this?"

Doyle stared again. "The steamer *City of Pargue*, bound from Liverpool to New York, three weeks out with a broken shaft. Principal passenger, Mr. Gordon Doyle; ditto lunatic, Mr. William Jarrett. These two distinguished travelers embarked together, but they are about to part, it being the resolute intention of the former to pitch the latter overboard."

I sat bolt upright. "Do you mean to say that I have been for three weeks a passenger on this steamer?"

"Yes, pretty nearly; this is the 3rd of July."

"Have I been ill?"

"Right as a trivet all the time, and punctual at your meals."

"My God! Doyle, there is some mystery here; do have the goodness to be serious. Was I not rescued from the wreck of the ship *Morrow*?"

Doyle changed color, and approaching me, laid his fingers on my wrist. A moment later, "What do you know of Janette Harford?" he asked very calmly.

"First tell me what *you* know of her?"

Mr. Doyle gazed at me for some moments as if thinking what to do, then seating himself again on the couch, said:

"Why should I not? I am engaged to marry Janette Harford, whom I met a year ago in London. Her family, one of the wealthiest in Devonshire, cut up rough about it, and we eloped—are eloping rather, for on the day that you and I walked to the landing stage to go aboard this steamer she and her faithful servant, a Negress, passed us, driving to the ship *Morrow*. She would not consent to go in the same vessel with me, and it had been deemed best that she take① a sailing vessel in order to avoid observation and lessen the risk of detection. I am now alarmed lest this cursed breaking of our machinery may detain us so long that the *Morrow* will get to New York before us, and the poor girl will not know where to go."

I lay still in my berth—so still I hardly breathed. But the subject was evidently not displeasing to Doyle, and after a short pause he resumed:

"By the way, she is only an adopted daughter of the Harfords. Her mother was killed at their place by being thrown from a horse while hunting, and her father, mad with grief, made away with himself the same day. No one ever claimed the child, and after a reasonable time they adopted her. She has grown up in the belief that she is their daughter."

"Doyle, what book are you reading?"

"Oh, it's called 'Denneker's Meditations.' It's a rum lot, Janette gave it to me; she happened to have two copies. Want to see it?"

He tossed me the volume, which opened as it fell. On one of the exposed pages was a marked passage:

"To sundry it is given to be drawn away, and to be apart from the body for a season; for, as concerning rills which would flow across each other the weaker is borne along by the stronger, so there be certain

---

① that she take：这是个虚拟语气的宾语从句，谓语动词用原形。

A Psychological Shipwreck

of kin whose paths intersecting, their souls do bear company, the while their bodies go fore-appointed ways, unknowing."

"She had—she has—a singular taste in reading," I managed to say, mastering my agitation.

"Yes. And now perhaps you will have the kindness to explain how you knew her name and that of the ship she sailed in."

"You talked of her in your sleep," I said.

A week later we were towed into the port of New York. But the *Morrow* was never heard from.

魂 游

〔美〕安布罗斯·比尔斯

  1874年夏，我为处理开在纽约的布朗森-贾勒特公司的事到了利物浦。我名叫威廉·贾勒特，合伙人叫泽纳斯·布朗森。去年公司破产后他一贫如洗，受不了，一命归西。
  我把事情办完后只觉筋疲力尽，想在海上多漂流几日，松一口气。漂亮的客轮很多，我没有乘，只搭了"明天号"帆船去纽约，我买的一大宗贵重货物也由"明天号"托运。这是一艘英国船，载客极少，只有我、一位英国姑娘和她的中年黑人女仆。一位出远门的英国姑娘带着这么个仆人很少见，后来我听她说才知道，仆人本是南卡罗来纳州一对夫妇的。有一天夫妇俩竟双双在德文郡死在姑娘的父亲家。这种怪事本来就叫人忘不了，更巧的是，后来姑娘还说那男的名叫威廉·贾勒特，与我同名同姓。我知道我有一位本家落在南卡罗来纳州，只不过我不认识，也不知道他们的情况。
  6月15日，"明天号"从默西河口起锚，航行半个多月，海上一直风平浪静，晴空万里无云。船长是一位很棒的海员，但仅此而已，除了吃饭，很少与我们来往，于是我和那位年轻姑娘（她叫珍尼特·哈福德）混得很熟。说实话，我们几乎形影不离。我内心常悄悄捉摸被她激起的一种奇怪的感情，一种没有外露、微妙而强烈，且使我总不愿离开她的感情，但没有捉摸出名堂来。我只知道这种感情不是爱情。由于心中有数，同时也知道她心地纯洁，一天晚上（我记得是7月3日）趁我俩坐在甲板上时，我笑着问她，能不能帮我解开心头之谜。

她先沉默好一会儿，脸扭向一边，我不禁担心，也许自己过于冒昧、莽撞。后来她的目光直逼我双眼，顿时使我脑中产生一种人所鲜知的幻觉。似乎在看着我的不是她的眼睛，而是深深躲在她眼睛里的许多人，有男有女，还有孩子。他们聚集在她的眼里，脸上带着熟悉而难以捉摸的表情，一齐透过她的眼直望着我。船、海、天空统统消逝了，见到的唯有这异乎寻常的幻景中的人物。突然，眼前一片黑。人是能逐渐适应暗淡的光线的，我在这片黑暗中慢慢看到原先在我周围的甲板、桅杆和绳索。哈福德小姐已经闭上了眼，靠在椅上，睡着了，她看的书摊开放在腿上。也不知出于什么动机，我朝书瞟了一眼，发现原来是《登内克之冥想》，一本珍贵而难懂的书，她手指指着的那一段是：

"各种人的灵魂可以暂时游离，脱离其身体。而且如同溪流交汇，弱者会依附于强者，所以有些曾萍水相逢的人的灵魂会不知不觉结伴而行，虽然身体各在一处。"

哈福德小姐站起来，身子直颤抖。太阳落下了，但天气并不冷。没有一丝风，天空既无云，也不见星。甲板上响起一阵急促的脚步声，船长闻声从船舱赶来，找着大副，大副正在看晴雨表。"天哪！"他嚷道。

一小时后，船沉了，珍妮特·哈福德随着沉船被无情的海水卷走，消失在夜色和浪花中，我抓也没抓住；我被桅杆上的绳索缠着，在海上漂流，也昏了过去。

我感觉到了灯光，醒了过来。我躺在一艘客轮的船舱里，四周的一切都显得眼熟。对面床坐着一个人，已脱了半身衣准备睡觉，但还在看一本书。我认出来是一位朋友，叫戈登·多伊尔，在利物浦上船那天遇见的。他买了"布拉格号"客轮票，还叫我与他结伴同行。

过了好一会儿我才叫他，他只"嗯"了一声，翻过一页书，没有瞧我一眼。

"多伊尔！"我又叫道，"他们救了她吗？"

他这才看了我一眼，一笑，像是遇上了有趣的事。他准是当我迷迷糊糊还没全醒。

"她？哪个她？"

"珍妮特·哈福德。"

他由觉得好笑转而觉得奇怪，眼睛直愣愣看着我，没有答话。

"那就等一会儿吧，"我便道，"等一会儿你一定会说。"

过了一会儿我问："这是什么船？"

多伊尔的眼又发直了。"'布拉格号'客轮，从利物浦驶往纽约，航行了三星期，现在轴坏了。船上有两位贵客，一位是我，戈登·多伊尔先生，一位是威廉·贾勒特先生，十足的神经病。这两人一道上的船，可现在要分手了，多伊尔横了一条心要把贾勒特扔下海去。"

我一骨碌坐起来。"这么说我在这条船上已坐了三个星期？"

"正是。今天已经7月3日了。"

"我生过病吗？

"结实得像头牛,每天三顿没少吃过一顿。"

"哎哟,这就怪了,多伊尔!你别开玩笑。我不是从'明天号'船上被救起来的吗?"

多伊尔变了表情,走到我身边,抓住我的手腕,好一会儿没出声,然后才平心静气地问:"你与珍妮特·哈福德是什么关系?"

"你先说说你与她是什么关系?"

多伊尔先生久久地注视着我,像在考虑怎样做妥当,然后才回到床上坐下,道:

"说就说吧!我是珍妮特·哈福德的未婚夫,一年前在伦敦相识。她家是德文郡的巨富,反对这门亲事,我们就私奔了。准确地说,是正在私奔途中,因为你和我在码头上这条船的那天,她带着贴心黑人女仆上了'明天号'船,马车就从我们跟前经过。她不愿与我乘同一条船,觉得搭帆船好,以免被别人发现而跟踪。我担心这要命的机器一坏,在路上耽误的时间太长,'明天号'船会比我们先到纽约,让她倒霉,不知道去哪儿。"

我躺在铺位上一动不动,几乎连呼吸也屏住了。但多伊尔看来还愿意继续谈这件事,过一会儿又开腔了:

"其实,她只是哈福德家的养女。她母亲在老家打猎时从马上掉下来摔死了,她父亲伤心过度,当天也断了气。她成了无依无靠的孤儿,不久以后他们收养了她。她不知情,到长大了还以为是他们的亲生女儿。"

"多伊尔,你在看什么书?"

"书名叫《登内克之冥想》。写得很玄,珍妮特有两本,给了我一本。你想看吗?"

他把书扔过来,书正好摊开,一页上有一段画了记号:

"各种人的灵魂可以暂时游离,脱离其身体。而且如同溪流交汇,弱者会依附于强者,所以有些曾萍水相逢的人的灵魂会不知不觉结伴而行,虽然身体各在一处。"

"她——她——爱看的书与众不同。"我好不容易才抑制住内心的激动,说道。

"现在该请你说说,你怎么知道她的名字,又怎么知道她上了哪条船。"

"是你自己在梦里把她的事说了出来。"我回答。

一星期后,我们到达了纽约港,但"明天号"从此杳无音讯。

An Attempt at Reform

August Strindberg

She had noticed with indignation that girls were solely brought up to be housekeepers for their future husbands. Therefore she had learned a trade which would enable her to keep herself in all circumstances of life. She made artificial flowers.

He had noticed with regret that girls simply waited for a husband who should keep them; he resolved to marry a free and independent woman who could earn her own living; such a woman would be his equal and a companion for life, not a housekeeper.

Fate ordained that they should meet. He was an artist and she made, as I already mentioned, flowers; they were both living in Paris at the time when they conceived these ideas.

There was style in their marriage. They took three rooms at Passy. In the centre was the studio, to the right of it his room, to the left hers. This did away with the common bedroom and double bed, that abomination which has no counterpart in nature and is responsible for a great deal of dissipation and immorality. It moreover did away with the inconvenience of having to dress and undress in the same room. It was far better that each of them should have a separate room and that the studio should be a neutral, common meeting-place.

They required no servant; they were going to do the cooking themselves and employ an old charwoman in the mornings and evenings. It was all very well thought out and excellent in theory.

"But supposing you had children?" asked the sceptics.

"Nonsense, there won't be any!"

It worked splendidly. He went to the market in the morning and did the catering. Then he made the coffee. She made the beds and put the rooms in order. And then they sat down and worked.

When they were tired of working they gossiped, gave one another good advice, laughed and were very jolly.

At twelve o'clock he lit the kitchen fire and she prepared the vegetables. He cooked the beef, while she ran across the street to the grocer's; then she laid the table and he dished up the dinner.

Of course, they loved one another as husbands and wives do. They said good night to each other and went into their own rooms, but there was no lock to keep him out when he knocked at her door; but the accommodation was small and the morning found them in their own quarters. Then he knocked at the wall.

"Good morning, little girlie, how are you today?"

"Very well, darling, and you?"

Their meeting at breakfast was always like a new experience which never grew stale.

An Attempt at Reform

They often went out together in the evening and frequently met their countrymen. She had no objection to the smell of tobacco, and was never in the way. Everybody said it was an ideal marriage; no one had ever known a happier couple.

But the young wife's parents, who lived a long way off, were always writing and asking all sorts of indelicate questions; they were longing to have a grandchild. Louisa ought to remember that the institution of marriage existed for the benefit of the children, not the parents. Louisa held that this view was an old-fashioned one. Mama asked whether she did not think that the result of the new ideas would be the complete extirpation of mankind? Louisa had never looked at it in that light, and moreover the question did not interest her. Both she and her husband were happy; at last the spectacle of a happy married couple was presented to the world, and the world was envious.

Life was very pleasant. Neither of them was master and they shared expenses. Now he earned more, now she did, but in the end their contributions to the common fund amounted to the same figure.

Then she had a birthday! She was awakened in the morning by the entrance of the charwoman with a bunch of flowers and a letter painted all over with flowers, and containing the following words:

"To the lady flower-bud from her dauber[①], who wishes her many happy returns of the day and begs her to honor him with her company at an excellent little breakfast—at once."

---

① dauber 此处即指写信人，是个谦词。英语 daub 相当于汉语"涂鸦"一词。

She knocked at his door—come in!

And they breakfasted, sitting on the bed—his bed; and the charwoman was kept the whole day to do all the work. It was a lovely birthday!

Their happiness never palled. It lasted two years. All the prophets had prophesied falsely.

It was a model marriage!

But when two years had passed, the young wife fell ill. She put it down to some poison contained in the wall-paper; he suggested germs of some sort. Yes, certainly germs[①]. But something was wrong. Something was not as it should be. She must have caught cold. Then she grew stout. Was she suffering from tumour? Yes, they were afraid that she was.

She consulted a doctor—and came home crying. It was indeed a growth, but one which would one day see daylight, grow into a flower and bear fruit.

The husband did anything but cry. He found style[②] in it, and then the wretch went to his club and boasted about it to his friends. But the wife still wept. What would her position be now? She would soon not be able to earn money with her work and then she would have to live on him. And they would have to have a servant! Ugh! those servants!

All their care, their caution, their wariness had been wrecked on

---

① 此处一语双关。germ 既有"细菌，微生物"的意思，又有"胚芽"的意思。
② style：指不同寻常之处。

the rock of the inevitable.

But the mother-in-law wrote enthusiastic letters and repeated over and over again that marriage was instituted by God for the protection of the children; the parents' pleasure counted for very little.

Hugo implored her to forget the fact that she would not be able to earn anything in future. Didn't she do her full share of the work by mothering the baby? Wasn't that as good as money? Money was, rightly understood, nothing but work. Therefore she paid her share in full.

It took her a long time to get over the fact that he had to keep her. But when the baby came, she forgot all about it. She remained his wife and companion as before in addition to being the mother of his child, and he found that this was worth more than anything else.

尝试改革

〔瑞典〕奥古斯特·斯特林堡

她看到女孩子都白养,长大了只能给丈夫当管家,很不服气。所以,她学会了一门本领,将来生活无论怎样变化都能自立:她会扎花。

他看到女孩子就等着嫁一个供养她的丈夫,觉得可惜,决心娶一个能自食其力、不依附于丈夫的自由独立的女人;这个女人与他处在平等地位,是终身伴侣,不是管家。

命运注定了他们要相逢。他是一位画家,而她又如我前面所说,会扎花。他们抱着相同的想法时同住在巴黎。

他们的夫妻生活有独特之处。他们在帕西租了三间房,当中一间作为工作室,右边是他的房间,左边属于她。这一来就没有了两人合用的卧室和双人床,断了祸根;要说祸根,这些东西可算是首屈一指的,许许多多寻欢作乐、乌七八糟的事都与它们密切相关。另外,穿衣脱衣不在同一间房,省得大家不方便。他们的办法好得多,一人一间房,工作画室共用,相见就在这儿。

他们不用仆人,饭菜自己烧,只在早晚请一个上了年纪的女人干杂活。一切都想得周到,满有道理。

"你们有了孩子怎么办呢?"持怀疑态度的人问。

"哪儿的话,决不会有!"

事情进行得顺利。他上午上市场,操办吃的,然后烧咖啡;她铺床,整理房间。然后两人坐下工作。

干累了,他们就谈天,互相帮着出主意,常常大笑,开心得很。

到12点钟,他生炉子,她洗菜、切菜;他烧牛肉时,她赶到街对过的杂货店买东西;摆桌子是她的事,端菜是他的事。

当然,他们仍然像夫妻一样恩爱。晚上互道晚安后各回自己的房间睡,只是如果他敲她的门,并不会被锁在门外。但这种情况很少,每到早上,他们总是各守本土。醒过来后他敲敲墙,问:

"早上好!小宝贝,今天怎么样?"

"很好,亲爱的。你呢?"

早餐见面每次都像是初会,新鲜得很,从不乏味。

晚上他们常一道出门,多为拜访同乡。她不反对抽烟,从不干涉。人人都说这是美满姻缘,从没见过哪对夫妻比他们幸福。

但新娘的父母着了急,又隔得远,只能写信,每次离不了问些不文雅的事。他们是等着抱外孙,说女儿路易莎该记住结婚是为了生孩子,不是为了自己快活。路易莎认为这是老观念。做母亲的问她有没有想到新观念的后果是人类会绝子灭孙,路易莎不这么认为,而且她对这个问题根本不感兴趣。她和丈夫都心满意足。久而久之,世人都看到这一对美满幸福的夫妇,羡慕得很。

生活是愉快的。他们谁也不主宰谁,开销两人共同负担。有时候他挣得多,有时候是她,但两人对共同积蓄的贡献最终相等。

转眼到了她的生日。早上醒来时她见干杂活的女人进来了,

捧着一束花,拿着一封信,信上画满了花,还写着:

"献给花蕾般的爱妻,谨祝生日愉快,并请共进早餐——速来!"

她敲敲他的门。"请进!"他说。

他们坐在床上吃早饭,是他的床!干零活的女人留了一整天,包揽了所有的活计。真是个快乐的生日!

他们的幸福有增无减,就这样过了两年,那些预言家的预言全错了。

好一对模范夫妻!

但两年过去后,妻子病了。她认为是中了墙纸的毒,他说是有细菌感染。对了,一定是细菌作怪。然而,出了反常的事。有些现象是不该有的。她一定是患了感冒。后来,她的身体变大了。难道她长了肿瘤吗?的确,他们担心是肿瘤。

她找了医生,回家时哭哭啼啼。当真她身体里长了东西,然而是一个有一天会见到阳光、会开花结果的东西。

丈夫可没有哭。他觉到这事新鲜,这家伙到他的俱乐部向朋友说了开来。妻子一个劲儿地哭。她的处境现在会怎样变呢?很快,她不能干活挣钱了,以后便只能靠他养活。他们还得请佣人!哎唷唷!那帮佣人!

他们用心良苦,最后遇上不可避免的事,气力全白费了。

但丈母娘的来信封封充满热情,还一再说,上帝注定结婚是为了生儿育女,至于父母乐不乐意,那是小事一桩。

丈夫雨果求妻子别再想以后不能挣钱的事。她养育孩子,不就是尽了她的全部本分吗?不就等于挣了钱吗?挣钱的正确理解不就是工作吗?所以,她就等于尽了自己的义务。

她怎么也想不通,为什么她非靠他供养不可。但孩子生下以后,她把一切忘得干干净净。她与以前一样,仍是他的妻子、伴侣,不同的是又成了他的孩子的母亲,而他觉得最可贵的正是这一点。

The Jewels of M. Lantin

Guy de Maupassant

M. Lantin, having met this young lady at a party given by his immediate superior, was literally enmeshed by love.

She was the daughter of a provincial tax collector who had died a few years previously. With her mother, she had come to Paris. Her mother became friendly with several middle-class families of the neighborhood in hopes of marrying off the young lady. Mother and daughter were poor, honorable, quiet, and gentle. The girl seemed to be the typical dream woman into whose hands any young man would yearn to entrust his entire life. Her modest beauty had an angelic quality, and the imperceptible smile which constantly graced her lips, seemed a reflection of her heart.

Everyone sang her praises; everyone who knew her repeated incessantly: "It will be a lucky fellow who wins her. You couldn't find a better catch!"

M. Lantin, now chief clerk of the Minister of the Interior, at a salary of 3,500 francs, asked and received her hand in marriage.

The Jewels of M. Lantin

He was unbelievably happy. She managed the house with such skill that their life was one of luxury. There was no delicacy, no whim of her husband's which she did not secure and satisfy; and her personal charm was such that, six years after their first meeting, he loved her even more than he had initially.

He begrudged her only two traits—her love of the theater and her passion for artificial jewels.

Her friends (she knew the wives of several minor functionaries) were always getting her seats for the fashionable plays, sometimes even for first nights; and she dragged her poor husband, willy-nilly, to these entertainments which completely wore him out, tired as he was[①] after a hard day's work. He begged her to agree to go to the theater with some lady friend of hers who would accompany her home. She took a long time to decide, claiming this a most inconvenient arrangement. At last, however, she agreed, and he was profoundly grateful to her.

Now, this taste for the theater naturally stirred in her the need to primp. Her toilette remained simple, to be sure—always modest but in good taste; and her gentle grace, her irresistible, humble, smiling grace seemed to acquire a new savor from the simplicity of her dress, but she became accustomed to wearing two huge rhinestone earrings, which looked like diamonds; and she had strings of artificial pearls around her neck, and wore bracelets of similar gems.

Her husband, who somewhat scorned this love of garish display,

---

① tired as he was: though he was tired。as 引导让步状语从句时，从句的表语需置其前。

said, "Dearest, when you haven't the means① to wear real jewelry, you should show yourself adorned only with your own grace and beauty; these are the true pearls."

But she, smiling quietly, would insist, "Can I help it? I love it so. This is my vice. I know, my dear, how absolutely right you are; but I can't really remake myself, can I? I think I would just idolize real jewelry."

And she would roll the pearls in her fingers. "See how perfect," she'd say. "You'd swear they were real."

Sometimes, during the evening, while they sat before the fire, she would bring out her jewel chest, put it on the tea table, and commence to examine the contents with passionate attention, as though there were some subtle and profound secret delight in this pursuit. She persisted in draping strings of pearls around her husband's neck; then she would laugh merrily, crying, "How silly you look, my darling!" And she would throw herself into his arms and kiss him wildly.

One wintry evening, when she had been at the opera, she came home shivering with cold. The next day she was coughing wretchedly. A week later she died.

Lantin nearly followed her into the tomb. His despair was such that, in a month's time, his hair turned completely white. He wept incessantly, his very soul seared by unbearable suffering, haunted by the memory, the smile, the voice—by the overwhelming beauty of his

---

① the means: means 此处指财产。注意其复数形式。

The Jewels of M. Lantin

deceased wife.

Even the passage of time failed to stem his grief. Frequently, at his office, while his colleagues were chatting idly, his cheeks would tremble and his eyes would fill with tears; he would grimace horribly and commence to sob.

He kept his wife's room intact, and sealed himself in every day to meditate. All her furniture and even her dresses remained just where they had been on the fatal day.

Living became difficult for him. His income which, under his wife's management, amply supplied the needs of both, now became insuffcient for him alone. Dazed, he wondered how she had been able to purchase the superb wines and delicacies which he could no longer afford.

He fell into debt and began to scurry around for money as does anyone suddenly plunged into poverty. One fine morning, finding himself penniless a full week before payday, he thought about selling something. Suddenly the idea swept over him of taking a look① at his wife's treasure trove, because, if the truth be told, he had always harbored some resentment towards this store of brilliants. The mere sight of them slightly tarnished the memory of his beloved.

It was a difficult business, searching through the case of jewels, because, even up to the very last days of her life, his wife had shopped stubbornly, bringing home some new bauble practically every night. He

---

① of taking a look: 是修饰 idea 的定语。

finally chose the magnificent necklace she seemed to have preferred, which, he figured, was worth six or seven francs, because, for artificial gems, it was really a masterpiece of craftsmanship.

With the jewels in his pocket he walked towards the Ministry, looking for a reliable jeweler.

Spotting a store, he entered—somewhat chagrined to be making this public display of his poverty and ashamed at attempting to sell so worthless an object.

He approached the merchant. "Excuse me. I wonder what value you would place on this piece."

The man took the necklace, examined it, turned it over, weighed it, called to his partner, talked to him in low tones, placed the necklace on the counter and scrutinized it carefully from a distance as though judging the effect[①].

M. Lantin, overwhelmed by this process, opened his mouth to protest: "Oh! I know that piece isn't worth anything," but just at that moment the storekeeper said:

"Monsieur, this piece is worth between twelve and fifteen thousand francs, but I cannot buy it until I learn exactly how you came into possession of it."

Lantin stared, wide-eyed, silent—uncomprehending. He finally stammered, "What? You are absolutely sure?"

The gentleman seemed offended by his attitude, and said wryly,

---

① the effect: effect 指人或事物给人的印象。

The Jewels of M. Lantin

"You may go elsewhere if you think you can do better. To me that is worth fifteen thousand at the very most. If you find no better offer, you may come back here."

M. Lantin, stupified, took the necklace and left, feeling a curious urge to be alone and undistrubed.

But, before he had gone far, he was seized with an impulse to laugh, and he thought, "Imbecile! What a fool! What if I had taken him at his word! What a jeweler—not to know the difference between real gems and fakes!"

And he entered another jewelry store on the Rue de la Paix. As soon as he saw the jewel, the dealer cried, "Of course! I know this necklace well; I sold it!"

Deeply disturbed, M. Lantin asked, "How much is it worth?"

"Sir—I sold it for twenty-five thousand francs. I'm ready to take it back for eighteen thousand, if you will tell me①—the law, you know—how you happened to receive it."

This time Lantin sat paralyzed with astonishment. He stutered, "But—but—examine it very closely, sir. I have always thought it was—artificial."

The jeweler asked, "Would you please tell me your name, sir?"

"Of course. I'm Lantin. I work at the Ministry of the Interior, and I live at 16 Rue des Martyrs."

The merchant opened his ledger, looked through it, and said,

---

① if you will tell me：此处 will 义为"愿意"，不是表示将来时态的助动词。

"This necklace was sent to Mme. Lantin, 16 Rue des Martyrs, on the twentieth of July, 1876."

And the two men stared at each other, the clerk dumbfounded; the jeweler scenting a robber.

The merchant said, "Would you mind letting me have this for a day? Naturally, I'll give you a receipt."

M. Lantin blurted out, "Of course!" And he left, folding the paper into his pocket.

Then he crossed the street, went back, saw that he had gone out of his way, returned past the Tuileries, saw again he had made a mistake, crossed the Seine, went back to the Champs-Elysées without a single clear notion in his head. He forced himself to think. His wife could not possibly have purchased such valuable jewelry. Absolutely not! Well then? A present? A present! From whom? For what?

He was brought up short, and he stood stock still①—there in the middle of the street. A horrible thought flashed across his mind. She? But all those other jewels were also gifts! He felt the earth shiver; a tree just before him seemed to crush him. He threw out his arms and fell, senseless, to the ground.

He regained consciousness in a nearby pharmacy to which passers-by had carried him. He asked that he be taken home, and he locked himself in.

He wept bitterly until nightfall—stuffing a handkerchief into his

---

① stock still: as still as a stock。也可说 as still as a log，此处的 stock 就是指木头。

The Jewels of M. Lantin

mouth to stifle his cries. Then he staggered to bed, wrung out with fatigue and chagrin, and he slept heavily.

A ray of sunshine woke him, and he got up slowly to go to his office. After such a blow, it would be hard to carry on with his work. He felt that he could be excused, and he wrote his superior a note. Then he thought that he ought to go back to the jeweler; and he crimsoned with shame. He could not possibly leave the necklace with that man. He dressed hurriedly and went out.

As he walked along, Lantin said to himself, "How easy it is to be happy when you're rich! With money you can even shake off your sorrows; you can go or stay as you please! You can travel and amuse yourself. If only I were really rich!"

Then he became aware of the fact that he was hungry, not having eaten since the previous evening. But his pockets were empty, and he reminded himself of the necklace. Eighteen thousand francs! Eighteen thousand francs! What a fortune!

He reached the Rue de la Paix, and he began pacing up and down opposite the shop. Eighteen thousand francs! More than twenty times he started to enter; but shame always halted him.

He was still hungry—famished—and without a sou. He finally made up his mind, raced across the street so as not to give himself time to think, and burst into the store.

As soon as he saw him, the merchant greeted him royally, offered him a chair with smiling courtesy. The partners then came in and sat down near Lantin, happiness beaming from their eyes and their lips.

The jeweler declared, "I am satisfied, Monsieur, and if you feel as you did yesterday, I am ready to pay you the sum agreed upon."

"Certainly," stammered Lantin.

The merchant took eighteen large notes from a drawer, counted them, gave them to Lantin, who signed a receipt and, with trembling hand, stuffed the money into his pocket.

Then, just as he was going out, he turned back towards the grinning shopkeeper, and, lowering his eyes, murmured, "I—I have some other gems—which came to me in the same way. Would you be willing to buy those from me?"

The jeweler nodded, "Of course, Monsieur."

One of the partners barely stifled a laugh, while the other was forced to leave the room to hide his mirth.

Lantin, impassive and stern, said, "I'll bring them to you."

When he returned to the store, an hour later, he had still not eaten. They set about examining the jewels piece by piece, assessing each one. Then they all went back to Lantin's house.

Now Lantin entered into the spirit of the business, arguing, insisting that they show him the bills of sale, and getting more and more excited as the values rose.

The magnificent earrings were worth twenty thousand francs; the bracelets, thirty-five thousand. The brooches, pins and medallions, sixteen thousand. The whole collection was valued at one hundred ninety-six thousand francs.

The merchant boomed out in a jolly voice, "That's what happens when you put your money into jewelry."

Lantin said solemnly, "That's one way to invest your money!" Then he left, after having agreed with the purchaser to have a second expert appraisal the following day.

When he was out in the street, he looked up at the Vendome Column. He felt like leaping up to the top. He felt light enough to play leapfrog with the statue of the Emperor perched up there in the clouds.

He went into an elegant restaurant to eat, and he drank wine at twenty francs a bottle.

Then he took a cab and rode around the Bois de Boulogne. He looked at the gleaming carriages, suppressing a desire to cry out, "I'm rich, too! I have two hundred thousand francs!"

He thought of his office. He drove up, entered his Chief's office solemnly, and announced, "Sir—I'm tendering my resignation! I've just inherited three hundred thousand francs!" He went around shaking hands with his colleagues, and telling them all about his plans for the future. Then he went out to dinner at the Café Anglais.

Finding himself seated alongside a distinguished-looking gentleman, he couldn't resist whispering to him, a little archly, that he had just inherited four hundred thousand francs.

For the first time in his life he enjoyed the theater and he spend the night carousing.

Six months later he remarried. His second wife was a most worthy woman, but rather difficult. She made his life unbearable.

兰廷先生的珠宝

〔法〕莫泊桑

兰廷先生在顶头上司的宴会上遇到这位姑娘就一头栽进了情网。

她是省里一位几年前去世的税务员的女儿,随母亲到了巴黎。她妈妈在邻里中结交了好几户中产家庭,指望把姑娘嫁出去。母女俩虽穷,但名声好,朴实,本分。姑娘是位最理想的人儿,无论哪个青年都巴不得守着这样的人过一辈子。她又貌美,又庄重,宛如天使,嘴角总挂着一丝淡淡的微笑,那微笑仿佛是她心灵的影像。

人人对她交口称赞,凡认识她的总要说了又说:"得有福气的人才能娶到她。比她强的你上哪儿找?"

后来兰廷先生当了内务部长的首席秘书,年俸3500法郎,才向她求婚结了亲。

你不知道他有多幸福。她非常善于当家理财,两口子生活居然过得阔阔绰绰。她对丈夫体贴入微,一思一念都能领会迎合。她非常有魅力,虽相识六年,他对她的爱较之当初却有增无减。

他对她不满的只有两点:她喜欢上剧院,爱戴假宝石。

凡有新剧上演，她的朋友们（她认识好几位小官员的夫人）总要邀她到场，有时还看首演；虽然丈夫辛苦一天已经有气无力，可她不管他愿不愿意，仍拉他去消遣，弄得他筋疲力尽。他央求她答应，只跟能陪她回家的女伴上剧院。她嫌这是下策，拖了很久没下决心。但是，她最终还是同意了，他对她感激万分。

由于喜爱上剧院，自然而然她需要打扮。诚然，她的装束依旧简单（总是朴实而大方），她那文静的气质，那动人、矜持的风度，那款款浅笑，似乎因为衣着的简单才别具品味。但是她变了，耳上总要戴两只莱茵石耳坠，看起来倒像两颗真钻石，脖子上还挂着几串人造珍珠，手上有手镯，也是类似的货色。

她丈夫似乎有些看不惯这种俗气花哨的爱好，说："心肝，要是你戴不起真宝石，还不如让人看看你的气质和美貌，这才是真正值钱的珠宝。"

但她不以为然地笑着，不肯依。"叫我有什么办法？我就爱这样。亲爱的，你说得对极了，这是我的坏习气，但我又不能脱胎换骨，对吧？我不过想真珠宝想得要命。"

她用手指玩着珍珠，说："看，多精巧！你不把它当真的才怪哩！"

夜晚，当两人坐在火炉前时，她常取出珠宝箱，放到茶桌上，一件件细细欣赏里面的东西，好像这样做其乐无穷。她还硬把一串串珍珠往丈夫的脖子上挂，开心地笑着，叫着："亲爱的，你这模样真有意思！"然后，就扑到他怀里，发疯似地吻他。

有一年冬天的一个夜晚，她看完新剧回来冷得直哆嗦。到第二天，咳得厉害。再过一星期，她死了。

兰廷就差没跟着她进坟墓。他悲痛欲绝，没出一星期，头发全白了。他不住地哭,难过得心都碎了;往事历历在目,他忘不了她的音容笑貌,亡妻的天姿国色总浮现在脑海里。

甚至时间的流水也没冲淡他的哀伤。在办公室里,往往同事们在谈天说地,他却脸颊颤抖眼含泪,现出一副苦相,呜咽起来。

他把妻子房间里的一切都保持原样,每天独自坐在里面沉思。所有家具,甚至衣服,在那个不幸的日子放在哪里,现在仍然放在哪里。

他的生活变得拮据起来。妻子当家时,他的收入两人花还绰绰有余,现在却不够一人的开销。他给弄糊涂了,猜不透为什么佳肴美酒她有钱买,而他却无法再问津。

他负债了,没逃出每个一朝落魄的人的困境,开始为了钱而团团转。有一天早上,风和日丽,他却一文不名,并且离发薪还差整整一星期,于是他想变卖点什么。突然,一个念头从他脑子里闪过:不妨看看妻子的百宝箱。说实在的,他对这箱珍宝一直感到不大痛快。瞧一眼不要紧,这一来他对爱妻的思念却减了一分。

翻珠宝箱还是件难事,因为妻子在临终前几天,仍执意要上商店,天天夜里带回一件新玩意。最后他拣了她喜爱的一条漂亮项链,算算,估计值六七个法郎;虽然这是一件赝品,但的确属于能工巧匠的杰作。

他把项链揣进衣兜往部里走,顺路找一个可靠的珠宝商。

他挑中一家店,走了进去,但想到因此要让人看出他的穷困,多少有些心酸;他要卖的又是件值不了几个钱的东西,也感到难为情。

他走近了店主:"劳驾,请看看这一件你能出什么价。"

那人接过项链，看了看，翻过来，掂掂分量，又叫来伙计，低声说了几句，再把项链放到柜台上，站在远处仔细打量，似乎在估计有几分像真的。

这一系列动作使兰廷先生憋不住了，张开嘴打算叫嚷："算了吧，我知道这东西不值钱！"但就在这时，店主说：

"先生，这东西值12,000到15,000法郎，但我得先弄清它的来路才会买。"

兰廷目瞪口呆。太不可思议！最后，话总算出了口："什么？你有绝对把握吗？"

那位先生似乎对他的态度有些恼火，没好气地说："你如果以为卖得上更好的价钱，就另找一家吧。我至多出15,000法郎，如果卖不到更好的价，你再回这儿来。"

兰廷先生莫名其妙，接过项链，走了，恨不得一个人躲起来，找个安静。

然而，没走多远，他又几乎要笑出声来，心想："笨脑袋！真傻！我该把他的话当真！还有这样的珠宝商，连真假宝石都分不出！"

他走进和平大道的另一家珠宝店。珠宝商一看到项链便嚷开了："没错！我认得这条项链，是我卖出去的！"

兰廷先生的心怦怦跳着，问："值多少钱呢？"

"先生，我卖出的价是25,000法郎，现在愿出18,000法郎买回，只是你得说——你知道规矩——说出它怎么到了你手里。"

这一次兰廷吃惊得不能动弹。他结结巴巴地说："可是——可是——你仔细瞧瞧，先生。我一直以为它是——是假的。"

珠宝商道："先生，请问尊姓大名？"

"我姓兰廷，在内务部工作，住先烈街16号。"

那商人翻开账簿，一页页查，说："这条项链于1876年7月12日送往先烈街16号兰廷夫人家。"

两人面面相觑，兰廷先生目瞪口呆，珠宝商只当看到了强盗。

珠宝商道："你能不能让它在我这儿搁一天？当然，我给你收条。"

兰廷先生脱口道："那行！"他出了店门，把收条叠好放进口袋。

接着，他横过马路，往回走，却发现走错了路，又掉转头，等过了杜伊勒里宫，又发现错了，于是从塞纳河桥回头往爱利舍大道走，一路上脑子活像一锅粥。他好不容易开始思索。他妻子不可能买这样贵重的珠宝。绝对不可能！那是怎么回事呢？是别人送的？送的！谁送的？？为什么送？？？

他停下来，站着一动不动，就呆在马路正中。一个可怕的念头掠过脑际。她？但是，别的珠宝也全是人家送的！他只觉得天旋地转，正对着他的一棵树仿佛朝他倒了下来。他摊开两手，倒在地上，人事不省。

他苏醒过来后，发现自己躺在附近一家药店里，原来是被过路人抬进来的。他请人护送他回家，然后锁上了房门。

他痛哭流涕，直到天黑；为了怕人听到哭声，他往嘴里塞了一块手帕。天黑以后东倒西歪地上了床，已经有气无力，沉沉地睡了过去。

这一觉他直睡到太阳照到了脸上。他慢慢儿起床，打算去上班。受到这样沉重的打击，坚持上班谈何容易。他觉得有理由请假，给上司写了张请假条。接着他想到该去珠宝商那儿，羞得脸发烧。真不该把项链留在店里。他匆匆穿好衣服，出了门。

兰廷一路走一路想:"成了富翁过得快活还不容易!有了钱你甚至能使悲伤烟消云散,想走就走,想留就留!你可以去旅行,去消遣。要是我当真成了富翁就好了!"

这时,他意识到还是前一天晚上吃的饭,肚皮已经饿了。可是,他的衣袋空空,这才又记起项链。18,000法郎!18,000法郎!多大一笔洋财!

他走到和平大道,却在珠宝店对过来回踱起步子来。18,000法郎!他打了20多次主意,想进店门,每一次因羞愧而畏缩不前。

他饥肠辘辘,腹内空空,袋内也空空,终于,他下了决心。为了不让自己有时间再犹豫,跑过马路,冲进了店里。

珠宝商一看见他,招呼得异常热情,陪着笑,恭恭敬敬请他坐。马上两个伙计进来了,在兰廷左右坐下,乐得眉开眼笑。

珠宝商说:"先生,太好了。如果你昨天的主意没有变,我这就付给你已说定的钱数。"

"好——好吧。"兰廷结结巴巴道。

那商人从抽屉取出18张大钞票,数过一遍,交给兰廷。兰廷的手颤抖着,在收据上签了字,把钱塞进口袋。

但是在快出店门时,他又转过身,向眉飞色舞的店主走来,眨着眼,轻声问:"我——我还有些宝石,来路也一样,你愿不愿买?"

珠宝商点点头:"那当然,先生。"

那两个伙计一个几乎要笑出声来,另一个为了遮掩自己的高兴劲儿,只得躲进另一间屋子。

兰廷没那股劲儿,满脸一本正经,说:"等等我给你们拿来。"

一小时以后,他回到店里,还是没吃没喝。那些珠宝几个人一件件看,一件件估价,最后它们又统统回了兰廷的家。

现在兰廷懂得生意经了，讨价还价，叫他们非拿卖货账目出来看不可，随着对方出价的增高，越来越兴奋。

大耳坠可卖2万法郎，手镯3.5万，各式胸针、别针、小像牌1.6万，全部财宝估价19.6万法郎。

珠宝商用高兴的声音嚷道："你花钱买宝石就会是这个结果。"

兰廷严肃地说："这是一种生财之道！"后来，他答应珠宝商第二天再找内行的人做第二次估价，走了。

到了大街，他抬头看着旺多姆圆柱，想纵身跳上柱顶，感到体轻如燕，可以和高耸入云的柱顶上的皇帝塑像玩跳蛙游戏。

他走进一家高级餐厅吃饭，喝20法郎一瓶的酒。

然后，他雇了辆马车，在布洛涅森林公园兜圈子。他看着闪闪亮的过往马车，真想大叫："我也是富翁了！我有20万法郎！"

他想到了自己的公务，便乘车上部里。他迈着庄重的步子走进部长办公室，宣告："大人，我请求辞职！我刚继承了30万法郎的财产！"又与同事们一一握手，把以后的打算告诉了他们。出了内务部，他往英国咖啡馆①吃午饭。

他发觉邻座是位仪表不凡的绅士，忍不住耍起小聪明，低声对那人说，他刚继承了40万法郎的财产。

他生平第一次爱上了剧院，晚上还喝得酩酊大醉。

半年后他又结了婚。第二个妻子是位十足的贵妇，但相当难对付，使他没法过日子。

---

① 19世纪巴黎最有名的餐厅。

The Boy Who Drew Cats

Koisumi Yakumo

A long, long time ago, in a small country village in Japan, there lived a poor farmer and his wife, who were very good people. They had a number of children, and found it very hard to feed them all. The elder son was strong enough when only fourteen years old to help his father; and the little girls learned to help their mother almost as soon as they could walk.

But the youngest, a little boy, did not seem to be fit for hard work. He was very clever—cleverer than all his brothers and sisters; but he was quite weak and small, and people said he could never grow very big. So his parents thought it would be better for him to become a priest than to become a farmer. They took him with them to the village-temple one day, and asked the good old priest who lived there if he would have their little boy for his acolyte, and teach him all that a priest ought to know.

The old man spoke kindly to the lad, and asked him some hard questions. So clever were the answers that the priest agreed to take the little fellow into the temple as an acolyte, and to educate him for the priesthood.

The boy learned quickly what the old priest taught him, and was very obedient in most things. But he had one fault. He liked to draw cats during study-hours, and to draw cats even where cats ought not to have been drawn at all.

Whenever he found himself alone, he drew cats. He drew them on the margins of the priest's books, and on all the screens of the temple, and on the walls, and on the pillars. Several times the priest told him this was not right; but he did not stop drawing cats. He drew them because he could not really help it. He had what is called "the genius of an artist," and just for that reason he was not quite fit to be an acolyte; —a good acolyte should study books.

One day after he had drawn some very clever pictures of cats upon a paper screen, the old priest said to him severely: "My boy, you must go away from this temple at once. You will never make a good priest, but perhaps you will become a great artist. Now let me give you a last piece of advice, and be sure you never forget it. *Avoid large places at night; —keep to small!* "

The boy did not know what the priest meant by saying, "*Avoid large places;—keep to small.*" He thought and thought, while he was tying up his little bundle of clothes to go away; but he could not understand those words, and he was afraid to speak to the priest any more, except to say goodby.

He left the temple very sorrowfully, and began to wonder what he

216

The Boy Who Drew Cats

should do. If he went straight home he felt sure his father would punish him for having been disobedient to the priest; so he was afraid to go home. All at once he remembered that at the next village, twelve miles away, there was a very big temple. He had heard there were several priests at that temple; and he made up his mind to go to them and ask them to take him for their acolyte.

Now that big temple was closed up but the boy did not know this fact. The reason it had been closed up was that a goblin had frightened the priests away, and had taken possession of the place. Some brave warriors had afterward gone to the temple at night to kill the goblin; but they had never been seen alive again. Nobody had ever told these things to the boy; —so he walked all the way to the village hoping to be kindly treated by the priests.

When he got to the village, it was already dark, and all the people were in bed; but he saw the big temple on a hill at the other end of the principal street, and he saw there was a light in the temple. People who tell the story say the goblin used to make that light, in order to tempt lonely travelers to ask for shelter. The boy went at once to the temple, and knocked. There was no sound inside. He knocked and knocked again; but still nobody came. At last he pushed gently at the door, and was quite glad to find that it had not been fastened. So he went in, and saw a lamp burning—but no priest.

He thought some priest would be sure to come very soon, and he sat down and waited. Then he noticed that everything in the temple was gray with dust, and thickly spun over with cobwebs. So he thought to himself that the priests would certainly like to have an acolyte, to keep the place clean. He wondered why they had allowed everything to get so dusty. What most pleased him, however, were some big white screens, good to paint cats upon. Though he was tired, he looked at once for a writing pad, and found one and ground some ink, and began to paint cats.

He painted a great many cats upon the screens; and then he began to feel very, very sleepy. He was just on the point of lying down to sleep beside one of the screens, when he suddenly remembered the words, "*Avoid large places; —keep to small!* "

The temple was very large; he was all alone; and as he thought of these words—though he could not quite understand them—he began to feel for the first time a little afraid; and he resolved to look for a *small place* in which to sleep. He found a little cabinet, with a sliding door, and went into it, and shut himself up. Then he lay down and fell fast asleep.

Very late in the night he was awakened by a most terrible noise— a noise of fighting and screaming. It was so dreadful that he was afraid even to look through a chink in the little cabinet; he lay very still, holding his breath for fright.

The light that had been in the temple went out; but the awful sounds continued, and became more awful, and all the temple shook. After a long time silence came; but the boy was still afraid to move. He did not move until the light of the morning sun shone into the cabinet through the chinks of the little door.

Then he got out of his hiding place vary cautiously, and looked about. The first thing he saw was that all the floor of the temple was covered with blood. And then he saw, lying dead in the middle of it, an enormous, monstrous rat—a goblin-rat—bigger than a cow!

But who or what could have killed it? There was no man or other creature to be seen. Suddenly the boy observed that the mouths of all the cats he had drawn the night before, were red and wet with blood. Then he knew that the goblin had been killed by the cats which he had drawn. And then also, for the first time, he understood why the wise old priest had said to him, "*Avoid large places at night;—keep to small.*"

Afterward that boy became a very famous artist. Some of the cats which he drew are still shown to travelers in Japan.

爱画猫的孩子

〔日〕小泉八云

很久很久以前,日本的一个小乡村有个贫苦农民,夫妻俩都非常善良。他们生了好些孩子,供给他们吃喝很不容易。大儿子身强力壮,14岁时就成了父亲的帮手,几个小女儿几乎刚学会走路就成了母亲的帮手。

但最小的儿子不像是干重活的料。他非常聪明,比哥哥姐姐都聪明,但身体弱、个子小,大家说他永远长不大。于是,他的父母想叫他当和尚,不要种地。一天,他们把他送到村子的庙里,请那儿的老和尚将他收作徒弟,教他当和尚。

老和尚对孩子说话和颜悦色,问了他几个难题。孩子答得很让人满意,和尚便收他进庙做了徒弟,教他当和尚。

老和尚的传授孩子领会很快,而且相当听话。但是他有一个缺点:爱在诵经的时候画猫,还在不该画的地方乱涂乱画。

只要师父不在,他就画猫,在经书的边缘上画,墙上画,柱子上画,屏风上画。好几次师父叫他别画,但他从没歇手。他爱画是因为忍不住要画。他有所谓"画家的天才",所以不宜当小和尚——当个好和尚应该攻读经文。

有一天，他在纸屏风上画了好几只活灵活现的猫，老和尚见了拉下面孔对他说："徒儿，你马上从我庙里出去吧。你当和尚不行，也许当画师有出息。你走之前我要对你叮嘱一件事，千万记住：夜晚靠小不靠大。"

孩子不明白师父说的"靠小不靠大"是什么意思，一边把衣服打成小包，一边反复思量，但怎样也猜不透这句话，又不敢问师父，只好拜别。

离开庙他觉得非常难过，不知怎么办好。如果回家，父亲准会责怪他不听师父管教，所以不敢回。忽然他想起12里路外的邻村有一座大庙，那儿有好几个和尚，便决心投奔，请他们收作徒弟。

其实那座大庙已经关闭，但孩子并不知道。原来，庙里出了妖怪，把和尚吓跑了，占了那地方，庙只好关门。后来有几个胆大的武士夜晚想去庙里除妖，但没有一个生还。这些事孩子没有听说，所以他直往那村子走，指望和尚热情收留。

进村以后天黑了，村里的人都已睡觉，但他看到大街另一头的山上有座大庙，庙里还有灯光。据说灯是妖怪点的，专为引诱过往行人投宿。孩子一直往大庙走，敲敲门，里面没有动静。他敲了又敲，还是不见人开门。于是他轻轻一推，高兴地发现门没有拴，便走了进去，看到点了一盏灯，但是没有和尚。

他以为过一会儿和尚会来，就坐下等着。这时他才看到庙里到处是厚厚一层灰，蜘蛛结满了网。于是他想，这儿的和尚一定肯收个徒弟，好把庙里打扫干净。他猜不透为什么会弄得到处都是灰。然而他最高兴的是这儿有几块大白屏风，上面好画猫。虽然他已经走累了，但马上找砚台，也果真找着了，研好墨，画起猫来。

他在屏风上画了许许多多猫以后，瞌睡上来了，正要躺在一幅大屏风旁睡，突然想起了师父的话：靠小不靠大。

寺庙很大，他只孤身一人，想起这话心里开始害怕起来，尽管他还猜不透这句话的意思。他决定找个"小"地方睡觉。他看到了一个小柜子，门是推拉的，钻进去，把门关上，躺下睡着了。

到深更半夜，他被一阵大吵大闹的声音惊醒了——是厮打和尖叫的声音，可怕极了。他躲在小柜子里，连从缝里瞧一眼都不敢，躺着一动不动，吓得气也不敢出。

庙里的灯灭了，但那可怕的声音还在响着，而且越来越可怕，整个庙都震动了。

过了很久，庙里恢复了平静，但孩子还不敢动弹。一直等到太阳照进了小柜的门缝里，他才从躲藏的地方小心翼翼钻了出来，四下一看，先看到满地是血，后看到大殿当中躺着只大老鼠精，比牛还大，原来就是那妖怪。

老鼠精怎么丧了命呢？既不见人，也不见什么动物。突然，孩子发现头天晚上他画的猫只只嘴上鲜血淋漓，这才明白妖怪是被他画的猫咬死的。这一来他也明白了聪明的老和尚为什么对他说"夜晚靠小不靠大"。

后来孩子成了一位大名鼎鼎的画家，他画的猫有的现在到日本的游客还能看到。

The Crime on Calle de la Persequida[①]

Palacio Valdes

"Here, as you see me, sits before you a murderer."

"How's that, Don Elias!" I exclaimed, laughing, as I filled his glass with beer.

Don Elias is the kindest individual, the most reserved and disciplined in the Telegraph Corps. He is incapable of going on strike even though his boss should order him to dust off his trousers[②].

"Yes, sir. There are circumstances in life—there comes a moment when the most peace-loving man ..."

"Come, come; tell me about this," I said, piqued with curiosity.

It was in the winter of '78. Because of reorganization I was out of a job and had gone to live in O.[③] with a married daughter of mine. My

---

① Calle de la Persequida: 法文,其意见译文。
② order him to dust off his trousers: 直译为"叫他掸裤子上的灰",意即做任何别人不愿做的事。
③ in O.: 此处 O 相当于汉语的"某地",不必译出。

life there was too easy—eat, stroll about, sleep. Sometimes I helped my son-in-law, who is employed by the Municipal Government, copying the secretary's minutes. We dined invariably at eight. After putting my granddaughter to bed—she was then three years old and is today a good-looking blonde, plump, one of those you like (I modestly lowered my eyes and took a gulp of beer)—and after that I used to spend the evening with Doña Nieves, a widow who lives alone on Persequida Street and to whom my son-in-law owes his job. She lives on her property in a huge old one-story house which has a dark entrance gate with a stone stairway. Don Gerardo Piquero also used to drop around; he had been Customs Administrator in Puerto Rico and was retired. The poor fellow died a couple of years ago. He'd get there around nine; I'd never get there until after nine-thirty. However, he'd pull out at ten-thirty sharp, while I'd stay on until eleven or later.

One night I left, as usual, at about this time. Doña Nieves is very economical and puts on a show of being poor when actually she owns enough property to do herself proud and live like a grand lady. She'd never set out any lamp to light the stairs or portal. When Don Gerardo or I departed, the maid would light the way with a lamp from the kitchen. As soon as we'd close the gate, she would put out the light and leave us in almost utter darkness, since there was scarcely any light penetrating from the street.

As I took the first step I felt what is vulgarly called a slap; that is to say with one heavy blow my hat was rammed down to my nose. I was paralyzed with fear and fell against the wall. I thought I heard tittering, and somewhat recovered from my fright I pulled off my hat.

"Who goes these?" I shouted in a loud and threatening voice.

No one replied. Rapidly I imagined various possibilities. Was I about to be robbed? Did some little hoodlums wish to entertain themselves at my expense? Could it be a friend playing a practical joke? I resolved to depart immediately, since the gate was open. When I reached the middle of the portal, I received a heavy blow on the thighs, delivered by the palm of a hand, and at the same time a group of five or six men blocked the gateway.

"Help!" I screamed in a strangled voice, retreating once again toward the wall. The men began to jump up and down in front of me with wild gesticulations. My terror knew no bounds.

"Where are you going at this hour, thief?" asked one.

"He must be going to steal a corpse. He's the doctor," said another.

It then occurred to me that they were drunk, and pulling myself together, I loudly exclaimed.

"Out, dogs! Let me by, or I'll kill one of you." At the same time I grasped an iron club which had been given me by a foreman in the Arms Factory and which I always carried about with me at night.

The men, paying no attention, continued dancing before me, using the same wild gestures. I could observe by the dim light from the street, that they kept one man in the foreground as the strongest and most determined behind whom the rest took shelter.

"Out of the way!" I shouted again, swinging my club like a windmill.

"Give up, dog!" they replied without ceasing their fantastic dance.

I was no longer in any doubt: they were drunk. Because of this conviction and because no weapons glittered in their hands, I became relatively calm. I lowered the club, and, endeavoring to give my words a note of authority, I said,

"Come on, now. Stop the clowning! Make way."

"Give up, dog! Are you going to suck blood from the dead? Are you going to cut off someone's leg? Tear off his ear! Tear out an eye! Pull his nose!"

These were the replies that came in answer to my request. At the same time they advanced upon me. One of them, not the one in the foreground, but another, reached over the shoulder of the first and, grabbing my nose, gave it such an awful yank that I cried out in pain. I leaped sideways, because my back was against the wall, and I managed to separate myself from them somewhat; I raised the club and, blind with rage, brought it down on the first fellow. He fell heavily to the ground without uttering a cry. The rest fled.

I was alone and waited anxiously for the wounded man to groan or to move. Nothing—not even a whimper; not even the slightest movement. Then it occurred to me that I might have killed him. The club was really heavy, and all my life my hobby has been keeping fit. I hurried, with trembling hands, to get out my match box and light a match ...

I can't describe to you what went through my mind at that moment. Stretched on the ground, face up, lay a dead man. Yes, dead!

I clearly read death on the pale features. The match fell from my hands and once again I was in darkness. I saw him only for a moment, but the spectre was so vivid that no detail escaped me. He was a heavy fellow with a black and tangled beard, a nose large and beaked; he wore a blue shirt, colored trousers, and sandals. On his head was a black beret. He appeared to be a workman from the arms plant—a gunsmith, as they call him around there.

I can tell you for certain that the things I thought of in one instant there in the darkness, I'd never have time to think of now in an entire day. I clearly foresaw what would happen: the death of that man divulged immediately throughout the city; the police laying hands on me; the consternation of my son-in-law; the dismay of my daughter; the wails of my granddaughter. Then imprisonment, the weary process dragging through months and perhaps years; the difficulty of proving that the deed was done in self-defense; the accusation of the district attorney naming me an assassin as always happens in such cases; my lawyer's defense citing my noble antecedents; then the verdict of the Court absolving me perhaps, perhaps condemning me to prison.

With one leap I landed in the street and ran to the corner, but then I realized I'd come without my hat, and I turned back. Once again I went through the portal with the greatest fear and revulsion. I lit another match and threw a sidewise glance at my victim in the hope of seeing him breathe. Nothing—there he lay in the same spot, rigid and yellowed, without a tinge of color in his face, which made me think that he had died of a cerebral concussion. I found my hat, ran my hand inside it to get it back in shape, and putting it on, got out of there.

But this time I took care not to run. The instinct of self-preservation had taken hold of me completely, and helped me to think up all ways of evading justice. I hugged the wall along the shadows, and as noiselessly as possible soon rounded the corner of Persequida Street to enter San Joaquin and return home. I endeavored to give my gait all the assurance and composure possible. But behold, there on Altavilla Street, just as I had begun to calm down, there unexpectedly appeared a police officer from the City Hall.

"Don Elias, could you kindly tell me ...?"

I heard no more. I leaped so far that I placed several yards between the constable and myself. Then, without glancing back I took off in a desperate mad race through the streets. I reached the outskirts of the city and halted, panting and perspiring. Then I regained my senses. What madness had I committed! That constable know me. Most probably he had approached me to ask me something concerning my son-in-law. My outlandish behavior had filled him with amazement. He may have thought I'd gone crazy; but by morning when news of the crime was known, he would surely start conjecturing and make his suspicions known to the judge. Suddenly I felt an icy chill.

Appalled, I walked toward and soon reached home. As I got in, I suddenly had a happy thought. I went straight to my room, put away the iron club in the closet and took up another cudgel which I had and went out again. My daughter appeared in the doorway, much surprised. I invented the pretext of a date with a friend at the Casino, and did in fact make my way hurriedly to this spot. There were still quite a few men gathered there in the room next to the billiard room who were part of the late conversation group. I sat down among them, put on a good-natured demeanor and was exceedingly jovial and gay, managing by all manner of devices to have them notice the light stick I carried in my hand. I would bend it into an arc; I'd switch it against my trousers. I'd brandish it like a foil, touch the back of one of the talkers to ask him anything at all. I'd let it fall to the floor. In short, nothing was left undone to call attention to the stick.

When at last the gathering broke up and I separated from my companions on the street, I was somewhat calmed. But once at home and in my room, I was seized with a mortal sorrow. I realized that these wiles would only serve to aggravate my situation should suspicion fall on me. Mechanically I undressed and remained sitting on the edge of my bed for a long while absorbed in dark thoughts. At length the cold forced me into bed.

I couldn't close my eyes. I turned and twisted a thousand times between the sheets, prey to a dreadful anxiety and fear which the silence and solitude rendered more acute. At each instant I expected to hear a pounding on the door and the constabulary's step upon the stair. Nevertheless, at dawn, sleep overcame me; that is to say, it was more like a deep lethargy from which my daughter's voice roused me.

"Father, it's already ten o'clock! Your eyes look terrible! Have you had a bad night?"

"On the contrary, I slept beautifully," I hastened to reply.

I didn't even trust my daughter. Then, affecting nonchalance, "Has the *Echo of Commerce* arrived yet?"

"What a question! I should say so!"

"Bring it to me."

I waited until my daughter had left and unfolded the newspaper with a trembling hand. I skimmed over it with anxious eyes, but could find nothing. Suddenly I read in big headlines, *The Crime on Persequida Street* and froze with fear. Then I looked again more closely. It had been a hallucination. It was an article entitled, "The Criterion of the Padres of the Province." At length, making a supreme effort to control myself, I managed to read the gossip column where I found a section that read:

Mysterious Occurrence

The male nurses at the County Hospital have the dubious practice of using the harmless inmates of this insane asylum to run various errands, among them that of transferring corpses to the Autopsy Room. Last night, four of these demented men, engaged in such an errand, found the garden gate which opens onto San Idelfonso Park ajar, and they escaped through it carrying the corpse with them. As soon as the Hospital Administrator became aware of the situation, he sent various emissaries in search of them, but to no avail. At one o'clock in the morning these four demented men returned to the hospital, but without the corpse. The latter was found by a watchman on

Persequida Street inside the gateway to Doña Nieves Menendez's home.

We implore the Dean of the County Hospital to take the necessary measures so that these scandalous goings-on are not repeated.

I let the paper fall from my hands and was stricken with convulsive laughter which worked itself into hysterics.

"So that, actually, you had really killed a man who was already dead?"

"Precisely."

佩塞基达街凶杀案

〔西〕帕拉西奥·瓦尔德斯

"我坐在你面前你还不知道,我是个杀人凶手。"

"哪儿的话,堂埃利亚斯!"我往他杯里倒啤酒,笑着说。

堂埃利亚斯这人最善良、最稳重、最守规矩,在电报局屈指可数。即使老板叫他擦屁股,他也不会撒手不干。

"一点不假,生活中有这种情况,到时候连最安分守己的人……"

"你说说究竟怎么回事?"我忍不住好奇地说。

事情发生在1978年。由于改组,我失业了,住到了一个结了婚的女儿家。生活过得挺自在,就吃吃饭,散散步,睡大觉。有时候我给在市政府工作的女婿抄写会议记录。每天在8点吃晚饭。安顿好外孙女儿睡觉以后——当时外孙女儿才3岁,今天成了丰满、漂亮的金发女郎,你一定喜欢(我不大好意思地低下头,喝了口啤酒)——那以后我便去寡妇堂娜涅韦斯那儿消磨时间。她一个人住在佩塞基达街,我女婿多亏她才有了那个职位。她自己有房产,住一栋老式大平房,前门黑黢黢,要上石阶梯。堂赫拉尔多·皮克罗也天天去。他当过波多黎各的海关官员，退了休。这老兄不幸两年前死了。他大约9点去那儿，我每次都在9点半以后去。然而他10点半准时告辞，我要待到11点或11点以后。

一天晚上，我与往常一样，也在这个时候走。堂娜涅韦斯非常节俭，表面看起来穷，其实有大笔财产，足可以摆阔气，过贵妇人生活。她从不在楼梯上或者大门口点灯，每次堂赫拉尔多和我走时，都叫女仆用厨房里的灯照路，还不等我们关门，就吹灭灯，我们只好摸黑，因为街上的亮光照不进来。

刚跨出一步，用俗话所说，我便挨了一巴掌，被人用力一击，帽子打歪到了鼻子上。我吓呆了，倒在墙边。我听到有人咯咯笑，定了定神，摘下了帽子。

"是谁？"我厉声喝道。

没有人答话。马上我想到了几种可能。是想打劫吗？还是几个小流氓拿我开心？难道哪位朋友开了个玩笑？门开着，我决定马上走。走到门当中时，腿上重重挨了一下，是有人伸开巴掌打的，跟着五六个人把门堵住了。

"救命啊！"我尖叫起来，又退到了墙边。这些人在我面前乱蹦乱跳，指手画脚，把我吓得半死。

"这深更半夜你去哪儿偷什么？"一个问。

"一定是去偷尸体，他是医生。"又一个说。

我这才明白他们是群酒鬼，放大了胆，高声叫：

"滚开，狗东西！让开路，看我不宰了你们！"说着我摸出了一根铁棒，是兵工厂一个领班送的，夜晚我总随身带着。

这些人没有理会，还是在我面前跳着，一个劲指手画脚。借着街上照来的微光我看见他们把一个人推在最前面。那是最有力气和胆量的人，别的人全仗他的势。

"滚开些！"我又叫，把铁棒舞得呼呼直响。

"得了吧，老兄！"他们不示弱，仍比划着乱蹦乱跳。

我用不着再怀疑，这群人准喝醉了。我算是看准了，再加上他们手里没有武器，我镇静了很多，放下铁棒，把声音尽量放威严些，说：

"收场了吧，别这么胡闹！让开！"

"得了吧，老兄！你是想喝死人身上的血？还是割什么人的腿？把他的耳朵拧下来！挖眼睛！揪鼻子！"

他们就这么回答了我。这还不算，他们逼近我，有一个人——不是最前面的那个，是另一个——从第一个人肩后伸出只手，抓住我的鼻子，使劲一拽，痛得我叫了起来。我是靠墙站的，只好往旁边一跳，离他们远了些。我举起铁棒，一气之下，打了站在最前面的那家伙。他没叫一声，扑通倒在地上，其他人一哄而散。

我就剩一个人了，等着受伤的家伙哼一哼，动一动，心里直发急。可是没有动静，他哼也不哼，动也不动。我这才想起也许我把他打死了。铁棒很有些分量，我这一辈子又一直注意锻炼身体，有把力气。我急忙掏出火柴，划了一根，手直发抖……

这一照我吓破了胆。一个死人直挺挺脸朝上躺着。就是死啦！他的脸惨白，一看就知道是死人。火柴从手上掉了，眼前又一片黑。我只看了那么一下，但把死人的模样看得一清二楚，可说是一览无余。他体格魁梧，黑胡子乱糟糟，长着大鹰钩鼻，穿着蓝衬衫、花裤、拖鞋，头上戴顶扁圆软羊毛小帽，像是哪家兵工厂的工人，当地人叫他们枪炮匠。

那一刻我在黑黢黢的地方想到的事比我现在一整天想到的

还多。我把会发生的事情清清楚楚全估计到了：死人一经发现马上会闹得满城风雨；警察把我抓起来；女婿呆若木鸡；女儿伤心透顶；小外孙女哭哭啼啼。然后进监狱，案件一拖就几个月甚至几年；要证明我纯系自卫很不容易；地方检察官遇上这类案件照例指控我凶杀；我的律师为我辩护，说我世代高贵；然后法庭宣判，也许宣告无罪，也许判我坐牢。

我一纵身跳到街上，朝角落跑，这才记起丢了帽子，又转身回来。我再一次提心吊胆、战战兢兢穿过大门，又划着一根火柴，瞟了吃我一铁棒的人一眼，希望看到他回过气来。枉然！他躺在老地方，硬邦邦，脸蜡黄，没有一点人色，像是死于脑震荡。我找到了帽子，把手伸进去理理平，又戴上，走了。

这一次我没有跑。我本能地但求能保全自己，想出了种种逃脱法网的办法。我贴着墙根轻手轻脚在暗处走，很快转个弯出了佩塞基达街，到了圣华金，打算回家。自然，我把步子尽量放稳。可事有凑巧，走到阿尔塔维勒街，我刚镇静了些，却突然闯出了市政厅的一名警官。

"堂埃利亚斯，请问你……？"

我没往下听，一跳，离开了警官好几码远。接着，我头也不回，发疯似地在街上跑，出了市区才停下，气喘吁吁，汗流浃背。这时我才清醒过来。我真发了疯！这位警官认识我，走过来很可能是问问我女婿的什么事。我莫名其妙的行为准叫他猜不透，只当我得了神经病，但第二天早上事情一暴露，他非怀疑上我，向法官报告不可。我一下子像是掉进了冰窖。

我提心吊胆地走着，没多久到家了。进家门时我突然想到了个好主意，一直走进自己的房间，把铁棒藏进柜里，另外拿了一根棍，又出门了。女儿莫名其妙，站到了门口。我想了个借口，说要去俱乐部会一位朋友，然后当真去了那儿。台球室的隔壁房间还有好些人没散，都是爱在夜晚聊天的人。我也坐了下来，假装镇静，有说有笑，挖空心思让他们注意我手里没多少分量的棍，一会儿把它弄弯，一会儿用它拍拍裤腿，一会儿在手里舞舞，像是舞一把钝剑，一会儿又敲敲别人的背，装作打听些事，一会儿又让它掉到地上。总之，为了引起别人对这根棍的注意，什么动作都做了出来。

最后聚会散了，我与会友们在街上分手后，心安了些。但一回到家，走进自己房间，突然又懊悔起来，想到一旦我被怀疑上，这些做法只会弄巧成拙。我机械地脱下衣服，在床沿坐了很久，越想越害怕，后来冷得受不住了才躺下。

我合不上眼，在被窝里翻来覆去，覆去翻来，又心焦又害怕，再加夜深人静，更加难受。我随时准备听到敲门声和警察上楼的脚步声。快天亮时总算睡着了，而且睡得昏昏沉沉，后来听到女儿的声音，醒了过来。

"爸爸，已经10点啦！你的眼睛怎么这么难看？是晚上没睡好吗？"

"没这事！睡得很香。"我忙回答。

我对女儿也放心不下了。我装作漫不经心的样子，问道："《商业回声报》来了吗？"

"那还用问？准来了。"

"你给我拿来。"

我等到女儿走了才颤颤巍巍打开报纸，急急忙忙扫了一眼，可是什么也没看清。突然间，我见到一条大字标题"佩塞基达街的凶杀案",吓得呆若木鸡。再仔细一瞧,原来是幻觉,社论的标题是"外省神父的标准"。我好不容易才镇静下来,在八卦专栏里发现了一篇文章,是这样写的:

怪　事

县立医院的男护士有个怪习惯,叫院内精神病房不具攻击性的精神分裂症患者跑腿当差,例如往解剖室送尸体。昨夜4名这样的病人被派了这种差事。他们发现通往圣伊德尔丰索公园的门开着,便搬着死尸溜了出来。院长得知这一情况后,派人四处查找,均未见踪影。凌晨1点精神病人回到医院,但尸体没有了。后来佩塞基达街的一巡夜人发现尸体躺在堂娜涅韦斯·梅嫩德斯家门口。

我们恳请县医院院长采取必要措施,杜绝此类不体面的事发生。

报纸从手上掉了下来,我大笑着,笑得发疯。
"这么说,你真杀了人,不过杀的是个死人?"
"一点不错。"

A Wicked Boy

Anton Chekhov

Ivan Ivanych Lapkin, a young man of nice appearance, and Anna Semionovna Zamblitskaia, a young girl with a little turned-up nose, went down the steep bank and sat down on a small bench. The bench stood right by the water among some thick young osier bushes. What a wonderful little place! Once you'd sat down, you were hidden from the world—only the fish saw you, and the water-tigers, running like lightning over the water. The young people were armed with rods, nets, cans of worms, and other fishing equipment. Having sat down, they started fishing right away.

"I'm glad we're alone at last," Lapkin began, looking around. "I have to tell you a lot of things, Anna Semionovna ... an awful lot ... when I saw you the first time ... You've got a bite ... then I understood what I'm living for, understood where my idol was—to whom I must devote my honest, active life ... that must be a big one that's biting ... Seeing you, I feel in love for the first time, feel passionately in love! Wait before you give it a jerk ... let it bite harder ... Tell me, my darling,

I adjure you, may I count on—not on reciprocity, no! I'm not worthy of that, I dare not even think of that—may I count on ... Pull!"

Anna Semionovna raised her hand with the rod in it, yanked, and cried out. A little silvery-green fish shimmered in the air.

"My Lord, a perch! Ah, ah ... Quickly! It's getting free!"

The perch got free of the hook, flopped through the grass toward its native element ... and plopped into the water!

In pursuit of the fish, Lapkin somehow inadvertently grabbed Anna Semionovna's hand instead of the fish, inadvertently pressed it to his lips ... She quickly drew it back, but it was already too late; their mouths inadvertently merged in a kiss. It happened somehow inadvertently. Another kiss followed the first, then vows and protestations ... What happy minutes! However, in this earthly life there is no absolute happiness. Happiness usually carries a poison in itself, or else is poisoned by something from outside. So this time, too. As the young people were kissing, a laugh suddenly rang out. They glanced at the river and were stupefied: a naked boy was standing in the water up to his waist. This was Kolia, a schoolboy, Anna Semionovna's brother. He was standing in the water, staring at the young people, and laughing maliciously.

"An-ah-ah ... you're kissing?" he said. "That's great! I'll tell Mama."

"I hope that you, as an honest young man ..." muttered Lapkin, blushing. "It's low-down to spy, and to tell tales is foul and detestable ... I assume that you, as an honest and noble young man ..."

"Give me a ruble and then I won't tell!" said the noble young man. "Or else I will."

Lapkin pulled a ruble out of his pocket and gave it to Kolia. Kolia squeezed the ruble in his wet fist, whistled, and swam off. And the young people didn't kiss any more that time.

The next day Lapkin brought Kolia some paints and a ball from town, and his sister gave him all her empty pill-boxes. After that they had to give him some cuff-links with dogs' heads on them. The wicked boy obviously liked all these things very much and, in order to get still more, he started keeping his eye on them. Wherever Lapkin and Anna Semionovna went, he went, too. He didn't leave them alone for a minute.

"The bastard!" Lapkin gnashed his teeth. "So little, and already such a real bastard! What's he going to be like later?!"

All through June, Kolia made life impossible for the poor lovers. He threatened to tell on them, kept his eye on them, and demanded presents; it all wasn't enough for him, and he finally started talking about a pocket watch. And what then? They had to promise the watch.

One time at dinner, when the waffle cookies were being passed, he suddenly burst out in a guffaw, winked an eye, and asked Lapkin:

"Shall I tell? Huh?"

Lapkin blushed terribly and started eating his napkin instead of the cookie. Anna Semionovna jumped up from the table and ran into the other room.

And the young people found themselves in this position until the end of August, until the very day when, at last, Lapkin proposed to Anna Semionovna. Oh, what a happy day that was! Having talking to the parents of his bride, and having received their consent. Lapkin first of all ran out into the garden and started looking for Kolia. Once he had found him, he almost sobbed from delight and seized the wicked boy by the ear. Anna Semionovna, who had also been looking for Kolia, ran up, and seized him by the other ear. And you really ought to have seen what joy was written all over the lovers' faces as Kolia cried and begged them:

"Dearest, darling, angles, I'll never do it again! Ow, ow! Forgive me!"

And afterwards they both admitted that during the whole time they had been in love with each other they had never once felt such happiness, such breath-taking bliss as during those moments when they were pulling the wicked boy's ears.

小缺德鬼

〔俄〕安东·契诃夫

英俊的小伙子伊万·伊万尼奇·拉普金带着小鼻子往上翘的姑娘安娜·谢苗诺夫娜·扎姆布利茨卡娅,走下陡峭的河岸,在一条小长凳上坐了下来。长凳紧靠水边,隐没在一个密密的小柳树丛中。多理想的小天地!你一坐下来,就与世隔绝了,看见你的只有鱼和在水面上窜得像闪电一样快的水虎。两个年轻人带着钓竿、网、装诱饵的小罐等工具,坐下后马上开始钓鱼。

"我们总算有机会在一起了,我真高兴。"拉普金向四周望一眼,开始说话,"安娜·谢苗诺夫娜,我有许多话要对你说……太多了……打第一次看见你起——鱼上钩了——我就知道了现在我是为什么而活着,知道了我的偶像在哪里,我该把我诚实、勤劳的一生献给谁——一定是条大家伙上钩了——就因为见到你,我心里第一次产生了爱,压抑不住的爱!——别忙着拉,让它再使劲咬一口——告诉我,亲爱的,我求求你,我能不能指望……不是指望你也这样,你别误会!那我不配,连想也不敢想,可我能不能指望——快拉!"

安娜·谢苗诺夫娜把拿钓竿的手一抬,一拉,叫了起来。一条闪亮的银灰色小鱼吊在半空中了。

"乖乖,一条鲈鱼!哟,哟——快!它要逃啦!"

鲈鱼脱了钩,在草上跳着,往河里溜,扑通一声,下水了!

拉普金追鱼时有意无意地没抓着鱼,而抓着了安娜·谢苗诺夫娜的手,还有意无意地把手送到嘴唇边……她赶忙往后缩,可是为时已晚,两人的嘴不经意中撞到一块儿,接起吻来。这事本是有意无意发生的。一个吻完了又来一个,接着是海誓山盟的话……多幸福的时刻!然而,在人们的生活中,没有绝对的幸福。幸福往往自带毒药,或者会招致毒药。这一次也不例外。两个年轻人正接吻时,突然有人大笑一声。他们往河边一看,傻了眼:一个光身子孩子站在齐腰深的水里。原来是安娜·谢苗诺夫娜的弟弟科利亚,还在上小学。他站在水里,眼睛直瞅着两个年轻人,不怀好意地大笑。

"哟,哟,哟……你们在接吻?"他说,"好家伙!我去告诉妈。"

"你是个好兄弟,我看你……"拉普金红着脸嘟嘟囔囔,"偷看可不光彩,告密更是可恶可鄙……听我说,如果你是走正道的孩子,是好样的……"

"拿一个卢布来我就不说,要不等着瞧。"好样的小家伙说。

拉普金从口袋里掏出一个卢布,给了科利亚。科利亚把钱攥在湿淋淋的手心里,打一声呼哨,游走了。这一来两个年轻人没再接吻。

第二天,拉普金从城里给科利亚买了几种颜料和一个球,他姐姐把自己的几个空药筒全送给了他。后来他们又被迫送了他几个有狗头的链扣。这些东西小缺德鬼显然喜欢得不得了。为不断招财进宝,他开始跟踪起他们来,拉普金和安娜·谢苗诺夫娜走到哪儿他跟到哪儿,一刻也没放过他们。

"这混蛋！"拉普金气得咬牙切齿，"才小小年纪，干缺德事就这么内行！长大以后还得了！"

6月里，科利亚叫这对情人没法过日子，闹了整整一个月。他扬言要告发他们，眼睛死死盯着他们，还敲竹杠。凡此种种不算，最后他竟开口勒索一只怀表。结果怎样呢？他们只好答应照给。

有一次吃饭时，等端上鸡蛋面包了，他突然打起哈哈来，眨眨眼，问拉普金：

"要我说吗？嗯？"

拉普金连耳根都红了，一口没咬到面包，却咬到了餐巾上。安娜·谢苗诺夫娜一下从椅子上站起来，跑进另一间屋子去了。

两个年轻人就这样活受罪一直受到8月底，也就是8月的最后一天，拉普金终于向安娜·谢苗诺夫娜求婚了。哦，那是多么幸福的一天！拉普金向意中人的父母提了亲，得到了同意，之后他干的第一件事就是跑到花园里找科利亚。他找到了他，高兴得几乎要哭了，一把拧住这小缺德鬼的一只耳朵。安娜·谢苗诺夫娜也在找科利亚，她跑了上去，拧住他的另一只耳朵。你真该看看科利亚哭着讨饶时这对情人脸上的痛快劲儿。只听他哀求着：

"爹呀！妈呀！天呀！我再不干啦！哎唷唷，饶了我吧！"

后来，他们俩都说，在他们相爱的整个时间里，要算拧着小缺德鬼的耳朵那阵儿最幸福、最开心。

Witches' Loaves

O. Henry

Miss Martha Meacham kept the little bakery on the corner (the one where you go up three steps, and the bell tinkles when you open the door).

Miss Martha was forty, her bank-book showed a credit of two thousand dollars, and she possessed two false teeth and a sympathetic heart. Many people have married whose chances to do so were much inferior to Miss Martha's.

Two or three times a week a customer came in in whom she began to take an interest. He was a middle-aged man, wearing spectacles and a brown beard trimmed to a careful point.

He spoke English with a strong German accent. His clothes were worn and darned in places, and wrinkled and baggy in others. But he looked neat, and had very good manners.

He always bought two loaves of stale bread. Fresh bread was five cents a loaf. Stale ones were two for five. Never did he call for anything but stale bread.

Once Miss Martha saw a red and brown stain on his fingers. She was sure then that he was an artist and very poor. No doubt he lived in a garret, where he painted pictures and ate stale bread and thought of the good things to eat in Miss Martha's bakery.

Often when Miss Martha sat down to her chops and light rolls and jam and tea she would sigh, and wish that the gentle-mannered artist might share her tasty meal instead of eating his dry crust in that draughty attic. Miss Martha's heart, as you have been told, was a sympathetic one.

In order to test her theory as to his occupation, she brought from her room one day a painting that she had bought at a sale, and set it against the shelves behind the bread counter.

It was a Venetian scene. A splendid marble palazzo (so it said on the picture) stood in the foreground—or rather forewater. For the rest there were gondolas (with the lady trailing her hand in the water), clouds, sky, and chiaroscuro in plenty. No artist could fail to notice it.

Two days afterward the customer came in.

"Two loaves of stale bread, if you blease[①]."

"You haf[②] here a fine bicture[③], madame," he said while she was wrapping up the bread.

"Yes?" says Miss Martha, revelling in her own cunning. "I do so admire art and" (no, it would not do to say "artists" thus early) "and

---

① blease: please, 此处说话者为德国人, 其说的英文带有德国口音, 较为生硬。
② haf: have
③ bicture: picture, 同注释①。

paintings," she substituted. "You think it is a good picture?"

"Der balace①," said the customer, "is not in good drawing. Der bairspective② of it is not true. Goot③ morning, madame."

He took his bread, bowed, and hurried out.

Yes, he must be an artist. Miss Martha took the picture back to her room.

How gentle and kindly his eyes shone behind his spectacles! What a broad brow he had! To be able to judge perspective at a glance—and to live on stale bread! But genius often has to struggle before it is recognized.

What a thing it would be for art and perspective if genius were backed by two thousand dollars in bank, a bakery, and a sympathetic heart to—But these were daydreams, Miss Martha.

Often now when he came he would chat for a while across the showcase. He seemed to crave Miss Martha's cheerful words.

He kept on buying stale bread. Never a cake, never a pie, never one of her delicious Sally Lunns.

She thought he began to look thinner and discouraged. Her heart ached to add something good to eat to his meagre purchase, but her courage failed at the act. She did not dare affront him. She knew the pride of artists.

Miss Martha took to wearing her blue-dotted silk waist behind the

---

① balace: palace，同第246页注释①。
② bairspective: perspective，同第246页注释①。
③ Goot: Good，同第246页注释①。

counter. In the back room she cooked a mysterious compound of quince seeds and borax. Ever so many people use it for the complexion.

One day the customer came in as usual, laid his nickel on the showcase, and called for his stale loaves. While Miss Martha was reaching for them there was a great tooting and clanging, and a fire-engine came lumbering past.

The customer hurried to the door to look, as any one will. Suddenly inspired, Miss Martha seized the opportunity.

On the bottom shelf behind the counter was a pound of fresh butter that the dairyman had left ten minutes before. With bread knife Miss Martha made a deep slash in each of the stale loaves, inserted a generous quantity of butter, and pressed the loaves tight again.

When the customer turned once more she was tying the paper around them.

When he had gone, after an unusually pleasant little chat, Miss Martha smiled to herself, but not without a slight fluttering of the heart.

Had she been too bold? Would he take offense? But surely not. There was no language of edibles. Butter was no emblem of unmaidenly forwardness.

For a long time that day her mind dwelt on the subject. She imagined the scene when he should discover her little deception.

He would lay down his brushes and palette. There would stand his easel with the picture he was painting in which the perspective was beyond criticism.

He would prepare for his luncheon of dry bread and water. He would slice into a loaf—ah!

Miss Martha blushed. Would he think of the hand that placed it there as he ate? Would he—

The front door bell jangled viciously. Somebody was coming in, making a great deal of noise.

Miss Martha hurried to the front. Two men were there. One was a young man smoking a pipe—a man she had never seen before. The other was her artist.

His face was very red, his hat was on the back of his head, his hair was wildly rumpled. He clinched his two fists and shook them forociously at Miss Martha. *At Miss Martha.*

"*Dummkopf!*" he shouted with extreme loudness; and then "*Tausendonfer!*" or something like it in German.

The young man tried to draw him away.

"I vill not go," he said angrily, "else I shall told her."

He made a bass drum of Miss Martha's counter.

"You haf shpoilt me," he cried, his blue eyes blazing behind his spectacles. "I vill tell you. You vas von *meddlingsome old cat!*"

Miss Martha learned weakly against the shelves and laid one hand on her blue-dotted silk waist. The young man took the other by the collar.

"Come on," he said, "you've said enough." He dragged the angry one out at the door to the sidewalk, and then came back.

"Guess you ought to be told, ma'am," he said, "what the row is about. That's Blumberger. He's an architectural draftsman. I work in the same office with him.

"He's been working hard for three months drawing a plan for a new city hall. It was a prize competition. He finished inking the lines yesterday. You know, a draftsman always makes his drawing in pencil first. When it's done he rubs out the pencil lines with handfuls of stale bread crumbs. That's better than India rubber.

"Blumberger's been buying the bread here. Well, today—well, you know, ma'am, that butter isn't—well, Blumberger's plan isn't good for anything now except to cut up into railroad sandwiches."

Miss Martha went into the back room. She took off the blue-dotted silk waist and put on the old brown serge she used to wear. Then she poured the quince seed and borax mixture out of the window into the ash can.

多情女的面包

〔美〕欧·亨利

玛莎·米查姆小姐的小面包店开在路口,就是你得上三级台阶,推开门后铃会响的那一家。

玛莎小姐40岁,有2000美元存款,镶着两颗假牙,生来一副好心肠。偏偏有许多条件大不如玛莎小姐的人倒先结了婚。

有位顾客一星期来两三次,玛莎小姐对这人产生了兴趣。这人是中年人,戴一副眼镜,下巴上棕色的长胡须修得溜尖。

这人说话带浓重的德国口音,衣服好几处穿破了,打了补丁,没破的地方不是皱就是鼓,但收拾得倒干净,而且彬彬有礼。

他每次只买两块陈面包,新鲜的要5分钱一块,而陈面包5分钱可以买两块。除了陈面包,别的东西他从不问津。

有一次,玛莎小姐发现他手指上沾了一点棕红色颜料,便断定他是位画家,而且穷得很。不用说,他住的是小阁楼,在阁楼里作画,啃陈面包,玛莎小姐店里好吃的东西只能空想想。

玛莎小姐在吃排骨、面包卷、果酱和喝茶时,常唉声叹气,惦念着那位在冷风吹的小阁楼里啃硬面包的文质彬彬的画家,就可惜他不能来分享她的佳肴。前面已经说过,玛莎小姐生来一副好心肠。

为了证实自己对他的身份猜得是否正确,玛莎小姐把她在一次拍卖时买来的一幅画从房里取了出来,挂到柜台后的架子上。

这是一幅威尼斯风景画,画了一座富丽堂皇的大理石宫殿(画上是这样标明的),建在水边。水上荡着几叶轻舟,一位女郎用手轻轻拨着水。另外还画了云、天空,大量使用了明暗对比法。如果是画家,绝不会注意不到。

两天后这位顾客又来了。

"请拿两块陈面包。"

玛莎小姐包面包时,他又说话了:"小姐,你这画很漂亮嘛!"

"当真?"玛莎小姐说,暗自得意巧计成功,"我喜欢艺术,喜欢画。"(现在说"喜欢艺术家"为时过早)接着她换了话题问:"你觉得这画画得好吗?"

"宫殿没画好,透视法运用得不合适。再见,小姐!"顾客道。

他拿起面包,一鞠躬,匆匆走了。

没错,他准是画家。玛莎小姐把画又拿回她房里。

他眼镜后的两只眼睛多温和、多善良呵!前额长得真宽!一眼能看出透视法运用不当,却只能啃陈面包过日子!然而,往往天才在得到承认之前不得不艰苦奋斗。

如果天才有2000美元银行存款、一个面包店、一个满心同情他的人……那么艺术与透视法将会有多辉煌的成就!然而,玛莎小姐,别想入非非了。

自那次以后,他常会隔着货柜跟她闲聊几句。他似乎爱听玛莎小姐的热心话。

他仍然只要陈面包,从没买过一块蛋糕,一块肉馅饼,一块可口的萨利伦饼。

她觉得他越来越瘦、越来越没精神了。玛莎小姐过意不去，想在他买的便宜货里加点好吃的，却又鼓不起勇气行动。她怕冒犯他。她理解艺术家的自尊。

玛莎小姐换了一件有蓝圆点的丝绸衣服站柜台。她还在后面房间里将榅桲子和硼砂放在一起熬，其汁有神奇功效，现在仍有许多人用此来美容。

有一天，那位顾客又来了，把一个5分的镍币往柜台上一放，照旧买陈面包。就在玛莎小姐伸手拿面包时，街上响起了哨声和叮叮当当的铃声，一辆消防车轰鸣而过。

遇到这种事谁都会站到门口看看，那位顾客也不例外。玛莎小姐灵机一动，抓住良机。

柜台后的底层货架上放着一磅新鲜奶油，刚送来10分钟。玛莎小姐拿起面包刀把两块陈面包都深深划了一刀，塞进好些奶油，再紧紧捏拢。

等那位顾客再走回柜台时，她已经在包面包了。

他闲谈了几句，话显得格外动听，然后走了。玛莎小姐心中暗笑，但也不是没有一点忐忑不安。

她是不是太胆大妄为？他会生气吗？当然不会。没一句话说到过吃的。况且送一点奶油也不算姑娘家有失体统的事。

这一天她心上老牵挂着这件事。她想象着他发现上了个小小的当后的情形。

他会放下笔和调色板。画架上搁着他在画的一张画，当然透视法用得无可挑剔。

他打算吃午饭了，还是干面包和开水。等他切开面包——哟！

玛莎小姐脸红了。吃面包时他会惦念起在面包里打了埋伏的人吗？他会……

前门的铃乱响起来，有人进来了，哇哇乱叫着。

玛莎小姐连忙赶到店堂里。进来了两个人。一个是年轻人，叼着根烟斗，她以前从没见过。另一个是她关心的画家。

他的脸涨得通红，帽子罩在后脑勺上，头发像一堆乱草。他攥紧两只拳头，向着玛莎小姐恶狠狠地挥。竟然向玛莎小姐挥！

"Dummkopf!"①他的叫声震得人耳发麻，然后又是"Tausendonfer!"②之类的话，像是德语。

年轻人使劲儿拽住他。

"我不走，"他气冲冲地说，"要找她算账！"

他把玛莎小姐的柜台当大鼓敲。

"你把我毁啦！"他大叫着，眼镜后的两只蓝眼睛直冒火，"你听着，谁叫你多管闲事来着！"

玛莎小姐有气无力地斜靠在货架上，一只手按在蓝圆点丝绸衣上。年轻人拽着那个人的衣领。

"得了吧，你也说够了。"他说，把大发雷霆的人拖到门外，然后自己又走回来。

"小姐，我想还是应该告诉你为什么他大吵大闹。"他说，"这人姓布卢姆伯格，是建筑设计师。我与他在同一个办公室。

"他辛辛苦苦干了三个月，为新市政大楼画图纸，是要参加比赛夺奖的，用墨水描线条昨天才描完。你不知道，设计师画图

---

① 德语，义为"蠢货"。
② 德语，骂人的话。

总是先用铅笔打草稿,定稿以后用陈面包屑擦去铅笔印,比用橡皮擦的效果好。

"布卢姆伯格老来这儿买面包。嗯——今天,嗯,今天,你知道,小姐,那奶油不——嗯,布卢姆伯格的图纸完全成了废纸,什么用也没有了。"

玛莎小姐回到后面的房间,脱下有蓝圆点的丝绸衣,穿回了原来那件棕色的哔叽布料衣服,把榅桲子和硼砂熬的汁倒进了窗外的垃圾箱里。

Her Lover

Maxim Gorky

An acquaintance of mine once told me the following story.

When I was a student at Moscow I happened to live alongside one of those ladies who—you know what I mean. She was a Pole, and they called her Teresa. She was a tallish, powerfully-built brunette, with black, bushy eyebrows and a large coarse face as if carved out by a hatchet—the bestial gleam of her dark eyes, her thick bass voice, her cabman-like gait and her immense muscular vigour, worthy of a fishwife, inspired me with horror. I lived on the top flight and her garret was opposite to mine. I never left my door open when I knew her to be at home. But this, after all, was a very rare occurrence. Sometimes I chanced to meet her on the staircase or in the yard, and she would smile upon me with a smile which seemed to me to be sly and cynical. Occasionally, I saw her drunk, with bleary eyes, touzled hair, and a particularly hideous smile. On such occasions she would speak to me:

"How d'ye do, Mr. Student!" and her stupid laugh would still further intensify my loathing of her. I should have liked to have changed my quarters in order to have avoided such encounters and greetings; but my little chamber was a nice one, and there was such a wide view from the window, and it was always so quiet in the street below—so I endured.

And one morning I was sprawling on my couch, trying to find some sort of excuse for not attending my class, when the door opened, and the bass voice of Teresa the loathsome, resounded from my threshold:

"Good health to you, Mr. Student!"

"What do you want?" I said. I saw that her face was confused and supplicatory ... It was a very unusual sort of face for her.

"Look ye, sir! I want to beg a favour of you. Will you grant it me?"

I lay there silent, and thought to myself:

"Gracious! An assault upon my virtue, neither more nor less. —Courage, my boy!"

"I want to send a letter home, that's what it is," she said, her voice was beseeching, soft, timid.

"Deuce take you!" I thought; but up I jumped, sat down at my table, took a sheet of paper, and said:

"Come here, sit down, and dictate!"

She came, sat down very gingerly on a chair, and looked at me with a guilty look.

"Well, to whom do you want to write?"

"To Boleslav Kashput, at the town of Svyeptsyana, on the Warsaw

Road. ..."

"Well, fire away!"

"My dear Boles ... my darling ... my faithful lover. May the Mother of God protect thee! Thou heart of gold, why hast thou not written for such a long time to thy sorrowing little dove, Teresa?"

I very nearly burst out laughing. "A sorrowing little dove!" more than five feet high, with fists a stone and more in weight[①], and as black a face as if the little dove had lived all its life in a chimney, and had never once washed itself! Restraning myself somehow, I asked:

"Who is this Bolest?"

"Bolés, Mr. Student," she said, as if offended with me for blundering over the name, "he is Bolés—my young man."

"Young man!"

"Why are you so surprised, sir? Cannot I, a girl, have a young man?"

She? A girl? Well!

"Oh, why not?" I said, "all things are possible. And has he been your young man long?"

Six years.

"Oh, ho!" I thought. "Well, let us write your letter. ..."

And I tell you plainly that I would willingly have changed places with this Bolés if his fair correspondent had been not Teresa, but

---

① a stone and more in weight: fists 的后置定语, 等于 which were a stone and more in weight。stone 在此处指计量单位, 英制, 等于 14 磅。

Her Lover

something less than she.

"I thank you most heartily, sir, for your kind services," said Teresa to me, with a curtsey. "Perhaps *I can show you* some service, eh?"

"No, I most humbly thank you all the same."

"Perhaps, sir, your shirts or your trousers may want a little mending?"

I felt that this mastodon in petticoats[①] had made me grow quite red with shame, and I told her pretty sharply that I had no need whatever of her services.

She departed.

A week or two passed away. It was evening. I was sitting at my window whistling and thinking of some expedient for enabling me to get away from myself. I was bored, the weather was dirty. I didn't want to go out, and out of sheer ennui I began a course of self-analysis and reflection. This also was dull enough work, but I didn't care about doing anything else. Then the door opened. Heaven be praised, someone came in.

"Oh, Mr. Student, you have no pressing business, I hope?"

It was Teresa. Humph!

"No. What is it?"

"I was going to ask you, sir, to write me another letter."

"Very well! To Bolés, eh?"

"No, this time it is from him."

---

① this mastodon in petticoats: 直译为"穿着女人衣的乳齿象(古代一种类似象的巨兽)"。

259

"What?"

"Stupid that I am! It is not for me, Mr. Student, I beg your pardon. It is for a friend of mine, that is to say, not a friend but an acquaintance—a man acquaintance. He has a sweetheart just like me here, Teresa. That's how it is. Will you, sir, write a letter to this Teresa?"

I looked at her—her face was troubled, her fingers were trembling. I was a bit fogged at first—and then I guessed how it was.

"Look here, my lady," I said, "there are no Boléses or Teresas at all, and you've been telling me a pack of lies. Don't you come sneaking about me any longer. I have no wish whatever to cultivate your acquaintance. Do you understand?"

And suddenly she grew strangely terrified and distraught; she began to shift from foot to foot without moving from the place, and spluttered comically, as if she wanted to say something and couldn't. I waited to see what would come of all this, and I saw and felt that, apparently, I had made a great mistake in suspecting her of wishing to draw me from the path of righteousness. It was evidently something very different.

"Mr. Student!" she began, and suddenly, waving her hand, she turned abruptly towards the door and went out. I remained with a very unpleasant feeling in my mind. I listened. Her door was flung violently to—plainly the poor wench was very angry ... I thought it over, and resolved to go to her, and, inviting her to come in here, write everything she wanted.

I entered her apartment. I looked round. She was sitting at the table, leaning on her elbows, with her head in her hands.

"Listen to me," I said.

Now, whenever I come to this point in my story, I always feel horribly awkward and idiotic. Well, well!

"Listen to me," I said.

She leaped from her seat, came towards me with flashing eyes, and laying her hands on my shoulders, began to whisper, or rather to hum in her peculiar bass voice:

"Look you, now! It's like this. There's no Bolés at all, and there's no Teresa either. But what's that to you? Is it a hard thing for you to draw your pen over paper? Eh? Ah, and *you*, too! Still such a little fair-haired boy! There's nobody at all, neither Bolés, nor Teresa, only me. There you have it, and much good may it do you!"

"Pardon me!" said I, altogether flabbergasted by such a reception, "what is it all about? There's no Bolés, you say?"

"No. So it is."

"And no Teresa either?"

"And no Teresa. I'm Teresa."

I didn't understand it at all. I fixed my eyes upon her, and tried to make out which of us was taking leave of his or her senses. But she went again to the table, searching about for something, came back to me, and said in an offended tone:

"If it was so hard for you to write to Bolés, look, there's your letter, take it! Others will write for me."

I looked. In her hand was my letter to Bolés. Phew!

"Listen, Teresa! What is the meaning of all this? Why must you get others to write for you when I have already written it, and you haven't sent it?"

"Sent it where?"

"Why, to this—Bolés."

"There's no such person."

I absolutely did not understand it. There was nothing for me but to spit and go. Then she explained.

"What is it?" she said, still offended. "There's no such person, I tell you," and she extended her arms as if she herself did not understand why there should be no such person. "But I wanted him to be ... Am I then not a human creature like the rest of them? Yes, yes, I know, I know, of course. ... Yet no harm was done to anyone by my writing to him that I can see. ..."

"Pardon me—to whom?"

"To Bolés, of course."

"But he doesn't exist."

"Alas! alas! But what if he doesn't? He doesn't exist, but he *might*! I write to him, and it looks as if he did exist. And Teresa—that's me, and he replies to me, and then I write to him again. ..."

I understood at last. And I felt so sick, so miserable, so ashamed, somehow. Alongside of me, not three yards away, lived a human creature who had nobody in the world to treat her kindly, affectionately, and this human being had invented a friend for herself!

"Look, now! you wrote me a letter to Bolés, and I gave it to someone else to read it to me; and when they read it to me I listened and fancied that Bolés was there. And I asked you to write me a letter from Bolés to Teresa—that is to me. When they write such a letter for me, and read it to me, I feel quite sure that Bolés is there. And life grows easier for me in consequence."

"Deuce take thee for a blockhead!" said I to myself when I heard this.

And from thenceforth, regularly, twice a week, I wrote a letter to Bolés, and an answer from Bolés to Teresa. I wrote those answers well. ... She, of course, listened to them, and wept like anything, roared, I should say, with her bass voice. And in return for my thus moving her to tears by real letters from the imaginary Bolés, she began to mend the holes I had in my socks, shirts, and other articles of clothing. Subsequently, about three months after this history began, they put her in prison for something or other. No doubt by this time she is dead.

My acquaintance shook the ash from his cigarette, looked pensively at the sky, and thus concluded:

Well, well, the more a human creature has tasted of better things the more it hungers after the sweet things of life. And we, wrapped round in the rags of our virtues, and regarding others through the mist of our self-sufficiency, and persuaded of our universal impeccability, do not understand this.

And the whole thing turns out pretty stupidly—and very cruelly. The fallen classes, we say. And who are the fallen classes, I should like to know? They are, first of all, people with the same bones, flesh, and blood and nerves as ourselves. We have been told this day after day for ages. And we actually listen—and the Devil only knows how hideous the whole thing is. Or are we completely depraved by the loud sermonizing of humanism? In reality, we also are fallen folks, and so far as I can see, very deeply fallen into the abyss of self-sufficiency and the conviction of our own superiority. But enough of this. It is all as old as the hills—so old that it is a shame to speak of it. Very old indeed— yes, that's where it is!

她的情人

〔苏〕马克西姆·高尔基

下面的故事是一位相识对我讲的：

我在莫斯科念书时，有个女人曾与我是邻居。你知道我说这话是什么意思。她是波兰人，大家叫她特雷莎。她个子高，粗壮，黑皮肤，浓眉毛，脸又大又粗，似乎是用斧头砍出来的，黑眼睛里露出凶光，说话声音沙哑低沉，一举一动像马车夫，有股子好力气，够得上标准的悍妇，叫我望而生畏。我住在顶层，她的小房间正好在我对面。我知道她在房间里时从不把门打开，不过她难得在房间里。有时候我在楼梯上或院子里碰到她，她见我一笑，我只觉得她的笑来得狡诈，带着讥讽。有时候我发现她喝得醉醺醺，眼神蒙眬，蓬头散发，笑起来特别难看。遇上这种时候她总是对我招呼：

"你好呀，大学士！"她那么一傻笑叫我更觉厌恶。我真想换房，以免跟这种人见面应酬，然而我住的小房间的确好，窗口视野开阔，楼下的街安安静静，也就马虎过去算了。

一天早上，我懒散地躺在床上，想找个不上课的借口，突然门开了，我最不愿见的特雷莎站在门口用低沉的嗓音说：

"你好呀,大学士!"

"有什么事?"我问,发现她脸上有为难的神色,像有事要求人,这倒是不常见的表情。

"是这么回事,先生!我想找你帮帮忙,不知行不行?"

我躺着没出声,暗想:

"天哪,这可不好办!别怕,老兄!"

"我想写封信回家,没别的。"她说,声音放轻了,带着胆怯,是在恳求我。

"活见鬼!"我心想。可是我仍起了床,坐到桌边,拿出张纸,说:

"进来坐。你说吧!"

她走进来,小心翼翼地坐到一张椅子上,难为情地望着我。

"说吧,你想写给谁?"

"写给博烈斯拉夫·卡什普特,住斯维耶普茨亚纳市华沙路。"

"开始吧!"

"亲爱的博烈斯……我亲爱的人……我忠实的情人。愿圣母保佑你!你有金子一样的心,可为什么这么久不写信给你伤心的小鸽子特雷莎?"

我几乎忍不住要笑。"伤心的小鸽子!"身高5英尺多,拳头像铁锤,而且比铁锤重,脸黑不溜秋,如果也算得上小鸽子,那准是一天到晚蹲在烟囱里,从来没洗过澡的小鸽子!我强忍着笑,问道:

"这位博烈斯特是什么人?"

"叫博烈斯,大学士先生。"她说,似乎不高兴我念错了他的名字,"他叫博烈斯,我的男朋友。"

"男朋友!"

"这有什么奇怪？我是姑娘家，就不能找男朋友？"

她是姑娘家？好家伙！

"当然可以！"我答道，"什么事都有可能。他与你交朋友多久了？"

"6年。"

"哎哟哟！"我暗想，"好吧，再往下写。"

不瞒你说，如果这位博烈斯的女朋友不是特雷莎，而是比她像样些的人，我倒愿意与他换个位置。

"先生，你帮了大忙，真不知怎样感谢才好。"特雷莎对我行了个礼，说，"你有什么事叫我干吗？"

"非常感谢，我没有。"

"有什么衬衣、裤子要缝缝补补吗？"

丑八怪这一问叫我很难堪，我不大客气地对她说，什么也用不着她干。

她走了。

过了一两个星期，有天晚上我坐在窗边吹口哨，想找个事消遣。我正发闷，天气又坏。我不愿出门，只是为了打发时间，进行起自我反省来。这事也没意思，但别的事我又统统不愿干。正在这时，门开了。谢天谢地，有人来了。

"哟，大学士，你没什么急着办的事吧？"

原来是特雷莎，倒霉！

"没有，怎么啦？"

"我想再请你写封信，先生。"

"好吧！又给博烈斯吗？"

"不是，这次是他写给别人。"

"怎么啦?"

"我真笨头笨脑!大学士先生,对不起,这次不是代我写,是代我的一位朋友写。要说嘛,也不是什么朋友,只是熟人,一位我认识的男性朋友。他有个女朋友在这儿,与我一样,叫特雷莎。就是这么回事。先生,你能不能给这位特雷莎写封信?"

我看看她,发现她一副尴尬相,手指在发抖。开始我不很明白,后来想想才恍然大悟。

"你得了吧,"我说,"根本就没有什么两个博烈斯和两个特雷莎,全是胡诌。别再往我这儿窜,我不想管你熟人的闲事,明白吗?"

她一听顿时紧张起来,不知所措,两只脚动着,却没迈开步,嘴接连发出叽叽声,想说话而说不出。我等着要看个究竟,发现原来我犯了个大错误,不该怀疑她想引我走斜路。显然她不是这个目的。

"大学士先生!"她说了声,突然手一挥,猛地转身出了门。我站着没动,心里感到内疚,竖起耳朵听着。她的房门砰地一响,一定是这可怜虫生了气……我经过反复考虑后决心去找她,请她上我这儿来,她想写什么我都给她写。

我走进她的房间,往四下一看,见她坐在桌边,两只手撑在桌上,抱着头。

"你听我说。"我说道。

每次故事讲到这里我总觉得别扭,成了呆子。哎!哎!

"你听我说。"我说道。

她一跳而起,向我冲来,两眼发亮,手搁到我肩上,开始轻声说话了——就是把她特有的粗嗓门压低了说。

“听我说吧，是这么回事：没有什么博烈斯，也没有特雷莎，可你管这干吗？你拿起笔写封信还会为难？嗯？你呀，你还是个毛孩子！没有什么博烈斯，也没有特雷莎，就我一个人。现在你全知道了，该放心吧？”

“对不起！”我说，没想到会受到这顿抢白，“怎么回事？真没有博烈斯？”

“是没有！”

“也没有特雷莎？”

“也没有，我就是特雷莎。”

我弄糊涂了，定睛瞧着她，想看看我们俩究竟是她还是我已经神智错乱。然而她回到桌边，找到了一件东西，又向我走来，没好气地说：

“叫你给博烈斯写封信这么为难，好吧，你把你写的拿去！别人会替我写。”

我一看，原来她手里拿的是我替她写给博烈斯的信。天哪！

“听我说，特雷莎！这是怎么回事？我已经替你写了封信，你不寄，又去找别人替你写。”

“往哪儿寄？”

“当然是寄给博烈斯。”

“没有这么个人。”

我越弄越糊涂，只好一走了之。这时她说出了谜底。

“是这么回事，”她声音里仍带着怨艾。“对你说了没这么个人！”她双手一摊，似乎自己也不明白为什么没有这么个人，“我只是想要有这么个人存在……我不跟别人一样，也是人吗？这还用说！我写信给他又没碍着别人……”

"对不起——写给谁?"

"就是博烈斯。"

"你不是说没这么个人吗?"

"哟,哟,哟!没有又怎么样?没有就不能当成有?我只当有这么个人,给他写信。我呢,就是特雷莎,他给我回信,我又给他写信……"

我终于明白了,感到十分难受、同情,也非常惭愧。她与我对门住着,不到三码远,在世上得不到任何人的关心、爱护,于是只好凭空设想出一个朋友!

"告诉你吧,你给我写了信给博烈斯以后,我请别人念给我听,边听边想真有一个博烈斯。我请你写封博烈斯给特雷莎的信,其实是写给我。要是有人给我写,给我念,我就把博烈斯当了真,觉得日子没那么难过。"

"天下还有这样的傻瓜!"我听了她的话想道。

从那以后,我每星期写两封信,一封是给博烈斯的,一封是博烈斯给特雷莎的复信。我把那些复信写得很动人。当然,每封她都细细听,哭得肝断肠裂,也就是扯开破锣似的嗓子嚎。博烈斯是假的,信是真的,感动得她眼泪直流。得了这个安慰后她给我补袜子、衬衫,还有别的破衣洞。过了三个月,她为了件事进了监狱,到现在肯定已经死了。

我的这位相识弹掉香烟上的灰,无限感慨地对天叹道:

越是享受惯了的人对生活越有苛求。我们由于自恃德行高尚,一尘不染,以己之长比人之短,并不了解这一点。

一切其实都是愚蠢而无情的。平常我们常说什么堕落了的人,可是我倒要问问,什么样的人算是堕落了的人?首先,他们与我们有同样的血、肉、骨、神经。多少年来,我们天天听到的是这本经。我们就那么规规矩矩听着,而只有魔鬼才知道一切有多么可怕。请想想,我们是不是完全被人道主义的高声说教毁了呢?其实,据我所见,我们也是堕落了的人,坠进了自以为是的深渊,只当我们高人一等。还是别说了吧。千百年来都是如此,提起反而有失体面。的确千百年来如此,这就是事实的真相。

Mrs. Packletide's Tiger

Saki

It was Mrs. Packletide's pleasure and intention that she should shoot a tiger. Not that the lust to kill had suddenly descended on her, or that she felt that she would leave India safer and more wholesome than she had found it, with one fraction less of wild beast per million of inhabitants. The compelling motive for her sudden deviation towards the footsteps of Nimrod[①] was the fact that Loona Bimberton had recently been carried eleven miles in an aeroplane by an Algerian aviator, and talked of nothing else; only a personally procured tiger-skin and a heavy harvest of Press photographs could successfully counter that sort of thing. Mrs. Packletide had already arranged in her mind the lunch she would give at her house in Curzon Street[②], ostensibly in Loona Bimberton's honour, with a tiger-skin rug occupying most of the foreground and all of the conversation. She had also already

---

① Nimrod: 圣经中一古代国王,因打猎英勇,常被后人用以指好猎手。
② Curzon Street: 位于伦敦,富人居住区。

designed in her mind the tiger-claw brooch that she was going to give Loona Bimberton on her next birthday. In a world that is supposed to be chiefly swayed by hunger and by love Mrs. Packletide was an exception; her movements and motives were largely governed by dislike of Loona Bimberton.

Circumstances proved propitious. Mrs. Packletide had offered a thousand rupees for the opportunity of shooting a tiger without overmuch risk or exertion, and it so happened that a neighbouring village could boast of being the favoured rendezvous of an animal of respectable antecedents, which had been driven by the increasing infirmities of age to abandon game-killing and confine its appetite to the smaller domestic animals. The prospect of earning the thousand rupees had stimulated the sporting and commercial instinct of the villagers; children were posted night and day on the outskirts of the local jungle to head the tiger back in the unlikely event of his attempting to roam away to fresh hunting-grounds, and the cheaper kinds of goats were left about with elaborate carelessness to keep him satisfied with his present quarters. The one great anxiety was lest[①] he should die of old age before the date appointed for the memsahib's[②] shoot. Mothers carrying their babies home through the jungle after the day's work in the fields hushed their singing lest they might curtail the restful sleep of the venerable herd-robber.

---

① lest: 引导一个表语从句, 等于 that。
② memsahib: 当时印度人对英国殖民者已婚妇女的尊称。

The great night duly arrived, moonlit and cloudless. A platform had been constructed in a comfortable and conveniently placed tree, and thereon crouched Mrs. Packletide and her paid companion, Miss Mebbin. A goat, gifted with a particularly persistent bleat, such as[①] even a partially deaf tiger might be reasonably expected to hear on a still night, was tethered at the correct distance. With an accurately sighted rifle and a thumbnail pack of patience cards the sportswoman awaited the coming of the quarry.

"I suppose we are in some danger?" said Miss Mebbin.

She was not actually nervous about the wild beast, but she had a morbid dread of performing an atom more service than she had been paid for.

"Nonsense," said Mrs. Packletide; "it's a very old tiger. It couldn't spring up here even if it wanted to."

"If it's an old tiger I think you ought to get it cheaper. A thousand rupees is a lot of money."

Louisa Mebbin adopted a protective elder-sister attitude towards money in general, irrespective of nationality or denomination. Her energetic intervention had saved many a rouble from dissipating itself in tips in some Moscow hotel, and francs and centimes clung to her instinctively under circumstances which would have driven them headlong from less sympathetic hands. Her speculations as to the

---

① such as: 此处 such 与 as 意义上分开。可认为 such 后省略了 bleat, 而 as 为关系代词，在其引导的定语从句中作主语。

market depreciation of tiger remnants were cut short by the appearance on the scene of the animal itself. As soon as it caught sight of the tethered goat it lay flat on the earth, seemingly less from a desire to take advantage of all available cover than for the purpose of snatching a short rest before commencing the grand attack.

"I believe it's ill," said Louisa Mebbin, loudly in Hindustani, for the benefit of the village headman, who was in ambush in a neighbouring tree.

"Hush!" said Mrs. Packletide, and at that moment the tiger commenced ambling towards his victim.

"Now, now!" urged Miss Mebbin with some excitement; "if he doesn't touch the goat we needn't pay for it." (The bait was an extra.)

The rifel flashed out with a loud report, and the great tawny beast sprang to one side and then rolled over in the stillness of death. In a moment a crowd of excited natives had swarmed on to the scene, and their shouting speedily carried the glad news to the village, where a thumping of tomtoms took up the chorus of triumph. And their triumph and rejoicing found a ready echo in the heart of Mrs. Packletide; already that luncheonparty in Curzon Street seemed immeasurably nearer.

It was Louisa Mebbin who drew attention to the fact that the goat was in death-throes from a mortal bullet-wound, while no trace of the rifle's deadly work could be found on the tiger. Evidently the wrong animal had been hit, and the beast of prey had succumbed to heart-failure, caused by the sudden report of the rifle, accelerated by senile decay. Mrs. Packletide was pardonably annoyed at the discovery; but, at any rate, she was the possessor of a dead tiger, and the villagers, anxious for their thousand rupees, gladly connived at the fiction that she had shot the beast. And Miss Mebbin was a paid companion. Therefore did Mrs. Packletide face the cameras with a light heart, and her pictured fame reached from the pages of the Texas Weekly Snapshot to the illustrated Monday supplement of the Novoe Vremya[①]. As for Loona Bimberton, she refused to look at an illustrated paper for weeks, and her letter of thanks for the gift of a tiger-claw brooch was a model of repressed emotions. The luncheon-party she declined; there are limits beyond which repressed emotions become dangerous.

From Curzon Street the tiger-skin rug travelled down to the Manor House[②], and was duly inspected and admired by the county, and it seemed a fitting and appropriate thing when Mrs. Packletide went to the County Costume Ball in the character of Diana. She refused to fall in, however, with Clovis's tempting suggestion of a primeval dance party, at which every one should wear the skins of beasts they had recently slain. "I should be in rather a Baby Bunting condition," confessed Clovis, "with a miserable rabbit-skin or two to wrap up in, but then," he added, with a rather malicious glance at Diana's proportions, "my figure is quite as good as that Russian dancing boy's."

"How amused every one would be if they knew what really happened," said Louisa Mebbin a few days after the ball.

---

① Novoe Vremya：俄文的音译，其义为"新时代"。
② the Manor House：manor house 本指领主的宅邸，此处指女主人公的乡间豪宅。

"What do you mean?" asked Mrs. Packletide quickly.

"How you shot the goat and frightened the tiger to death," said Miss Mebbin, with her disagreeably pleasant laugh.

"No one would believe it," said Mrs. Packletide, her face changing colour as rapidly as though it were going through a book of patterns before post-time①.

"Loona Bimberton would," said Miss Mebbin. Mrs. Packletide's face settled on an unbecoming shade of greenish white.

"You surely wouldn't give me away?" she asked.

"I've seen a weekend cottage near Dorking that I should rather like to buy," said Miss Mebbin with seeming irrelevance. "Six hundred and eighty, freehold. Quite a bargain, only I don't happen to have the money."

Louisa Mebbin's pretty weekend cottage, christened by her "Les Fauves", and gay in summer-time with its garden borders of tiger-lilies, is the wonder and admiration of the friends.

"It is a marvel how Louisa manages to do it," is the general verdict.

Mrs. Packletide indulges in no more big-game shooting.

"The incidental expenses are so heavy," she confides to inquiring friends.

---

① as though it were going through a book of patterns before post-time: book of patterns 为介绍赛马场各骑师所穿上衣的小册子，post-time 指赛马的出发时间。赛马前观众因下了赌注，心情紧张，有种种猜测。

帕克尔泰夫人打老虎

〔英〕萨基

帕克尔泰夫人满心想打一只老虎。这倒不是因为她突然起了杀心，或者觉得每100万人中少了几头野兽，印度会安全、太平些。她心血来潮别的事不干而要去当个猎人的原因是看到卢娜·比姆伯顿前不久坐着一位阿尔及利亚人驾驶的飞机上天飞了11英里，便张口不离这件事；唱对台戏的办法只有一个：亲手打只老虎，剥下虎皮，让新闻界大登特登其照片。帕克尔泰夫人还盘算好了，要在柯曾街的府第设宴，特地邀请卢娜·比姆伯顿，把虎皮毯摆在最显眼的位置，让来客赞不绝口。她还打定了主意，等到卢娜·比姆伯顿生日那天，把虎爪做的胸针送给她。现在世人大都为食为爱所主宰，而帕克尔泰夫人例外，她的行为和思想主要被对卢娜·比姆伯顿的恨所左右。

事情办得很顺利。帕克尔泰夫人出了1000卢比赏金，但求有机会既能打到老虎，又无生命之虞，也不会伤筋劳骨，而凑巧邻村是个理想的地方。有只生来就威风凛凛的老虎，因为上了年纪，越来越不中用了，再也抓不到林中走兽，只好常来村里吃些小家畜。眼见能挣到1000卢比，村里人人动了好打猎和捞钱的天性：林子的四周日日夜夜有小孩守着，万一老虎想走到别的地方找吃的，就把它引回来；不值钱的山羊东丢一头，西丢一头，看上去像是无意走失的，其实是为使老虎对现在的住地感到心满意足。他们怕就怕没等到夫人定好的打虎日子，老虎就死了。做母亲的白天在地里干一天活，干完抱着孩子回家走过林子时，压低了声音唱，唯恐惊醒偷牛的山大王的睡梦。

那个了不起的夜晚终于来到了，皓月当空，天上没有一丝云。树上搭了个台，选的是一棵地点方便的大树，帕克尔泰夫人和她出钱雇的女伴梅宾小姐蹲在台上。隔台不近不远处系着只羊，生性爱咩咩叫个不停，夜晚又静，老虎哪怕耳背，也准听得见。步枪是分毫不差瞄好了的，这位女猎人还带了副小巧的供单人解闷玩的扑克牌，就等猎物来。

"我们会不会有危险哟？"梅宾小姐问。

其实，她并不怕那老虎，而是怕少拿钱多做事，多做哪怕芝麻大的事也不愿意。

帕克尔泰夫人道："别瞎说，这虎老掉了牙，想跳都跳不上台来。"

"既然是老掉牙的虎，你该少些钱，1000卢比太多。"

无论对谁，不管其国籍与教派如何，只要牵涉到钱，路易莎·梅宾总是采取一种老大姐式的保护态度。在莫斯科住旅馆时，由于她力谏，少白送好些小费，省了许多卢布。还有一些时候，稍有同情心的人本也会解囊相助的，她却本能地把法郎和生丁牢牢守着。她正猜测虎皮虎骨会跌价时，虎来了。虎一看到系着一只羊，马上趴在地上。看样子不像是想法隐蔽，而是要先喘一口气，再猛扑过去。

"分明是一只有病的虎!"路易莎用印度语大声说,就是要让躲在近边的一棵树上的村长听明白。

帕克尔泰夫人嘘了一声,只见虎开始慢慢往羊靠近。

"快,快!"梅宾小姐心有些急了,催促道,"如果虎没碰着羊,我们就不用花冤枉钱。"(诱饵的钱是另外算的)

枪发出一声巨响,斑皮大兽往旁边一跳,一滚,不动弹了。当地人马上兴奋得一窝蜂拥上来,欢叫着。在村里的人一听,知道有好消息,立即敲起手鼓,也欢庆胜利。他们的得意和高兴在帕克尔泰夫人心里引起了共振,柯曾街的宴会似乎已指日可待。

还是路易莎·梅宾眼尖,发现羊在致命的地方中了一枪,挣扎着,马上会死,而老虎身上倒是找不着枪子眼。显然,不该挨枪的家伙挨了一枪,而虎是因年老体衰,突然听到枪响,死于心力衰竭的。不难理解,这一发现使帕克尔泰夫人很扫兴;但话又说回来,死虎还是归她所有;村里人想得1000卢比,睁一只眼闭一只眼,都说她一枪打死了一只老虎。梅宾小姐呢,毕竟是出了钱雇的女伴。于是帕克尔泰夫人还是带着轻松的心情面对照相机,从美国《得克萨斯每周快照》到俄国《新时代》有照片的星期一增刊,都登了她的照片,名扬四海。再说卢娜·比姆伯顿,她接连好几星期不肯看有照片的报纸,收到老虎爪做的胸针后,写了一封感谢信,是一封典型的忍气吞声的信。宴会她谢绝了;忍气有个限度,超过限度会闹出事来。

虎皮毯在柯曾街炫耀过后又拿到了乡下的府邸,全郡名流细细过目,赞赏不已,到郡里举行化装舞会时,帕克尔泰夫人挑了狩猎女神狄安娜这个角色装扮起来似乎就成为理所当然的事了。然而,对克洛维斯提出的举行原始人化装舞会,人人穿最近刚打来的野兽皮的建议，她没有表示赞同。克洛维斯也承认："如果我只披着一两张小兔子皮，那会像个刚从娘肚里出来什么也没包的人。不过嘛——"他不怀好意地瞥了狄安娜的身材一眼，补上一句，道："我的身材满可以与那个在跳舞的俄国小伙子比。"

舞会后几天，路易莎·梅宾说："如果底细让人知道了，那才好玩哩！"

"你说什么底细？"帕克尔泰夫人赶紧问。

"就是你一枪打死了羊，吓死了虎。"梅宾小姐说完乐得笑了。那笑声却使听的人感到不入耳。

"这话没人会信。"帕克尔泰夫人说，脸上一阵红一阵白，变化多端。

"卢娜·比姆伯顿会信。"梅宾小姐说。帕克尔泰夫人的脸最后变得白里透青，很难看。

"你该不会出卖我吧？"她问。

"我看中了多金附近一栋周末小别墅，很想买。"梅宾小姐装作漫不经心地说，"只要680卢比，是不动产，划得来，就可惜手头缺这笔钱。"

路易莎·梅宾把漂亮的周末小别墅命名为"野兽"，花园四周种的是虎皮百合①，一到夏天美极了！她的朋友看了好生奇怪和羡慕。

"路易莎如何能享到这样的福真叫人捉摸不透。"这已成了公论。

帕克尔泰夫人再也不热衷打大野兽了。

有朋友问起时，她私下透露说："意想不到的开销太大了。"

---

① 学名卷丹，橙色大花，有大量黑色斑点，所以俗称虎皮百合。文中别墅的名字及这种植物都是有用意的。

The Ant and the Grasshopper

William Somerset Maugham

When I was a very small boy I was made to learn by heart certain of the fables of La Fontaine, and the moral of each was carefully explained to me. Among those learned was *The Ant and the Grasshopper*, which is devised to bring home to the young the useful lesson that in an imperfect world industry is rewarded and giddiness punished. In this admirable fable (I apologise for telling something which everyone is politely, but inexactly, supposed to know) the ant spends a laborious summer gathering its winter store, while the grasshopper sits on a blade of grass singing to the sun. Winter comes and the ant is comfortably provided for, but the grasshopper has an empty larder: he goes to the ant and begs for a little food. Then the ant gives him her classic answer:

"What were you doing in the summer time?"

"Saving your presence[①], I sang. I sang all day, all night."

---

① Saving your presence: 旧式英语中的道歉话。

The Ant and the Grasshopper

"You sang. Why, then go and dance."

I do not ascribe it to perversity on my part, but rather to the inconsequence of childhood, which is deficient in moral sense, that I could never quite reconcile myself to the lesson. My sympathies were with the grasshopper and for some time I never saw an ant without putting my foot on it. In this summary (and as I have discovered since, entirely human) fashion I sought to express my disapproval of prudence and common-sense.

I could not help thinking of this fable when the other day I saw George Ramsay lunching by himself in a restaurant. I never saw anyone wear an expression of such deep gloom. He was staring into space. He looked as though the burden of the whole world sat upon his shoulders. I was sorry for him: I suspected at once that his unfortunate brother had been causing trouble again. I went up to him and held out my hand.

"How are you?" I asked.

"I'm not in hilarious spirits," he answered.

"Is it Tom again?"

He sighed.

"Yes, it's Tom again."

"Why don't you chuck① him? You've done everything in the world for him. You must know by now that he's quite hopeless."

I suppose every family has a black sheep. Tom had been a sore trial to his for twenty years. He had begun life decently enough: he

---

① chuck：俚语，意为"抛弃"。

went into business, married and had two children. The Ramsays were perfectly respectable people and there was every reason to suppose that Tom Ramsay would have a useful and honourable career. But one day, without warning, he announced that he didn't like work and that he wasn't suited for marriage. He wanted to enjoy himself. He would listen to no expostulations. He left his wife and his office. He had a little money and he spent two happy years in various capitals of Europe. Rumours of his doings reached his relations from time to time and they were profoundly shocked. He certainly had a very good time. They shook their heads and asked what would happen when his money was spent. They soon found out: he borrowed. He was charming and unscrupulous. I have never met anyone to whom it was more difficult to refuse a loan. He made a steady income from his friends and he made friends easily. But he always said that the money you spent on necessities was boring; the money that was amusing to spend was the money you spent on luxuries. For this he depended on his brother George. He did not waste his charm on him. George was respectable. Once or twice he fell to Tom's promises of amendment and gave him considerable sums in order that he might make a fresh start. On these Tom bought a motorcar and some very nice jewellery. But when circumstances forced George to realise that his brother would never settle down and he washed his hands of him, Tom, without a qualm, began to blackmail him. It was not very nice for a respectable lawyer to find his brother shaking cocktails behind the bar of his favourite restaurant or to see him waiting on the box-seat of a taxi outside his

The Ant and the Grasshopper

club. Tom said that to serve in a bar or to drive a taxi was a perfectly decent occupation, but if George could oblige him with a couple of hundred pounds he didn't mind for the honour of the family giving it up. George paid.

Once Tom nearly went to prison. George was terribly upset. He went into the whole discreditable affair. Really Tom had gone too far. He had been wild, thoughtless and selfish, but he had never before done anything dishonest, by which George meant illegal; and if he were prosecuted he would assuredly be convicted. But you cannot allow your only brother to go to gaol. The man Tom had cheated, a man called Cronshaw, was vindictive. He was determined to take the matter into court; he said Tom was a scoundrel and should be punished. It cost George an infinite deal of trouble and five hundred pounds to settle the affair. I have never seen him in such a rage as when he heard that Tom and Cronshaw had gone off together to Monte Carlo the moment they cashed the cheque. They spent a happy month there.

For twenty years Tom raced and gambled, philandered with the prettiest girls, danced, ate in the most expensive restaurants, and dressed beautifully. He always looked as if he had just stepped out of a bandbox[①]. Though he was forty-six you would never have taken him for more than thirty-five. He was a most amusing companion and though you knew he was perfectly worthless you could not but enjoy

---

① looked as if he had just stepped out of a bandbox: bandbox 本指装帽子或衣领的薄板箱或盒子，整个短语是比喻用法，意为样子看起来干净、漂亮。

his society. He had high spirits, an unfailing gaiety and incredible charm. I never grudged the contributions he regularly levied on me for the necessities of his existence. I never lent him fifty pounds without feeling that I was in his debt. Tom Ramsay knew everyone and everyone knew Tom Ramsay. You could not approve of him, but you could not help liking him.

Poor George, only a year older than his scapegrace brother, looked sixty. He had never taken more than a fortnight's holiday in the year for a quarter of a century. He was in his office every morning at nine-thirty and never left it till six. He was honest, industrious and worthy. He had a good wife, to whom he had never been unfaithful even in thought, and four daughters to whom he was the best of fathers. He made a point of saving a third of his income and his plan was to retire at fifty-five to a little house in the country where he proposed to cultivate his garden and play golf. His life was blameless. He was glad that he was growing old because Tom was growing old too. He rubbed his hands and said:

"It was all very well when Tom was young and good-looking, but he's only a year younger than I am. In four years he'll be fifty. He won't find life too easy then. I shall have thirty thousand pounds by the time I'm fifty. For twenty-five years I've said that Tom would end in the gutter. And we shall see how he likes that. We shall see if it really pays best to work or be idle."

Poor George! I sympathised with him. I wondered now as I sat down beside him what infamous thing Tom had done. George was evidently very much upset.

"Do you know what's happened now?" he asked me.

I was prepared for the worst. I wondered if Tom had got into the hands of the police at last. George could hardly bring himself to speak.

"You're not going to deny that all my life I've been hard-working, decent, respectable and straightforward. After a life of industry and thrift I can look forward to retiring on a small income in gilt-edged securities. I've always done my duty in that state of life in which it has pleased Providence to place me."

"True."

"And you can't deny that Tom has been an idle, worthless dissolute and dishonourable rogue. If there were any justice he'd be in the workhouse."

"True."

George grew red in the face.

"A few weeks ago he became engaged to a woman old enough to be his mother. And now she's died and left him everything she had. Half a million pounds, a yacht, a house in London and a house in the country."

George Ramsay beat his clenched fist on the table.

"It's not fair, I tell you, it's not fair. Damn it, it's not fair."

I could not help it. I burst into a shout of laughter as I looked at George's wrathful face. I rolled in my chair, I very nearly fell on the floor. George never forgave me. But Tom often asks me to excellent dinners in his charming house in Mayfair, and if he occasionally borrows a trifle from me, that is merely from force of habit. It is never more than a sovereign.

蚂蚁和蟋蟀

〔英〕威廉·萨默塞特·毛姆

我很小的时候就背诵过拉封丹的寓言，听人细细解释过每篇的寓意。其中有一篇名叫《蚂蚁和蟋蟀》，告诫年轻人要将有日思无日，要勤劳，别轻浮。这个很有教益的寓言（请原谅我在此絮烦，诸位一定知道这个寓言，虽不一定说得清楚）说的是：蚂蚁夏天忙忙碌碌，准备食粮过冬，而蟋蟀坐在草叶上对着太阳唱歌。冬天来了，蚂蚁不愁吃，蟋蟀饿着肚皮。它找上蚂蚁的门，求蚂蚁给它一点吃的。蚂蚁的回答很巧妙：

"你夏天干什么去了？"

"请原谅，我在唱歌，一天到晚唱。"

"好呀，你那时候唱歌，现在就去跳舞吧！"

我并不是要标新立异，而是年幼无知，领会不了其中的寓意，总是抱着另一种看法。我同情蟋蟀，有一段时间看到蚂蚁便用脚踩，用这种干脆的（现在我觉得这是人独有的）办法，表示我不赞成谨小慎微、规规矩矩。

几天前，我遇见乔治·拉姆齐独自在餐馆吃饭，不由想起了这个寓言。我看到他无精打采，比谁心情都不好，两眼直发愣，似乎天塌下来压到了他一个人的肩上。我同情他，马上猜准是他那不成器的小兄弟又出了事，走过去，伸出一只手。

"你好！"我说。

"我心情不大好！"他说。

"又为了汤姆吗？"

他叹了口气。

"没错，又为汤姆。"

"你就别管他了。你对他已仁至义尽，现在也该明白他已无可救药了。"

我想家家都有个不成器的人。20年来，汤姆已叫他的家人伤透了脑筋。刚开始时他还满可以，有正经事干，结了婚，有两个孩子。拉姆齐家的人都是体体面面的人，不难猜想，汤姆·拉姆齐也会干一番出息、光彩的事业。然而，没料到有一天他说，他讨厌辛辛苦苦干，不喜欢妻子儿女拖累，要痛痛快快享受。谁劝他都不听。他抛开妻子，扔下办公室的工作。他有些钱，在欧洲各国的首都逍遥了两年。他家的人对他的所作所为常有所耳闻，非常不安，当然他玩得痛快。他们直摇头，担心他的钱花完了会落到什么结果。不久以后，他们发现他自有办法——借钱。他逗人喜爱，脸皮厚。谁开口借钱我都不难推脱，唯有他开口借却推托不了。朋友们的接济成了他的可靠收入，而他交朋友又轻而易举。但他总是说，如果你的钱只用在必不可少的开销上，那么花得没意思；如果有了钱享受一番，那才够味。他有钱享受靠的是亲哥哥乔治，他在哥哥身上的功夫从没白花过。乔治是位君子。有一两次他因汤姆答应浪子回头，给了他大笔钱，让他重新起家。汤姆用这些钱买了辆汽车和一些漂亮的宝石。种种事情使乔治绝望了,知道兄弟不会安分过日子,不肯再理他。汤姆无情无义,马上对他进行讹诈。当然,一位堂堂的律师不能眼睁睁看着同胞兄弟在自己爱去的餐馆的酒吧间后摇鸡尾酒,或者坐在他俱乐部外的出租汽车里等乘客。汤姆说到酒吧间当服务员和开出租车都是正当职业,但如果乔治给他200镑钱,为了一家人的体面,他也可以不干这种事。乔治只好出钱。

有一次汤姆几乎锒铛入狱。乔治着急了,打听了这件不光彩的事的本末。汤姆这一次做得太过分。之前他放荡,没头脑,又只顾自己,但从没有干过不名誉的事——乔治说的不名誉的事就是犯法的事。这次如果追究起来,他一定会被判有罪。但你总不能看着你唯一的亲兄弟下大牢而不闻不问吧?受汤姆诈骗的人姓克朗肖,气不过,决定到法院控告,说汤姆是无赖,应绳之以法。乔治费尽九牛二虎之力,又花了500镑,才算把事情了结。谁知等支票一兑现,汤姆和克朗肖马上一道去了赌城蒙特卡洛,快快活活逛了一个月。乔治知道后气得要死,我亲眼见到的。

20年来汤姆嫖赌逍遥,吃喝玩乐,穿得漂漂亮亮,总是一副公子哥儿相。他已年到46,可是你会只当他还不上35。他很有交际手腕,尽管你知道他是个浪子,却总情不自禁喜欢他。他精神十足,无时不开心,又十分可爱。每次他找我要钱做必要开销,我总是解囊相助,给了他50镑还只当自己欠了他的债。汤姆·拉姆齐了解所有人,所有人也了解汤姆·拉姆齐。你会不赞成他的行为,但又不由得会喜爱他。

可怜的乔治,比败家子兄弟只大一岁,看起来却有60岁。25年来,一年里他从没有享受过两星期的假日,每天上午9点半进办公室,下午不到6点不出来。他诚实,肯干,办事可靠。他有一位贤妻,连想都没想过做对不起她的事;生了四个女儿,对她们体贴入微。他的收入三分之一积攒了下来。打算到55岁退休后,住到乡下的一栋小别墅里,打打高尔夫球,在花园里养养花。他过的生活无可挑剔。他渐渐老了,心里反而高兴,因为他老了汤姆也老了。他搓搓手说:

"汤姆年轻漂亮时不发愁,但他仅仅比我小一岁。再过四年,他也是50岁的人了,到那时日子会很难过。我到50岁有3万镑积蓄。这25年里我老说汤姆到头来要进贫民窟,我们等着瞧他受那罪吧。到头来,辛辛苦苦干的人好,还是游手好闲的人好,我们会亲眼瞧见。"

乔治真可怜!我同情他。我坐在他身边,心想一定是汤姆干出了什么丢人现眼的事。一看就知道乔治非常苦闷。

"你猜猜,又闹出什么名堂啦?"他问我。

我想一定是出了大祸,说不定汤姆最后落到了警察手里。乔治几乎气得有话说不出。

"你知道得清清楚楚,我一辈子辛辛苦苦,规规矩矩,老老实实,受人敬重。劳累节俭了一生,指望退休后靠着一份买金边证券的小收入过日子总不算过分吧?我一直安分守己过日子,总对得起天地良心吧?"

"那当然。"

"你也知道得清清楚楚,汤姆一贯游手好闲、荒唐透顶,是个不成器的家伙。要是他进了收容所,也不算过分吧?"

"那当然。"

乔治的脸涨得通红。

"几个星期前他与一个老太太订了婚,那人做他老娘绰绰有余。没想到现在那女的死了,全部财产归了他,有50万镑积蓄,一艘游艇,两栋房子,一栋在伦敦,一栋在乡下。"

乔治·拉姆齐握紧拳头,在桌上咚地捶了一拳。

"老天没眼,真没眼!妈的,老天没眼!"

我不是有意,看到乔治气歪了脸,忍不住放声大笑起来,笑得前仰后合,差一点从椅子上滚下来。乔治从此恨透了我,但汤姆常邀我去梅费尔阔气的住所里美餐一顿。偶尔他还向我借点钱,那是因为积习难改,数目绝不超过1英镑。

Three Letters ... and a Footnote

Horacio Quiroga

Sir:

I am taking the liberty of sending you these lines, hoping you will be good enough to publish them under your own name. I make this request of you because I am informed that no newspaper would accept these pages if I sign them myself. If you think it wiser, you may alter my impressions by giving them a few masculine touches, which indeed may improve them.

My work makes it necessary for me to take the streetcar twice a day, and for five years I have been making the same trip. Sometimes, on the return ride, I travel in the company of some of my girl friends, but on the way to work I always go alone. I am twenty years old, tall, not too thin, and not at all dark-complexioned. My mouth is somewhat large but not pale. My impression is that my eyes are not small. These outward features which I've estimated modestly, as you have observed, are nevertheless all I need to help me form an opinion of many men, in fact so many that I'm tempted to say all men.

You know also that you men have the habit before you board a streetcar of looking rapidly at its occupants through the windows. In that way you examine all the faces (of the women, of course, since they are the only ones that have any interest for you). After that little ceremony, you enter and sit down.

Very well then; as soon as a man leaves the sidewalk, walks over to the car and looks inside, I know perfectly what sort of fellow he is, and I never make a mistake. I know if he is serious, or if he merely intends to invest ten cents of his fare in finding an easy pick-up. I quickly distinguish between those who like to ride at their ease, and those who prefer less room at the side of some girl.

When the place beside me is unoccupied, I recognize accurately, according to the glance through the window, which men are indifferent and will sit down anywhere, which are only half-interested and will turn their heads in order to give us the once-over slowly, after they have sat down; and finally, which are the enterprising fellows who will pass by seven empty places so as to perch uncomfortably at my side, way back in the rear of the vehicle.

Presumably, these follows are the most interesting. Quite contrary to the regular habit of girls who travel alone, instead of getting up and offering the inside place to the newcomer, I simply move over toward the window to leave plenty of room for the enterprising arrival.

Plenty of room. That's a meaningless phrase. Never will the three quarters of a bench abandoned by a girl to her neighbor be sufficient. After moving and shifting at will, he seems suddenly overcome by a surprising motionlessness, to the point where he seems paralyzed. But that is mere appearance, for if anyone watches with suspicion this lack of movement, he will note that the body of the gentleman, imperceptibly, and with a slyness that does honor to his absent-minded look, is slipping little by little down an imaginary inclined plane toward the window, where the girl happens to be, although he isn't looking at her and apparently has no interest in her at all.

That's the way such men are: one could swear that they're thinking about the moon. However, all this time, the right foot (or the left) continues slipping delicately down the aforementioned plane.

I'll admit that while this is going on, I'm very far from being bored. With a mere glance as I shift toward the window, I have taken the measure of my gallant. I know whether he is a spirited fellow who yields to his first impulse or whether he is really someone brazen enough to give me cause for a little worry. I know whether he is a courteous young man or just a vulgar one, whether a hardened criminal or a tender pickpocket, whether he is really a seductive Beau Brummel[①] (the seduisant and not the seducteur of the French) or a mere petty masher.

At first view it might seem that only one kind of man would

---

① 花花公子布鲁梅尔，19世纪初伦敦名流领袖，高大而英俊，以衣着打扮讲究著称，引领当时上层社会穿衣时尚。现已成爱打扮男子的代名词。

perform the act of letting his foot slip slyly over while his face wears a hypocritical mask, namely the thief. However that is not so, and there isn't a girl that hasn't made this observation. For each different type she must have ready a special defense. But very often, especially if the man is quite young or poorly dressed, he is likely to be a pickpocket.

The tactics followed by the man never vary. First of all the sudden rigidity and the air of thinking about the moon. The next step is a fleeting glimpse at our person which seems to linger slightly over our face, but whose sole purpose is to estimate the distance that intervenes between his foot and ours. This information acquired, now the conquest begins.

I think there are few things funnier than that maneuver you men execute, when you move your foot along in gradual shifts of toe and heel alternately. Obviously you men can't see the joke; but this pretty cat and mouse game played with a size eleven shoe at one end, and at the other, up above, near the roof, a simpering idiotic face (doubtless because of emotion), bears no comparison so far as absurdity is concerned with anything else you men do.

I said before that I was not bored with these performances. And my entertainment is based upon the following fact: from the moment the charmer has calculated with perfect precision the distance he has to cover with his foot, he rarely lets his gaze wander down again. He is certain of his measurement and he has no desire to put us on our guard by repeated glances. You will clearly realize that the attraction for him lies in making contact, and not in merely looking.

Very well then: when this amiable neighbor has gone about halfway, I start the same maneuver that he is executing, and I do it with equal slyness and the same semblance of absent-minded preoccupation with, let us say, my doll. Only, the movement of my foot is away from his. Not much; a few inches are enough.

It's a treat to behold, presently my neighbor's surprise when, upon arriving finally at the calculated spot, he contacts absolutely nothing. Nothing! His size eleven shoe is entirely alone. This is too much for him; first he takes a look at the floor, and then at my face. My thought is still wandering a thousand leagues away, playing with my doll; but the fellow begins to understand.

Fifteen out of seventeen times (I mention these figures after long experience) the annoying gentleman gives up the enterprise. In the two remaining cases I am forced to resort to a warning look. It isn't necessary for this look to indicate by its expression a feeling of insult, or contempt, or anger: it is enough to make a movement of the head in his direction, toward him but without looking straight at him. In these cases it is better always to avoid crossing glances with a man who by chance has been really and deeply attracted to us. There may be in any pickpocket the makings of a dangerous thief. This fact is well known to the cashiers who guard large amounts of money and also to young women, not thin, not dark, with mouths not little and eyes not small, as is the case with yours truly,

M. R.

Dear Miss:

Deeply grateful for your kindness. I'll sign my name with much pleasure to the article on your impressions, as you request. Nevertheless, it would interest me very much and purely as your collaborator to know your answer to the following questions: Aside from the seventeen concrete cases you mention, haven't you ever felt the slightest attraction toward some neighbor, tall or short, blond or dark, stout or lean? Haven't you ever felt the vaguest temptation to yield, ever so vague, which made the withdrawing of your own foot disagreeable and troublesome?

H. Q.

Sir:

To be frank, yes, once in my life, I felt that temptation to yield to someone, or more accurately, that lack of energy in my foot to which you refer. That person was *you*. But you didn't have the sense to take advantage of it.

M. R.

三封信与一条脚注

〔乌拉圭〕奥拉西奥·基罗加

先生：

　　冒昧地给你写这封信，希望你能帮忙，同意将此信以你的名义发表。我提出这个请求是因为据说文章如果署上我自己的名字，哪家报纸也不愿刊载。如果你认为必要，不妨将此信修改修改，添几笔有关男性的描写，使文章更好些。

　　由于要上班，我每天得坐两趟电车，5年来都这么跑。在回家的路上有时与几个小姐妹同车，但在上班的路上，总是一个人。今年我20岁，个子高，但不是瘦得可怜，皮肤根本谈不上黑，嘴比较大，但不缺少血色。我觉得我的眼睛也不小。你知道，我这样说并没有把我的外貌估计过高。但不提及我的外貌，我就无法评价许多男人，其实，是太多的男人，甚至是所有男人。

　　你也知道，你们男人有个习惯：上电车前在车窗外把里面的乘客先扫上一眼。这一扫，你们看到了所有人的脸（当然是女人的脸，因为你们关心的唯有女人）。做完这个小动作之后，你们才上车坐下。

　　不瞒你说，哪个男人一离开人行道，走到电车边，往里一瞧，我准知道他的底细，十拿十稳。我知道他是真坐车，还是想花1毛钱买张车票，看看有没有容易上钩的；我能一眼分辨出要舒舒服服坐车的人和偏要挤到姑娘身边的人。

如果我旁边的座位空着，从窗外人的眼神我能准确地判断哪些人无心，坐在哪儿都行；哪些人兴趣不浓，只会在坐下以后转过头慢慢打量我们一番算了；哪些人是打着主意的，会走过七八个空位子不坐，要到车后与我挤在一起。

可以说，这些人是最有趣的人。我与其他单身坐车的姑娘不同，不会站起来把新上来的人请进里边座位，只是挪到靠窗位置，让出足够的地盘给打着主意的人。

足够的地盘并不足够，即令姑娘让出四分之三的地方，旁边的人还嫌小。他先动来动去，后来突然变得安静，似乎是在座位上瘫痪了。但这是假象，谁要是起了疑心，注意观察这位端坐不动的人，准会发现，尽管表面装得漫不经心，这位君子的身子不知不觉地、巧妙地、一点一点往窗口靠。窗边坐的是一位姑娘，他眼没朝她看，似乎对她根本没有兴趣。

这些男人就是这样，别人只当他们的心挂念着天涯海角的事。其实，他们右边（或左边）的一只脚不停地悄悄往之前我所说的方向移动着。

我可以承认，他这样做时，我满不在乎。我往窗口靠时，瞥上一眼就目测出了身边风流郎君是个什么样的人。我能看出他是个知趣的人，试探一次不成就拉倒，还是个厚脸皮，会给我找些麻烦；能看出他是个懂礼貌的人，还是个粗俗的人；是一个惯犯，还是个刚上路的扒手；是个迷人的时尚帅哥，还是个小小的采花蝶。

初看，似乎只有一种人会面上装得若无其事，而脚却悄悄地移过来，那就是小偷。然而实际情况不是这样，哪位姑娘都不这样看。对于不同类型的人，她必须进行不同的防范。但往往特别是年纪很轻或衣着不像样的，以小偷居多。

男人采取的策略千篇一律。首先是正襟危坐，装作想天涯海角的事。然后飞快地瞥我们一眼，似乎留意的是我们的脸，实际上唯一目的是估计他的脚与我们的脚之间的距离。估计出以后，开始了征战。

你们男人交替着把脚尖和脚跟一点一点移，那模样真是滑稽透顶。当然你们自己不觉得可笑，但你们干的最荒唐的事数来数去要算这一件。想想吧，你们脚上穿着11码的大鞋，头几乎顶着汽车的顶篷，却玩猫捉老鼠的游戏，脸像白痴一样，还傻笑。

前面我说过，我并不在乎这些名堂。我有个办法开心，是这样的：那鬼迷心窍的家伙把脚要移动的距离算准了以后，便再也不朝下看。他很有把握，不想左一眼右一眼让我们起戒心。你会明白，他并不是想看我们两眼了事，一定要碰着我们才甘心。

不瞒你说，等身边这位热心人功夫用到一半时，我学着他的样，也移动起脚来，跟这家伙同样巧妙，同样装作若无其事，比如假装玩着我的布偶。只是他的脚来了，我的脚就让开。相隔不用远，几英寸就行。

过了不久，我的邻座终于到达算准了的目的地，可是扑空。他好生奇怪，我看了却得意。扑空！他11码的大鞋子什么也没捞着，忍不住了，先看看下面，再看看我的脸。我只装作没事一般玩着布偶，但这家伙心中有数。

17次中有15次（这个数据来自长期的经验），这位不规矩的先生只好罢休。另外两次我还得用眼睛示警。这一眼用不着带叫人难堪、鄙视或愤怒的表示，只要把头朝他一偏就行，并不正眼瞧。偶尔也有当真对我们钟情的人，这样做就可避免与他们目光接触了。扒腰包的人也有可能成为胆大妄为的贼，腰缠万贯的出纳员很懂得这一点，年轻姑娘也懂，给你写信的不瘦、不黑、嘴不太小、眼不太小的我就懂。

M. R.

小姐：

　　非常感谢你的信任。我非常高兴按你的要求，在你谈体会的文章上签上我的名字。但是还有几个问题，是我深感兴趣的，我想单纯作为你的合作者听听你的回答：除了你说到的17次情况外，你有没有对某位邻座曾稍稍产生过兴趣，无论是高是矮，是白是黑，是壮是瘦？你有没有起哪怕一丁点顺从之心，而觉得把你的脚往一边缩是不可取或失策的呢？

H. Q.

先生：

　　坦率地说，有的，就一次。哦，我想顺从某个人，或者更确切些说，正如你所说，我的脚没有了力气。这个人就是你。但你没领会，错过了良机。

M. R.

The Ghosts

Lord Dunsany

The argument that I had with my brother in his great lonely house will scarcely interest my readers. Not those, at least, whom I hope may be attracted by the experiment that I undertook, and by the strange things that befell me in that hazardous region into which so lightly and so ignorantly I allowed my fancy to enter. It was at Oneleigh that I had visited him.

Now Oneleigh stands in a wide isolation, in the midst of a dark gathering of old whispering cedars. They nod their heads together when the North Wind comes, and nod again and agree, and furtively grow still again, and say no more awhile. The North Wind is to them like a nice problem among wise old men; they nod their heads over it, and mutter it all together. They know much, those cedars, they have been there so long. Their grandsires knew Lebanon, and the grandsires of these were the servants of the King of Tyre and came to Solomon's court. And amidst these black-haired children of grey-headed Time stood the old house of Oneleigh. I know not how many centuries had lashed against it their evanescent foam of years; but it was still unshattered, and all about it were the things of long ago, as cling strange growths to some sea-defying rock. Here, like the shells of long-dead limpets, was armour that men encased themselves in long ago; here, too, were tapestries of many colours, beautiful as seaweed; no modern flotsam ever drifted hither, no early Victorian furniture, no electric light. The great trade routes that littered the years with empty meat tins and cheap novels were far from here. Well, well, the centuries will shatter it and drive its fragments on to distant shores. Meanwhile, while it yet stood, I went on a visit there to my brother, and we argued about ghosts. My brother's intelligence on this subject seemed to me to be in need of correction. He mistook things imagined for things having an actual existence; he argued that second-hand evidence of persons having seen ghosts proved ghosts to exist. I said that even if they had seen ghosts, this was no proof at all; nobody believes that there are red rats, though there is plenty of first-hand evidence of men having seen them in delirium. Finally, I said I would see ghosts myself, and continue to argue against their actual existence. So I collected a handful of cigars and drank several cups of very strong tea, and went without my dinner, and retired into a room where there was dark oak and all the chairs were covered with tapestry; and my brother went to bed bored with our argument and trying hard to dissuade me from making myself uncomfortable. All the way up the old stairs as I stood at the bottom of them, and as his candle went winding up and up, I heard him still trying to persuade me to have supper and go to bed.

It was a windy winter, and outside the cedars were muttering I know not what about; but I think they were Tories of a school long dead, and were troubled about something new. Within, a great damp log upon the fireplace began to squeak and sing, and struck up a whining tune, and a tall flame stood up over it and beat time, and all the shadows crowded round and began to dance. In distant corners old masses of darkness sat still like chaperones and never moved. Over there, in the darkest part of the room, stood a door that was always locked. It led into the hall, but no one ever used it; near that door something had happened once of which the family are not proud. We do not speak of it. There in the firelight stood the venerable forms of the old chairs; the hands that had made their tapestries lay far beneath the soil, the needles with which they wrought were many, separate flakes of rust. No one wove now in that old room—no one but the assiduous ancient spiders who, watching by the deathbed of the things of yore, worked shrouds to hold their dust. In shrouds about the cornices already lay the heart of the oak wainscot that the worm had eaten out.

Surely at such an hour, in such a room, a fancy already excited by hunger and strong tea might see the ghosts of former occupants. I expected nothing less. The fire flickered and the shadows danced, memories of strange historic things rose vividly in my mind; but midnight chimed solemnly from a seven-foot clock, and nothing happened. My imagination would not be hurried, and the chill that is with the small hours had come upon me, and I had nearly abandoned myself to sleep, when in the hall adjoining there arose the rustling of silk dresses that I had waited for and expected. Then there entered two by two the high-born ladies and their gallants of Jacobean times. They were little more than shadows—very dignified shadows, and almost indistinct; but you have all read ghost stories before, you have all seen in museums the dresses of those times—there is little need to describe them; they entered, several of them, and sat down on the old chairs, perhaps a little carelessly considering the value of the tapestries. Then the rustling of their dresses ceased.

Well—I had seen ghosts, and was neither frightened nor convinced that ghosts existed. I was about to get up out of my chair and go to bed, when there came a sound of pattering in the hall, a sound of bare feet coming over the polished floor, and every now and then a foot would slip and I heard claws scratching along the wood as some four-footed thing lost and regained its balance. I was not frightened, but uneasy. The pattering came straight towards the room that I was in, then I heard the sniffing of expectant nostrils; perhaps "uneasy" was not the most suitable word to describe my feelings then. Suddenly a herd of black creatures larger than bloodhounds came galloping in; they had large pendulous ears, their noses were to the ground sniffing, they went up to the lords and ladies of long ago and fawned about them disgustingly. Their eyes were horribly bright, and ran down to great depths. When I looked into them I knew suddenly what these creatures were, and I was afraid. They were the sins, the filthy, immortal sins of those courtly men and women.

How demure she was, the lady that sat near me on an old-world chair—how demure she was, and how fair, to have beside her with its jowl upon her lap a sin with such cavernous red eyes, a clear case of murder. And you, yonder lady with the golden hair, surely not you— and yet that fearful beast with the yellow eyes slinks from you to yonder courtier there, and whenever one drives it away it slinks back to the other. Over there a lady tries to smile as she strokes the loathsome furry head of another's sin, but one of her own is jealous and intrudes itself under her hand. Here sits an old nobleman with his grandson on his knee, and one of the great black sins of the grandfather is licking the child's face and has made the child its own. Sometimes a ghost would move and seek another chair, but always his pack of sins would move behind him. Poor ghosts, poor ghosts! How many flights they must have attempted for two hundred years from their hated sins, how many excuses they must have given for their presence, and the sins were with them still—and still unexplained. Suddenly one of them seemed to scent my living blood, and bayed horribly, and all the others left their ghosts at once and dashed up to the sin that had given tongue. The brute had picked up my scent near the door by which I had entered, and they moved slowly nearer to me sniffing along the floor, and uttering every now and then their fearful cry. I saw that the whole thing had gone too far. But now they had seen me, now they were all about me, they sprang up trying to reach my throat; and whenever their claws touched me, horrible thoughts came into my mind and unutterable desires dominated my heart. I planned bestial things as these creatures leaped around me, and planned them with a masterly cunning. A great red-eyed murder was among the foremost of those furry things from whom I feebly strove to defend my throat. Suddenly it seemed to me good that I should kill my brother. It seemed important to me that I should not risk being punished. I knew where a revolver was kept; after I shot him, I would dress the body up and put flour on the face like a man that had been acting as a ghost. It would be very simple. I would say that he had frightened me—and the servants had heard us talking about ghosts. There were one or two trivialities that would have to be arranged, but nothing escaped my mind. Yes, it seemed to me very good that I should kill my brother as I looked into the red depths of this creature's eyes. But one last effort as they dragged me down—"If two straight lines cut one another," I said, "the opposite angles are equal. Let AB, CD, cut one another at E, then the angles CEA, CEB equal two right angles (prop. xiii). Also CEA, AED equal two right angles."

I moved toward the door to get the revolver; a hideous exultation arose among the beasts. "But the angle CEA is common, therefore AED equals CEB. In the same way CEA equals DEB. *Q.E.D.*" It was proved. Logic and reason re-established themselves in my mind, there were no dark hounds of sin, the tapestried chairs were empty. It seemed to me an inconceivable thought that a man should murder his brother.

鬼

〔爱尔兰〕邓萨尼勋爵

我与弟弟在那所冷清清的大房子里进行的一场辩论,读者一定不爱听。至少有些人不爱,因为我猜他们会被我的经历所吸引,被我在幻觉莫名其妙地闯进那危险地方时见到的奇怪现象所吸引。我去看望他的地方叫奥尼莱因。

现在的奥尼莱因与世隔绝,到处是黑压压、沙沙响的古杉。北风吹来时它们一齐点头,点头,偷偷地长得更大,一时间什么也不说了。年长智高的人也有许多难以回答的问题,北风对于古杉来说就是一个谜。北风来了它们频频点头,谈起北风只能轻声轻气。这些杉树见多识广,在这儿生长的时间很长。它们的祖宗知道黎巴嫩,祖宗的祖宗给泰尔王[①]当过差,去过所罗门[②]的王宫。在白头时间老人的黑发子孙中立着古老的住宅奥尼莱因。我说不上它经历了多少世纪的风风雨雨,只知道它没有垮,整个屋子里的东西都已年深月久,好像不怕海浪的岩石上的附着物已年

---

① 泰尔是古腓尼基南部一海港,在今之黎巴嫩。
② 圣经记叙的以色列贤明国王。

深月久一样。这里有古代人披挂的甲胄,像是帽贝的壳,帽贝早死了,壳却留了下来。还有绣帷,颜色多种多样,像海藻一样好看。现代装饰见不到一星半点,甚至见不到维多利亚早期的家具,见不到电灯。这里也没有空餐盒和廉价小说,可见历年不是商队的必经之路。当然,若干世纪后这所房子会倒塌,连断壁残垣最后都要消失得无影无踪,可是现在它还安然无恙,我就是在这所房子里看望我弟弟的。我们争论了有没有鬼,我觉得他对这个问题的看法欠妥。他把幻觉当成现实,认为有人见过鬼便足以证实鬼的存在。我认为即便有人见过,也不足为凭,就像很多人在神情恍惚时见过红老鼠,却没有谁相信真有红老鼠。最后我说要亲眼见见,仍然表示不相信真有鬼。于是我抓了一把香烟,喝了几杯浓茶,没有吃饭,回房休息了。房间里的家具是橡木的,已经发黑,每张椅上铺着坐垫。弟弟与我舌战一场,倦了。他苦心劝我别饿肚子,可是无用,只好去睡。我站在古屋弯弯曲曲的楼梯下,还听到他拿着蜡烛边上楼边劝我吃了饭再睡。

  这年冬天风大,屋子外的杉树不知在叨咕着什么,我想大概它们属于一个早已消亡的保守派,因为看不惯某件新鲜事,牢骚满腹。屋子里一大段搁在炉子上的湿木头吱吱叫起来,唱起来,声调低沉,接着木头上冒出高高的火焰,火焰打着拍子,房间里的影子一齐跳起舞来。火堆远处的角落黑乎乎,不会动,仿佛是舞场少女的陪娘。在一个最暗的角落里有一道门,总是锁着。它通往大厅,但谁也不从这儿出入,原因是这道门边曾出过事,是不宜外扬的,我们别提吧。火光照着古色古香的老式座椅,织椅垫的人早已长眠地下,化成了尘埃。现在这间房子里没有人编编织织了,干这工作的只有勤勤恳恳的老蜘蛛,它们眼见昔日的伙

鬼

伴一个个作古，在织着装殓它们的尸衣。尸衣把壁板包了起来，蛀虫吃空的橡木板就包在里面。

在这样一个时刻，在这样一个房间，一个肚皮空空，喝了浓茶的人很有可能见到以往房主人的鬼魂。我有充分准备。火光跳动着，影子也跳动着，历史上记载的许多奇怪事件活灵活现浮现在脑海里，但等到一座七英尺高的时钟庄重地敲过十二点时，还不见任何动静。我没再多想，只觉得午夜的寒气逼人，渐渐要睡着了。正在这时，一门之隔的大厅里响起了我原等待的窸窸窣窣的罗裙声。接着詹姆斯一世时代①的贵妇挽着情侣成双成对进来了。这些人只不过是影子，几乎看不清楚，只知气派十足。你一定看过鬼故事，也在博物馆里见过当时的服装，把它们描述一番用不着。一共好几对，进来后在椅子上一屁股坐下来，于是窸窸窣窣的罗裙声没有了。椅垫很值钱，这样坐下似乎太随便了些。

好了，我见到了鬼，但既不害怕，也不相信真有鬼。我正要从椅子上站起来睡觉，突然大厅里响起了吧嗒吧嗒的声音，是赤脚走在光滑的地板上的声音。好几次有的脚走滑了，我听到有爪子在地板上擦过，大概是什么四脚动物失了足又重新站稳。我不害怕，却不安起来。吧嗒吧嗒的声音一直往我坐的房间来了，接着果然听到了鼻子发出的哼声。也许，"不安"并不是形容我当时心情的最合适字眼。一群比警犬大的黑东西闯了进来，大耳朵往下垂着，鼻子在地上嗅，跑到往日的贵人跟前，讨好卖乖。它们的眼发亮，亮得可怕，深深凹进眼窝里。我仔细一看，马上明白了这些畜牲是什么东西，害怕起来。它们是罪恶，是这些仪表

---

① 指1603—1625年詹姆斯一世当权的时代。

311

堂堂的男男女女干的肮脏的缺德事。

坐在我旁边一张老式椅上的贵妇人庄重极了，又庄重又美丽，身边蹲着条狗，下巴靠在她膝上，两只红眼睛深深陷进去，一看而知是谋杀罪变的。还有这一位，留着金发的这一位——当然也可说不是这一位。黄眼睛畜牲从她身边跑开，找上另一位贵人，而且每次被一位赶走，它就另找一位。有一位贵妇边笑边摸别人畜牲头上的乱毛，她自己的畜牲见了眼红，钻过来让她摸。有位年老的贵族把孙儿抱在膝上，他的一条大黑畜牲舔着孩子的脸，把孩子当成己出。有时有的鬼魂会起身换个座位，但他的一帮畜牲总是紧跟着。可怜啊可怜！两百年来，这群鬼魂一定无数次想摆脱身边的畜牲，也一定为自己的罪恶找过无数口实，然而罪恶无法摆脱，也无口实可找！突然，有一只畜牲发现了我的气味，狂吠起来；别的畜牲马上丢下自己的主人，向汪汪叫的那只跑过来。这帮家伙在我进来的门附近找到了我的气味，用鼻子在地上嗅着，慢慢往我这儿走，走几步乱叫一阵。我发现大事不妙。但它们这时已经看见了我，围住了我，一齐跳起来，想咬断我的喉管。无论哪条畜牲的爪子碰到我，我脑子就产生邪念，内心就起歹意。它们在我前后左右跳着，我尽打坏主意，而且打得巧妙。我有气无力地护着喉管，被这帮长毛畜牲团团围住，打头阵的家伙中有一头是红眼睛的谋杀罪。突然间我起了杀亲兄弟的意图，还想到干了必须逃脱法网。我知道手枪放在哪里。一枪打死他之后，我给他穿衣服，往脸上抹面粉，伪造他装神弄鬼的模样。这办法简单得很。我就说他把我吓得胆战心惊，反正佣人们都听到了我们辩论有没有鬼。还有一些细节需要安排，但我考虑得周到，定会万无一失。一点不假，我看着那家伙深陷进去的红眼睛时，起了杀亲兄弟的意图。然而就在眼见要被拖下水时，我得救了。我心里在想着："两条直线相交时两对角相等。假设线段AB与线段CD相交于E点，那么CEA角与CEB角之和等于两直角（即180°），CEA角与AED角之和也等于两直角。"

我往门边走，想拿枪，这群畜牲兴高采烈。"但是CEA角为公有，所以AED角等于CEB角。同理，CEA角等于DEB角。"一道题做出来了，我恢复了逻辑思维和理智。罪恶变成的恶犬消失了，椅子上的鬼魂不见了。我认为起心谋杀亲兄弟是不可思议的事。

A Dangerous Guy Indeed

Damon Runyon

It is maybe a matter of thirty-five years ago that a young fellow by the name of Morgan Johnson comes to my old home town and starts in living there.

In those days back in my old home town it is not considered polite to ask a man where he comes from, and as Morgan Johnson never mentions the place himself nobody ever knows. Furthermore, he never tells much of anything about himself outside of this, so he is considered something of a mystery.

He is a hard-looking citizen in many respects, what with having a scar across his nose, and a pair of black eyebrows which run right together, and black hair, and black eyes, and a way of[①] looking at people, and the first time he goes down Santa Fe Avenue thirty-five years ago, somebody or other says:

"There is a very dangerous man."

---

① have a way of: 此处 way 指人的某种习惯。

A Dangerous Guy Indeed

Well, the next time Morgan Johnson goes down Santa Fe Avenue somebody who hears what is said about him the first time, says to somebody else:

"There is certainly a very dangerous man."

By and by everybody who sees Morgan Johnson with the scar across his nose, and his black eyes, and all, says:

"There is a dangerous man."

Finally it is well known to one and all[①] back in my old home town that Morgan Johnson is a dangerous man, and everybody is most respectful to him when he goes walking up and down and around and about, looking at people in that way of his.

If he happens into a saloon where an argument is going on, the argument cools right off. If he happens to say anything, no matter what it is, everybody says it is right, because naturally nobody wishes any truck with a dangerous man.

This scar on Morgan Johnson's nose shows that he has been in plenty of trouble sometime or other, and the fact that he is alive and walking up and down in my old home town out West shows that he can take care of himself.

He never states how he comes to get this scar, but finally somebody says they hear he gets it in a fight with ten very bad men one night in New York, one of them zipping a bullet across his nose, and that Morgan Johnson finally kills all ten.

---

① one and all: everybody

Who starts this story nobody knows, but Morgan Johnson never denies it, even when the number of parties he kills gets up to as high as twenty. In fact Morgan Johnson never denies anything that is said about him, being something of a hand for keeping his mouth shut, and minding his own business.

Well, sir, he lives in my old home town out West for many years, and is often pointed out to visitors to our city by citizens who say:

"There is a very dangerous man, indeed."

By the time Morgan Johnson is getting along toward fifty years old, some people start shivering the minute he comes in sight and never stop shivering until he goes on past.

Then one day what happens but Morgan Johnson is going along the street when a little old guy by the name of Wheezer Gamble comes staggering out of the Greenlight saloon, this Wheezer Gamble being nothing but a sheepman from down on the Huerfano River.

He is called Wheezer because he wheezes more than somewhat[①], on account of having the asthma, and he is so old, and so little that nobody ever thinks of bothering him even though he is nothing but a sheepman. He comes to town once a month to get his pots on, and this day he staggers out of the Greenlight is the first of the month.

The whiskey they sell in the Greenlight saloon is very powerful whiskey, and often makes people wish to fight who never think of fighting before in their life, although, of course, nobody ever figures it

---

① more than somewhat: very much

is powerful enough to make a sheepman fight. But what does Wheezer Gamble do when he sees Morgan Johnson, but grab Morgan by the coat, to hold himself up, and say to Morgan like this:

"So you are a dangerous man, are you?"

Well, everybody who sees this come off feels very sorry for poor old Wheezer because they figure Morgan Johnson will chew him up at once and spit him out, but Morgan only blinks his eyes and says:

"What?"

"They tell me you are a dangerous man," Wheezer says. "I am now about to cut you open with my jack-knife and see what it is that makes you dangerous."

At this he lets go Morgan's coat and outs with a big jack-knife, which is an article he uses in connection with cooking and skinning dead sheep and one thing and another, and opens it up to carve Morgan Johnson.

But Morgan Johnson does not wait to be carved. The minute he sees this knife he turns around and hauls it, which is a way of saying he leaves. Furthermore, he leaves on a dead run, and everybody says that if he is not a fast runner that day he will do until a fast one comes along.

Of course, Wheezer Gamble cannot chase him very far, being old, and also drunker than somewhat and Morgan Johnson never stops until he is plumb out of town. The last anybody sees of him he is still going in the direction of Denver and the chances are he reaches there, as he is never seen in my old home town again.

Then it comes out that the story about him being dangerous is by no means true, and furthermore that he does not kill ten men back in New York or any men whatever. As for the scar across his nose, somebody says that he gets it from being busted across the nose by a woman with a heavy pocketbook which Morgan Johnson is trying to pick off her arm.

The chances are this story is no truer than the story about him killing the ten men, but that is the story everybody back in my old home town believes to this day.

My Grandpap often speaks of Morgan Johnson, and says it goes to prove something or other about human nature. My Grandpap says you can say a man is a good man or a bad man, and if you say it often enough people will finally believe it, although the chances are when it comes to a showdown he is not a good man or a bad man, as the case may be.①

My Grandpap says he always suspects Morgan Johnson is not a dangerous man, but if you ask my Grandpap why he does not prove it the same as Wheezer Gamble, my Grandpap says like this:

"Well," he says. "You know there is always the chance that he may be just what they say. There is always that chance, and I am never any hand for going around trying to bust up traditions if there is a chance they may be true."

---

① as the case may be：义为"看情况而定"，习惯用语。

十足的祸害

〔美〕达蒙·鲁尼恩

大约35年前,一个名叫摩根·约翰逊的年轻人来到我家乡,住了下来。

当时,在我的老家,问人的来历被认为是不礼貌的行为,而且摩根·约翰逊自己从来也不提,所以无人知道他从何处来。这还不算,他对自己的身世一概讳莫如深,因此被看成了神秘人物。

他在许多方面叫人见着就害怕:鼻子上横着一条伤疤,两条浓眉连到了一起,黑头发,黑眼睛,爱朝人看。35年前第一次走在圣菲路时,有人就说:

"这人是个祸害。"

就这样,摩根·约翰逊第二次走在圣菲路时,听到了第一次那话的人对另一个人说:

"这人的确是个祸害。"

渐渐地,凡是看到了摩根·约翰逊鼻子上的伤疤和黑眼睛等特征的人,无不说:

"来了个祸害。"

最后,在我老家无人不晓摩根·约翰逊是个祸害,他无论走到哪个角落,用他独特的眼光打量人时,个个对他敬而远之。

要是他进了哪个酒馆,本来人们谈得正起劲,也会一下子就冷场。要是他说些什么,不管是什么话,大家都点头称是;既是祸害,谁也不想与他顶撞。

摩根·约翰逊鼻子上的伤疤说明,他不知什么时候遇过大祸,而他居然活着,还在西部我老家的街上出没,因此他必然有一套防身术。

他从没说过这个伤疤是怎么来的,后来终于有人打听到了底细:在纽约时,一天晚上他与10个坏家伙干仗,其中一个一枪擦伤了他的鼻子,但摩根·约翰逊最后却要了这10个人的性命。

此说从何人何处开始不得而知,但摩根·约翰逊从不否认,甚至说他杀的人增加到20个时也不否认。实际上,无论别人说他什么,摩根·约翰逊都不否认,总是闭着嘴,只管自己的事。

诸位,他在美国西部我的老家一住就是好些年,镇上要是来了客人,本地人常指着他说:

"这人是个祸害,一点不假。"

到摩根·约翰逊年近50时,有人见到他就发抖,一直要抖到他走远。

后来,有一天摩根·约翰逊在大街上走,碰着一个叫"气喘病"的小老头跌跌撞撞从绿灯酒馆出来。这家伙根本没什么了不起,不过是韦尔法诺河边的一个羊倌。

他害着气喘病,总是上气不接下气,所以得了"气喘病"的诨名。年岁很大,个子很小,尽管只是个微不足道的羊倌,谁也犯不着欺侮他。每月他到镇上来两趟,就为喝酒,从绿灯酒馆跌跌撞撞出来那天他是一个月里头一趟进城。

绿灯酒馆卖的是烈性威士忌,一辈子从来没起过心干仗的人喝了酒常常会想与人干仗。不过,要说酒烈到会使羊倌也想干仗,那当然还不至于。可偏偏这个气喘病就想。他看见摩根·约翰逊后,一把揪住摩根的衣服,踮起脚,冲着摩根问道:

"你是个祸害,对吗?"

看到这情景的人全替老气喘病担心,以为摩根·约翰逊会一口气把他吞下去,嚼碎了又吐出来,可是摩根仅眨眨眼,说:

"怎么?"

"听说你是个祸害,"气喘病说,"今天我要把你的肚皮划开,看看里面藏了什么祸水。"

说着他敞开摩根的衣服,摸出把大折叠刀,打开来,要划破摩根·约翰逊的肚皮,平常他下厨房、剥羊皮及做诸如此类的事,用的正是这把刀。

摩根·约翰逊没等他开膛,一看见亮出刀,马上转身一溜烟跑了。他没命地跑着,人人都说,那天他要是不算飞毛腿,那就没谁算得上飞毛腿。

气喘病有了一把年纪,又醉醺醺,当然追不了几步。摩根·约翰逊却没有停,一直跑到了镇外很远很远。有人看到他往丹佛方向走,很可能一直走到了丹佛,因为从此以后他再没在我老家露过面。

这一来,说他是祸害的话没人相信了,而且,他也没有在纽约杀过10个人,连一个也没杀过。至于鼻子上的伤口,有人说是因为摩根·约翰逊想挽一个女人的手,那女人把本厚厚的书顺手扔过去,砸破了他的鼻子。

这种传闻与他杀过10个人的传闻同样不可靠,但到现在为止，我老家的人个个都相信。

我爷爷常谈起摩根·约翰逊，认为这件事多多少少能说明人的天性。爷爷说，你可以把一个人说成好人，也可以把一个人说成坏人，说多了，大家都会相信，即使最后事情的结果证明他不是好人或坏人，那也没有关系。

我爷爷说他一直怀疑摩根·约翰逊不是祸害，但是如果你问他为什么不像老"气喘病"那样去证实一下，爷爷就这样回答：

"这嘛——你知道，大家没把他说错的可能性同样存在。可能性是半对半，既然大家也许说对了，人人习惯了的说法我何必起心推翻呢？"

The Guardian Angel

André Maurois

When Jeanne Bertaut died, at thirty, we all thought that Victor Bertaut's career was ended. A determined worker and one of the finest orators of his generations, Victor by all signs seemed destined for political success. But those of us who, like myself, had been through school and in the service with him knew his weaknesses too well to think that he had within him the makings of a statesman. We certainly knew him capable of getting himself elected deputy and of dazzling the Chamber with his verbal fireworks. But we couldn't possibly visualize him heading a ministry, working harmoniously with his colleagues, or winning the respect of the nation. His defeats were no less spectacular than his triumphs. He had too great a fondness for women and had a bland confidence in his powers of seduction. In debate, always convinced of being right, he was completely incapable of considering the merits of his opponents' arguments. In addition, he was subject to such outbursts of rage that he frequently alienated the very men whom he needed.

For these reasons I felt that his success, despite his brilliance, would be limited. That is until the day when, to my great surprise, he married Jeanne. I never learned how he got to know her. What was surprising was not that he had met her, but that he appreciated her. She was as different from him as possible—calm as he was furious; moderate as he was fanatical; indulgent as he was sharp; reticent as he was garrulous. And she seemed to have set herself—and succeeded at—the double task of conquering him and changing him. Much less beautiful than his other women, she had an undeniable fresh charm, blooming health, a frank regard, and a gay smile.

I must admit that I could never have anticipated Bertaut's ability to discover, much less to appreciate such hidden virtues. But I was wrong. From the time she married her great man. Jeanne and he were never apart. She worked with him, went to the Chamber daily, accompanied him on the rounds of his constituency, and finally, with great tact, advised him in such a manner that he could not take offense.

Bertaut's position in his party was transformed by the marriage. No longer did the political bigwigs say: "Bertaut? Yes—very brilliant—a good talker—but a crackpot!" Now they nodded in approval: "Bertaut? A bit young perhaps, but very promising." Sometimes he'd burst out again—but a word from Jeanne, a handshake—and all would be smoothed over. As for the "great lover"—he was faithful to one woman—his own.

This success and good fortune was cut short by Jeanne's death. I remember returning from the cemetery with Bertrand Schmitt, the novelist, and one of the couple's best friends.

"She made him over from head to toe," he said. "She saved him from himself. Without her he'll go to Hell with himself again. Well, we'll have to wait and see."

For some months, outside of writing to assure Bertaut that I would assist him if and when he desired, I did not disturb his grief. He reappeared at the Palais-Bourbon in October when the Chamber reconvened. His colleagues greeted him with sympathy, but they soon found him as hard to get along with as before. Even more difficult, for an icy bitterness was added to his former rages. I, however, had nothing to complain about. We dined together a couple of times a month; he treated me with a sulky affection which was not unpleasant. But he never mentioned his wife, and developed, in this regard, a cynicism which I interpreted as defense.

When, in December, the Ministry resigned, the newspapers announced that Briand, charged with forming a new cabinet, had offered Victor, Deputy from Drôme, the office of Postmaster General. Shortly after his name appeared in the official list, I went to congratulate Victor. I found him in one of his bad moods.

"Keep your congratulations," he snapped. "I've taken part in only two Council meetings—and I'll probably resign. I've had furious battles with Finance and with Public Works. Anyway, this Ministry is a shambles. Everyone's in charge except me—the Minister."

For a few days after that I expected, daily, to read of Bertaut's resignation. This did not occur. The following week I encountered

Bertrand Schmitt, and, of course, we spoke of Victor:

"Have you heard about his amazing experience?" asked Schmitt. "Concerning the letter?"

"What letter?" said I.

"Ah, what a subject for a novel," sighed Schmitt. "I don't know if you know that Bertaut, a fledgling in office, started acting like a bull in a china shop[①]."

"Yes, yes," I said.

"And you know that Briand is patient—but even his patience has its limits. And when Bertaut insulted poor Cheron—before the entire Chamber, the President was about to demand his resignation. Then there was a real coup de theatre. To the surprise of all his colleagues, our intransigent Victor voluntarily apologized to Cheron in such an outspoken, sincere, repentant manner that Cheron himself went to Briand to plead for him. And, of course, everything has been patched up."

"How," I asked, "do you explain this reversal of character?"

"Victor himself explained it to me," Schmitt said. "The day after the run in with Cheron, as he was leaving his house, his secretary gave him a letter marked PERSONAL which had just arrived. With surprise, emotion, and even terror he thought he recognized Jeanne's handwriting. He ripped open the envelope—the letter was, beyond a doubt, from his wife. He read me some passages from it; naturally, I

---

① acting like a bull in a china shop: 瓷器易碎，公牛进了瓷器店自然一动就闯祸，形容人鲁莽。根据上下文，此短语可活译为"且不知天高地厚"。

The Guardian Angel

didn't memorize them, but as a novelist it's easy for me to reconstruct such things. In effect, Jeanne had written:

"Dearest—at first you'll be upset at receiving a letter from me. Be reassured—this is not a letter from the tomb, nor from Hades. Before entering the clinic, feeling very weak and not knowing whether or not the operation would succeed, I thought, naturally, of you. I tried to imagine what would become of you if I did not survive. I know you, my dear, better than you know yourself, and I am a little afraid for you. I am certainly not your equal, dear, but I have acted as a brake for you. A brake is essential to a racer.

"There is nothing, I said to myself, to keep me from being with you in spirit, so I wrote this letter for you. I am confiding it to the care of a friend with instructions to deliver it to you only if certain things which I feel may occur really do happen. In that case, if I have not erred, you will find written here the things I would have said were I present. The proof of the correctness of my prophecies rests in the fact that this letter is now in your hands. Stretch out near me, my sweet; hold my hand; rest your head upon my shoulder and listen as you always used to ···"

"Are you making this up, Bertrand?"

"Even if all the words are not hers, the thoughts are those of Jeanne Bertaut. She had foreseen both honors and disputes. And she advised generosity, moderation, and frankness."

"And that's why he went to see Cheron?"

"That's why he apologized."

When I saw Bertaut the following week, he confirmed Schmitt's story. His guardian angel, caressing him with her wing, affected him strongly, and I thought I saw his hard shell of cynicism crack and vanish. I was not wrong. Several of Victor's colleagues commented upon the happy effects of this message.

For several months all went well for Bertaut. He straightened things out in the Post Office Department. All France sang his praises. His star was in the ascendant. When the Briand cabinet fell, Bertaut left for a vacation in Morocco. There he fell under the spell of Dora Bergmann, explorer and poet, who had wandered disguised as an Arab scout, through North Africa, and who had aroused considerable talk. Now none of us had ever expected or wanted Victor, a young man, to remain wedded to a memory. His choice, however, did perturb us. In her strange fashion, Dora Bergmann was beautiful—and talented. But her past and her reputation were not such as inspire confidence. She had had several affairs, always with officers or high officials of the Colonial Service; it was even suspected that she was a foreign agent. Be that as it may, there was nothing more certain to ruin a man's prestige and opportunities for advancement than any intimacy with this adventuress.

When Bertaut returned to Paris, with Dora Bergmann in tow, some of us tried to advise him. The rule, alas, holds true without exception—who tires to protect a friend from a woman he loves, loses friend

The Guardian Angel

without touching the woman. Victor, furious, cast Bertrand Schmitt, and me, among others, out of his life. Talk of his affair spread through parliamentary circles, and harmed him grievously.

"There's only one hope," I said to Bertrand one evening. "And that's that Jeanne anticipated something like this and that Bertaut will receive a warning from her. I fell that only she has sufficient authority over him to make him open his eyes."

"I am certain that such a letter will arrive," said Bertrand. "After all Jeanne could have assumed that such a woman as Dora would swoop down upon Victor. She could have left a letter to handle just such an emergency."

Despite my scoffing at the novelist, the facts proved Schmitt correct. We were delighted, one fine day, to see Victor leave hurriedly for his district. He told no one; left no explanation. He buried himself in his small country house near Montelimar. Dora Bergmann followed him; he refused to see her. She persisted, raved, pleaded, withdrew. The papers announced that she was going to explore the Rio de Oro[①]. Voictor was saved.

When he returned to Paris, he was delighted to see me.

And he told me about the second letter from beyond the grave. He had found it one morning in his mail. Jeanne advised him that if some imprudent love affair really threatened him, he should flee the very moment he received the letter. "I know you, my love," she wrote.

---

① the Rio de Oro: 里奥-德奥罗, 位于非洲西北部, 原为西班牙殖民地。

"If you remain—if you see the woman again, you will fall victim to your sense of honor, your desires, and your pride. At a distance your own intelligence will prevail. You will suddenly perceive clearly what, at close range, you missed seeing. So don't hesitate; don't stop to consider. Fold up this letter instantly, put it in your pocket, pack your bag and leave for Drôme immediately!"—And he had obeyed her.

"That's the extent of the trust I placed in my wife's wisdom," he said.

But I wondered if he would be shielded throughout his life by this dead woman.

All his life? No. But two years later, when he was hesitant about remarrying, Bertaut received a third letter which approved the idea and shaped his decision. Had Jeanne left any others? Or had the first wife, with that curious foreknowledge of her husband's destiny, abdicated before the accession of the second? We will never know.

Bertrand Schmitt says that once, in 1936, when Bertaut, minister, found himself confronted by a delicate matter of conscience, he hopefully awaited the advice of his guardian angel. This time, however, the message did not come. Bertaut made the decision, alone, and was wrong. That was the end of his political career.

But in his country retreat, ruling his small family domain, with his second wife who, annually, presents him with a child, Bertaut does not seem unhappy. And it may be that it is just this sort of good fortune his posthumous counsellor wished for him.

保护神

〔法〕安德烈·莫洛亚

当让娜·贝尔托30岁那年去世时,我们大家都认为维克托·贝尔托的事业也跟着完了。由于维克托的魄力和顶呱呱的口才,他在政治上似乎前程远大。但是一些与他同过窗、共过事的人,包括我在内,也了解他的弱点,并不认为他有政治家的才干。我们知道他无疑能当选议员,用如簧巧舌在议会使满座佩服,但他领导不了一个部门,与同事难以相处,在人们心目中树立不了威信。他的过失与成就同样一目了然。他太贪女色,又以为自己有些引人上钩的本领。在辩论中,总自以为是,全然不考虑对方所言的道理。而且,动不动就发火,得罪的人往往是他正需要的人。

由于这些原因,我认为他尽管聪明,却前程有限。没想到后来他与让娜结了婚,我的这一看法也随之变了。我不知道他与她是怎样认识的。叫人奇怪的并不是他结识了她,而是他看中了她。她与他处处不同:一个遇事沉着,一个脾气暴躁;一个性情温和,一个过于偏激;一个心胸宽阔,一个不肯饶人;一个难得开口,一个叽叽喳喳。似乎她有心干而且干成了两件事:使他倾倒，使他变个模样。她没有其他与他有过关系的女人漂亮，但自有一种青春美、健康美，一种质朴的魅力，一种叫人开心的美。

我必须承认，我不可能预见贝尔托择偶的天才，更不能预见他会欣赏这些内在的优点。总之，是我错了。让娜与她的伟人结婚以后，两人从没分开过。她参与他的工作，天天去议会，陪他巡视他的选区，最后巧妙地给他出谋划策，使他拒绝不得。

结婚以后贝尔托在党内的印象变了。以往政界的显要人物说："贝尔托吗？对，很聪明，能说会道，可就是爱乱来！"现在他们则点头称赞："贝尔托吗？也许年轻了些，但前程远大。"有时候他会老毛病发作，但只要让娜说一句话，握一握手，火气便消了。"伟大的爱情"这话不假，他只忠实于一个女人——他的妻子。

让娜一死，贝尔托成就算到了顶，好运走到了头。我记得，我与著名小说家、夫妇俩最要好的朋友贝特朗·施米特从墓地回来时，他说：

"她使他完全变了样，改掉了自身的缺点。没有了她，他会旧病复发的，我们等着瞧吧。"

好几个月里，我除了写信对贝尔托说在他需要我帮忙的地方和时候，一定出力外，没有打断他的哀思。10月国会复会，他又在波旁宫露面了。同事们向他表示慰问，但没多久便发现他像以往一样难相处，甚至更糟糕，因为除了旧日的火气，还多了内心的痛苦，待人冷冰冰。然而，我没有什么可埋怨的。一个月里我们好些次同桌吃饭，他与我在一起只闷闷不乐，还不至于闹得不痛快。但他从不提起妻子，而且在这方面变得与众不同，我想是唯恐触痛了创伤。

12月，内阁辞职了，报界报道白里安负命组织新政府。白里安委任德龙省选出的议员维克托为邮政部长。名单正式公布后不久，我去向他表示祝贺，结果发现他很不高兴。

"且慢说恭贺的话，"他没好气地说，"我仅仅参加了两次内阁会议，说不定会辞职。我与财政部和公共工程部大干了一场。这个部是烂摊子。人人管事，只有我这个部长不管事。"

他说这话以后接连几天，我天天以为会登出贝尔托的辞职消息，却没有看到。第二周我遇见贝特朗·施米特，自然谈起了维克托。

"你听说了他遇到的一件怪事吗？就是那封信。"施米特问。

"什么信？"我说。

"可以作为写小说的题材了！"施米特感叹道，"贝尔托虽当了官，却只是个羽毛未丰满的鸟，且不知天高地厚。你听说了吗？"

"听说了，听说了。"我说。

"白里安是个耐心人，但他的耐心也有限度。贝尔托当着全体议员谩骂谢龙，总统打算要求他辞职。可后来出现了戏剧性的变化。谁也没想到，从不让步的维克托主动向谢龙道歉，态度诚惶诚恐。谢龙受了感动，亲自找白里安说情，这一来当然万事全消。"

"你知道他的性格为什么会发生这样大的变化吗？"

"维克托亲口对我说明了底细。"施米特说，"就在与谢龙发生冲突的第二天，他正要离开家时，秘书交给他一封写着'亲启'的信，是刚到的。他认出是让娜的笔迹，又吃惊，又激动，甚至还害怕。他撕开信封一看，信果真是妻子写的。他念了一部分给我听，当然我背不出原文，但我是小说家，不难重述其内容。让娜的信大概是这样写的：

最亲爱的：

你一接到我的信一定会莫名其妙。别担心，这不是坟墓里来的信，也不是阴司地府来的信。在进医院之前，我只觉身体非常虚弱，也不知道手术是否成功，自然要想到你。我曾想，如果我不能活下去，你会变得怎样。亲爱的，我比你自己还要了解你，有些替你担心。亲爱的，当然我不等于你，但我一直充当了你的刹车。跑得太快的车是离不了刹车的。

我曾想过，什么也不能把我与你在精神上隔离开，所以我给你写了这封信。我将把它交给一位朋友，嘱咐他在我预料的情况果真发生时寄给你。所以，要是我没估计错，你会在信上看到如果我还活着一定会对你说的话。这封信现在已送到了你手里，这就证明我的预料正确。过来吧，我的爱人。握住我的手，把头靠在我肩上，像以往那样听着……"

"贝特朗，这全是你瞎编的吧？"

"哪怕这些话不是让娜·贝尔托的原话，意思绝没有变样，她把荣升和纠纷都预见到了。她还叫他待人宽厚、温和、坦率。"

"他去找谢龙就因为这个原因？"

"这一来他道歉了。"

第二个星期我见到贝尔托时，他证实了施米特的话。他的保护神在庇佑他，使他很受感动，我看得出他愤世嫉俗的保护壳已开始土崩瓦解。我没有看错，维克托的好几位同事都说这封信起了作用。

贝尔托顺顺当当过了几个月。他把邮政部的工作处理得井井有条，全法国都称赞他。他福星高照。白里安内阁倒台后，贝尔托去摩洛哥度假。在那儿他迷上了多拉·贝格曼。多拉·贝格曼是位探险家、诗人，装成阿拉伯人，游遍北非，风头出尽。维克托年纪轻轻，我们估计他不会，也不希望他一辈子郁郁想念已经去世的妻子，然而他现在的选择的确叫我们放心不下。多拉·贝格曼是有异国风度的美人，而且有才能，但她的往事和名声令人很不满意。她的风流韵事不少，有关系的全是殖民事务部的军官和高级官员，甚至有人怀疑她是外国间谍。无论怎么说吧，谁要是与这种危险人物过往太密，谁的威信就会扫地以尽，前程断送无疑。

贝尔托带着多拉·贝格曼回到巴黎后，我们有的人好言规劝他。然而，朋友爱上了女人，想拖朋友一把的人不但奈何不了女人，反而会失去朋友，这是一条规律，无一例外。维克托大发雷霆，与贝特朗·施米特、我还有其他人统统断绝了往来。国会议员对他的事议论纷纷，形势于他极为不利。

一天晚上，我对贝特朗说："如果让娜预料到这种事，贝尔托收到她的信，那么事情还有一线希望。我认为只有她才有本领说服他，使他睁开眼。"

"别急，这封信会来。"贝特朗说，"让娜不会猜不到有多拉这样的女人，使他鬼迷心窍。她很可能留下了一封信，在这种紧要关头才发出。"

我笑小说家瞎猜，而事实却证明了他的话是对的。有一天天气晴朗，我们看到维克托急匆匆往他所在的选区跑。他没有告诉任何人，也没有写留条，躲进了蒙特利马尔附近的乡间别墅。多拉·贝格曼追了过去，他闭门不见。她不罢休，大吵大闹，又是哀求，最后退了兵。报纸报道她要去里奥-德奥罗探险。维克托得救了。

回到巴黎，他见到我时高高兴兴。

他告诉我第二封信也不是坟墓里来的，是一天上午邮局送来的。让娜叫他在被不明智的爱情冲昏头脑时，一收到她的信便远走高飞。她在信上写道："亲爱的，我了解你。如果你不走，如果你还见到这个女人，你考虑的是你的面子、欲望、自尊。离开她以后，你的理智会占上风。近距离看不到的，在远距离你会突然看到。所以别犹豫，别迟疑，马上叠好这封信，放进衣袋里，收拾东西，往德龙省去！"他听从了她的劝告。

"我对妻子的聪明就有这样信任。"他说。

但是我想，他该不会一辈子仰信亡妻的庇佑吧？

真的是一辈子吗？不。只是又过了两年，贝尔托打算续弦，却又举棋不定，这时收到了第三封信，得到赞许，下了决心。让娜有没有留下其他信呢？是不是他的第一个妻子有惊人的先见之明，知道丈夫命里注定的事，不等第二个妻子进门就让位了呢？我们不得而知。

贝特朗·施米特说，1936年，有一次贝尔托任部长职务时遇上了一件棘手的事，满以为保护神会有妙计。然而，这一次信没有来。贝尔托独自做了决定，结果失误，他的政治生涯从此告终。

离职以后他回到乡下，当个小家庭的一家之长，第二个妻子每年给他生一个孩子，贝尔托似乎没有什么不愉快。也许，这就是他在阴曹的高参希望他享有的福分。

Kong at the Seaside

Arnold Zweig

Kong got his first glimpse of the sea as he ran on the beach, which stretched like a white arc along the edge of the cove. He barked vociferously with extravagant enthusiasm. Again and again, the bluish-white spray came dashing up at him and he was forbidden to hurl himself into it! A tall order for an Airedale terrier with a wiry brown coat and shaggy forelegs. However, Willie, his young god, would not permit it; but at any rate he could race at top speed across the firm sand, which was still damp from the ebbing waters, Willie following with lusty shouts. Engineer Groll, strolling after, noticed that the dog and his tanned, light-haired, eight-year-old master were attracting considerable attention among the beach-chairs and gaily striped bathing-houses. At the end of the row, where the sky was pale and dipped into the infinite—whereas it was vividly blue overhead and shed relaxation, happiness, and vigor on all these city people and their games in the sand—some controversy seemed to be in progress. Willie was standing there, slim and defiant, holding his dog by the collar. Groll hurried over. People in bathing suits looked pretty much alike, social castes and classes intermingled. Heads showed more character and expression, though the bodies which supported them were still flabby and colorless, unaccustomed to exposure and pale after a long winter's imprisonment within the darkness of heavy clothing. A stoutish man was sitting in the shade of a striped orange tent stretched over a blue framework; he was bending slightly forward, holding a cigar.

"Is that your dog?" he asked quietly.

A little miss, about ten years old, was with him; she was biting her underlip, and a look of hatred for the boy and the dog flashed between her tear-filled narrow lids.

"No," said Groll with his pleasant voice, which seemed to rumble deep down in his chest, "The dog belongs to the boy, who, to be sure, is mine."

"You know dogs aren't allowed off the leash," the quiet voice continued. "He frightened my daughter a bit, has trampled her canals, and is standing on her spade."

"Pull him back, Willie," laughed Groll. "You're quite right, sir, but the dog broke away and, after all, nothing serious has happened."

Willie pushed Kong aside, picked up the spade and, bowing slightly, held it out to the group. Its third member was a slender, remarkable pretty young lady, sitting in the rear of the tent; Groll decided she was too young to be the mother of the girl and too attractive to be her governess. Well gotten up, he reflected; she looks like Irish with those auburn eyebrows.

No one took the spade from the boy, and Willie, with a frown, stuck the toy into the sand in front of the girl.

"I think that squares it, especially on such a beautiful day," Groll smiled and lay down. His legs behind him, his elbows on the sand, and his face resting on his hands, he looked over the hostile three. Willie has behaved nicely and politely; how well he looks with his Kong. The dog, evidently not as ready to make peace, growled softly, his fur bristling at the neck, then he sat down.

"I want to shoot his dog, Father," the girl suddenly remarked in a determined voice; "he frightened me so." Groll noticed a gold bracelet of antique workmanship about her Wrist—three strands of pale green-gold braided into the semblance of a snake. These people need a lesson. I shall give it to them.

Groll nodded reassuringly at his boy, who was indignantly drawing his dog closer to him. Those grown-ups seemed to know that the girl had the upper hand of them, or, as Groll told himself, had the right to give orders. So he quietly waited for the sequel of this charming conversation; after all, he was still there to reprimand the brat if the gentleman with the fine cigar lacked the courage to do so because the sweet darling was not accustomed to proper discipline.

"No one is going to shoot my dog," threatened Willie, clenching his fists; but, without deigning to look at him, the girl continued:

"Buy him from the people, Father; here is my checkbook." She actually took the thin booklet and a fountain-pen with a gold clasp from a zipper-bag inside the tent.

"If you won't buy him for me, I'll throw a soup-plate right off the table at dinner; you know I will, Father." She spoke almost in a whisper and was as white as chalk under her tan; her blue eyes, over which the sea had cast a greenish glint, flashed threateningly.

The gentleman said: "Ten pounds for the dog."

"The dog is not mine; you must deal with my boy. He's trained him."

"I don't deal with boys. I offer fifteen pounds, a pretty neat sum for the cur."

Groll realized that this was an opportunity of really getting to know his eldest. "Willie," he began, "this gentleman offers you fifteen pounds for Kong so he may shoot him. For the money, you could buy the bicycle you have been wanting since last year. I won't be able to give it to you for a long time, we're not rich enough for that."

Willie looked at his father, wondering whether he could be in earnest. But the familiar face showed no sigh of jesting. In answer he put an arm about Kong's neck, smiled up at Groll, and said: "I won't sell him to you, Father."

The gentleman in the bathing suit with his still untanned pale skin turned to Groll. Apparently the argument began to interest him. "Persuade him. I offer twenty pounds."

"Twenty pounds," Groll remarked to Willie; "that would buy you the bicycle and the canoe, which you admired so much this morning, Willie. A green canoe with double paddles for the water, and for the land a fine nickel-plated bicycle with a headlight, storage battery, and new tires. There might even be money left over for a watch. You only have to give up this old dog by handing the leash to the gentleman."

Willie said scornfully: "If I went ten steps away, Kong would pull him over and be with me again."

The beautiful and unusual young lady spoke for the first time. "He would hardly be able to do that," she said in a clear, sweet, mocking voice—a charming little person, thought Groll—and took a small Browning, gleaming with silver filigree work, out of her handbag. "This would prevent him from running very far."

Foolish of her, thought Groll. "You see, sir, the dog is a thoroughbred, pedigreed, and splendidly trained."

"We've noticed that."

"Offer fifty pounds, Father, and settle it."

"Fifty pounds," repeated Groll, and his voice shook slightly. That would pay for this trip, and if I handled the money for him, his mother could at last regain her strength. The sanatorium is too expensive, we can't afford it. "Fifty pounds, Willie! The bicycle, the watch, the tent—you remember the brown tent with the cords and tassels—and you would have money left to help me send mother to a sanatorium. Imagine, all that for a dog! Later on, we can go to the animal welfare society, pay three shillings, and get another Kong."

Willie said softly: "There is only one Kong. I will not sell him."

"Offer a hundred pounds, Father. I want to shoot that dog. I shouldn't have to stand such boorishness."

The stoutish gentleman hesitated a moment, then made the offer.

"A hundred pounds, sir," he said huskily. "You don't look as though you could afford to reject a small fortune."

"Indeed, sir, I can't," said Groll, and turned to Willie. "My boy," he continued earnestly, "a hundred pounds safely invested will within ten years assure you of a university education. Or, if you prefer, you can buy a small car to ride to school in. What eyes the other boys would make! And you could drive mother to market; that's a great deal of money, a hundred pounds for nothing but a dog."

Willie, frightened by the earnestness of the words, puckered up his face as though to cry. After all, he was just a small boy of eight and he was being asked to give up his beloved dog. "But I love Kong, and Kong loves me," he said, fighting down the tears in his voice. "I don't want to give him up."

"A hundred pounds—do persuade him, sir! Otherwise my daughter will make life miserable for me. You have no idea," he sighed—"what a row such a little lady can kick up."

If she were mine, thought Groll, I'd leave marks of a good lesson on each of her dainty cheeks; and after glancing at his boy, who, with furrowed brow, was striving to hold back his tears, he said it aloud, quietly, clearly, looking sternly into the eyes of the girl. "And now, I think, the incident is closed."

Then a most astounding thing happened. The little girl began to laugh. Evidently the tall, brown man pleased her, and the idea that anyone could dare to slap her, the little lady, for one of her whims fascinated her by its very roughness.

"All right, Father," she cried; "he's behaved well. Now we'll put the check-book back in the bag. Of course, Father, you knew it was all in fun!"

The stoutish gentleman smiled with relief and said that, of course, he had known it and added that such a fine day was just made to have fun. Fun! Groll didn't believe it. He knew too much about people.

Willie breathed more freely and, pretending to blow his nose, wiped away two furtive tears. He threw himself down in the sand next to Kong, happily pulled the dog on top of himself, and began to wrestle with him; the shaggy brown paws of the terrier and the slim tanned arms of the boy mingled in joyful confusion.

However, Groll, while he somewhat reluctantly accepted a cigar and a light from the strange gentleman and silently looked out into the blue-green sea, which lay spread before him like shimmering folds of silk with highlights and shadows—Groll thought: Alas for the poor! If this offer had come to me two years ago when my invention was not yet completed and when we lived in a damp flat dreaming of the little house we now have, then—poor Willie!—this argument might have had a different outcome, this struggle for nothing more than a dog, the love, loyalty, courage, and generosity in the soul of an animal and a boy. Yet, speaking in terms of economics, a little financial security was necessary before one could indulge in the luxury of human decency. Without it—he reflected—no one should be asked to make a decision similar to the one which has just confronted Willie and me; everyone was entitled to that much material safety, especially in an era which was so full of glittering temptations.

The little girl with the spade put her slim bare feet into the sand outside of the tent and called to Willie: "Help me to dig new ones." But her eyes invited the man Groll, for whose approval she was striving.

She pointed to the ruined canals. Then, tossing her head, she indicated Kong, who lay panting and lazy in the warm sunshine, and called merrily: "For all I care, he can trample them again."

The whistle of an incoming steamboat sounded from the pier.

康康在海边

〔德〕阿诺尔德·茨维格

　　康康跑上海湾边成弧形展开的白沙滩，第一次看到了海。它使劲儿狂吠着。淡蓝色的浪花一次又一次向它飞来，可惜的是它不能一纵身跳下去。对于身上长着棕色硬毛，前腿长着蓬松松软毛的小猎狗来说，这禁令很严。他的小主人威利决不会答应，但无论如何它在刚退潮的沙滩上尽情快跑是可以的，威利只得一边追，一边高声喊。工程师格罗尔溜达着跟在后面，发现躺在沙滩椅上和有鲜艳彩条的更衣室外的许多人都眼盯着这条狗和它的皮肤晒黑、头发浅黄的八岁小主人。在人群的尽头，天空发白，延伸到无限远，而头顶的天空蓝得清澈，使所有这些城里人感到轻松、快乐、精神，在沙滩上玩得格外痛快。也就是在人群的尽头，似乎发生了一场口角。威利站在那儿，小小的个子，却正气鼓鼓，牵着狗的项圈。人们穿着游泳服时看起来都差不多，分不出属哪个社会阶层、阶级。头的特点明显些，又有表情，虽然支撑头的身体在厚厚的衣服里闷了一个漫长的冬天后肌肉松软，缺少血色，不习惯阳光。一个身子还算健壮的人坐在一个撑在蓝架子上的橘黄色彩条帐篷下；他手拿一根烟，身子稍稍向前倾。

"这是你的狗吗?"他心平气和地问。

他身边有个小女孩,大约十岁,咬着下嘴唇,眯缝着眼,泪水汪汪,看来是恨死了这男孩子和狗。

"不是。狗是孩子的。当然,孩子是我的。"格罗尔回答,声音挺好听,仿佛是从胸腔里发出的。

"你知道,狗的皮带是不能放开的。"心平气和的人继续说,"它吓了我女儿一跳,踏坏了她挖的水沟,现在还站在她的铁铲上。"

"威利,把狗牵走。"格罗尔笑道,"先生,你说得不错。不过,是狗自己挣脱了皮带。再说,也没闹出什么大事。"

威利把康康牵到一边,捡起铁铲,弯弯腰,伸出铁铲想叫人接。帐篷里的第三个人是一位苗条、相当漂亮的年轻女人,坐在后边。格罗尔料想她必定不是小女孩的妈妈,因为年纪太轻;也不可能是家庭教师,因为太漂亮。他觉得她的穿着也阔气;眉毛是赤褐色的,像爱尔兰人。

没有人接孩子手中的铁铲。威利眉头一皱,把这玩具插到了小女孩跟前的沙子里。

"这就得啦,也别辜负了今天的好天气吧。"格罗尔笑着躺下来,把腿伸直,手托着脸,肘撑在沙里,看了看三个还怒气未消的人。威利的表现不错,有礼貌。他牵着康康,模样逗人看。这狗还不肯罢休,轻声叫,脖子上的毛竖着。叫过几声它蹲了下来。

"爸爸,我要一枪打死这条狗,它把我吓坏啦。"小女孩突然说,听声音态度坚决。格罗尔发现她戴了个古式金手镯,由三条淡色绿金扭成蛇形。这些人不知好歹,这次就教训他们一下。

格罗尔的孩子牵着狗站在他身边,憋着一肚子气,格罗尔向他点点头示意别害怕。两个大人似乎满以为小女孩占了上风,要不然,格罗尔猜,就是认为该她要怎样就怎样。所以他默不出声地等着看这场戏怎样唱下去;如果抽高档香烟的人没有勇气训斥小丫头,那他就准备出马,看来这宝贝不大懂礼数。

"看谁敢打死我的狗!"威利握紧拳,不示弱。但小女孩没有再看他,又说道:

"爸爸,就向人家买吧,我的支票本在这儿。"果然,她从帐篷里的一个拉链袋里拿出了一个薄本本和一支带着金扣的钢笔。

"如果你不给我买这条狗,中午吃饭我就掀桌上的汤盘。你看我敢不敢,爸爸!"她是小声说这话的,晒黑了的脸发白,被海抹上了一层淡绿色的蓝眼睛露出威胁的目光。

那男的说:"我出10英镑,把狗卖给我。"

"狗不是我的,你得与我儿子谈买卖。狗是他养大的。"

"我不与孩子谈买卖。就15镑吧,这要算是好价钱,满对得起这条恶狗了。"

格罗尔把这事看成一个真正了解他的大孩子的良机,说:"威利,这位先生愿意出15英镑买康康,好一枪把它打死。有了这么多钱,你去年就想要的自行车可以买回来了。你要等我买还不知等到哪一天,我们家没钱,买不起。"

威利看着爸爸,怀疑他不是当真。但是,在爸爸熟悉的面孔上看不出开玩笑的迹象。他特意伸出只手搂着康康的脖子,冲格罗尔一笑,说:"爸爸,我不会把它卖给你。"

穿游泳衣的先生还没有把缺少血色的皮肤晒黑,他转身看着格罗尔,显然对孩子的话有了兴趣:"你劝劝他,我出20镑。"

"20镑了!"格罗尔对威利说,"你买了车还可买个独木舟,今天上午你不是很想要独木舟吗，威利？带双桨的绿色独木舟好在水上玩，陆地上你有镀锡的漂亮自行车，带前灯，装干电池，新轮胎。也许，多下的钱还可以买块表。就看你舍不舍得这条狗，把皮带交给这位先生。"

威利鄙夷地说："我站在十步外，康康会从他手里跑开，又回到我这儿来。"

那漂亮、不寻常的年轻女人第一次说话了："那可办不到。"她的声音清脆动听而带着讥讽。格罗尔觉得她倒是个可爱的小姑娘。她从手提包里摸出一支包着闪亮的银丝的勃朗宁手枪："这东西不会让它跑多远。"

格罗尔心里暗笑她的愚蠢："先生，这狗是纯良种狗，又训练有素。"

"这我们看得出来。"

"爸爸，出50镑吧，50镑算了。"

"50镑！"格罗尔重复了遍，声音有些颤抖。这笔钱够跑这一趟的旅费，如果他代儿子处理这笔钱，儿子的母亲便总算有了恢复体力的希望。疗养院收费太高，他们出不起。"50镑，威利！自行车、表、帐篷，就都有了。你记得带绳索和流苏的那个棕色帐篷吗？如果你把剩下的钱交给我，我可以送妈妈上疗养院。想想吧，一条狗卖这么多钱。以后我们上动物福利协会，只要拿三先令就可以再买一个康康。"

威利轻声说："康康只有一个，我不卖。"

"出100镑吧，爸爸。我要打死这条狗。我们不应让它这么胡闹。"

身体还算健壮的人犹豫了一下，升了这个价。"100镑，先生。"他的声音发哑,"能发这么一笔小财,我看你不会反对。"

"那倒是真的,先生。"格罗尔说,转身看着威利,"孩子,100镑如果存到一个可靠的地方,十年后你上大学不用愁。要不然,如果你愿意,可以买一辆小汽车,坐车上学。同学们会多羡慕!你还可以开汽车送妈妈上市场。这可是一大笔钱,一条狗就卖一百镑,划得来。"

威利听到这些话是出自内心的,心急了,嘴一扁想哭。毕竟他只是个八岁的小娃娃,却被逼着卖心爱的狗。"我喜欢康康,康康也喜欢我。"他说,听声音是强忍着才没有哭出来,"我就不卖!"

"100镑!先生,劝劝他吧!要不然,我女儿会跟我闹别扭。你还不知道——"他叹口气,"这小丫头闹起来有多厉害。"

格罗尔心想,这如果是他的女儿,一定在她粉嫩的脸蛋上一边给一记耳光。他看了儿子一眼,儿子一脸哭相,在强忍着眼泪。他用严厉的眼光直视着小女孩,平心静气,然而大声、干脆地说:"好啦,我看事情就到此收场吧。"

这一说,出乎意料的事发生了。小女孩大声笑起来。显然她喜欢上了这个高高的、深色皮肤的人。她是千金小姐,竟然有人敢为了她一时兴起想干的事打她的耳光,她倒喜爱这种粗鲁。

"算了吧,爸爸!"她嚷道,"他是好样的。我们把支票本放回袋里。你也知道这是闹着玩的,爸爸!"

身体还算健壮的那人松了口气,笑了,说他当然早知道,还说在这样的好天气就该闹着玩。闹着玩!格罗尔不相信。他了解各种各样的人。

威利也不担心了,假装擤鼻涕,偷偷揩去两滴眼泪。他扑到康康旁边的沙里,高兴地把狗高高举起来,又跟狗扭打着,狗毛茸茸的棕色爪子和孩子深肤色的小手臂高兴地搅在一起。

然而格罗尔的心情不同,他有些不大情愿地接过这位不相识的人递过来的一根烟,又让他点着火,默默地望着帐篷外深绿色的海水。他眼前的大海像闪光的百褶软绸,有亮的部分,也有暗的部分。格罗尔感慨的是穷人之苦!如果是在两年前,那时他的发明还没有完成,他还住在一套潮湿的公房,梦想着能有一栋他家现在住的那样的小房子,有人出这样一笔钱,那么,这场嘴皮战,这场不仅是为了一条狗,而是考验一个动物和一个孩子心灵深处的爱、忠诚、勇气和气概的争斗,很可能会出现一个不同的结果——就得委屈威利了!然而,从经济学的角度来说,人只有在金钱有了比较可靠的保障时,才能谈到应有的自尊。他想道,如果没有这种保障,就不该叫任何人做他和威利刚才面临的选择;人人都应该得到这样的保障,特别是在一个时时会遇上让人眼花缭乱的物质诱惑的时代。

小女孩拿着铁铲,赤着双小脚,走到帐篷外叫威利道:"你来帮我挖新水沟吧。"但她的眼直往大人格罗尔这儿瞅,希望格罗尔能同意。

她指指踏坏了的水沟,然后头一偏,看着懒洋洋地躺在太阳下喘气的康康,高高兴兴说:"没关系,让它再来踩吧。"

码头上传来一声进港轮船的汽笛声。

Germans at Meat

Katherine Mansfield

Bread soup was placed upon the table. "Ah," said the Herr Rat, leaning upon the table as he peered into the tureen, "that is what I need. My 'magen'[①] has not been in order for several days. Bread soup, and just the right consistency. I am a good cook myself" —He turned to me.

"How interesting," I said, attempting to infuse just the right amount of enthusiasm into my voice.

"Oh yes—when one is not married it is necessary. As for me, I have had all I wanted from women without marriage." He tucked his napkin into his collar and blew upon his soup as he spoke. "Now at nine o'clock I make myself an English breakfast, but not much. Four slices of bread, two eggs, two slices of cold ham, one plate of soup, two cups of tea—that is nothing to you."

He asserted the fact so vehemently that I had not the courage to refute it.

---

① 德语，义即"胃"。

All eyes were suddenly turned upon me. I felt I was bearing the burden of the nation's preposterous breakfast—I who drank a cup of coffee while buttoning my blouse in the morning.

"Nothing at all," cried Herr Hoffman from Berlin. "Ach, when I was in England in the morning I used to eat."

He turned up his eyes and his moustache, wiping the soup drippings from his coat and waistcoat.

"Do they really eat so much?" asked Fräulein Stiegelauer. "Soup and baker's bread and pig's flesh, and tea and coffee and stewed fruit, and honey and eggs, and cold fish and kidneys, and hot fish and liver. All the ladies eat, too, especially the ladies?"

"Certainly. I myself have noticed it, when I was living in a hotel in Leicester Square," cried the Herr Rat. "It was a good hotel, but they could not make tea—now—"

"Ah, that's one thing I *can* do," said I, laughing brightly."I can make very good tea. The great secret is to warm the teapot."

"Warm the teapot," interrupted the Herr Rat, pushing away his soup plate. "What do you warm the teapot for? Ha! ha! that's very good! One does not eat the teapot, I suppose?"

He fixed his cold blue eyes upon me with an expression which suggested a thousand premeditated invasions.

"So that is the great secret of your English tea? All you do is to warm the teapot."

I wanted to say that was only the preliminary canter, but could not translate it, and so was silent.

The servant brought in veal, with sauerkraut and potatoes.

"I eat sauerkraut with great pleasure," said the Traveller from North Germany, "but now I have eaten so much of it that I cannot retain it. I am immediately forced to—"

"A beautiful day," I cried, turning to Fräulein Stiegelauer. "Did you get up early?"

"At five o'clock I walked for ten minutes in the wet grass. Again in bed. At half-past five I fell asleep, and woke at seven, when I made an 'overbody' washing! Again in bed. At eight o'clock I had a cold-water poultice, and at half-past eight I drank a cup of mint tea. At nine I drank some malt coffee, and began my 'cure.' Pass me the sauerkraut, please. You do not eat it?"

"No, thank you. I still find it a little strong."

"Is it true," asked the Widow, picking her teeth with a hairpin as she spoke, "that you are a vegetarian?"

"Why, yes; I have not eaten meat for three years."

"Im-possible! Have you any family?"

"No."

"There now, you see, that's what you're coming to! Who ever heard of having children upon vegetables? It is not possible. But you never have large families in England now; I suppose you are too busy with your suffragetting. Now I have nine children, and they are all alive, thank God. Fine, healthy babies—though after the first one was born I had to—"

"How *wonderful*!" I cried.

"Wonderful," said the Widow contemptuously, replacing the hairpin in the knob which was balanced on the top of her head. "Not at all! A friend of mine had four at the same time. Her husband was so pleased he gave a supper-party and had them placed on the table. Of course she was very proud."

"Germany," boomed the Traveller, biting round a potato which he had speared with his knife, "is the home of the Family."

Followed an appreciative silence.

The dishes were changed for beef, red currants and spinach. They wiped their forks upon black bread and started again.

"How long are you remaining here?" asked the Herr Rat.

"I do not know exactly. I must be back in London in September."

"Of course you will visit München?"

"I am afraid I shall not have time. You see, it is important not to break in my 'cure.'"

"But you *must* go to München. You have not seen Germany if you have not been to München. All the Exhibitions, all the Art and Soul life of Germany are in München. There is the Wagner Festival in August, and Mozart and a Japanese collection of pictures—and there is the beer! You do not know what good beer is until you have been to München. Why, I see fine ladies every afternoon, but fine ladies, I tell you, drinking glasses so high." He measured a good washstand pitcher in height, and I smiled.

"If I drink a great deal of München beer I sweat so," said Herr Hoffman. "When I am here, in the fields or before my bath, I sweat, but

I enjoy it; but in the town it is not at all the same thing."

Prompted by the thought, he wiped his neck and face with his dinner napkin and carefully cleaned his ears.

A glass dish of stewed apricots was placed upon the table.

"Ah, fruit!" said Fräulein Stiegelauer, "that is so necessary to health. The doctor told me this morning that the more fruit I could eat the better."

She very obviously followed the advice.

Said the Traveller: "I suppose you are frightened of an invasion, too, eh? Oh, that's good. I've been reading all about your English play in a newspaper. Did you see it?"

"Yes." I sat upright. "I assure you we are not afraid."

"Well, then, you ought to be," said the Herr Rat. "You have got no army at all—a few little boys with their veins full of nicotine poisoning."

"Don't be afraid," Herr Hoffman said. "We don't want England. If we did we would have had her long ago. We really do not want you."

He waved his spoon airily, looking across at me as though I were a little child whom he would keep or dismiss as he pleased.

"We certainly do not want Germany," I said.

"This morning I took a half bath. Then this afternoon I must take a knee bath and an arm bath," volunteered the Herr Rat; "then I do my exercises for an hour, and my work is over. A glass of wine and a couple of rolls with some sardines—"

They were handed cherry cake with whipped cream.

"What is your husband's favorite meat?" asked the Widow.

"I really do not know," I answered.

"You really do not know? How long have you been married?"

"Three years."

"But you cannot be in earnest! You would not have kept house as his wife for a week without knowing that fact."

"I really never asked him, he is not at all particular about his food."

A pause. They all looked at me, shaking their heads, their mouths full of cherry stones.

"No wonder there is a repetition in England of that dreadful state of things in Paris," said the Widow, folding her dinner napkin. "How can a woman expect to keep her husband if she does not know his favorite food fater three years?"

"Mahlzeit!"

"Mahlzeit!"

I closed the door after me.

餐桌上的德国人

〔英〕凯瑟琳·曼斯菲尔德

面包汤摆上了桌。拉特先生把身子凑过去往碗里瞧瞧："太好啦，我正想吃。这些天我的胃不舒服。面包汤，稀稠正好。我烧菜也是能手。"他转身看着我。

"真有意思！"我说，声气里装出带着应有的热情。

"是这样。不成家的话必须会这一手。要说我嘛，没结婚，就把需要女人干的事全学会了。"他把餐巾掖进衣领里，边说边吹吹他跟前的汤。"现在每天九点我自己动手做一顿英国早餐，但不算丰盛。四片面包，两个鸡蛋，两片冷火腿，一份汤，两杯茶，这对你来说不在话下。"

他把话说得非常肯定，我没有勇气反驳。

突然所有人的眼光投向了我。顿时我感到蒙受了不白之冤，本来早上我只边扣衣服边喝一杯咖啡，现在却成了英国有数的大肚皮。

"根本不在话下？"柏林来的霍夫曼先生大声道，"以前我去英国时早上也吃一顿。"

他抬起眼，翘起胡须，揩去滴在上衣和背心上的汤。

"他们真吃那么多吗?"施蒂格劳尔小姐问,"又是汤,又是面包,又是猪肉,还有茶、咖啡、水果、蜜糖、鸡蛋、冷鱼伴腰子、热鱼伴肝……女的也这么吃,还吃得更多吗?"

"当然啦!我住在莱斯特广场亲眼见的。"拉特先生道,"旅店的设施倒很好,可是他们不会沏茶。现在——"

"这我倒会!"我高兴地笑着说,"我沏的茶味道非常好,奥妙全在茶壶要热。"

"茶壶要热?"拉特先生推开汤盘,打断我的话,"为什么茶壶要热?哈,哈!太妙啦!难道连茶壶一道吃下去吗?"

他的一双蓝眼睛直盯着我,现出咄咄逼人的神气。

"你们英国人沏茶的奥妙就在这里?在一把热茶壶?"

我本想说那只是个预备步骤!但用德语表达不出,所以没有出声。

佣人端上了嫩牛肉,还有泡菜、马铃薯。

德国北方来的旅行家说:"我很爱吃泡菜,可惜现在吃得太多,已经腻了。马上我只得——"

我转身对施蒂格劳尔小姐大声说:"今天天气好,你起得早吗?"

"五点钟起床,在有露水的草地上散了十分钟步,又上床睡了。我在五点半睡着了,醒来时已经是七点,擦了个澡,又睡了。八点敷了冷水药膏,八点半喝了杯薄荷茶,九点喝了些麦芽咖啡,开始'治疗'。请把泡菜递给我。你不要吃吗?"

"谢谢,不吃。我总觉得有些受不了。"

"听说,"寡妇一边用发针剔牙一边问,"你吃素不吃荤吗?"

"是啊!我三年没吃过肉了。"

"这不可能!你有孩子吗?"

"没有。"

"原来是这么回事。你的毛病就出在这里!有谁听过光吃素的人能生孩子?不可能!不过,英国从来没有什么大家庭,我看你们太热衷于女权。我生了九个孩子,谢天谢地全活着。孩子个个都棒,身体好,虽说生了第一胎以后我只好——"

"真不简单!"我大声道。

"不简单!"寡妇轻蔑地说,把发针插回头顶上梳得端端正正的发髻,"什么不简单?我有位朋友一胎生了四个。她丈夫高兴极了,设了宴席待客,把孩子全摆到餐桌上。当然啦,她得意洋洋。"

"德国是孩子之家。"旅行家用刀叉起一个马铃薯,往嘴里一送,嚼着。

接着是一阵表示赞同的沉默。

牛肉、红醋栗、菠菜又上了桌。他们把餐叉在黑面包上揩揩,又吃了起来。

"你打算在这儿住多久?"拉特先生问。

"我也说不准,反正九月得回伦敦。"

"一定会去慕尼黑吧?"

"恐怕没有时间。你知道,我的'治疗'不能中断。"

"慕尼黑非要去一趟不可,不去慕尼黑,德国算是白来了。所有的展览都在慕尼黑举行,德国艺术和精神的精华集中在慕尼黑。八月是瓦格纳①演奏会,还有莫扎特演奏会,有日本的图片展览——还有啤酒!要喝好啤酒非去慕尼黑不可。每天下午我都看到雍容华贵的女人,不瞒你说,这些女人喝起来用的是这么高

---

① 1813—1883,德国作曲家。

的大杯子。"他比划了一个放在洗脸架上的水罐的高度,引得我笑了。

"慕尼黑的啤酒我喝得太多,会浑身出汗。"霍夫曼先生说,"到了这儿,要是在野外,或者说洗澡前,也出一身汗,舒服得很,但在城里就两回事了。"

一说出汗,他便用餐巾揩了揩脖子、脸,又轻轻擦擦耳朵。

熟杏子端上了桌,是一个玻璃盘盛的。

"哟,水果!"施蒂格劳尔小姐嚷道,"想身体好得吃水果。就在今天上午医生还对我说,水果我吃得越多越好。"

当然她听从了医生的叮嘱。

旅行家说:"看来你们也怕人家的军队打进来,是吗?这很好呀!报纸上关于你们英国的报道我篇篇都看。你看不看?"

"看。"我坐直了说,"告诉你吧,我们不怕。"

"你们倒是应该怕,"拉特先生说,"你们没有像样的军队,就那么几个毛孩子,还中了尼古丁毒。"

"别害怕,"霍夫曼先生说,"我们不想征服英国。如果想,我们早占领了。说真的,我们并不想要你们国家。"

他随意地把调羹一挥,看着桌子对过的我,仿佛我是一个去留皆可由其任意处置的小孩。

"当然我们也不想要你们德国。"我说。

"今天上午我洗了身子,今天下午洗两条腿,两只手臂。"拉特先生说,"洗完了活动一小时,我的事便算完了。喝杯酒,吃两卷面包,外加些沙丁鱼——"

奶油樱桃饼上了桌。

"你丈夫最爱吃什么肉?"寡妇问。

"我说不上。"我答道。

"真说不上?你们结婚多久了?"

"三年。"

"你肯定没有说实话!连他最爱吃什么肉也不知道,你怎能管家?这样当妻子连一个星期也混不下去。"

"是实话,我从来没有问过他,他一点也不挑食。"

一阵沉默。几个人一齐看着我,直摇头,嘴里塞满了樱桃核。

"难怪巴黎乱七八糟的事英国也多得很。"[①]寡妇叠着餐巾,说,"如果在一起生活了三年妻子还不知道丈夫最爱吃什么肉,那还算什么妻子。"

"吃吧!"

"吃吧!"

我随手关上了门。

[①] 巴黎乱七八糟的事指巴黎离婚的人多。寡妇认为夫妻在一起生活了三年,妻子还不知道丈夫爱吃什么,势必离婚,所以英国也会像巴黎一样,离婚的人多。

Mr. Preble Gets Rid of His Wife

James Thurber

Mr. Preble was a plump middle-aged lawyer in Scarsdale. He used to kid with his stenographer about running away with him. "Let's run away together," he would say, during a pause in dictation. "All righty," she would say.

One rainy Monday afternoon, Mr. Preble was more serious about it than usual.

"Let's run away together," said Mr. Preble.

"All righty," said his stenographer. Mr. Preble jingled the keys in his pocket and looked out the window.

"My wife would be glad to get rid of me," he said.

"Would she give you a divorce?" asked the stenographer.

"I don't suppose so," he said. The stenographer laughed.

"You'd have to get rid of your wife," she said.

Mr. Preble was unusually silent at dinner that night. About half an hour after coffee, he spoke without looking up from his paper.

"Let's go down in the cellar," Mr. Preble said to his wife.

"What for?" she said, not looking up from her book.

"Oh, I don't know," he said. "We never go down in the cellar any more. The way we used to."

"We never did go down in the cellar that I remember," said Mrs. Preble. "I could rest easy the balance of my life if I never went down in the cellar." Mr. Preble was silent for several minutes.

"Supposing I said it meant a whole lot to me," began Mr. Preble.

"What's come over you?" his wife demanded. "It's cold down there and there is absolutely nothing to do."

"We could pick up pieces of coal," said Mr. Preble. "We might get up some kind of a game with pieces of coal."

"I don't want to," said his wife. "Anyway, I'm reading."

"Listen," said Mr. Preble, rising and walking up and down. "Why won't you come down in the cellar? You can read down there, as far as that goes[①]."

"There isn't a good enough light down there," she said, "and anyway, I'm not going to go down in the cellar. You may as well make up your mind to that."

"Gee whiz!"[②] said Mr. Preble, kicking at the edge of a rug. "Other people's wives go down in the cellar. Why is it you never want to do anything? I come home worn out from the office and you won't even go down in the cellar with me. God knows it isn't very far—it isn't as if

---

① as far as that goes：习惯用语，义为"就目前情况来说""实际上"。
② Gee whiz：也拼作 Geewhiz，小孩用感叹词，表示惊奇。

I was asking you to go to the movies or some place."

"I don't want to *go*!" shouted Mrs. Preble. Mr. Preble sat down on the edge of a davenport.

"All right, all *right*," he said, he picked up the newspaper again. "I wish you'd let me tell you more about it. It's—kind of a surprise."

"Will you quit harping on that subject?" asked Mrs. Preble.

"Listen," said Mr. Preble, leaping to his feet. "I might as well tell you the truth instead of beating around the bush. I want to get rid of you so I can marry my stenographer. Is there anything especially wrong about that? People do it every day. Love is something you can't control ..."

"We've been all over that," said Mrs. Preble. "I'm not going to go all over that again."

"I just wanted you to know how things are," said Mr. Preble. "But you have to take everything so literally. Good Lord, do you suppose I really wanted to go down there and make up some silly game with pieces of coal?"

"I never believed that for a minute," said Mrs. Preble. "I knew all along you wanted to get me down there and bury me."

"You can say that now—after I told you," said Mr. Preble. "But it would never have occurred to you if I hadn't."

"You didn't tell me; I got it out of you," said Mrs. Preble. "Anyway, I'm always two steps ahead of what you're thinking."

"You're never within a mile of what I'm thinking," said Mr. Preble.

"Is that so? I knew you wanted to bury me the minute you set foot

Mr. Preble Gets Rid of His Wife

in this house tonight." Mrs. Preble held him with a glare.

"Now that's just plain damn exaggeration," said Mr. Preble, considerably annoyed. "You knew nothing of the sort. As a matter of fact, I never thought of it till just a few minutes ago."

"It was in the back of your mind," said Mrs. Preble. "I suppose this filing woman put you up to it."

"You needn't get sarcastic," said Mr. Preble. "I have plenty of people to file without having her file. She doesn't know anything about this. She isn't in on it. I was going to tell her you had gone to visit some friends and fell over a cliff. She wants me to get a divorce."

"That's a laugh," said Mrs. Preble. "*That's* a laugh. You may bury me, but you'll never get a divorce."

"She knows that! I told her that," said Mr. Preble. "I mean—I told I'd never get a divorce."

"Oh, you probably told her about burying me, too," said Mrs. Preble.

"That's not ture," said Mr. Preble, with dignity. "That's between you and me. I was never going to tell a soul."

"You'd blab it to the whole world; don't tell me," said Mrs. Preble. "I know you." Mr. Preble puffed at his cigar.

"I wish you were buried now and it was all over with," he said.

"Don't you suppose you would get caught, you crazy thing?" she said. "They always get caught. Why don't you go to bed? You're just getting yourself worked up over nothing."

"I'm not going to to bed," said Mr. Preble. "I'm going to bury you in the cellar. I've got my mind made up to it. I don't know how I could make it any plainer."

"Listen," cried Mrs. Preble, throwing her book down, "will you be satisfied and shut up if I go down in the cellar? Can I have a little peace if I go down in the cellar? Will you let me alone then?"

"Yes," said Mr. Preble. "But you spoil it by taking that attitude."

"Sure, sure, I always spoil everything. I stop reading right in the middle of a chapter. I'll never know how the story comes out—but that's nothing to you."

"Did I make you start reading the book?" asked Mr. Preble. He opened the cellar door. "Here, you go first."

"Brrr," said Mrs. Preble, starting down the steps. "It's *cold* down here! You *would* think of this, at this time of year! Any other husband would have buried his wife in the summer."

"You can't arrange these things just whenever you want to," said Mr. Preble. "I didn't fall in love with this girl till late fall."

"Anybody else would have fallen in love with her long before that. She's been around for years. Why is it you always let other men get in ahead of you? Mercy, but it's dirty down here! What have you got there?"

"I was going to hit you over the head with this shovel," said Mr. Preble.

"You were, huh?" said Mrs. Preble. "Well, get that out of your mind. Do you want to leave a great big clue right here in the middle of everything where the first detective that comes snooping around will find it? Go out in the street and find some piece of iron or something—something that doesn't belong to you."

"Oh, all right," said Mr. Preble. "But there won't be any piece of iron in the street. Women always expect to pick up a piece of iron anywhere."

"If you look in the right place you'll find it," said Mrs. Preble. "And don't be gone long. Don't you dare stop in at the cigar store. I'm not going to stand down here in this cold cellar all night and freeze."

"All right," said Mr. Preble. "I'll hurry."

"And shut that *door* behind you!" she screamed after him. "Where were you born—in a barn?"[①]

---

① be born in a barn 是个习语，义为"行为粗鲁"。此处译文取中国人在这种情况下常说的一句话，以求文学翻译的生动。

普雷布尔先生杀妻

〔美〕詹姆斯·瑟伯

普雷布尔先生是位胖胖的中年人,在斯卡斯代尔当律师。他常与速记员说着玩,叫她跟他跑。"我们一道跑吧!"工作说到一半时,他会搁下来这么一句。"跑就跑吧。"她总是答道。

有个星期一下午,天下着雨,普雷布尔先生的神态比往常认真,说道:

"我们一道跑吧。"

"跑就跑吧。"速记员说。普雷布尔先生把口袋里的钥匙弄得哗啦响,望着窗外。

"我太太巴不得甩开我。"他说。

"会跟你离婚?"速记员问。

"离婚倒不会。"他说。速记员笑出了声。

"那你得把你太太甩开。"她说。

当天晚上,普雷布尔先生吃晚饭时沉默得反常。喝过咖啡后约半小时也一句话没说,低头看报。

"我们往地窖去一趟吧。"普雷布尔先生开腔后对太太说。

"去干什么?"她问,没放下手里的书。

"我也说不上。"他道,"我们连一次也没去过了。以前是常去的。"

"我记得以前也没有去过。"普雷布尔太太说,"要是我一次也不去地窖,下半辈子准会太平。"普雷布尔先生又沉默好几分钟。

"你知道我提起这话是因为有要紧的事吗?"普雷布尔先生又说话了。

"你究竟怎么啦?"他太太问,"地窖里冷,又连一丁点大的事也没有。"

"去拿几块煤,"普雷布尔先生说,"拿几块煤来我们好玩玩游戏。"

"我不想去,"他太太说,"再说我要看书。"

"你听我说!"普雷布尔先生说着站了起来,来回走着,"你跟我去一趟有什么关系?要说看书,到地窖里也能看。"

"那儿光线不好。不管怎么着,我就是不想去地窖。你死了这条心吧。"她说。

"好厉害!"普雷布尔先生说,踢了踢一条地毯的边。"人家的太太都下地窖,为什么你就什么事也不干?我上班累得筋疲力尽,回了家叫你跟我去一趟地窖也不干。去地窖又用不着走多远,总不比我叫你陪我上电影院或者去别的什么地方吧?"

"我不想去!"普雷布尔太太放大了嗓门,说完坐到一张长沙发上。

"好吧,好吧!"他说,又把报纸拿了起来,"你最好是听我说说,把话说明白些。你——你想不到的事。"

"你别跟我再啰嗦了,行不行?"普雷布尔太太说。

"你听着!"普雷布尔先生一跃而起,"我就对你实话实说,不再拐弯抹角了吧。我想把你甩开,跟我的速记员结婚。这该没有错到哪儿去吧?这种事天天有。产生了爱情你身不由己了……"

"我们都谈过这事了,我不想再提。"普雷布尔太太说。

"我只是希望你知道事情到了什么地步。"普雷布尔先生说,"不过你得把一切都当真。哼!你猜猜,叫你到那儿干什么?就因为发了傻,要拿几块煤玩玩?"

"我根本没相信这话,"普雷布尔太太说,"我早知道你打的主意是把我骗到那儿埋了。"

"我把底细告诉了你,你当然会这样说。"普雷布尔先生说,"如果我不说穿,你怎么也想不到。"

"你没有告诉我,是我逼出来的。"普雷布尔太太说,"不管怎样,反正你的心思不说也瞒不了我。"

"我的心思你没有哪次猜得着。"普雷布尔先生说。

"当真?今天晚上,你一跨进家门我就知道你想把我埋了。"普雷布尔太太狠狠瞪了他一眼。

"这完全是瞎吹,"普雷布尔先生说,恼火透了,"这种事你半点也不知道。其实,这个主意我才刚打。"

"可是由来已久,我看就是那整理案卷的女人使你起了坏心。"普雷布尔太太说。

"就别说带刺的话了吧。"普雷布尔先生说,"我不叫她理案卷还有许多人理。她不知道这件事,跟她没关系。我本想告诉她你去朋友家做客,从悬崖上摔了下来。她想叫我离婚。"

"真是开玩笑!"普雷布尔太太说,"真是开玩笑!你把我埋了可以,但休想离婚。"

"她知道啦！我早对她说了。"普雷布尔先生道，"我是说——我告诉过她我离不了婚。"

"哼，那你就很可能也告诉她要把我埋了。"普雷布尔太太道。

"没这回事，"普雷布尔先生庄重地说，"这事就你知我知，对谁我也没有说过。"

"你藏不住话，逢人都会说，就别骗我了吧。"普雷布尔太太说，"我知道你的脾气。"普雷布尔先生吸了口烟。

"我巴不得现在就把你埋了，来个干脆利落。"他说。

"你就不想想会被抓起来？你疯了吗？"她问，"那些人一个个都抓住了。干吗不去睡觉？你是在没事胡搅。"

"我不想睡。"普雷布尔先生说，"我要把你埋在地窖里，已经打定了主意，这你总够明白了吧？"

普雷布尔太太把书一放，嚷道："行啦！我就到地窖去，你总该满意，可以闭上嘴了吧？我去了地窖可不可以享点太平？你放得过我了吧？"

"那当然，不过这一来你把事情就弄糟了。"

"那还用说！件件事都让我弄糟。一本书我没看完就放下了，结尾怎么样我是再也没法知道了，可是这对你无所谓。"

"难道书是我叫你看的吗？"普雷布尔先生问。他打开地窖门："请吧，你先下去。"

"哟哟哟，"普雷布尔太太说着往下走，"这儿真冷！亏你想得出来，一年里挑了这个时候。别人家的男人要埋老婆总是赶在夏天。"

"这种事不可能你想何时就何时，"普雷布尔先生说，"我直到今年秋天快完了才爱上这姑娘。"

"要是换上别人，早就爱上她了。她已经来了好些年，为什么你事事让别人抢在你前面？哎哟，这地方真脏！你在那儿放了什么？"

"我就用这把铁铲一铲子敲在你头上把你敲死。"普雷布尔先生说。

"哼，你要这样干？"普雷布尔太太说，"得了吧，别打这主意。难道你要等侦探一来就在这儿找到一个重要线索？到大马路上去，捡点铁器或者别的什么来，反正得是别人的东西。"

"那好，那好！"普雷布尔先生说，"不过，大马路上没有铁器捡。你们女人就这个样，以为随便哪儿都有铁器捡。"

"走对了地方就有的捡，"普雷布尔太太说，"快去快回。我看你敢走到哪家香烟店又进去耽搁一阵！让我在地窖里待上一整夜冻得发僵我可不干。"

"行，我会赶快。"普雷布尔先生说。

"把门关好！你怕夹了尾巴呀？"他刚转身走，她就叫了起来。

Fard

Aldous Huxley

They had been quarrelling now for nearly three-quarters of an hour. Muted and inarticulate, the voices floated down the corridor, from the other end of the flat. Stooping over her sewing, Sophie wondered, without much curiosity, what it was all about this time. It was Madame's voice that she heard most often. Shrill with anger and indignant with tears, it burst out in gusts, in gushes. Monsieur was more self-controlled, and his deeper voice was too softly pitched to penetrate easily the closed doors and to carry along the passage. To Sophie, in her cold little room, the quarrel sounded, most of the time, like a series of monologues by Madame, interrupted by strange and ominous silences. But very now and then Monsieur seemed to lose his temper outright, and then there was no silence between the gusts, but a harsh, deep, angry shout. Madame kept up her loud shrillness continuously and without flagging; her voice had, even in anger, a curious, level monotony. But Monsieur spoke now loudly, now softly, with emphases and modulations and sudden outbursts, so that his contributions to the squabble, when they were audible, sounded like a series of separate explosions. Bow, wow, wow-wow-wow, wow—a dog barking rather slowly.

After a time Sophie paid no more heed to the noise of quarrelling. She was mending one of Madame's camisoles, and the work required all her attention. She felt very tired; her body ached all over. It had been a hard day; so had yesterday, so had the day before. Every day was a hard day, and she wasn't so young as she had been. Two years more and she'd be fifty. Every day had been a hard day since she could remember. She thought of the sacks of potatoes she used to carry when she was a little girl in the country. Slowly, slowly she was walking along the dusty road with the sack over her shoulder. Ten steps more; she could manage that. Only it never was the end; one always had to begin again.

She looked up from her sewing, moved her head from side to side, blinked. She had begun to see lights and spots of color dancing before her eyes; it often happened to her now. A sort of yellowish bright worm was wriggling up towards the right-hand corner of her field of vision; and though it was always moving upwards, upwards, it was always there in the same place. And there were stars of red and green that snapped and brightened and faded all round the worm. They moved between her and her sewing; they were there when she shut her eyes. After a moment she went on with her work; Madame wanted her camisole most particularly tomorrow morning. But it was difficult to see round the worm.

Fard

There was suddenly a great increase of noise from the other end of the corridor. A door had opened; words articulated themselves.

"... bien tort, mon ami, si tu crois que je suis ton esclave. Je ferai ce que je voudrai."①

"Moi aussi."② Monsieur uttered a harsh, dangerous laugh. There was the sound of heavy footsteps in the passage, a rattling in the umbrella stand; then the front door banged.

Sophie looked down again at her work. Oh, the worm, the coloured stars, the aching fatigue in all her limbs! If one could only spend a whole day in bed—in a huge bed, feathery, warm and soft, all the day long ...

The ringing of the bell startled her. It always made her jump, that furious wasplike buzzer. She got up, put her work down on the table, smoothed her apron, set straight her cap, and stepped out into the corridor. Once more the bell buzzed furiously. Madame was impatient.

"At last Sophie. I thought you were never coming."

Sophie said nothing; there was nothing to say. Madame was standing in front of the open wardrobe. A bundle of dresses hung over her arm, and there were more of them lying in a heap on the bed.

"Une beauté à la Rubens," her husband used to call her when he was in an amorous mood. He liked these massive, splendid, great women. None of your flexible drainpipes for him. "Helene Fourmont"

---

① 法文。
② 法文。

was his pet name for her.

"Some day," Madame used to tell her friends, "some day I really must go to the Louvre and see my portrait. By Rubens, you know. It's extraordinary that one should have lived all one's life in Paris and never have seen the Louvre. Don't you think so?"

She was superb tonight. Her cheeks were flushed; her blue eyes shone with an unusual brilliance between their long lashes; her short, red-brown hair had broken wildly loose.

"Tomorrow, Sophie," she said dramatically, "we start for Rome. Tomorrow morning." She unhooked another dress from the wardrobe as she spoke, and threw it on to the bed. With the movement her dressing-gown flew open, and there was a vision of ornate underclothing and white exuberant flesh. "We must pack at once."

"For how long, Madame?"

"A fortnight, three months—how should I know?"

"It makes a difference, Madame."

"The important thing is to get away. I shall not return to this house, after what has been said to me tonight, till I am humbly asked to."

"We had better take the large trunk, then, Madame; I will go and fetch it."

The air in the box-room was sickly with the smell of dust and leather. The big trunk was jammed in a far corner. She had to bend and strain at it in order to pull it out. The worm and the coloured stars flickered before her eyes; she felt dizzy when she straightened herself. "I'll help you to pack, Sophie," said Madame, when the servant returned, dragging the heavy trunk after her. What a death's-head the old woman looked nowadays! She hated having old, ugly people near her. But Sophie was so efficient; it would be madness to get rid of her.

"Madame need not trouble." There would be no end to it, Sophie knew, if Madame started opening drawers and throwing things about. "Madame had much better go to bed. It's late."

No, no. She wouldn't be able to sleep. She was to such a degree enervated. These men ... What an embeastment! One was not their slave. One would not be treated in this way.

Sophie was packing. A whole day in bed, in a huge, soft bed, like Madame's. One would doze, one would wake up for a moment, one would doze again.

"His latest game," Madame was saying indignantly, "is to tell me he hasn't got any money. I'm not to buy any clothes, he says. Too grotesque. I can't go about naked, can I?" She threw out her hands. "And as for saying he can't afford it, that's simply nonsense. He can, perfectly well. Only he's mean, mean, horribly mean. And if he'd only do a little honest work, for a change, instead of writing silly verses and publishing them at his own expense, he'd have plenty and to spare." She walked up and down the room. "Besides," she went on, "there's his old father. What's he for, I should like to know? 'You must be proud of having a poet for a husband,' he says." She made her voice quaver like an old man's. "It's all I can do not to laugh in his face. 'And what beautiful verses Hegesippe writes about you! What passion, what fire!'" Thinking of the old man, she grimaced, wobbled her head, shook her finger, doddered on her legs. "And when one reflects that poor Hegesippe is bald and dyes the few hairs he has left." She laughed. "As for the passion he talks so much about in his beastly verses," she laughed—"that's all pure invention. But, my good Sophie, what are you thinking of? Why are you packing that hideous old green dress?"

Sophie pulled out the dress without saying anything. Why did the woman choose this night to look so terribly ill? She had a yellow face and blue teeth. Madame shuddered; it was too horrible. She ought to send her to bed. But, after all, the work had to be done. What could one do about it? She felt more than ever aggrieved.

"Life is terrible." Sighing, she sat down heavily on the edge of the bed. The buoyant springs rocked her gently once or twice before they settled to rest. "To be married to a man like this. I shall soon be getting old and fat. And never once unfaithful. But look how he treats me." She got up again and began to wander aimlessly about the room. "I won't stand it though," she burst out. She had halted in front of the long mirror, and was admiring her own splendid tragic figure. No one would believe, to look at her, that she was over thirty. Behind the beautiful tragedian she could see in the glass a thin, miserable, old creature, with a yellow face and blue teeth, crouching over the trunk. Really, it was too disagreeable. Sophie looked like one of those beggar women one sees on a cold morning, standing in the gutter. Does one hurry past, trying not to look at them? Or does one stop, open one's purse, and give them one's copper and nickel—even as much as a two-franc note, if one has no change? But whatever one did, one always felt uncomfortable, one always felt apologetic for one's furs. That was what came of walking. If one had a car—but that was another of Hegesippe's meannesses—one wouldn't, rolling along behind closed windows, have to be conscious of them at all. She turned away from the glass.

"I won't stand it," she said, trying not to think of the beggar women, of blue teeth in a yellow face; "I won't stand it." She dropped into a chair.

But think of a lover with a yellow face and blue uneven teeth! She closed her eyes, shuddered at the thought. It would be enough to make one sick. She felt impelled to take another look: Sophie's eyes were the color of greenish lead, quite without life. What was one to do about it? The woman's face was a reproach, an accusation. And besides, the sight of it was making her feel positively ill. She had never been so profoundly enervated.

Sophie rose slowly and with difficulty from her knees; an expression of pain crossed her face. Slowly she walked to the chest of drawers, slowly counted out six pairs of silk stockings. She turned back towards the trunk. The woman was a walking corpse.

"Life is terrible," Madame repeated with conviction, "terrible, terrible, terrible."

She ought to send the woman to bed. But she would never be able to get her packing done by herself. And it was so important to get off tomorrow morning. She had told Hegesippe she would go, and he had simply laughed; he hadn't believed it. She must give him a lesson this time. In Rome she would see Luigino. Such a charming boy, and a marquis, too. Perhaps ... But she could think of nothing but Sophie's face; the leaden eyes, the bluish teeth, the yellow, wrinkled skin.

"Sophie," she said suddenly; it was with difficulty that she could prevent herself screaming, "look on my dressing table. You'll see a box of rouge, the Dorin[①] number twenty-four. Put a little on your cheeks. And there's stick of lip salve in the right-hand drawer."

She kept her eyes resolutely shut while Sophie got up—with what a horrible creaking of the joints!—walked over to the dressing table, and stood there, rustling faintly through what seemed an eternity. What a life, my God, what a life! Slow footsteps trailed back again.

She opened her eyes. Oh, that was far better, far better.

"Thank you, Sophie. You look much less tired now." She got up briskly. "And now we must hurry." Full of energy she ran to the wardrobe. "Goodness me," she exclaimed, throwing up her hands, "you've forgotten to put in my blue evening dress. How could you be so stupid, Sophie?"

---

① Dorin 指所说化妆品品牌。

胭　脂

〔英〕奥尔德斯·赫胥黎

他们已经吵了将近三刻钟，声音从房间的另一头沿着走廊传来，只是听不清楚，听不真切。索菲对这种事早已习以为常，低头做着针线活，但猜不透这次为了什么，她听到最多的是太太的声音。太太气得尖叫，声泪俱下，一阵接一阵发作。老爷克制些，低沉的声音不容易穿过门传到走廊的另一头。索菲坐在自己冷冰冰的小房间里，听到的往往不像是吵嘴，而是太太的独白，一段接一段，当中插着难以思议的、不祥的寂静。但老爷也有好几次压不住火气，那么，一段独白之后出现的便不是寂静，而是男低音愤怒的吼叫。太太的嗓门保持高频率，没有降过调，显得格外单调，即使在大发雷霆时也听不出变化。老爷说起话来忽而声大，忽而声小，有轻重缓急，抑扬顿挫，所以只要听得见，他拌嘴的发作是有节奏的，像条狗慢慢叫——汪，汪汪汪，汪！

索菲听了一会儿吵架的声音后没心听了。她在缝太太的短上衣，不能分心。她觉得疲倦，周身痛。这一天她干得辛苦，昨天也是，前天也是，天天辛苦，而岁月又不饶人。再过两年她便是50岁的人了。从记事起她就天天累死累活。她想起在乡下时还小小年纪就要扛一袋袋马铃薯。她驮着袋子在土路上慢慢地、慢慢地往前走。再走十步,没问题。只不过再走十步并没有到头,十步完了又是十步。

她放下手里的针线活,把头左右转转,眨眨眼睛。她眼前早已开始冒出一些花花点点,现在次数越来越多。一条浅黄色的发亮的虫在她右眼角边爬着。它不停地往上爬,爬,但爬来爬去还在原地。这条虫的四周有红色的和绿色的星星,忽隐忽现,忽明忽暗。它们在她的手与眼之间游移,闭上眼还能看到。歇了一会儿她又缝起来,太太等着第二天上午穿她的短上衣。然而,她看得清的只有那条虫。

突然走廊另一头的声音变大了。门开了,话听得一清二楚。

"你错了,朋友。如果你把我当奴隶,那我偏要想怎么干就怎么干。"

"我也一样。"老爷发出一阵粗鲁的、难听的笑声。走廊里响起了沉重的脚步声,接着伞架上也有了响动,最后是前门砰地一响。

索菲又低头做活计。不好!又见到了虫子,红绿星星,四肢直发酸。要是能躺上一天该多舒服!如果在暖和、松软的鸭绒床垫上躺整整一天……

一阵铃声惊醒了她。每次她听到那铃黄蜂似地狂响都要跳起身来。她起身后把针线活放到桌上,抹抹围裙,整整帽子,到了走廊里。铃再次狂响起来,太太不耐烦了。

"索菲,你总算来了呀!我只当不会来呢!"

索菲没答话,她无话可答。衣柜开着,太太站在柜前,手上挽着一大堆衣服,床上还放着一大堆。

胭　脂

老爷在温情脉脉时总说太太是鲁本斯①画中的大美人。他喜爱那些丰腴的美人，看不中干豆角似的女人。他对她的爱称是"海伦娜·弗尔曼"。

太太多次对朋友说过："哪一天我当真得去卢浮宫看看'我'的画像，是鲁本斯画的。在巴黎住了一辈子的人如果没去过卢浮宫，那就是白住了。你说对不对？"

今天夜晚她非同寻常，脸发红，两道长睫毛间的蓝眼睛格外亮，棕里透红的短发乱糟糟。

"索菲，明天我们去罗马，明天上午去。"她得意地说，边说边从衣柜又取下一件衣服扔到床上。就因这么一扔，她的睡衣撑开了，露出了漂亮的贴身衣和雪白丰满的肉体。"我们得马上整理行装。"她说。

"去多久，太太？"

"或者两星期，或者三个月，谁知道！"

"两星期不同于三个月，太太。"

"只要能走就行。今晚受了这窝囊气我决不回来，除非是来求我。"

"那我们带大箱子，太太。我去拿吧。"

堆放箱箱笼笼的房间里有股灰尘和皮革味，难闻得很。大箱子塞在一个角落里，拖出来要猫着腰，费一把力气。那条虫和红红绿绿的星在眼前一隐一现，她直起身子时只觉得头一阵晕。"索菲，我帮你收拾吧。"太太见她把大箱子拖过来了，说。这女

---

① 鲁本斯（1577—1640），佛兰德斯著名画家。他画中的女人多肥硕、丰满，他为第二任妻子海伦娜画的画像非常有名。

人现在上了年纪，看起来像个骷髅。她不愿让丑老婆子跟着。然而，索菲手脚麻利，开销她不合算。

索菲知道，如果太太动手开抽屉，扔东西，那就没法收场，说："不用太太费力了。天晚了，请太太休息吧。"

这可不成！她睡不着，已经给气昏了。这些男人……哪是什么好东西！没人给他们当奴隶，没人受得了这种气。

索菲在收拾行李。心想得躺一整天，在太太那样的又大又软的床上躺。睡了醒，醒了睡。

太太气冲冲地说："他近来的一个花招是说没有钱，什么衣服我也不能买。天下奇闻！我总不能赤身裸体，对吧？"她双手一摊，"要说买不起，那真是瞎扯。他阔得很啦！糟就糟在他不成器，太不成器。如果他不写什么歪诗，自己掏钱印，去找点正经事干，他的钱花不完。"她在房间里走来走去。"还有他家那老爷子。我真弄不清，他安的什么心。"她又开腔了，"他说：'你的丈夫是诗人，你应该觉得荣耀。'"她的嗓门直发抖，是学老年人的声气，"我好不容易才忍住没当他的面笑。他还说：'埃热西佩歌颂你的诗写得多好！多有感情，多热乎！'"想到那老爷子，她又是皱眉，又是摇头，又是抖手指头，又是跺脚。"你还不知道啦，那埃热西佩秃了顶，没剩下几根头发还要染青。"她大笑着。"他大谈特谈他的歪诗里有什么感情，全是吹牛。"她笑着。"哟，索菲，你的脑子哪儿去啦？那件绿衣服又旧又难看，你为什么要往箱子里放？"

索菲二话没说，把衣服又拿出了箱子。这女人偏赶今天晚上一副难看相，究竟是怎么回事呢？她的脸发黄，牙发黑。太太哆嗦起来，害怕了。她该打发她去睡。然而，行李总得收拾。不收拾能行吗？她心里更烦了。

"日子不好过呀！"她叹口气，一屁股坐到床上，弹簧震了一两下才稳下来。"嫁给这样一个人，我准老得快，胖得快。我没一次做过对不起他的事，可现在他这样对待我！"她又站起身，在房间里乱转。"我不再客气了！"她嚷道。她走到穿衣镜前，欣赏着自己漂亮、迷人的身段。看到她的人没一个会相信她已年过三十。她发现镜子里的不幸的大美人后有一个可怜的瘦老婆子，脸蜡黄，牙发黑，跪在一口大箱子边。这真太不相称。索菲那模样像个冬天大清早站在大街上的叫花婆。谁要是看到她，究竟是装作没见，三步并两步地溜之大吉呢？还是停下来，打开钱包，给一个铜板，甚至一张两法郎的钞票呢（如果他没有零钱的话）？溜走也好，给钱也好，反正谁心里都不好受，会怨自己倒霉。走路难免遇到这种事。如果有车——这又得怪埃热西佩不成器——往车里一坐，窗关着，一溜烟过去，根本就注意不到叫花婆了。她转过身，不再照镜子。

"我不会客气！"她说，极力想忘掉蜡黄脸、黑牙齿的叫花婆，"我不会客气！"她坐到了一张椅子上。

见到这蜡黄的脸，一嘴错乱不齐发黑的牙，还有什么心情想情人！她闭上眼，打了个寒颤。叫谁也受不了。她不由自主地又看了一眼：索菲的绿眼睛呆滞无神。怎么办呢？这女人的脸使人感到不安、内疚。而且，她一见就觉得恶心。她更烦躁了。

索菲吃力地、慢慢地从地上爬起来，脸上现出痛苦的表情。又慢慢地走到抽屉柜前，慢慢拿出六双丝袜，再回到大箱子边。除了会走路，别的她活像具死尸。

"日子真难过呀！"太太又感叹道，"难过，难过，真难过！"

她本想打发索菲去睡,只可惜她一个人收拾不好行李,明天上午又非走不可。她对埃热西佩说要走,他听了一笑置之,不相信。这次她决心叫他知道她的厉害。到罗马后她去找路易吉诺,这小伙子长得帅,还是侯爵。也许……但是她脑子里老浮现出索菲的脸,脸上呆滞的眼睛,发黑的牙齿,打皱的黄皮肤。

"索菲!"她叫道(要她克制住不大声叫,很难办到),"你到我的梳妆台看看,那儿有盒胭脂,是多林24,你往脸上擦一点。右边的抽屉里还有一支口红。"

她紧闭着眼,没看索菲怎样站起身,但听见了她的关节发出咔的一声响;也没看她怎样走到梳妆台前,怎样站在那儿,但听见了她的衣服沙沙响,似乎响了很久很久。天啊,这是什么日子,什么日子啊!她又听到她回来的脚步声,才睁开眼睛。哟,好多了,好多了!

"谢谢你,索菲,你显得精神多了。"她赶快站起来,"我们得抓紧时间。"她急冲冲跑到衣柜边,两手一摊,嚷了起来:"哎呀呀,你忘了收拾我的蓝色晚礼服。索菲,你怎么这么笨呀!"

The Bedchamber Mystery

C. S. Forester

Now that a hundred years have passed, one of the scandals in my family can be told. It is very doubtful if in 1843 Miss Forester (she was Eulalie, but being the eldest daughter unmarried, she, of course, was Miss Forester) and Miss Emily Forester and Miss Eunice Forester ever foresaw the world of 1943 to which their story would be told; in fact it is inconceivable that they could have believed that there ever would be a world in which their story could be told blatantly in public print. At that time it was the sort of thing that could only be hinted at in whispers during confidential moments in feminine drawing rooms; but it was whispered about enough to reach, in the end, the ears of my grandfather, who was their nephew, and my grandfather told it to me.

In 1843 Miss Forester and Miss Emily and Miss Eunice Forester were already maiden ladies of a certain age. The old-fashioned Georgian house in which they lived kept itself modestly retired, just like its inhabitants, from what there was of bustle and excitement in the High Street of the market town. The ladies indeed led a retired life; they went to church a little, they visited those of the sick whom it was decent and proper for maiden ladies to visit, they read the more colorless of the novels in the circulating library①, and sometimes they entertained other ladies at tea.

And once a week they entertained a man. It might almost be said that they went from week to week looking forward to those evenings. Dr. Acheson was (not one of the old ladies would have been heartless enough to say "fortunately," but each of them felt it) a widower, and several years older even than my great-great-aunt Eulalie. Moreover, he was a keen whist player and a brilliant one, but in no way keener or more brilliant than were Eulalie, Emily, and Eunice. For years now the three nice old ladies had looked forward to their weekly evening of whist—all the ritual of setting out the green table, the two hours of silent cut-and-thrust play, and the final twenty minutes of conversation with Dr. Acheson as he drank a glass of old Madeira② before bidding them good night.

The late Mrs. Acheson had passed to her Maker somewhere about 1830, so that it was for thirteen years they had played their weekly game of whist before the terrible thing happened. To this day we do not know whether it happened to Eulalie or Emily or Eunice, but it happened to one of them. The three of them had retired for the night, each to her separate room, and had progressed far toward the

---

① the circulating library：指可以外借的图书馆，有时借书收费。
② old Madeira：Madeira 为葡萄牙属群岛，位于大西洋中，盛产葡萄酒。此处即指该地所产葡萄酒。

The Bedchamber Mystery

final stage of getting into bed. They were not dried-up old spinsters; on the contrary they were women of weight and substance, with the buxom contours even married women might have been proud of. It was her weight which was the undoing of one of them, Eulalie, Emily or Eunice.

Through the quiet house that bedtime there sounded the crash of china and a cry of pain, and two of the sisters—which two we do not know—hurried in their dressing gowns to the bedroom of the third—her identity is uncertain—to find her bleeding profusely from severe cuts in the lower part of the back. The jagged china fragments had inflicted severe wounds, and most unfortunately, just in those parts where the injured sister could not attend to them herself. Under the urgings of the other two she fought down her modesty sufficiently to let them attempt to deal with them, but the bleeding was profuse, and the blood of the Foresters streamed from the prone figure face① downward on the bed in terrifying quantity.

"We shall have to send for the doctor," said one of the ministering sisters; it was a shocking thing to contemplate.

"Oh, but we cannot!" said the other ministering sister.

"We must," said the first.

"How terrible!" said the second.

And with that the injured sister twisted her neck and joined in the

---

① the prone figure face：此处 prone 义为"俯卧的"，figure 仍指身体，但 face 并不指脸，而是指身体朝上部分。

conversation. "I will not have the doctor," she said. "I would die of shame."

"Think of the disgrace of it!" said the second sister. "We might even have to explain to him how it happened!"

"But she's bleeding to death," protested the first sister.

"I'd rather die!" said the injured one, and then, as a fresh appalling thought struck her, she twisted her neck even further. "I could never face him again. And what would happen to our whist?"

That was an aspect of the case which until then had occurred to neither of the other sisters, and it was enough to make them blench. But they were of stern stuff[①]. Just as we do not know which was the injured one, we do not know which one thought of a way out of the difficulty, and we shall never know. We know that it was Miss Eulalie, as befitted her rank as eldest sister, who called to Deborah the maid, to go and fetch Dr. Acheson at once, but that does not mean to say that it was not Miss Eulalie who was the injured sister—injured or not, Miss Eulalie was quite capable of calling to Deborah and telling her what to do.

As she was bid. Deborah went and fetched Dr. Acheson and conducted him to Miss Eunice's bedroom, but, of course, the fact that it was Miss Eunice's bedroom is really no indication that it was Miss Eunice who was in there. Dr. Acheson had no means of knowing; all he saw was a recumbent form covered by a sheet. In the center of the sheet a round hole a foot in diameter had been cut, and through the hole the

---

① stern stuff: 此处 stern 义为 "严格的"，stuff 指人的性格。

The Bedchamber Mystery

seat of the injury was visible.

Dr. Acheson needed no explanations. He took his needles and his thread from his little black bag and he set to work and sewed up the worst of the cuts and attended to the minor ones. Finally he straightened up and eased his aching back.

"I shall have to take those stitches out," he explained to the still and silent figure which had borne the stitching stoically without a murmur. "I shall come next Wednesday and do that."

Until next Wednesday the three Misses Forester kept to their rooms. Not one of them was seen in the streets of the market town, and when on Wednesday Dr. Acheson knocked at the door Deborah conducted him once more to Miss Eunice's bedroom. There was the recumbent form, and there was the sheet with the hole in it. Dr. Acheson took out the stitches.

"It has healed very nicely," said Dr. Acheson. "I don't think any further attention from me will be necessary."

The figure under the sheet said nothing, nor did Dr. Acheson expect it. He gave some concluding advice and went his way. He was glad later to receive a note penned in Miss Forester's Italian hand[①]:

Dear Dr. Acheson,

> We will all be delighted if you will come to whist this week as usual.

---

① Italian hand: 指流行于中世纪的一种书法,被视为好书法。

When Dr. Acheson arrived he found that the "as usual" applied only to his coming, for there was a slight but subtle change in the furnishings of the drawing room. The stiff, high-backed chairs on which the three Misses Forester sat bore, each of them, a thick and comfortable cushion upon the seat. There was no knowing which of the sisters needed it.

闺房秘事

〔英〕C. S. 福雷斯特

时间已过去一百年，有件家丑现在扬扬也无妨了。福雷斯特小姐（她名叫尤拉莉娅，只因是未嫁的长女，当然该称为福雷斯特小姐）、埃米莉·福雷斯特小姐和尤妮斯·福雷斯特小姐大概不会预见到，到了1943年，她们的秘事会公之于众。其实，要是有谁对她们说，世道要大变，她们的秘事以后可以用白纸黑字公开，她们是决不会相信的。当时这种事只能在女人堆里谈知心话时咬着耳朵悄悄说，可是就因为说得太多，最后让我祖父知道了。我祖父与她们是堂亲，后来又告诉了我。

1843年，福雷斯特家姐妹仨都成了大龄姑娘。她们住在佐治亚的老式房子里，比不得住在镇上的大街，能见到热闹。三位小姐可以说是深居简出，只上上教堂，探望探望未出阁闺女可以探望的病人，谈谈图书馆里的正经小说，偶尔请同性朋友喝喝茶。

一星期里她们有一次接待一位男宾。说句不算过分的话，她们每星期都眼巴巴盼着这一晚。这人是艾奇逊大夫，年龄比大姑奶奶尤拉莉娅都长好几岁，已经丧偶。老姑娘们个个好心肠，没有说"幸好"已经丧偶，然而实际上却是这样想的。另外，他爱玩惠斯特牌，技巧高明，只是比三姐妹逊色。惠斯特牌每星期打一个夜晚，程序是先摆好绿色桌子，然后默不出声地你争我夺玩上两小时，临了与艾奇逊大夫攀谈20分钟，大夫喝完一杯陈年马德拉白葡萄酒便起身告辞。一年又一年，周周如此，三位规规矩矩的老姑娘就盼着这一晚。

艾奇逊太太升天是在1830年，从那时算到那件要命的事发生，前后共13年，她们坚持每星期玩一次惠斯特牌。直到今天，我仍说不上遭殃的是尤拉莉娅，还是埃米莉，或者尤妮斯，但总没出这三人。夜深了，她们各自回房休息，而且已经上床。三人都不是干瘪的老处女，恰好相反，倒有些斤两，鼓鼓的胸部叫已婚妇女见了都羡慕。尤拉莉娅、埃米莉、尤妮斯三位无论是谁出的事，反正就出在体重大。

到睡觉的时间，本来屋子里安安静静，却突然听到一声瓷器哐啷响，一声惨叫，三姐妹中的两个（我们不知道是哪两个）顾不得换睡衣，急忙跑到另一个（也不知道是谁）的房间里，只见另一个的下半身背后开了好几道口，直淌血。大伤口是瓷器碎片划出来的，而最糟的是，都划在受伤的人手够不着的地方。她被另外两人催逼不过，只好依从，让她们堵伤口的血，可是没有堵住，福雷斯特家小姐的血从身上淌到了床上，有一大摊。

"非请医生不可了！"在堵伤口的姐妹俩中有一个说——可这是犯忌讳的事，不堪设想。

"那——那可不行！"另一个说。

"非请不可！"第一个说。

"我的天哪！"第二个说。

受伤的一个听到这里扭转头，插话了："我不要请！请来了羞死人。"她说。

"你想想多丢人！"第二个说。"我们怎么向他交代如何弄成了这样子呢？"

"血再流下去没命啦！"第一个不依。

"没命就没命吧！"受伤的一个说。这时，她想到了另一件不妙的事，把脖子伸得更长，扭转头："我是再也见不着他了，惠斯特牌我们怎么玩下去哟！"

这话说得有理，另外两个没有想到，一听傻了眼。不过，她们不是随随便便的人。有一个想出了万全之策，但我们不知道是谁，就像我们不知道受伤的是谁一样。我们只知道尤拉莉娅因为三姐妹中居长，吩咐了女佣德博拉马上请艾奇逊大夫来，但这不等于受伤的不是尤拉莉娅。无论受没受伤，反正尤拉莉亚还有力气使唤德博拉。

德博拉领命把艾奇逊大夫请来，带进尤妮斯的房间。当然，大夫进她房间不见得房间里躺的就是她。艾奇逊大夫是认不出来的，他只看见躺着个人，身上盖了块布，布当中剪了直径1英尺的洞，洞里露出的是伤口。

艾奇逊大夫没多说，从小黑包里掏出针和线，先缝上大伤口，再在小伤口敷上药。最后他挺了挺身子，只觉得腰酸背痛。

"以后还要拆线，我星期四来。"他对躺着的人说。躺着的人一动不动，没有出声。可怜缝伤口时她一直不哼是咬紧牙关才熬过来的。

福雷斯特家的三位小姐一直守在家里，守到星期四。镇上的大街没见她们的踪影。星期四艾奇逊大夫登门时，德博拉把他又领进了尤妮斯的房间。有人在里面躺着，盖了块布，布上挖了洞。艾奇逊大夫拆了线。

"伤口愈合很好,以后用不着看了。"艾奇逊大夫说。

布单下的人没吱声,艾奇逊大夫也没指望她吱声。他最后叮嘱了些该注意的事,走了。过了些时候他接到一张便条,是福雷斯特小姐的漂亮手迹,写着:

艾奇逊大夫:
本星期惠斯特牌会照旧,请赏光。

艾奇逊大夫来了之后发现,原来牌会的"照旧"只是照旧有他来,客厅的摆设却有个细小而微妙的变化。三位福特斯特小姐坐的硬高背靠椅上,都铺了个舒舒服服的厚坐垫,只是不知三位中哪一位是真需要。

Over the Hill[①]

John Steinbeck

Sligo and the kid took their forty-eight hour pass listlessly. The bars close in Algeria at eight o'clock, but they got pretty drunk on wine before that happened and they took a bottle with them and lay down on the beach. The night was warm, and after the two had finished the second bottle of wine they took off their clothes and waded out into the quiet water and then squatted down and sat there with only their heads out. "Pretty nice, eh, kid," said Sligo. "There's guys used to pay heavy dough for stuff like this, and we get it for nothing."

"I'd rather be home on Tenth Avnoo,"[②] said the kid. "I'd rather be there than anyplace. I'd like to see my old lady. I'd like to see the World Series this year."

"You'd like maybe a clip in the kisser,"[③] said Sligo.

"I'd like to go into the Greek's and get me a double chocolate

---

① Over the Hill: 口语中用语，义为"开小差"。
② Tenth Avnoo: Tenth Avenue, 按不准确发音所拼。
③ a clip in the kisser: clip 此处指 "a quick, sharp blow", 英语口语; kisser 指 face, 俚语。

malted with six eggs in it," said the kid. He bobbed up to keep a little wavelet out of his mouth. "This place is lonely. I like Coney."

"Too full of people." said Sligo.

"This place is lonely," said the kid.

"Talking about the Series, I'd like to do that myself," said Sligo. "It's times like this a fella① gets kind of② tempted to go over the hill."

"S'posen you went over the hill—where the hell would you go? There ain't no place to go."

"I'd go home," said Sligo. "I'd go to the Series. I'd be first in the bleachers③, like I was in '40."

"You couldn't get home," the kid said; "there ain't no way to get home."

The wine was warming Sligo and the water was good. "I got dough④ says I can get home," he said carelessly.

"How much dough?"

"Twenty bucks⑤."

"You can't do it," said the kid.

"You want to take the bet?"

"Sure I'll take it. When you going to pay?"

"I ain't going to pay; you're going to pay. Let's go up on the beach

---

① fella: fellow, 按不准确发音所拼。
② kind of: almost, 口语中用法。
③ bleachers: 指球场上的露天座位。
④ dough: 指money, 俚语。
⑤ bucks: 指dollars, 俚语。

and knock off a little sleep ..."

At the piers the ships lay. They had brought landing craft and tanks and troops, and now they lay taking in the scrap, the broken equipment from the North African battlefields which would go to the blast furnaces to make more tanks and landing craft. Sligo and the kid sat on a pile of C-ration boxes and watched the ships. Down the hill came a detail with a hundred Italian prisoners to be shipped to New York. Some of the prisoners were ragged and some were dressed in American khaki because they had been too ragged in the wrong places. None of the prisoners seemed to be unhappy about going to America. They marched down to a gangplank and then stood in a crowd awaiting orders to get aboard.

"Look at them," said the kid, "they get to go home and we got to stay. What you doing, Sligo? What you rubbing oil all over your pants for?"

"Twenty bucks," said Sligo, "and I'll find you and collect, too." He stood up and took off his overseas cap and tossed it to the kid. "Here's a present, kid."

"What you going to do, Sligo?"

"Don't you come follow me, you're too dumb. Twenty bucks, and don't you forget it. So long, see you on Tenth Avnoo."

The kid watched him go, uncomprehending. Sligo, with dirty pants and a ripped shirt, moved gradually over, near to the prisoners, and then imperceptibly he edged in among them and stood bareheaded, looking back at the kid.

An order was called down to the guards, and they herded the prisoners toward the gangplank. Sligo's voice came plaintively. "I'm not supposed to be here. Hey, don't put me on dis ship."

"Shut up, wop," a guard growled at him. "I don't care if you did live sixteen years in Brooklyn. Git up that plank." He pushed the reluctant Sligo up the gangplank.

Back on the pile of boxes the kid watched with admiration. He saw Sligo get to the rail. He saw Sligo still protesting and fighting to get back to the pier. He heard him shrieking, "Hey, I'm Americano. Americano soldier. You canna poot me here."

The kid saw Sligo struggling and then he saw the final triumph. He saw Sligo take a sock at a guard and he saw the guard's club rise and come down on Sligo's head. His friend collapsed and was carried out of sight on board the ship. "The son-of-a-gun," the kid mumured to himself. "The smart son-of-a-gun. They can't do nothing at all to him and he got witnesses. Well, the smart son-of-a-gun. My God, it's worth twenty bucks."

The kid sat on the boxes for a long time. He didn't leave his place till the ship cast off and the tugs pulled her clear of the submarine nets. The kid saw the ship join the group and he saw the destroyers move up and take the convoy under protection. The kid walked dejectedly up to the town. He bought a bottle of Algerian wine and headed back toward the beach to sleep his forty-eight.

开小差

〔美〕约翰·斯坦贝克

斯莱戈与小伙子的两天假过得没劲。阿尔及利亚的酒吧间8点关门,他们没等关门便已喝了七八分,然后又拿了瓶酒,往沙滩上一躺。夜里天仍热,两人喝完第二瓶后,脱掉衣服,躺进平静的水里,坐着,只露出头。"嗯,够舒服吧,小伙子?"斯莱戈说,"有人像这样享受得花一大叠钞票,我们连一根毫毛也不用拔。"

"没有我老家的十马路好,"小伙子说,"哪儿也比不上那地方。我想我妈,还想看今年的世界棒球系列赛。"

"大概你想吃一记耳光吧?"斯莱戈说。

"我想去希腊人的店里喝双料巧克力饮料,还要往里加六个鸡蛋。"小伙子说,他伸了伸脖子,不让海水冲进嘴里,"这地方太僻静,我喜欢科尼。"

"科尼人太多。"斯莱戈说。

"这地方太僻静。"小伙子说。

"要说看系列赛,我也想,"斯莱戈道,"到这种时候,谁都憋不住想开小差。"

"就算开成了,你还能往哪儿去?根本没地方去。"

"我回家,看系列赛去,"斯莱戈说,"像1940年那样,第一个进场。"

"你回不了家,没办法回。"小伙子说。

酒性在斯莱戈身上渐渐发作了,海水舒适宜人。"打赌吧,我回得了。"他不在意地说。

"赌多少钱?"

"20美元。"

"你回不了。"小伙子说。

"你打不打赌?"

"当然赌!你什么时候兑现?"

"不是我兑现,是你兑现。我们到海滩上去睡一会儿吧……"

好些船停泊在码头,运来了登陆艇、坦克、军队,现在又准备把破破烂烂,就是在北非战场打坏了的装备运走,送到鼓风炉里,再造出新坦克和登陆艇来。斯莱戈和小伙子坐在一堆箱子上,看着船。山下过来了一小队人,押着100名意大利俘虏,乘船去纽约。有的俘虏穿得破破烂烂,有的换了美国卡其制服,因为原来的太破,连羞于见人的地方都遮不住。要去美国了,不高兴的俘虏一个都没有。他们走到跳板边停住了,站成一群,等候命令上船。

"你瞧他们,"小伙子说,"他们要回家了,我们倒只能留下。你怎么啦,斯莱戈?干吗把油往裤子上揩?"

"别忘了20美元,"斯莱戈说,"我会找着你,钱也别想少。"他站起来,摘下帽子扔给了小伙子,"送给你啦,小伙子。"

"你要干吗,斯莱戈?"

"别跟着我,你这人笨头笨脑。20美元,别忘了呀!再见吧,我们在十马路会面。"

小伙子眼看他走了,心里觉得奇怪。斯莱戈穿着油污裤子,一件破衬衫,慢慢靠近了那群俘虏,然后又神不知鬼不觉地挤到当中,站着,光着脑袋,回头看了看小伙子。

命令传来,押送俘虏的士兵把俘虏往跳板上赶。斯莱戈不肯上,只听他嚷道:"我不是这一伙的。喂,别把我往船上赶。"

"得啦吧,黑鬼[①]!"一名押送的士兵喝道,"你就是在布鲁克林[②]住过16年也不关我屁事!上船吧。"尽管斯莱戈不愿走,他还是把斯莱戈推上了跳板。

小伙子坐在一堆箱子上看着,佩服得很。他眼睁睁看到斯莱戈走到了栏杆边,还不肯依,要回码头上。他听到他尖声嚷着:"哎呀,我是美国人,美国士兵!你们不能把我推到这儿来!"

小伙子看到斯莱戈在反抗,后来又看到了他巧计成功。他看到斯莱戈狠狠向一个士兵打去,又看到士兵的棒子扬起来,落到斯莱戈的脑袋上。他的朋友倒下了,被抬上船,见不着了。"滑头鬼!"小伙子心想,"好厉害的滑头鬼!他们奈何不了他,他有的是证人。哼,好厉害的滑头鬼!乖乖,我这20美元输得心服口服。"

小伙子在箱子上坐了很久,直等到船解缆,被拖船拖出了防护网才走。小伙子看到这条船进了船队,又看到几艘驱逐舰开了过去,为船队护航。他无精打采地往城里走,买了瓶阿尔及利亚酒,又回到沙滩睡觉,他两天的假还没休完。

---

① 原文为 wop,指从南欧到美国的深色皮肤人,尤指意大利人。
② 布鲁克林是美国纽约的一个区。

Charles

Shirley Jackson

The day my son Laurie started kindergarten he renounced corduroy overalls with bibs and began wearing blue jeans with a belt. I watched him go off the first morning with the older girl next door, seeing clearly that an era of my life was ended, my sweet-voiced nursery-school tot replaced by a long-trousered, swaggering character who forgot to stop at the corner and wave good-bye to me.

He came home the same way, the front door slamming open, his hat on the floor, and the voice suddenly becomes raucous shouting, "Isn't anybody *here*?"

At lunch he spoke insolently to his father, spilled his baby sister's milk, and remarked that his teacher said we were not to take the name of the Lord in vain.

"How *was* school today?" I asked, elaborately casual.

"All right," he said.

"Did you learn anything?" his father asked.

Laurie regarded his father coldly. "I didn't learn nothing," he said.

Charles

"Anything," I said. "Didn't learn anything."[①]

"The teacher spanked a boy, though," Laurie said, addressing his bread and butter. "For being fresh[②]," he added, with his mouth full.

"What did he do?" I asked. "Who was it?"

Laurie thought, "It was Charles," he said. "He was fresh. The teacher spanked him and made him stand in a corner. He was awfully fresh."

"What did he do?" I asked again, but Laurie slid off his chair, took a cookie, and left, while his father was still saying, "See here, young man."

The next day Laurie remarked at lunch, as soon as he sat down, "Well, Charles was bad again today." He grinned enormously and said, "Today Charles hit the teacher."

"Good heavens," I said, mindful of the Lord's name. "I suppose he got spanked again?"

"He sure did," Laurie said. "Look up," he said to his father.

"What?" his father said, looking up.

"Look down," Laurie said. "Look at my thumb. Gee, you're dumb."[③] He began to laugh insanely.

"Why did Charles hit the teacher?" I asked quickly.

"Because she tried to make him color with red crayons," Laurie

---

① 这句话是 Laurie 的母亲纠正 Laurie 语法错误的话,汉译时由于英汉语词法与语法的差别,无法照原句译出。
② fresh: 此处为俚语,义即"爱捣蛋的"。
③ thumb 与 dumb 发音很近。这句话是儿子跟父亲捣蛋说的话。

said. "Charles wanted to color with green crayons so he hit the teacher and she spanked him and said nobody play with Charles but everybody did."

The third day—it was Wednesday of the first week—Charles bounced a see-saw on the head of a little girl and made her bleed, and the teacher made him stay inside all① during recess. Thursday Charles had to stand in a corner during story-time because he kept pounding his feet on the floor. Friday Charles was deprived of blackboard privileges because he threw chalk.

On Saturday I remarked to my husband, "Do you think kindergarten is too unsettling for Laurie? All this toughness and bad grammar, and this Charles boy sounds like such a bad influence."

"It'll be all right," my husband said reassuringly.

"Bound to be people like Charles in the world. Might as well meet them now as later."

On Monday Laurie came home late, full of news.

"Charles," he shouted as he came up the hill; I was waiting anxiously on the front steps. "Charles," Laurie yelled all the way up the hill, "Charles was bad again." "Come right in," I said, as soon as he came close enough. "Lunch is waiting."

"You know what Charles did?" he demanded, following me through the door. "Charles yelled so in school they sent a boy in from first grade to tell the teacher she had to make Charles keep quiet, and so

---

① all：此处为副词，修饰 during recess。

Charles had to stay after school. And so all the children stayed to watch him."

"What did he do?" I asked.

"He just sat there," Laurie said, climbing into his chair at the table. "Hi, Pop, y'old dust mop."①

"Charles had to stay after school today," I told my husband. "Everyone stayed with him."

"What does this Charles look like?" my husband asked Laurie. "What's his other name?"

"He's bigger than me," Laurie said. "And he doesn't have any rubbers and he doesn't ever wear a jacket."

Monday night was the first Parent-Teachers meeting, and only the fact that the baby had a cold kept me from going; I wanted passionately to meet Charles' mother. On Tuesday Laurie remarked suddenly, "Our teacher had a friend come to see her in school today."

"Charles's mother?" my husband and I asked simultaneously.

"Naaah,"② Laurie said scornfully. "It was a man who came and made us do exercises, we had to touch our toes. Look." He climbed down from his chair and squatted down and touched his toes. "Like this," he said. He got solemnly back into his chair and said, picking up his fork, "Charles didn't even *do* exercises."

"That's fine," I said heartily. "Didn't Charles want to *do* the

---

① pop 是孩子在家中对父亲的熟称。Pop 与 mop 音相近，整句话又是一句俏皮话。
② Naaah：Nah 的拖音。nah 为口语中用词，等于 no。

exercises?"

"Naaah," Laurie said. "Charles was so fresh to the teacher's friend he wasn't *let* do exercises."

"Fresh again," I said.

"He kicked the teacher's friend," Laurie said. "The teacher's friend told Charles to touch his toes like I just did and Charles kicked him."

"What are they going to do about Charles, do you suppose?" Laurie's father asked him.

Laurie shrugged elaborately. "Throw him out of school, I guess," he said.

Wednesday and Thursday were routine; Charles yelled during story hour and hit a boy in the stomach and made him cry. On Friday Charles stayed after school again and so did all the other children.

With the third week of kindergarten Charles was an institution in our family; the baby was being a Charles when he filled his wagon full of mud and pulled it through the kitchen; even my husband, when he caught his elbow in the telephone cord and pulled telephone, ashtray, and a bowl of flowers off the table, said, after the first minute, "Looks like Charles."

During the third and fourth weeks it looked like a reformation in Charles; Laurie reported grimly at lunch on Thursday of the third week, "Charles was so good today the teacher gave him an apple."

"What?" I said, and my husband added warily, "You mean Charles?"

"Charles," Laurie said. "He gave the crayons around and he picked up the books afterward and the teacher said he was her helper."

"What happened?" I asked incredulously.

"He was her helper, that's all," Laurie said, and shrugged.

"Can this be true, about Charles?" I asked my husband that night. "Can something like this happen?"

"Wait and see," my husband said cynically. "When you've got a Charles to deal with, this may mean he's only plotting."

He seemed to be wrong. For over a week Charles was the teacher's helper; each day he handed things out and he picked things up; no one had to stay after school.

"The PTA meeting's next week again," I told my husband one evening. "I'm going to find Charles's mother there."

"Ask her what happened to Charles," my husband said. "I'd like to know."

"I'd like to know myself," I said.

On Friday of that week things were back to normal. "You know what Charles did today?" Laurie demanded at the lunch table, in a voice slightly awed. "He told a little girl to say a word and she said it and the teacher washed her mouth out with soap and Charles laughed."

"What word?" His father asked unwisely, and Laurie said, "I'll have to whisper it to you, it's so bad." He got down off his chair and went around to his father. His father bent his head down and Laurie whispered joyfully. His father's eyes widened.

"Did Charles tell the little girl to say *that*?" he asked respectfully.

"She said it *twice*," Laurie said. "Charles told her to say it *twice*."

"What happened to Charles?" my husband asked.

"Nothing," Laurie said. "He was passing out the crayons."

Monday morning Charles abandoned the little girl and said the evil word himself three or four times, getting his mouth washed out with soap each time. He also threw chalk.

My husband came to the door with me that evening as I set out for the PTA meeting. "Invite her over for a cup of tea after the meeting," he said. "I want to get a look at her."

"If only she's there," I said prayerfully.

"She'll be there," My husband said. "I don't see how they could hold a PTA meeting without Charles's mother."

At the meeting I sat restlessly, scanning each comfortable matronly face, trying to determine which one hid the secret of Charles. None of them looked to me haggard enough. No one stood up in the meeting and apologized for the way her son had been acting. No one mentioned Charles.

After the meeting I identified and sought out Laruie's kindergarten teacher. She had a plate with a cup of tea and a piece of chocolate cake; I had a plate with a cup of tea and a piece of marshmallow cake. We maneuvered up to one another cautiously, and smiled.

"I've been so anxious to meet you," I said. "I'm Larurie's mother."

"We're all so interested in Laurie," she said.

"Well, he certainly likes kindergarten," I said. "He talks about it all the time."

"We had a little trouble adjusting, the first week or so," she said primly, "but now he's a fine little helper. With occasional lapses, of course."

"Laurie usually adjusts very quickly," I said. "I suppose this time it's Charles's influence."

"Charles?"

"Yes," I said, laughing, "you must have your hands full in that kindergarten, with Charles."

"Charles?" she said. "We don't have any Charles in the kindergarten."

查尔斯

〔美〕雪莉·杰克逊

我儿子劳里上幼儿园的第一天,便宣布不再穿带围兜的灯芯绒背带裤,而是换上了系腰带的牛仔裤。那天早上,他跟着邻居家一个比他年岁大的女孩离开了家;我眼望着,不由感到自己的生活又翻过了一页。这孩子原来声音清脆,只上托儿所,现在转眼成了个穿长裤、走路神气十足的小家伙,到拐弯的地方也不回头向我挥挥手告别。

回家时他的表现同样变了——砰地撞开门,帽子往地上一扔,声音突然粗了起来,嚷道:"这儿就没人啦?"

吃饭时他对父亲说话大模大样,把小妹妹的牛奶打翻了,却振振有词:老师说过,我们不要开口上帝,闭口上帝。

"今天幼儿园里怎么样?"我装作漫不经心地问。

"没什么。"他说。

"学到了什么吗?"他父亲问。

劳里很不热乎地看看父亲,说:"我什么也没学。"

"怎么?"我又问,"什么也没学?"

"只怪老师打了一个小朋友的屁股,"劳里边说边吃奶油面包,头也没抬,"他捣蛋。"他又说了一句,嘴里塞得满满的。

"他怎么啦?叫什么名字?"我问。

劳里想了想,说:"叫查尔斯。他捣蛋。老师打了他的屁股,叫他在一个角落里罚站。他太淘气了。"

"他究竟怎么啦?"我又问。可是劳里拿了块甜饼,从椅子上爬下来溜走了。他父亲没发现,还说:"你听着,小子!"

第二天劳里在吃饭时一坐下便说:"哼,查尔斯今天可表现不好。"他开心地笑着,"今天是查尔斯打了老师。"

"天哪!"我不敢提起上帝,说,"那他的屁股又挨打了吧?"

"当然啦!"劳里说。"你往上瞧。"他对他爸爸说。

"瞧什么?"他爸爸说着抬起头来。

"你往下瞧。"劳里说,"嘻,你瞧我的大拇指,你瞧我的拇指大。"他咯咯笑起来。

"为什么查尔斯要打老师?"他追问道。

"老师叫他用红蜡笔涂色,他要用绿蜡笔涂色,就打了老师。老师揍了他,叫大家别跟他玩,可大家偏要跟他玩。"

第三天,就是第一个星期的星期三,查尔斯把跷跷板一扳,打破了一个小孩的头,老师罚他站到屋子里,一直没让他出来玩。星期四那天,在听故事时查尔斯不住地跺脚,又挨罚了,一个人站在墙角里。星期五,查尔斯被剥夺了上黑板的权利,就因为乱扔粉笔。

到星期六,我对丈夫说:"你看,让劳里上幼儿园是不是会学坏?这么粗野,说话乱七八糟,那查尔斯更是个坏榜样。"

"没关系,"我丈夫满有把握地说,"查尔斯这样的孩子哪儿都有,今天遇上与明天遇上是一样。"

星期一劳里回来得晚，要说的新闻也多。"查尔斯——"他边上坡边叫唤，我站在门口的台阶上正等得心焦，"查尔斯——"他一路上拉大嗓门嚷，"查尔斯又表现不好啦！"

"快进来，就等你吃饭。"他一走近了我便说。

"你猜，查尔斯怎么啦？"他边说边跟着我进了家门，"查尔斯跑到小学里大喊大叫，人家要一个一年级学生来告诉老师，让老师叫他别再吵。查尔斯就留校了，幼儿园的小朋友也都留校了，看着他。"

"他怎么来着？"我问。

"他坐着没动。"劳里说，爬到桌子边坐下，"嘻，爸——爸，爸爸就是拖——把！"

我告诉丈夫："今天查尔斯留校了，小朋友跟着也都留校了。"

"查尔斯什么模样？"我丈夫问劳里，"他姓什么？"

劳里说："比我个子大。他不穿橡胶鞋，连短外衣也不穿。"

星期一晚上本要开家长会，我因为小儿子受了凉，没有去成。其实我很想见见查尔斯的妈妈。星期二劳里的话题变了："今天我们老师来了位朋友，来找她。"

"是查尔斯的妈妈吗？"我和丈夫异口同声问。

"才不是呐！"劳里不屑地说，"是来教我们做操的人，要我们够脚趾头。你们看！"他从椅上爬下来，双腿蹲下，伸手够脚趾。"就这样。"他说。他满神气地又坐到椅上，拿起叉，说："查尔斯连操也没做。"

"那怎么行！"我大声说，"查尔斯连操也不肯做吗？"

"不——是！"劳里说，"查尔斯跟老师的朋友捣蛋，老师没让他做。"

"又捣蛋！"我说。

"他踢了人家，"劳里说，"老师的朋友叫查尔斯够脚趾，就是我刚才这么够，可查尔斯踢了他。"

"你看他们会把查尔斯怎么办？"劳里的爸爸问劳里。

劳里把肩一耸，说："赶他出幼儿园呗！"

星期三、星期四照旧出了乱子。查尔斯在听故事时大喊大叫，还打了一个孩子的肚子，把人家打哭了。星期五查尔斯又留校了，所有的孩子也跟着没走。

到劳里上幼儿园的第三个星期，"查尔斯"在我家成了代号。小儿子把泥堆到自己的车里，推进厨房，我们便叫他查尔斯。甚至，我丈夫的手肘不小心挂着电话线，把电话机、烟灰缸、花瓶全弄到了地上时，他也骂自己："活像个查尔斯！"

在第三、第四个星期，查尔斯似乎有了长进。第三个星期的星期四，劳里在吃饭时有气无力地报告："查尔斯今天表现特别好，老师奖了他一个苹果。"

"当真？"我问。我丈夫担心没听清，说："你是说查尔斯？"

"是查尔斯，"劳里说，"他把蜡笔发给小朋友，后来又收图书，老师夸他是个好帮手。"

"究竟怎么啦？"我将信将疑地问。

"就只夸他是个好帮手。"劳里说完一耸肩。

这天晚上我问丈夫："查尔斯真会这样吗？他能变得这样快？"

"等着瞧吧，"我的丈夫不以为然，说，"要是你也对付个查尔斯，可得小心他在玩花招儿。"

他的话似乎错了，因为查尔斯给老师当帮手接着当了整整一星期，每天的东西收收发发全是他，也不见有人留校。

一天晚上，我对丈夫说："下星期又开家长会，我去见见查尔斯的妈妈。"

"问问他查尔斯怎样变好了,我很想听听。"我丈夫说。

"我也想。"我说。

到星期五,情况发生了逆转。"你们猜,查尔斯今天怎么啦?"劳里吃饭时间,声音中带着两分胆怯,"他叫一个小朋友说了句话,小朋友说了,老师就用肥皂给她洗嘴巴,查尔斯就笑了。"

"什么话?"他爸爸没细想,问。劳里说:"我只能对你悄悄说,是句脏话,太脏。"他从椅上下来,走到桌子对过爸爸那儿。他爸爸低下头来听,劳里边说边笑。爸爸瞪大了眼。

"查尔斯叫小朋友说这种话?"他吃惊地问。

"她说了两次,"劳里说,"查尔斯叫她说两次。"

"查尔斯受了什么处罚?"我丈夫问。

"什么也没有,"劳里说,"他在发蜡笔。"

星期一上午,那脏话查尔斯没叫小女孩说,却自己说了三遍,每次老师都用肥皂给他洗了嘴巴。他还扔了粉笔。

晚上我去开家长会,丈夫把我送到门边。"开完会请她来喝杯茶,"他说,"我想见见她。"

"那得她也去开会。"我没把握地说。

"她一定会去,"我丈夫说,"家长会离了查尔斯的妈妈,我看他们开不成。"

我开会时心不在焉,仔细打量每一位母亲的脸,想看出谁表面镇静而内心为查尔斯不安。结果,没有发现一张脸反常。会上,谁也没有因为儿子捣蛋而站起来表示歉意,谁也没提起查尔斯。

散会以后,我凭自己的判断认出了劳里的老师。她的茶盘里放着一杯茶和一块软糖。我们都拘谨地向对方走过去,微微笑着。

"我很想见见您,"我说,"我是劳里的妈妈。"

"我们大家都关心劳里。"她说。

"他很喜欢幼儿园,在家就爱说幼儿园的事。"

"刚来的那一两个星期我们费了些力气教他改掉坏毛病,"她是一本正经说这话的,"现在好了,成了小帮手。不过,偶尔还会出出岔子。"

"劳里做了错事总改得快,"我说,"偶尔犯错恐怕是受了查尔斯的影响。"

"查尔斯?"

"是的,"我笑着说,"你们幼儿园有了查尔斯一定够忙了。"

"查尔斯?"她问道,"我们幼儿园根本没有一个孩子叫查尔斯。"

附　录

作家简介

　　比德派（Bidpai，？—？），古代印度王宫首席学者、著名寓言作家。"比德派"是英文Bidpai的音译，而英文Bidpai也只是一个不准确的音译。有一本梵文寓言集的阿拉伯文译本以Bidpai作为书名，而且该书曾译成欧洲多国文字。第一个英文译本是从意大利文转译的，新版英译本出版于1980年。

　　薄伽丘（Boccaccio，1313—1375），意大利文艺复兴时期作家，人文主义的重要代表，与诗人但丁、彼特拉克并称为佛罗伦萨文学"三杰"。生于商人家庭，反对封建专制，拥护共和政体。写有长篇小说、长诗、中篇小说等。代表作《十日谈》是欧洲文学史上第一部现实主义作品，包括100篇故事，反映当时意大利社会生活，表达人文主义思想。其作品对以后欧洲文学中短篇小说有较大影响。

　　理查德·斯梯尔（Richard Steele，1672—1729），英国作家，曾就读于牛津大学，1700年左右开始笔墨生涯。曾写过几部喜剧，在对婚姻、爱情的描写中表现了中产阶级的道德观，但真正使他在文学界取得地位的是他的小品文。1708年，他创办了著名杂志《闲谈者》(The Tattler)，后来又与人合办杂志《旁观者》(The Spectator)，批评当时风尚，讨论家庭问题。两度担任国会议员，1718年受封为爵士。

奥利弗·哥尔斯密（Oliver Goldsmith，1730—1774），英国作家，生于牧师家庭。学过神学但未能获牧师职位，行过医但养不活自己。成名作是《威克菲牧师传》，也是他唯一的一部长篇小说。然而，他同时是散文家、诗人、剧作家。其作品反映了18世纪英国农村的贫困、农民的苦难，也常有劝善的说教和浓厚的伤感情调。

海因里希·冯·克莱斯特（Heinrich von Kleist，1777—1811），德国诗人、剧作家、小说家，生前郁郁不得志，死后才享殊荣，德国著名的文学奖克莱斯特奖就是以其姓氏而命名。在普鲁士政府机关供过职，与人合办过报纸、杂志。1810年，其所创办的《柏林晚报》因批评普鲁士政府亲拿破仑的政策，反对拿破仑侵略，受到政府干涉。1811年自杀。他主要创作喜剧作品，代表作为《破瓮记》，最著名的短篇小说是《智利地震》。

华盛顿·欧文（Washington Irving，1783—1859），美国作家。出生那年正逢美国独立战争胜利，后来他成为美国最早的著名作家之一。一生作品不少，但都是短篇小说、杂记、历史传记等，未写过长篇小说。最有名的短篇小说是《瑞普·凡·温克尔》和《睡谷的传说》。

纳撒尼尔·霍桑（Nathaniel Hawthorne，1804—1864），美国心理分析小说的开创者，美国文学史上首位写作短篇小说的作家，被称为美国19世纪最伟大的浪漫主义小说家，亨利·詹姆斯、爱伦·坡、赫尔曼·麦尔维尔等文学大师都深受其影响。生于清教徒家庭，读大学时与著名诗人朗费罗同窗。成名作为《红字》，后来也成为世界文学经典，书中反对清教徒的传统教义，但深受宗教思想影响，认为人类有罪恶的天性。

埃德加·爱伦·坡（Edgar Allen Poe，1899—1949），美国小说家、诗人、文艺批评家，美国浪漫主义思潮时期的代表人物。父母是流浪艺人。在美国的名作家中，他是第一个单靠写作谋生的，在他那个时代，弄得生活拮据。短篇小说数量很多，代表作有《怪诞故事集》《黑猫》《莫格街凶杀案》等。作品色彩阴暗，充满恐怖气氛。由于一些著名小说情节离奇，多描写犯罪心理或变态心理，被认为是侦探小说的先驱。

赫尔曼·梅尔维尔（Herman Melville，1819—1891），美国作家。生于富商家庭，但15岁就开始工作。做过银行职员、农场工人、乡村教师。对其创作影响最大的经历是随捕鲸船出海和在太平洋岛上与波利尼亚人在一起的生活。代表作为《白鲸》。除小说外，还写过好多诗歌。

陀思妥耶夫斯基（Fyodor Dostoevsky，1821—1881），俄国作家。生于一个医生家庭，家境并不富裕。曾就读于军事工程学院，但对文学有浓厚兴趣。1884年因参加革命团体被判死刑，行刑前改判流放。患有癫痫症，终身受病痛折磨。长篇代表作有《罪与罚》《白痴》《被侮辱与被损害的》等。其小说创作主题大致可归结为三个方面：一是描写被欺凌与被侮辱者，展示隐藏在贫民窟阴暗角落里人物的不幸与悲苦；二是描写自我分裂的人，揭示多重人格；三是表现人性的复归。

列夫·托尔斯泰（Leo Tolstoy，1828—1910），俄国作家。出生于贵族家庭，但是受法国启蒙运动思想影响，对沙皇专制不满。16岁入大学学习法律和东方语言，但中途辍学。23岁参军，并在此时开始写作。63岁时，俄国最高教育机关宣布他为"邪教徒和叛教者"。其长篇小说《战争与和平》《安娜·卡列尼娜》《复活》等真实而广泛地反映了他所处那个时代俄国社会的现实，使他成为世界最伟大的作家之一。这些作品也为我国读者所熟悉。

比昂斯滕·比昂松（Björnstjerne Björnson，1832—1910），挪威剧作家、诗人、小说家、社会活动家。1903年获诺贝尔文学奖。生于牧师家庭，当过新闻记者、剧场经理。曾参加挪威民族独立运动，当过政党领袖。早期剧作《战役之间》等多采用历史题材，后发表《挑战的手套》等问题剧，企图通过道德教育改良社会。后期作品带有宗教神秘色彩，有颓废主义倾向。

里卡多·帕尔马（Ricardo Palma，1833—1919），秘鲁作家。27岁时流亡智利，从事新闻工作。六年后回国，参加民族解放运动。他的创作生涯以写诗歌、戏剧、翻译雨果的作品开始。代表作是《秘鲁传说》,在拉丁美洲文学史中占有重要地位。

马克·吐温(Mark Twain,1835—1910),美国作家,美国批判现实主义文学的奠基人。真名萨缪尔·朗亨·克里曼斯。生于地方法官家庭,当过排字工、领港员、淘金工人和记者。1852年在波士顿的幽默周刊《手提包》上发表第一篇作品时,还是个排字工。1863年开始使用"马克·吐温"的笔名。其作品的风格是深刻的幽默与辛辣的讽刺相结合,优美的抒情与政论相结合。最著名的长篇有《汤姆·索亚历险记》《哈克贝利·费恩历险记》《王子与贫儿》。

维利埃·德·利尔-亚当(Villiers de L'Isle-Adam,1838—1889),法国诗人、剧作家、短篇小说家。出生于贵族家庭,但家境并不富裕,且本人也一生拮据。1881年曾试图竞选国会议员,但连候选人也未当上。他直到去世前五年作品才为人所知。主要成就在短篇小说,代表作是短篇小说集《无情的故事》。作品属反自然主义,既有神秘与恐怖,又有浪漫主义,对当时的社会道德进行了尖锐讽刺。

阿方斯·都德(Alphonse Daudet,1840—1897),法国小说家、剧作家。14岁开始写诗和第一部小说。17岁时父母财产损失无余,都德只好在一所学校当了半年看门人。其作品主要反映法国南部生活,有长篇小说《磨坊书简》、短篇小说《星期一的故事》、剧本《亚尔勒女郎》等。同时代人都承认他是位天才人物。他的短篇小说《最后一课》曾选入我国语文课本,广为人知。

附录：作家简介

托马斯·哈代（Thomas Hardy，1840—1928），英国小说家、诗人。早期和中期的创作以小说为主，继承和发扬了维多利亚时代的文学传统；晚年以其诗歌开拓了英国20世纪的文学。哈代说他的作品是"性格和环境小说"。28岁时写成第一部小说，送各家出版社均被退稿。三年后出版第一部作品。长篇小说有16部，最重要的作品有《还乡》《德伯家的苔丝》等6部，优秀短篇小说集有3部，诗集有10部。

安布罗斯·比尔斯（Ambrose Bierce，1842—1914），作家，美国最有影响的记者之一，报道多而面广。19岁从军，南北战争中任记者。最有名的长篇小说是《魔鬼词典》，被人列为美国文学百部杰作之一。短篇小说代表作是《鹰溪桥上》，主要短篇小说集有两部，为《士兵与平民的故事》和《这种事可能吗？》。作品中多荒诞离奇的心理现象。1913年71岁高龄时去墨西哥，想亲历墨西哥革命，但不知所踪，至今仍是个谜。

奥古斯特·斯特林堡（August Strindburg，1849—1912），瑞典作家，瑞典现代文学的奠基人。当过小学教师和记者。13岁丧母，后受继母虐待，成年后又有过三次婚姻挫折，且郁郁不得志。所以他成了反叛者和批判者，但在书中竭力反对妇女个性解放。其剧本在世界文坛享有盛誉，一生创作了60多部。代表作要数《朱丽小姐》。所写小说数量也多，以《女仆之子》最为有名。

莫泊桑（Guy de Maupassant，1850—1893），法国小说家。出身于一个没落贵族家庭。13岁入神学院，不久因犯上被开除。

423

随即去卢昂读书，打算长大了学法律。参加过普法战争，战后在海军供职，与福楼拜、左拉等大文豪相识。一生创作近300篇短篇小说和6部长篇小说。但是，其短篇小说比长篇小说更有名，与俄国的契诃夫、美国的欧·亨利同为世界三大短篇小说巨匠。代表作《项链》曾选入我国中学教科书。

小泉八云（Koisumi Yakumo，1850—1904），日本作家、翻译家，希腊与英国血统混血儿。生于爱尔兰都柏林，原名拉夫卡迪奥·赫恩（Lafcadio Hearn）。人生历经曲折，先后遭遇父母离世，缺乏信仰，孤苦漂泊。40岁到日本，45岁取得日本国籍，随妻姓小泉，起名八云。他对把日本的文化、文学介绍到西方做过重要贡献。相信有幽灵存在，其代表作为《怪谈》，典型反映了这种思想，奠定了其灵异文学鼻祖的地位。

帕拉西奥·瓦尔德斯（Palacio Valdes，1853—1938），西班牙著名小说家。曾在马德里大学学习法律，对科学也有过兴趣，其写作生涯以评论开始，曾主编《欧洲评论》，有四卷评论集。长篇小说有《何塞》《消失的村庄》等10余部，有的表现出现实主义，有的表现出乐观精神，有的具有狄更斯式的幽默和自然主义色彩。其短篇小说集的英语版出版于1935年。

安东·契诃夫（Anton Chekhov，1860—1904），俄国作家。生于小商人家庭。莫斯科大学医学系毕业，做过医生。20岁开始发表作品，所写小说中短篇题材多样，寓意深刻，笔调幽默，最善于揭示日常生活的悲剧。短篇小说尤为著名，与法国的莫泊桑、美国的欧·亨利同为世界三大短篇小说巨匠。代表作有《套中人》《变色龙》《小公务员之死》等。

欧·亨利（O. Henry，1862—1910），美国作家，仅写短篇小说，与法国的莫泊桑、俄国的契诃夫并肩为世界三大短篇小说巨匠。欧·亨利只是作家的笔名，其真名为威廉·西德尼·波特（William Sydney Porter）。幼时家境贫寒，只读过几年书。1896年在银行工作时因失误遗失少量款项，被指挪用公款入狱，在狱中开始创作短篇小说。作品共270篇，笔调幽默，结局出人意外而完全在情理之中。代表作有《警察与赞美诗》《最后一片叶子》《圣贤的礼物》等。《圣贤的礼物》为其最优秀的小说，曾以"礼物"为篇名入选我国中学教材。

马克西姆·高尔基（Maxim Gorky，1868—1936），苏联作家，原名阿列克赛·马克西姆维奇·彼什科夫（Alexei Maximovich Peshkov）。生于木工家庭，当过学徒、码头工、面包师，流浪俄国各地。24岁开始发表作品。三年后因参加革命工作几次被捕。1905年与列宁会面。1934年当选苏联作家协会主席。曾五次获诺贝尔文学奖提名，却始终未获奖。主要长篇小说有《母亲》，自传体三部曲《童年》《在人间》《我的大学》。

萨基（Saki，1870—1916），英国作家，真名赫克托·休·芒罗（Hector Hugh Munro）。1896年开始为伦敦《威斯敏斯特评论报》写政治讽刺小品。主要成就在短篇小说，有"短篇小说大师"的美誉，被一些人与欧·亨利相提并论。故事风趣，笔调幽默。

主要作品集有《雷金纳德》《克拉维斯纪事》《野兽和超级野兽》。第一次世界大战爆发时，他本已超过应征年龄，却走向了战场，最终遇德军狙击手身亡。

威廉·萨默塞特·毛姆（William Somerset Maugham，1874—1965），英国小说家、剧作家、文艺批评家。共写了21部长篇小说，190篇短篇小说，30个剧本，还有大量评论。其短篇小说受莫泊桑影响较深，故事性强，描写细腻，文字简练，拥有大量读者。代表作是《人性的枷锁》。1920年到中国，写了游记《在中国的屏风上》，并以中国为背景写了一部长篇小说《彩巾》。

奥拉西奥·基罗加（Horacio Quiroga，1878—1937），乌拉圭作家、诗人，在拉丁美洲国家很有影响。出生于一个中产阶级家庭。读书时兴趣广泛，爱好文学、化学、摄影、机械，开始工作后又喜欢上了哲学。擅长写短篇小说和童话。作品大多描写人和动物在原始森林生存的艰苦，也善于描写心理疾病。有短篇小说集《别人的罪行》《爱情、疯狂和死亡的故事》。晚年倾向神秘主义。

邓萨尼勋爵（Lord Dunsany，1879—1957），爱尔兰诗人、剧作家、小说家。参加过第一次世界大战，战后在雅典任英国文学教授。其作品常带神神鬼鬼的神秘色彩。多产，有诗歌、戏剧、小说、回忆录等50余卷，第一本短篇小说集是《裴伽纳的诸神》。

附录：作家简介

达蒙·鲁尼恩（Damon Runyon，1880—1946），美国作家，仅读到中学。其父办过一家报纸，并任编辑。亲戚中有多位是记者。鲁尼恩本人在美国旧金山、纽约及墨西哥当过记者。第一次世界大战时到欧洲任随军记者。写过大量短篇小说，多饶有风趣。短篇小说集有《鲁尼恩优秀小说选》等16部，故事中的很多主角都用绰号而不用名字，有20篇小说改编成了电影。他的作品特别受纽约人喜爱。

安德烈·莫洛亚（André Maurois，1894—1961），法国小说家、传记作家，父亲是工厂主，他自己也管理过父亲的工厂。曾任法兰西学院院士兼秘书长。第一次世界大战时曾任英法两国军队的联络员和翻译，这一经历后来成了他的第一部小说《布朗勃尔上校的沉默》的素材，此书使他一举成名。其短篇小说往往具有哲理，构思独特。其传记小说闻名于西欧，有《雪莱传》《拜伦传》《雨果传》等。

阿诺尔德·茨维格（Arnold Zweig，1887—1968），德国小说家、剧作家。生于犹太制革工人家庭。早期创作有印象主义色彩，第一次世界大战后，转而对社会做尖锐批判。1928年发表长篇小说《中士格里沙案件》，一举获得世界声誉。长篇小说、短篇小说、戏剧、随笔等创作均多。希特勒统治时期流亡国外，第二次世界大战后回到东德。

凯瑟琳·曼斯菲尔德（Katherine Mansfield，1888—1923），英国短篇小说女作家。生于新西兰，5岁才到英国。成名作是《幸福》与《园会》。她善于刻画细节，以象征手法描写周围事物，但其作品往往笼罩阴郁气氛。35岁时死于肺结核。

詹姆斯·瑟伯（James Thurber，1894—1961），美国作家。6岁时在一次玩耍中遇意外致左眼失明。当过报务员、记者。1937年开始专业从事写作。其作品有长篇小说、短篇小说、戏剧，以讽刺幽默见长，最有名的短篇小说《沃尔特·米蒂的秘密生活》中的主人公现在已是美国家喻户晓的人物。尤其擅长刻画大都市中的小人物，笔法简练新奇，荒唐之中有真实，幽默之中有苦涩，被人们称作"在墓地里吹口哨的人"。

奥尔德斯·赫胥黎（Aldous Huxley，1894—1963），英国小说家、散文家，《天演论》作者托马斯·赫胥黎的孙子。17岁即写完一部小说，但未出版。第一部作品《铬黄》发表于1921年。其一系列小说反映了西方上层社会知识分子对人类前途的幻灭心理。他最著名的代表作是《美丽新世界》，该书是20世纪最经典的反乌托邦文学之一。

C. S. 福雷斯特（Cecil Scott Forester，1899—1966），真名塞西尔·路易斯·特劳顿·史密斯（Cecil Louise Troughton Smith），英国作家，多产。生于埃及开罗，在伦敦长大。在伦敦时曾学过医，但半途而废，转而从事写作。最有名的作品是12卷小说《怒海英雄》。其他小说有24部，如《非洲女王》《将军》。作品很讲究细节的精确，内容也多惊险故事，许多被人改编为电影。

附录：作家简介

约翰·斯坦贝克（John Steinbeck，1902—1968），美国小说家。母亲是教师，自幼受其熏陶，对欧洲古典文学感兴趣。1935年第四部小说《煎饼坪》出版后才受到人们重视。一生共创作长篇小说16部，短篇小说集2部，代表作是《愤怒的葡萄》。1962年获诺贝尔文学奖。1966年初，斯坦贝克作为纽约《新闻日报》的战地记者前往越南。许多作品以美国的土地和人民为题材，刻画了富于同情心和人情味的真实可信的人物形象，展现了他们生活的图景。

雪莉·杰克逊（Shirley Jackson，1919—1965），美国女作家，出版过6部长篇小说和一部短篇小说集，但最出名的却是她的短篇小说《摸彩》。她的短篇小说常以一个女人为中心，而这个女人往往受其情人之害。在其所处的年代，她被认为是一个流行文学作家。近年来，她受到批评界越来越多的关注，作品被归入美国经典文学之列。她生前拒绝接受采访，认为她想说的话在自己的作品中都已讲述清楚。